I0691653

The Dreaming

TOOLS OF JUSTICE

JAIME SAMMS
and
SARAH MASTERS

Tools of Justice
ISBN # 978-0-85715-988-5
©Copyright Jaime Samms and Sarah Masters 2012
Cover Art by Posh Gosh ©Copyright March 2012
Interior text design by Claire Siemaszkiewicz
Total-E-Bound Publishing

TOOLS OF JUSTICE

Dedication

Jaime, a beautiful, sparkling star in my world
—Sarah

Chapter One

Barry floated a bit, on drink or desire, not quite connected to himself as his lover laid the tie over his closed eyes and tied it. "Really?" A bit of his hair caught in the knot, and he squirmed.

"Really. Trust me." A tongue slicked over his ear, and the squirm turned to reaching.

He should recognise the voice, thought maybe he did. Something shifted. A scent, making him think of blood or rust, drifted by like cigarette smoke. He stood still – nude, blind and bound – and the voice chuckled softly.

"Ready, baby?"

He nodded, straining to find the familiar – so close he could almost reach a name, a face…something he knew. The hands that had tied his behind him, lowered him until his chest rested on something hard under an inadequate layer of padding.

"Relax."

Easier said than done. Barry let out a breath.

"It isn't going to hurt. Promise."

"Tag?"

"Shhh." A hand ran through his hair.

Had Barry caught the scent of Old Spice? The particular drag of Tag's bad leg?

"What's next, Tag? Tell me."

"You'll see."

There was a sound behind him — shuffling, grunting — then frigid air engulfed him. He shivered, glanced over his shoulder as though his covered eyes could make out what was going on.

"What?"

The hands that touched him next weren't Tag's. They were too rough, too demanding, and he flinched, made a move to stand. The hands pushed him back.

"Tag?"

"Shh." The sound seemed so far away, too little for comfort or reassurance.

Cold air swirled around him. He struggled to stand, but whoever held him was too strong.

"Don't. Tag, don't go!" Panic squeezed out rational thought, and he strained. The only answer was a tighter grip on the back of his neck and one of those rough hands running up the inside of his thigh. "Tag!"

The hand moved to clamp over his mouth, leaving him struggling for air. His bare feet on the cold cement chilled him, toes ineffectual claws, gripping nothing. No more floating. Only shivering, cold, and a gag — its straps cutting into his cheeks — and no idea how it had got there. The ball clogged his words, turned his begging to garbled, tear-washed nothing. He shouted inarticulate sounds no one was going to hear. Struggling only earned him bruises and didn't stop the invasion of those rough fingers or the wave of pain from being stretched too far, too fast.

The hand came back, around the front of his neck this time.

This wasn't how it was supposed to be. Not how he wanted to go — bound and gagged and fucked, for Tag to find his body like that.

Blackness darker than the blindfold sucked him under...

He awoke screaming.

He always awoke screaming. His voice had gone raw from it, and he only barely remembered the terror that haunted the dark. He glared at the obnoxious red glow of the clock. Not quite five. His gaze shifted to the bottle distorting the numbers, but, for once, he turned away from it, untangled himself from the sweaty sheets, and shuffled off to the bathroom.

* * * *

An hour later, a good portion of the tar-like station coffee he'd tried to pour himself landed on the table beside his chipped mug. He sopped it up with the last of the napkins and tossed the sloppy mess into the trashcan. What was left of it, he took to his desk. It might taste like all hell, but it would scour the fuzz off his tongue. The computer hummed when he turned it on, the sound a comfort in the dim stillness of the deserted police station. Maybe he could get a few reports finished before his shift started. Better paperwork than the four walls of his empty apartment.

He wasn't sure how long the screen had been staring back at him, or how long the flying toasters had been careening around the black void, when he blinked back from his stupor.

"Hey, Wiki."

He jumped at his partner's hot breath on the back of his neck.

"Still daydreaming about Tag banging you within an inch of your life?" He thumped Barry on both arms.

The coffee cup slipped from Barry's grasp. The last few, cold sips dashed out across his desk and spattered the screen, the keyboard, and his pants.

Ross snickered and plopped down in his seat across from Barry. A glare only quieted the man's mirth—it didn't banish it.

"Fuck off."

"Hey. I tease because I care."

Barry relegated his response to single digit sign language.

"Seriously, dude. You have got to move on." Ross shook his head and jabbed at the ON button of his monitor. "That ship has sailed, man."

"Sank, more like," Barry muttered, conceding to truth.

"Whittaker!" Captain Taggart's voice sliced through the room, and Barry winced. "My office."

"Used to like the sound of that," he murmured as he gave his splattered khakis one last dab and rose. Ross didn't snicker this time, and Barry patted his shoulder as he passed. "Just call me Davey Jones."

A memory of his latest dream shuddered through him as his fingers curled around the door handle to Tag's office. He was already in a cold sweat when he stepped inside and pulled the door closed behind him. It was impossible to meet his captain's eye with the irrational thoughts of blame, completely unearned, grinding through him.

"Wiki?"

Barry's head popped up from where he'd been studying a dried splash of coffee on the linoleum.

"You okay? You look like—"

"Fine. What'd you want?"

Tag frowned.

"Sir."

A heavy sigh filled the room and settled around them.

Tag finally retrieved a folder from his desk. "New case." He handed it to Barry. "Dead guy, missing girl."

Barry took the folder, flipped it open, glad for the new focus. "Do we like her for it?"

"Doubt it. Little thing like that?" Tag shook his head.

Barry understood the comment when he saw the pictures of the victim.

"Beaten to a bloody pulp," Tag confirmed, as if the visual wasn't enough. "Garrotted. Missing woman's about five foot two, ninety pounds on a rainy day. She didn't do that."

"Who did?"

Tag's eyebrows went up. "That would be the case, wouldn't it?"

"And no idea where she is now?"

"If I had to guess? Run. Whoever did this had to be one scary son of a bitch."

Barry nodded, gaze still skimming the file. "I know this guy."

Tag nodded. "Reporter. Calvin Landry, wrote for some local rumour rag." He poked at another, much thicker file still sitting on his desk, flipped the folder open, and picked up a picture, which he handed to Barry. "He was following this case. Pain in the ass, but not a bad guy. This was the last murder he ran a story on. That girl there" — he tapped the picture of a gagged and bound woman lying lifeless on a cold, cement floor in what looked to be a garage — "looks an awful lot like Calvin's girlfriend. Now he's dead, his girlfriend is fuck knows where, and I don't like where this is going one bit. If Calvin pissed this guy off, and this kind of girl is his type…"

Barry stared at the photo of the dead girl. She was young, had been pretty. He handed it back to Tag.

"She was raped — "

"Strangled," Barry whispered.

"That was COD, yeah…"

Tag's voice faded out behind the whirlwind of violent memory. Barry shook. Papers drifted down around him. "You were there."

Tag shuffled forward, his bum foot slapping awkwardly on the linoleum.

Barry started and looked up.

"I went to the scene, yes." Tag paused. "Barry?"

Barry stared at him, a bit of shellshock still ricocheting around in his head, making it hard to focus, impossible to speak.

"You had a dream," Tag said.

Barry didn't have to answer.

"I'm giving this to Cornwall and Riggs. Go home. Get some sleep."

"Fuck you." Barry dropped to one knee and scooped the papers back into their folder. "You have to let me do this."

"You can barely focus. You're too close. Those dreams — "

"Make me the perfect candidate to find her."

Tag was shaking his head already, though. "I know what those dreams do to you, Barry."

"No, you don't." Barry leaned in to his face, tapped him on the chest with the corner of the folder. "You left."

Tag backed off and sank onto the edge of his desk. At least he didn't argue that point.

"I don't know where they come from, or why I have them, Tag, but you have to let me use them," Barry insisted.

"What they do to you, though..."

"They do whether I use them or ignore them. If something good can come..."

Captain Taggart nodded. "But if I think you're in trouble, I'm pulling you."

Barry scooped the fat file off his boss's desk and turned to the door. "I'll find her, Tag."

* * * *

Black shadows flitted around Barry. Every time they stopped there was pain, but they never slowed enough for him to strike back or even defend himself. Every time they connected, they left a part of him broken and bleeding until he was a quivering heap of helplessness on the cold floor. The screaming and begging in the background was endless.

Then came the garrotte. Knowing it was a dream didn't make it any better...

He clawed his way up from the abyss, gasping for enough air to scream.

The clock's red glow spread almost to the edge of his pillowcase. 2:27. Not quite an hour since he'd fallen, exhausted, onto his pillow. He turned away, kicked the tangled sheets off the end of the bed, and rolled onto his side. His hand contacted skin, and he sat up.

"Shit."

Bleary blue eyes blinked at him. "Hey."

Barry shifted warily, putting space between himself and the man in his bed.

"You okay?" The man reached a long-fingered hand towards him.

"Uh..." He stared at the fine fingers, striving for some memory of the feel of them roving over his skin.

The hand dropped. "That was some dream."

"Yeah." He studied the mussed blond spikes of the guy's hair and tried to remember his name.

"So..." The guy glanced around the bed, snagged his briefs from where they'd caught between the mattress and the wall, and shimmied down after the sheets. "I guess..." He slipped into his underwear and glanced back at Barry. "I gotta go. You know?"

"Yeah."

Jeans, shirt, sweater. Barry watched him, saw the clock tick over the minute.

"So. See you 'round."

"Sure."

Jacket and boots. He disappeared out the bedroom door. A minute later, the apartment door clicked open and thumped shut again.

Barry flopped back. The clock winked at him through the warm amber hue of the rum sitting on the bedside table. He caressed the bottle, wrapped his fingers around it, and the feel of the smooth glass — cool and solid under his touch — grounded him in the familiar, safe realm of his life. But he didn't pick it up. Drink made the dreams hazy. Sex sometimes left him with enough endorphins to make it to morning. Not this time. He rolled to face the wall, and at some point drifted back into the shadows.

The shadows moved so fast. He ducked as they came at him and held his hands up to ward off the blow. It only sliced through his bonds. Something soft floated down over his head. Silk hid him from view as he cringed from the footsteps rushing past, retreating. The only sounds left were soft, squelching thuds, and the snap of bone under the eerie silence of the swirling shadows.

He wondered if he'd imagined the face — dark, blank, framed in a wild spray of black fronds... Just more shadows flying about in a deadly mêlée he didn't want to see clearly.

Then it stopped. Only a low gurgling noise, a mask of death, and fingers clawing, blood oozing, and that dark, blank face staring at him.

He ran.

The memory of the receding footsteps led him out into the black night. Wet pavement froze his feet, doorways shielded him, but every shadow sent him fleeing. Nowhere was safe. One turn too many brought him headlong into a broad chest, and a hard grip closed over his arms. He didn't fall, only because the grip closed painfully and held him up. He'd run too far, too long — he couldn't breathe and couldn't bear to look up and see that empty face staring back at him this time…

When he finally dragged himself upright, he realised the grating sound wasn't his own breathing, but the harsh blare of his alarm.

* * * *

Barry didn't even make it to his desk before Tag was calling him into his office. He slumped onto the couch. "Where's Ross?"

"Coffee." Tag dropped his pen and his glasses onto the paperwork he'd been doing and stood.

Barry peered through the blinds, but the coffee maker sat empty, and Ross was nowhere to be seen.

Tag saw the motion and qualified, "Real coffee. Not that shit."

He let the blinds go. The couch received his sigh and his weight in its familiar embrace. "So. I got paperwork. We can do this when he gets back." He didn't get up, though. Getting up seemed like too much of a chore.

"How'd you sleep?" Tag perched on the edge of his desk and crossed his arms over his chest. His gaze slipped right past Barry's belligerence like only he could manage.

"How do you think?" Barry asked at last.

"You look like shit."

Barry smiled, a stiff grimace that showed his teeth but no mirth. "Is that what this is about?"

"You wanted to do this," Tag reminded him.

"I know." Barry pinched the bridge of his nose between his finger and thumb. "And I can't help but point out that even if I do dream something useful, it'll never hold up."

"But it could lead us to the girl. Or whoever killed this guy."

Barry looked up. "Yesterday you were all for kicking me off the case."

Tag's hands fell to his sides. He jammed them deep into his pockets. "We've got nothing, Barry." There it was—his willingness to use Barry's 'gift' but only if he had no other choice.

Barry closed his eyes, and Tag droned on.

"We found the vic's blood—and his girlfriend's, but we already know who she is—and a minuscule sample so corrupted it doesn't even read as human."

"How does someone do that and not leave blood evidence?"

"Wish we knew. At least it would be a lead."

The shadow of a bird flitted past the window, and Barry flinched, shivered. He sank deeper into the crevices of the sofa to stare out the window. "His girlfriend ran. You were right about that. Barely dressed. A shirt or something. Not hers."

"Where did she run to?"

Barry shrugged.

"Nothing on the perp?"

"What do you want, Tag?" He looked over, finally meeting his boss's gaze, and found only a thin, icy skin of cop attitude over a well of worry. Just once, he wanted to be the perp in a dream and not the victim. Just once. "Dead is dead," he whispered.

Tag was quiet for one beat too long, and Barry wondered if he'd heard.

"This guy is now hunting down an innocent girl because she saw him commit murder," Tag said. The arms crossed back over his chest.

Maybe he hadn't heard.

Good. Barry wasn't sure he could explain why he'd said it or what it meant, anyway.

"Gimme something on the perp, Barry. Anything. One tiny lead. A tattoo, a smell—"

"Black hair." Barry dropped his gaze to the coffee stain. "Maybe."

"That's it?"

"Not like it's a science, Tag." He slumped against the leather with a sigh, tipping his head back on the cushions. Worn cowhide embraced him like an old lover. One who could keep the dreams at bay. Just for a bit. An hour. One nap.

"Long? Short? Straight? Curly?" Tag started to pace.

Barry turned to the window to watch shadows dance over the façade of the building across the street. "Straight. Longish. Asian, maybe? Native? If I could give you more…"

"I know," Tag relented, clapping Barry on the shoulder.

"I should see the scene."

Tag frowned, about to protest, but Barry held up a hand. "It'll help. The dreams are still lagging. Doesn't do us any good to see what we already know happened. I need to see the place. Maybe I'll remember…"

"Remember what?"

Barry shivered and blocked the thought of that blank face from his mind. In the light of day, he recalled it as more desperate than deadly. "Where she ran. It's just a jumble of dark and cold. I need a reference." He sighed and let his head fall back again. "Fuck, I'm tired."

Taggart nodded. "Use the office. I'll be back in an hour and we'll go check it out." He stood, straightened the sleeves of his shirt, already rolled halfway to his elbows. "Maybe…"

A beat of silence.

Barry had already closed his eyes. He didn't bother to open them. "Maybe what?"

"Nothing. Forget it."

"Forgotten." Barry slouched over, curling his feet up onto the couch, too tired for guessing or finding another argument to keep him on the case. The dreams chose the tragedy, and he had to see them through or they would torment him forever. He had enough unsolved darkness against his soul. This one was too big to ignore, and with or without his ex-lover's approval, he was going to find the girl, find the killer, and find the answer to that desperate, haunted look.

Chapter Two

Tag stuck his head in his office, careful not to make any sudden, loud noises. He was immediately transported back a year and half to the apartment he'd shared with Barry, and the times he'd tiptoed around it to keep from waking him. He was sound asleep now, and Tag slipped inside, closed the door behind him and tripped the lock. He didn't like the idea of exposing Barry's vulnerability to anyone else. Not many understood him, and Tag saw no reason to invite more discord into his lover's life than he already endured.

"Ex-lover," he reminded himself in a quiet, sad voice, even as he crouched in front of the couch and pushed some of the heavy, dark curls out of Barry's face. "You need a haircut, Wiki."

The man continued to sleep, his face calm, with no sign that anything unpleasant was going on in his head. It was good to see him resting. Good to get close to him without the barbs and defensiveness springing between them. Not that he blamed Barry. Tag *had* left.

"And if I thought you would believe me, or understand my reasons, I would explain it, Wiki, I swear. But you wouldn't. It was always us against the world, but it couldn't last like that. You couldn't last. This is the only way I could think of to protect you." With a little sigh, he gave in to his desire and pressed his lips lightly to Barry's temple. "I'm sorry. I wish I could figure out a better way. I really do."

It was bad enough they had to be so careful about when and where they let their proclivities — and their relationship — show. Barry's 'gift', if you could call it that, only made everything worse for him. His only peace was found in stopping the things he dreamed about, and getting kicked off the force would put an end to that. It wasn't something Tag could sit back and watch happen.

Not wishing to take any further risk of waking him, Tag stood and quietly moved away to sit behind his desk and organise the files they would need for their crime scene visits. It would have to be this afternoon. The crime lab had done all they could collecting evidence. There was no point in cordoning the places off any longer. They were going to have to release both the abandoned garage, where they had found the dead girl, and Landry's house.

He was casting about for something else to do by the time Barry finally stirred.

"Well. Welcome back, Wiki."

Barry grunted and sat up, drawing a hand over his face and pushing his mussed hair back. "Hey."

Tag watched him, trying not to notice how this rumpled look suited him so well, or how much he wanted to get up and go over there and rumple it some more. "There's coffee." He pointed to the coffee maker on a side table by the door. "I promise it's a lot better than the shit they serve out there." He bobbed his head at the closed door.

"Thanks." Barry got up and shuffled to the fresh brew. "You want?"

"Sure."

"How long did I sleep?"

"Couple hours."

"You should have woke me." Barry brought a steaming mug to Tag's desk and set it down.

"You needed to rest."

Barry pressed his lips together. "Thanks."

"You're welcome."

Once Barry settled on the couch with his own coffee, Tag sat back in his chair, trying to calm his nerves.

"Let's do this like we used to. Tell me everything you remember. Every dream since this started."

"What do you mean since it started? I dream all the time."

"I know you, Wiki. You've been good lately. It's only been bad for a couple weeks. If we do this systematically, like we used to, we can get to the bottom of it before you get too strung out."

"You make it sound easy."

"Honestly. Do you think I like seeing you this way?"

"Should I think you care? You left me to deal with this on my own a long time ago, Tag." He got up to pace the confines of the room. "Why decide to help now?"

"I never stopped helping, Wiki. I just stopped watching the self-destruct sequence play out."

"Well." Barry flopped onto the couch. "Thank you so much for that."

Tag sank into the accommodating leather chair and closed his eyes, as though not seeing the defeat in

Barry's eyes would make it go away. Or make it so he wasn't mostly responsible for it.

"I can't take it back, Barry. However much I might want to, you won't let me, so can we just get on with what we have to do now?"

"Yes. Absolutely." He popped up, took a swig of the coffee, and set the rest on the desk. A quick swipe of his hands through his hair and a tuck of his loose shirttails, and he was unlocking the door. "We have crime scenes to visit. You want to drive, or should I?"

Tag gave up trying to get him to talk. Even when they'd been close, Barry hadn't liked to put what he went through in those dreams into words. "I'll drive. That way you can concentrate on what you're seeing."

"Sure."

In the car, Barry sat and stared out of the windshield, gripping the armrest like he might tear it off. "You were there."

"What?"

"In the dream. The first one. You were there. Why were you there?"

"Because I was at the crime scene?"

"No. In the dream." Barry looked at him, and Tag's breath caught. "You're always there. It always starts out with you. With us. Not..."

"Not what?"

Barry gave him a stiff smile. "Not murder. Just us. And then...it goes all wrong."

"Like we did."

"I don't know." He shook himself. "Doesn't matter. They all end the same."

"It's what happens between the beginning and the end we need to focus on. Everything you can remember. There might be something in there we can use." Tag consciously loosened his grip on the wheel.

He wasn't sure how he felt about Barry dreaming about him, about being associated with those murderous nightmares.

He watched Barry, trying to pay attention to every little nuance and not run them off the road at the same time. It would have been a lot easier to have this conversation in the office, but Wiki never made it easy.

"Tying, gagging, rape, and murder. What more is there? We already know it happened. We have a body and a crime scene."

"Wiki… Barry. Please. I know you hate this. I know. But you have to talk to me. Every little detail about the murder of the woman Landry was investigating. We—"

"The floor was cold," Barry snapped. "She didn't have shoes."

"She didn't have anything on."

"But she had bare feet for a really long time. It was freezing. My—*her* toes were aching, like she'd been on that cold floor for days. The guy was big. Strong. He had this…I don't know…bar or something. I couldn't see what it was. He put…" Barry ran his hands over his thighs and shuddered. "He used a tie to cover her eyes. Like, a necktie. And to tie her wrists too."

"How do you know it was a tie?"

"I just do. I wear one every day. I know how they feel." Another shudder ran through him. "And he wears Old Spice."

Tag made a mental note to forgo his cologne and buy new shaving cream. It wasn't necessary to remind Barry of the dreams every time he stepped into the office.

"What about the bar?" Tag asked. "You mentioned a bar. What did he use it for?"

Barry rubbed a hand over his chest and spoke slowly, his voice low, his gaze fixed straight ahead as he described being tied, bent over and everything that followed. His voice and hands were shaking by the time he'd finished, and Tag no longer felt the need to hold back his own emotions. He pulled the car into the parking lot of a boarded-up car dealership and turned off the engine.

"Barry—"

"What are you doing?" Barry shifted in his seat, scrunching against his door and eyeing Tag suspiciously.

"Let me help."

"Drive the damn car and get me to the scene. That's how you can help."

"Barry—"

"No!" Barry snarled and faced forward. "No. I can't. Just drive."

Tag heaved a sigh and started the car. What was there to say to that?

The scene didn't give them much more information than they already had. A cold, deserted garage with a bare concrete floor offered no new information. Tag watched as Barry slowly shuffled around the room, occasionally lifting his face, as though he were smelling the air.

"This." He ran his hand over what looked like a makeshift engine stand. The bare metal of the cross bar was slightly rusted, and Barry drew his hand back quickly, his nostrils flaring and his eyes showing too much white. "There was something covering it. Material. A towel maybe." He rubbed his chest as he had in the car. "He wanted to hurt them. He wanted them scared and hurting. Almost like..." His lips tightened, and his eyes glazed as he dropped into thought.

Tag moved a few steps closer, experience teaching him that this moment when Barry put the dream together—the beginning and the ultimate end—was the hardest part for him.

"I know why you were in it. He...keeps them a while. Wants them to think...not that they're safe. Just...that they're alive, that it's okay as long as they're alive. Wants them to hope. It's the hope he wants to kill first."

Tag didn't know what that had to do with him. Unless he was supposed to represent the hope, the false safety.

"As soon as the decision was made, soon as I knew he was going to do it, you were gone from the dream." Barry looked at him, no expression in his eyes. "That's it. That's all I got."

He turned abruptly and strode out of the building, back into the sunlight to lean on the car.

Tag took one last look around the place. There was nothing left of what had happened here except the memories Barry would have to live with.

"I'm going to figure this one out, Barry. I swear." He didn't voice the promise he wanted to make to himself. It was impossible to know if he could keep it. Judging by Barry's continuing anger, he didn't think it was likely.

* * * *

The house where Calvin Landry had died was across town. Under normal circumstances, the two murders might never have been connected. All the previous deaths had happened in the vicinity of the abandoned garage, clearly within the killer's comfort zone. The fact that he had ventured this far afield was significant. This kill was out of the ordinary. It meant something had happened to make him break from established patterns. Either he would fuck up and they would have him, or he would fall off the face of the earth, and their only hope then would be Barry and his dreams. As it was, Barry's dreams were all they had to connect the two crimes.

The only difference between the garage and the house was that the garage had been clean. That had been a brutal but bloodless murder. Here, the stench of death and fear still hung in the air, detectable the moment they entered the house. Dried pools and dark stains of blood spatter covered everything. Calvin had not died easily. His murder went beyond brutal. No matter how many times Tag had seen it, the reminder of just how hard it was to kill someone who didn't want to die—the amount of blood and fight in a person—never ceased to amaze and horrify him.

He'd spent as little time as possible inside the house on the first inspection and was reluctant to go back now, but there was no question of letting Barry go in alone. Once the scene was released, the cleaners would come. Tag doubted that the ghosts of memory could ever be scrubbed away with any amount of bleach—and the blood would remain, unseen but there all the same.

They nodded once to the uniform standing on the porch and, when Barry hesitated, Tag covered his pause by reaching for the door himself and pulling it open. "We'll make this quick," he told the cop. "No company, please."

The guy nodded and resumed his watch as Barry slipped inside and Tag closed the door behind him.

When Barry shrank back, Tag was ready, letting the shorter man press against him. "I know," he murmured. Even he had felt the heavy weight of what had happened here when he'd stepped inside the first time.

Barry's eyes flitted about the room, as though he were watching a movie only he could see. His pale cheeks and wide eyes showed the horror more than the low drone of words that spilled past his lips, describing what his dream had shown him— essentially nothing. At least, nothing more than they already knew.

For a few heartbeats after he'd stopped talking, Barry remained where he was, back hard against Tag's chest. Only the close proximity let Tag feel the delicate, constant tremor running through Barry. He was wound so tight his body literally vibrated.

"Come on. Let's get you out of here." He reached for the door, but Barry shook his head, then shook him off.

"Have to do something."

He moved to the stairs and went up, heading straight for the master bedroom. "His girlfriend was here." He pointed to the bed. "They must have heard something." He leaned over and peered behind the brass headboard. After a minute, he nodded. "Silk rope. They had a kinky side. The ropes were on her for play."

"She was tied?"

"It was confusing. I thought…the perp cut her loose, but I think it was Landry. They were playing, heard something, and he cut the ropes and threw his shirt over her. He was in a hurry. I think he knew the guy. He knew she was in danger. That's why he fought so hard, hoping she had time to get away."

"And?"

"She didn't run fast enough."

Barry hurried out of the room and down the stairs, speeding out of the door, Tag on his heels. They almost jogged down the street. Tag followed down a side alley and paused when Barry did, peering into a doorway and muttering under his breath. Halfway to the next set of lights, Barry stopped abruptly and looked around.

"Here."

A few steps brought them to the kerb, and Barry closed his eyes, no doubt chasing down a bit of the dream he thought he'd forgotten. Finally, he turned a frustrated expression on Tag. "A kitchen."

"What?"

"I don't know. I remember a kitchen." He pointed at the house. "Not that one. Just...cheap. Tiny. Seventies." Finally he shook his head. "I'm done. I can't..."

"Okay." Tag took Barry by the arm and steered him back towards the car.

For once, Barry didn't flinch away or tell him to bugger off. He accepted the hand on his arm and even let Tag open the door for him. Once back behind the wheel, Tag knew better than to hesitate. He started the car and pulled away from the kerb.

"I'm sorry, Tag." Barry laid his head back on the headrest. "I wasn't much help. I need to catch up, get ahead."

Tag bit his lip to keep quiet. Getting ahead of the curve meant the dreams only depicted what might happen, rather than what already had. Granted, it was frustrating to watch him go through the horror and not be able to glean anything they didn't already know, but watching him drive himself frantic trying to prevent the dreams that hadn't happened yet was infinitely worse. Especially if he failed to stop it.

"Don't try and tell me not to push."

"I wasn't going to." Tag pulled to a stop sign and glanced over. Barry still had his head back, his eyes closed. "I didn't want to leave, Barry." He watched his ex-lover's features tighten, his lips whiten around the edges, but he ploughed on anyway. He needed to get the reasons out, to warn him, and maybe find some closure for both of them.

"They were looking too closely at how we were solving those cases. They would have investigated you. I couldn't let them put you through that, with everything else. When the captain position came up, I knew if I had it, I could protect you. But I'd never get it—"

"If you were chained to me."

"I wanted to explain. I tried. Then that case came along. I had to make it clear I was cutting my ties. There just wasn't time."

"There's been a year and a half since you moved up." Still Barry didn't budge, look at him or even open his eyes. He sounded defeated, like he no longer cared.

The case in question had never been solved, but it had nearly driven Barry off the deep end. He'd taken months to recover. Tag remembered nights sleeping with the lights on and a bottle beside their bed. He'd done more damage control by keeping Barry's drinking and absences as inconspicuous as possible, but his suggestion that Barry find professional help had been their last argument. He'd known then the only way to save both their jobs was to make sure he made captain and to find Barry a partner who could keep him in check.

He had hopes his current choice, Jeremy Ross, would work out. He'd proven to be completely at ease with the sexual history Tag and Barry shared, and he was open to the idea that maybe there was more to the human brain than a mere five senses could explain.

"I know," Tag conceded at last. "You tell me how I should have explained after the fact without pissing you off even more."

Barry tipped his head to look at Tag as the car rolled forward again. "You couldn't." His eyes were dark, haunted, and Tag would have given up the job, the security…everything to go back a year and be the one to bring the light back.

"Maybe if you'd told me at the time," Barry said. "Maybe if I'd been given a choice."

"What kind of choice was it, Wiki? If I didn't do what I did, you'd be out of a job."

"A choice between you and this shit job wouldn't have been a choice."

This time his gaze glittered with loss, and all the air rushed out of Tag.

"I didn't know," he whispered.

"You didn't ask."

Barry turned to face forward again, and the remainder of the trip back to the station was made in silence.

Chapter Three

Hidden—that's what they thought they were, but Leyton knew better. Those killers, their crimes unsolved, their existence unknown except for the evidence they left behind.

Leyton had picked them off one by one, had watched as they fled their crime scenes. But he pursued, sometimes leaving months between announcing his presence so they gained a false sense of security.

I know when they're going to do it. Just like it was me thinking. I see them planning, getting ready, and instinctually know where to go in order to follow them. Dreams...they come so vividly, guiding me, pushing me to kill...

He laughed, the sound echoing through the treetops, a dry boom that sent him giddy. Lifting his binoculars, he stared through them into the distance. The latest killer had camped perhaps half a mile away in a clearing surrounded by trees. From his tree-branch vantage point, Leyton studied his comings and goings—the same pattern every time—and the familiar and much-wanted surge birthed inside him. *At last!* It had taken a while for this euphoria to visit, that certain knowledge that soon, very soon, he would take another evil man away, only to return him to his bed...dead.

Birds twittered, their melody a beautiful complement to his musings and the burn that spread within. Ah, such a stupendous moment this time of enlightenment was, as though he were reborn with every new mission, evolving into a stronger, more fearsome man. And they feared him — that much was obvious. Their shrieks upon finding him in their homes made them crazy, chanting around the gag he stuffed in their mouths.

A well-known movement flickered past his eye line, and Leyton followed it. His victim — *Charles, I'll call him Charles* — walked with such ease, such abandonment, as though he hadn't been stalking women over the past few weeks. As though he didn't have a woman in his caravan now, probably tied up, duct tape across her sweet lips. This man had made a mistake. Hadn't expected the woman's boyfriend to be there too... Leyton wanted her, had wanted her from the first time he'd seen her running down the street in a white shirt and nothing else, frightened for her life. But he'd have to wait until the time was right.

She came out of the caravan — wrists bound, mouth, as he'd suspected, covered with tape — and helped Charles pile kindling to form the basis of their fire. Blonde hair spilled down, a sheet of ripe corn, and she tossed it back along with her head, looking up at the sky in a silent prayer to God...who wouldn't be saving her just yet. He imagined her voice and wished she would pray for him — Leyton.

One day she would.

Charles ripped off the tape and said something into her ear. Her eyes widened, and she nodded, continuing with her task.

Leyton twisted the binocular dial and zoomed in on her. Christ, she was a beauty. All lithe limbs and creamy skin. And those lips, bow-like and tempting, had his cock straining in his pants. He needed her, wanted her—body splayed beneath him as he filled her cunt—and given time he would have her. No doubt about that.

Charles slid his finger beneath her chin and tilted her face—for a kiss? Anger boiled inside Leyton, a spiral of it wending its way through his body, spreading, leaching his happiness at seeing her again. He clenched his teeth, finger pads sore from his harsh grip on the binoculars, and wrenched the spy-piece away.

No one touched his woman. Not like that. Not... *No!*

He bowed his head, a growl of ire burrowing out of him, bursting from his lips despite his efforts to keep it inside. Releasing his hold on the binoculars, he left them hanging around his neck and scrambled down from the tree. On solid ground, he ran to his black VW camper and climbed inside, kneeling next to his bunk. Hands shaking, he patted beneath and pulled out his leather pouch, undoing the buckle and unfolding the flaps. Instant calm stole over him at the sight of his tools—those gleaming steel instruments of power that enabled him to do his work. He inhaled deeply—the action soothing his ragged nerve edges—and revelled in the infusion of well-being.

Everything would be all right now. The path that branched off from his main road formed in his mind, the last fork before he attained his ultimate goal—the woman. Charles stood on that imaginary path, the sun gleaming on his long black hair, highlighting his clean straight smile and easy pose, his olive skin — native, he was of native origin.

Goddamn you!

Leyton closed his eyes and focused on his plans, fingertip smoothing up and down his machete blade. He would follow the tried and tested route — the one that had worked every time in the past — but, all the same, he loved thinking about it, loved the anticipation. Eyes wide, he slid the red-handled pliers from their slot and climbed onto his bunk. What a beautiful accomplice it had always been, wrenching teeth from sockets with ease. He stroked the silver grippers and stared up, pulse thudding in his ears. Colour photographs taped into a montage covered the VW's ceiling, each of his victims shown in a series of shots from life to death. Red, so much red against pale skin, welts and cuts a tremendous accompaniment to toothless mouths and ripped lips. He adored the chase, the removal of those men from their beds, and the kills, but the replacement of the corpses...ah, what a superb moment.

Charles stood in the way of the dream Leyton had for himself and her. He smiled. Once he approached her and explained, she would understand. The image of her filled his mind, and he closed his eyes to drink her in. Freckles dotted the bridge of her nose, and blue eyes the colour of forget-me-nots stared back at him, their sparkle proof of newfound love — a love he would inspire in her with his announcement of their being together. Oh yes, she'd want him, need him, and together they would travel — his VW their haven, the cocoon that would keep her safe from prying eyes and groping hands.

No one must see her, touch her. Only him.

"Only me, my beautiful. Only me."

His cheeks flushed with another sudden onset of anger. Her name. What was it? *Lorelei, I'll call her Lorelei...* He hoped it wasn't a portent of her reeling him in only to dash him against the rocks, leaving him to drown. A shudder rippled through him at the prospect, and he sat up, heart thudding, disorientation claiming him. It wasn't an omen, was it? No, surely not. He exhaled slowly, telling himself it was just a name, nothing to do with her personality. From what he'd seen, she wasn't that type at all. Yet that blonde hair and those blue eyes...

Lorelei, the woman from the myths, she —

No! I won't entertain it. My Lorelei is a pure, good person. She may have been sullied by that man, but I will remedy that. I will make her chaste again.

Leyton leant forward and slipped the pliers back into his pouch. He closed the flaps and secured the buckle, pushing his tools beneath the bunk. Insecurity ate at his innards, and the urge to see Lorelei again overtook him. He stood, stumbling out of his camper on unsteady legs, upset that such a small thing could unnerve him. Why had he allowed it? Wasn't he stronger now? Stronger than the boy he once was?

"Nothin' but a strange little boy, Leyton, that's what you are. Come to Mother. Let me make your face nice and pretty."

Leyton palmed his cheeks as he ran to the tree, willing the past away. The smooth surface of his scars stood out, stubble growing in the dips and swells between them. Mother hadn't made his face pretty. No, she'd ruined it, the criss-cross of her knife her way of keeping him with her. They'd roamed the country in her camper van from as far back as he could remember, with no one to stop her hurting him. No one to care.

He climbed back to his branch and lifted the binoculars, feasting on the sight of Lorelei, who poked a now-raging fire with a metal pole. Sparks flew with each jab, and she appeared in a trance, her gaze fixed on the flames. Was she wishing for a better love than the one she had now with Charles? Yes...yes she was, only she didn't yet know the faceless man who would sweep her off her feet and remove her from her life of captivity — into another with Leyton.

Lorelei deserves riches, the finest home, and I'll give them to her.

The hum of the hunt sped through him. That and seeing Lorelei lost in a world of her own calmed the rage that thoughts of his mother always brought and eviscerated his momentary panic. She swayed — he hoped to a song only she could hear — and rubbed her belly. Leyton's stomach rumbled.

Hungry too, my sweet?

Charles moved away from her to a pair of low stools outside his caravan. He looked up at Lorelei, staring at her naked legs. Charles didn't care for her. No, if he did, she wouldn't still be wearing the bloodstained white shirt. She turned swiftly, as though from being called, then dropped the pole and walked towards Charles. Sitting on the ground, her wrists bound with loops of rope and a short length between them, she took a chopping board from him and began cutting potatoes he handed her, plopping them into a large pot. Blonde hair shrouded her face from his view. Leyton sighed his annoyance and scrabbled back down the tree. He locked up his camper and sat in the driver's seat, intent on visiting the nearby town and collecting a full canister of gas for his stove. He didn't relish cooking outside tonight, the lure of fast food too much to ignore, so he inched out of his hiding place and onto the main road.

He arrived in Rusholm quickly, it only being two miles from his campsite, and parked in a supermarket lot. Reaching to the passenger seat, he swiped up his baseball cap and secured it on his head, the brim pulled low. Why he bothered he didn't know — the brim never did much in the way of hiding his scars. Still, the cap gave him a little more confidence. He climbed out of his van and locked up.

A burger joint belched steam from a steel funnel beside the supermarket, and he headed there, already smelling the fare. Once inside, having ignored the initial shocked looks from diners, he ordered a burger and fries and took a seat in the corner by the window. He contemplated his next move. Should he approach the caravan tonight, when Charles took his usual stroll around the campsite alone?

A sliver of gherkin skin jammed between two back molars, and he winced, chewing on the other side until he'd swallowed. Fishing the skin out, he placed it on his burger wrapper and continued his meal, mind toying with his dilemma. Lorelei might need time to grow accustomed to his face, so maybe it *was* better that he approached tonight. While Charles strolled, Leyton would enter the caravan, introduce himself as her saviour. He'd be kind, stroke her pretty face, and tell her how much he loved her. She'd remember that when in the midst of grief and feel relieved that he would be taking Charles' place. Yes, he would speak with her later.

Mind made up, he finished his meal and folded his burger wrapper into a tight square, then flattened the fries carton. He strode to the bin and deposited his litter, placing the tray on top of the others, irked that the previous person had left a scattering of salt on theirs. Back in the queue, he waited patiently for his turn and ordered a coffee to go.

Outside, the heat from the cup burning his hand, he walked to his VW to drink in peace and quiet. Dusk had fallen while he'd been in the burger joint, the first sighting of stars struggling to be seen in the gloom. He imagined Charles' campfire lighting their faces while they ate their meal.

Coffee finished, he headed into the supermarket, confident he'd find the gas he wanted. They'd started stocking it in places like this a while back. Before that, he'd had to acquire it from camping stores or petrol stations, and that had proved a bind.

The tug of Lorelei pulled at him now, and he hurried through the self-service till and out into the parking lot. Gas canister heavy, he carried it over one shoulder, cursing as a woman stepped in his path and caught him off-guard. Leyton rasped out an apology—better he do that than argue, wasting precious time away from his love—and pushed on, relieved to reach his van without further incident. Canister secure in the passenger seat, the belt holding it tightly in place, he eased out of his parking space and drove back to his hidden spot. Once there, he drew to a stop and rummaged in the net bag attached behind his seat, bringing out a pair of night-vision goggles.

Back in the tree, he stared down at Charles' campsite. Just as he'd imagined, she sat eating in front of the flames, her face rendered orange in the firelight, her wrists still bound. He took off his cap and donned the goggles, scoping the site. There Charles was, leaning against his caravan doorway, one leg bent, the other straight, reminding Leyton of a flamingo. He smoked a cigarette — such a nasty habit — and blew the smoke from lips that had no business belonging to a man, the bow of the top one much like Lorelei's.

He needs to go. Soon. I can't allow him near her for much longer.

Leyton stared at Charles' face and envisaged it ruined by his scalpel, the cheekbone schlepped off by his machete. Blood oozed from the wounds and dripped off the man's chin, soaking his white shirt with crimson delight. Leyton's fingers twitched, and he almost felt the tools in his hands, handles warm from his heated touch. A touch that would smooth away Lorelei's tears and bring her happiness in his bunk.

One day she'd look at Leyton with desire in her eyes. Him saving her would make her so grateful.

"Who the hell would want to look at you?" Mother said, her cackling laughter turning into spiteful fingers that gripped his heart and squeezed. *"No one. And that's why you'll stay with me. I'm the only one who could love you. The only one who can bear to look at you."*

"Go away, Mother," Leyton snapped.

Lorelei stood and collected bowls, awkward with her hands so close together, and took them to a wooden barrel for washing. Charles brought out a pipe from his shirt pocket and inserted the stem into the corner of his mouth. Smoke puffed up, merging with that of the fire, and he tapped his foot on the ground.

Lorelei walked away from the fire, finding a hidden spot at the end of the caravan. She leaned her back against it, obviously needing time alone. Charles followed and pressed into her, hands braced above her head on the van. She turned her face away, eyes closed and mouth pursed.

"My woman. She's mine!" Leyton rasped, his throat closing with emotion.

Irked, he jumped down from his perch and ambled to his van, collecting his tool pouch and locking the vehicle. With long strides, he loped through the field, his journey easy with the goggles over his eyes. He neared the trees surrounding Charles' campsite and took care with each step, mindful he was close enough that his footsteps might be heard. He couldn't afford any cracking twigs alerting them to his presence. No, Charles was free and easy right now. Leyton stifled a laugh and walked on, the campfire visible as the trees thinned.

A few feet from the tree line, Leyton peered through the foliage and found what he sought. His woman and that man, still leaning against the van, only now that man's hands roved up and down her buttocks.

He breathed out through flared nostrils and clenched his teeth.

"I'll get you," he whispered to Charles.

Oh yes, I'll get you all right.

Chapter Four

Jessica stepped out of the caravan, the slight chill in the air springing goosebumps on her arms. That hateful man had removed the cuffs, placing a steel band around one wrist attached to a long metal chain secured to a ring on the wall inside the van. He told her she could have partial freedom now, and although she wished for total liberty, what he gave her was better than being cramped inside. Rubbing her arms, she stood on the grass, eyeing the area. Her captor had fallen asleep inside. She breathed in the cool night air, pleased to be able to do so.

She began to walk in a circle around the doused fire, the grass cold on her bare feet, the chain tinkling. Her mind went back to when she'd fled, frightened beyond belief, the stench of blood in her nose. Tears pricked her eyes in remembrance. She'd been at Cal's place, dressed in his white shirt after they'd made love. Someone had knocked on the door—the man, God, it had been the man—and Cal had gone to answer it. The man had burst inside, killing Cal with frenzied jabs of his knife then beating him to a pulp, and she had tried so hard to stop it, to make the nightmare go away. Cal had slumped to the floor, and the man turned his steely gaze on her, whispering that he wanted her, had wanted her for a long time, and stepped towards her, the glint of lust in his eyes.

She'd screamed, rushed past him, uncaring that he held the knife—nothing mattered now Cal was gone—and streaked down the street, barely feeling the bite of small stones on her feet. That hateful man had followed, caught her by the hair, and dragged her to his car. She'd screamed, screamed so loud her throat swelled, but no one came to help. She remembered thinking, *Where is everyone? This place is usually so busy!*

He had taken her to this campsite, to the caravan that smelt of sour, unwashed bodies, and had told her she was his now. He'd been watching her a *long* time…

She sighed, shoving the painful memories away. If she thought too much she'd go crazy, and she needed to remain calm. But how could she when he made it clear he wanted her like…that? She stopped and studied the camp. Embers still glowed in the fire, tendrils of smoke snaking into the air, and the scent of the dying heat pervaded the site.

How quiet it was. It gave her time to think, to commune with nature, and try to understand the horrors. She walked on, towards the edge of the clearing. *His* car stood in the darkness—a battered red Pontiac Firebird—and she turned back to face his van. A faint light glowed behind the thin curtains of the side window. He'd told her he liked to read by candlelight and usually doused the flame before sleep—he couldn't afford to lose the van.

Jessica picked up her pace, rounding the car and hoping the chain reached as far as she wanted to walk.

The darkness was deeper in the space between the van and the surrounding forest. She stepped over jutting tree roots and into the trees, but the chain snapped taut, yanking her wrist. She cried out quietly and turned back to the clearing.

A shuffle sounded to her left, and she whipped her head around to peer into the trees. Heart thumping hard, she embraced herself and walked on, sure it was only a night creature ambling around for food. It had sounded like a badger's steps, and if it wasn't for the man's intent to have her as his, she wouldn't have taken any notice. She shuddered at the thought that she was next on his list, a long list he'd told her about. Women he'd raped then killed. A lump filled her throat at the unfairness—she hadn't hurt anyone in her life. She didn't deserve to die because of someone's warped reasoning.

The camp was swamped by silence once more, save for her footsteps and steady breathing. Jessica decided to make another lap of the clearing then retire for the night. *His* candle was doused now, and she crept past his window, reticent to give him any reason to jolt out of bed and investigate should she make a sudden noise. She didn't relish the idea of looking down the barrel of his gun or seeing his glinting blade.

The faint tang of cloves wafted past—so faint she'd swear she'd imagined it. She looked up, her final lap complete, the scent of cloves stronger. The thought of returning to the van sickened her, but she was so tired she had no choice—unless she wanted to sleep out here.

Just one more lap, then I'll go inside.

She cocked her head and sniffed. *Yes, definitely cloves.*

A sharp crack sounded—a breaking twig?—and she gasped, her hand flying to her mouth, the chain's tinkle loud in the dark. She stared all around, her senses on full alert, her mind screaming for her to run to the van and lock the door. Laughter burbled inside her then. Run to the van? Run to *him*?

But what if he came out and I didn't see? If I get to the van... He has a phone in there...

Another waft of cloves reached her along with the soft breeze, and the hairs on her nape stood on end. She hadn't imagined that smell. No, it was there— spicy and pungent. In reverse, she walked in the direction of the van, sights on the tree line and mindful of the dying fire in her path. She quickly glanced back to judge how far she had left to go and where the fire was exactly, then turned back to face the trees.

A figure stood in the clearing, strange goggles covering his eyes and a cap pulled low over his brow. She stifled a scream, breaths coming hard and fast, and stared at the man, who now walked towards her, hands out as though beseeching her to remain quiet.

Is that him?

Hands splayed star-shaped beside her, she turned to run, head lightening and adrenaline fuelling her legs.

"Wait!"

She frowned at the new voice and stopped, spinning to face the man. He stepped closer, the moonlight casting one half of him in shadow, the other half a pale stripe. Heart thudding, she swallowed, narrowing her eyes as his face came into view. Another scream died in her throat, and she teetered on the brink of running, but her feet remained in place. Pink scars marred his cheeks and chin, some crossing over others. Was he a police officer? No, that was too coincidental. Too fanciful. Too much like her trying to convince herself she would be all right, that she'd get away without *him* killing her.

"It's me." He laughed, a soft, comforting sound, and moved nearer. If he held out his arm he'd almost be able to touch her. He took off his cap and goggles.

He thinks I know him?

Midnight eyes stared at her. She gasped as he stepped closer. So many scars, knobby compared to the rest of his face. What had happened to him?

"Who… What… Your face…"

He held out a hand, and she took it, so relieved someone had found her.

"An accident, that's all. Nothing to be afraid of. I've come to save you," he said, smiling with teeth that looked alien in his mouth. Too large. Too crooked.

She rushed into his open arms, pressing her face to his cold jacket. Lifting her head, she stared into his eyes, purposely avoiding sight of the scars. "There's a man…in the caravan. He killed my boyfriend, brought me here." She pulled back a little and raised her manacled arm. "He did this. He's going to…he said…"

"Shh. It's all right. You're safe now, Lorelei."

She frowned. *Lorelei?*

Leyton breathed in her scent—lemons, she smelt of lemons—and stared down at her, unable to believe he held her in his arms. He'd longed for this, hoped she would take to him, and he smiled, pleased that following his instincts had been right.

"My name's Jessica. Quickly, please! Get this off me. Get me out of here."

He stared at the moon's reflection in her eyes. "I can do that."

"Oh, God, hurry!"

Leyton pressed her head to his chest, twining his fingers in her silky soft hair. *Beautiful, so beautiful...* "It's okay."

Lorelei tried to lift her head, but he clamped his hand to the back of it and held it still. She stiffened, and he cursed himself for his action. He shouldn't be scaring her. That didn't figure in his plans. Releasing her, he frowned as she stepped back quickly—too quickly for his liking—and he scrabbled to find a way to ease her again.

He walked backwards a little way. "I need to get my tools."

She clasped her hands in front of her, and he wished one of those hands was his, her soft skin against his palm. With a glance at the van, she bit her lower lip then faced him again.

"But what if he wakes? What if he comes out here while you're gone?" She paused then rushed on. "You won't be able to save me. He's got a gun. A knife. He..." Her sigh blew a strand of hair away from her mouth.

"I understand. It's okay. I won't be long."

She smiled, nodded, and stepped forward. "Please...hurry!"

"All right. No worries." He smiled, the burn raging through him. He stood so close, so damn close to that van and *that man*. Jesus Christ, he could *taste* the thrill. Slipping the goggles over his eyes and replacing his cap, he said, "I'll be off, then."

She tilted her head, regarding him intently, the blue of her eyes rendered grey through the goggles. "Why do you wear those?" she whispered, pointing to his face. "They look kind of creepy."

"An accident. I need to be able to see in the dark. Stepped on a trap once and got my face caught up in its teeth." The lie tripped easily from his tongue, but a ball of regret at having to dupe her settled in his gut.

"Oh, God. I'm sorry. Sorry I asked, brought back memories."

"Hey, no problem." Leyton raised his hand in farewell, wanting to clasp her to him once more but not daring to push his luck. She seemed tense, wary of him, and who could blame her? She was walking out of the frying pan and into the damn fire.

He reversed into the trees, leaving her standing there worrying the neckline of her shirt, her big eyes watching him go, a look of fright on her face. His body hollowed, like a piece of him had been ripped away, and he guessed their parting played a role in that. His vision blurred as he thought of leaving her, but he forced himself to turn, crashing through the forest a short way until he reached the tree where he'd left his tool pouch.

Leyton hugged the pouch to his chest and stumbled back to the camp. She waited where he'd left her, relief seeping into her features when she spotted him. Taking a deep breath, he steadied his emotions, focusing on what he had to do next.

We belong together. Everything will go to plan.

More confident now, he motioned for her to hold up her wrist, then pulled a small set of metal cutters out of his tool case. He snipped the chain, and the sound of it falling to the ground with a dull thud was like a symphony to his ears. He gripped her hand, tugging her through the forest, elation surging through him that their life together had now begun. They broke through a gap in the trees and headed for his VW. Unlocking the side door, he stepped inside, ushered her in and secured it, then placed his pouch on the bunk. He opened it, rubbing his fingers across the machete blade. The cold steel calmed him further, and he smiled as her lemon scent filled the space.

He closed the pouch and hid it beneath his bed, then reached across to close the curtains on the windows above. Opposite stood a small sink with a tiny worktop beside it, and beneath that he stored his stove, gas, water, and food in the cupboard. Weary now, he shut the curtains over the sink and those at the rear of his van. He turned to her and smiled.

"You're safe now. I'll take you to the police soon. First you must change out of that shirt. Have a wash. I'll make you coffee."

She stared at him, mistrust in her eyes, and his stomach bunched. He must make her trust him. Make her want to stay. His adult life had been lonely as he'd trailed killers, ridding the world of badness. Some would say *he* was bad, but no, he wasn't. Not like *them*. No.

She eyed him again, hands clasped in front of her, one foot covering the other in a shy schoolgirl pose. He coaxed, he acted gentle, and eventually she gave in, undressing with her back to him, donning one of his clean T-shirts. They talked, side by side on his bunk, the quilt covering their legs. She told him of her ordeal, and he soothed her fears, mentioning the police again to keep up the charade.

Cocooned, she huddled under the covers, sleep coming on fast.

Fully content for the first time in years, Leyton drifted off, a smile on his face.

Chapter Five

Barry crouched at the head of his bed, staring off into the dark. The red glow of the clock illuminated a small half-circle of the table, glinting in fractured bits off the whisky left in the bottle beside it. The glass in his hands shook. The ice had melted a long time ago. Part of him wanted the oblivion enough alcohol would offer. Part of him was loath to undo all the hard work Tag had done pulling him out of the bottle. So he clung to the edge and desperately tried not to fall back in.

"Losing battle, Tag," he muttered. For a while, he watched the watery whisky slosh around in the tumbler, fascinated by the shapes on the side of the glass as it rolled up and slid back down. That's how he felt. Clinging. The dreams were like gravity, though, sucking him back, whether he wanted to fall or not.

The terror wasn't even the worst part. At some point, you realise it's just a dream. Sure, someone had lived it, had died that way, but you couldn't think about that. You could only thank God it wasn't you.

You're still alive. It was just a dream. No. The worst part was waking up alone, sweating, shaking, and no arms to wrap around you, and no voice whispering that it was okay...you were safe. No one could hurt you.

"Fuck, I'm getting old." He peered at the clock again, this time concentrating enough to let the actual numbers seep into his brain. "Three-thirty."

Too early to go in to work, especially on a Saturday, and he couldn't think anyway. Too late to go find a club and a willing bed mate. The 'ugly lights' would be on by now. In the dim lighting of a pick-up joint he could pass, but once the bar closed and the lights came on, it would be obvious he was no catch in this state. He didn't have the stomach to bring home someone drunk enough to think he was worth it. He was so tired. The sudden, irrational urge to scream and throw the glass against the wall surged through him. He held on until it passed, till his fingers ached and his head throbbed.

"Sorry, Tag. I just need..." *You.*

Setting the glass down beside the bottle, Barry stumbled from the bedroom, stuffed his bare feet into his shoes, and grabbed his apartment keys. He should call first.

He didn't.

He didn't remember his car keys until he was standing beside the old Ford, gazing in at the steering wheel.

"Damn."

Up and down the street, the night noises — distant sirens, a street sweeper on the next block, and the hum of traffic...the city breathing in its half-sleep — drifted around him in a steady rhythm.

He'd walk. Walking was good. It took energy, made him tired, and maybe he would be able to sleep without dreaming. Ten blocks to Tag's peeling-stucco apartment building took half an hour, and he didn't remember much of it. Or didn't want to. The darkness had been too reminiscent of the dreams he couldn't solve. Yawning doorways passed in a blur—like maws, opened and toothless...just dark, endless abysses where safety was an illusion. He was panting and sweating when he reached a shaking finger for the intercom button on the side of the faded pink building. Maybe he'd run. His feet were slippery inside his worn Docs, and trickles of dampness slid down his spine.

"What?" Taggart's sleepy, irritated voice crackled loudly out of the speaker.

"Tag?" Barry's own voice sounded breathless, shaky by comparison.

"Shit. Wiki?"

Barry pressed the button again and nodded, trying to catch his breath.

"It's open."

A loud buzz sounded, and Barry pushed through the doors into the shabby, threadbare lobby. He took the wide central staircase up the two floors and headed left down the puke-green hallway under the humming lights. Taggart's door stood open a sliver, and as he approached, it opened fully.

"Come on in."

"Sorry to wake you, Tag."

"Wasn't sleepin'."

Someone shuffled out of the bathroom and lifted a head of blond curls to stare at him. The stranger smirked, clapped Tag on the back, and waved the shirt in his hand at Barry. "Busy place." Turning to Tag, he tilted his head to one side. His lascivious grin made Barry's stomach churn slightly. "See you again sometime?"

Tag made a non-committal sound and walked him deliberately past Barry towards the door. Whatever other pleasantries were exchanged, Barry didn't hear them. He tried very hard not to hear or acknowledge any of it.

"So?" The door thumped closed, and Tag turned to lean on it. "Dreams?"

"Can't sleep," Barry muttered.

"Won't sleep."

"Would you?"

Tag shook his head and rubbed a hand over the back of his neck. The gesture flooded Barry with memories of when they had been partners in bed and out.

"I'm sorry for interrupting. It was..." *You or the bottle.* How many times had he used that excuse? Barry let out a breath. "I didn't want to show up at the station stinking of whisky."

Taggart peered at him from a head-bowed position. "On a Saturday?"

Barry just shrugged. "Have to solve this, stop it... I needed..."

"I know."

He did too. He knew exactly what Barry wanted. He could see it in the way Tag hugged his arms close and curled in on himself, unwilling to reach out for fear of inadvertently making the wrong offer. Or maybe worried Barry would snap his hand off. He hadn't exactly been open or welcoming in the past year.

After another few heartbeats, he spoke again. "That's good, Barry." His voice creaked over the words, tight and tense. "Better me than the bottle. My couch is your couch. You know that."

What sucked was that Barry couldn't even get mad anymore, and it wasn't worth the incessant pain of hoping for a different answer. What had he really expected? Tag had done everything he could. He'd stuck it out as long as he could. The truth was, Barry Whittaker was a liability and no one really wanted to be his partner. It was dangerous work at the best of times. Being partnered with a nutcase who only slept half as much as he should and carried a gun was the worst kind of Russian roulette.

"Come on." Tag pulled him by the arm across the room. "Shower. I'll make up the couch."

Not what he'd hoped for, but even the sympathy fucking had stopped a long time ago. Barry nodded and headed for the bathroom. He tried hard not to notice the rumpled bed sheets and obvious wet spot gracing the pale blue cotton. Odd moment to remember he'd bought those sheets, setting up house with Tag. Seemed like a lifetime ago.

Under the hot spray, divested of day-old clothes he'd long since soaked in stress and sweat, Barry began to feel much more human, a little foolish, and a lot horny. The stranger Tag had shown out of his apartment without so much as an introduction hadn't been at all bad-looking, but then, Tag had always been good at drawing in the lookers. Imagining what they'd been up to was enough to get Barry hard and make him growl with frustration. He didn't want to imagine Tag with someone else. It was a weird mix of excitement and revulsion that had him picturing the blond with his head down and his ass up, and Tag nailing him. It *shouldn't* excite him, but it did, even as the wish that he was the one being nailed squeezed the breath and the life out of him. He didn't have the right to wish...

"I'm an idiot." Still, he ran his fingers over his erection, leaned his shoulder blades on the wall, and tipped his head back. The feel of the water falling over him was calming, a replacement for hands he couldn't have. His palm pressed to his chest, as if he could hold the cracks inside closed. Smooth skin against his palm was just a reminder of the crinkle of sensation when he ran his hands over Tag's hairy, barrel chest.

"Not the same," he muttered as he forced his eyes closed and curled his fingers around himself. Maybe not, but it was release. It was a way to clear his head, and if he could hear Tag on the other side of the door — smell him, his soap and aftershave permeating his space — it was as close as he was going to get. It was going to have to do.

Breathing in a short, panting rhythm the flimsy bathroom door probably didn't mask, it took too long to get there.

"Tag." He whispered the name as quietly as he could and called up the memories — the feel of strong hands on him, of Tag deep inside, his weight and force, and the way it was safe under him, easy to forget for a while. Memories were a poor substitute but enough to get off. He stifled a grunt, flailed with his free hand for support, and braced it with a rattle and thump on the shower doors as his cum shot and spiralled away with the water down the drain.

"Wiki?" Tag's voice outside jarred him upright.

"Yeah." Too gruff.

"Everything all right?"

"Be right out." Not much better. He watched a bit of spunk slide down the door, made a move to wipe it away, and stopped.

"Serve ya right if I leave it there." He lifted one lip in a silent snarl, splashed water across the door, turned off the taps, and stepped out.

"Barry, there're no towels in there."

Of course not. He glanced around and groaned.

"I'm coming in."

Barry turned his back to the door as it opened, and Tag came inside.

"Just leave it—"

The towel was draped over his shoulders, and Tag's strong hands remained there too. "We'll figure this out."

Barry nodded but said nothing.

For a minute, Tag's heat and presence were close, his head resting against the back of Barry's, his hands firm on his shoulders. The air hummed with a million things neither of them said, and then Tag was backing out, leaving him alone.

* * * *

Alone. He was always alone. Even with…with what? With who?

A hand on the back of his head, stroking. He shook. Nails scraped across his scalp. He couldn't stop shaking. Fingers tangled in his hair, pulled until his head was tipped up as far as it would go. The hand was so strong. The voice…

"Open."

He shook his head, clamped his lips closed. That voice. Female, but hard, cold, unlike anything he'd dreamed before, and still with an eerie sense of familiarity to it that wormed into his gut. Beyond knowing this was a dream, that sense of familiarity terrified him. The voice should be…gentler. Fingers tightened until shaking his head 'no' yanked at his hair and made his eyes tear up. He felt it part from his scalp

55

and stopped moving. Whoever held him shook him by the hair, and his heart shredded. It shouldn't be like this.

"Please," he said.

"Open!"

"Please don't." His own voice was tiny by comparison. He was tiny. Helpless. His breath caught on a sob even as he tried not to think he was dreaming in the skin of a child.

"Too late."

A finger pried into his mouth. Not a finger. Something cold, hard. He struggled, no longer caring about his hair. It was coming. It would hurt. The clank of metal against his teeth was loud inside his head. Then there was just pain.

When his vision cleared, everything had changed. A clammy breeze blew across his tear-stained face, trapping his hair in the dampness. A chain rattled lightly with his movement, and the heavy weight on one wrist told him where it was attached. He was no longer in the same dream. He was older, bigger, still terrified.

He tried looking around, but it was too dark to see where the other end of the chain led. Anticipation of Bad Things whispered through the breeze, trickled through his hair like unwanted fingers.

The shift threw him off. The last dream hadn't ended, and here he was in some other victim's skin watching someone...something coming towards him. A figure approached out of the dark, hunched, its face distorted out of proportion by scars and...something...covering its eyes.

He squinted, shut his eyes tight, as though everything would be clear when he opened them again. It wasn't. It was like looking through a set of night goggles. The figure approaching was a wavering cloud of blues and greens, as though it possessed no warmth of its own. He shuddered in revulsion. Hope couldn't come in a package like that...

He blinked and everything changed again. He was lying on a hard, creaking bed surrounded by the scent of stale smoke and old beer. He listened in the darkness, but the *sounds that should have been there were absent. He just didn't know what those sounds should be, didn't know what he was listening for.*

"What's missing?" he whispered.

No one answered.

There was no one, nothing but the vague scent of lemons under the other stench.

He sat up, and a shape loomed out of the dark. A leering, maniacal, contorted face he should recognise. His stomach churned. He tried to get up but found himself once again on his knees, that hand tight in his hair. The face shifted closer. It was a woman. He smelt cloves. Someone...

"You'll stay now..." She leered at him.

"Mother?"

Pain. Just pain and absolute terror, the scent of piss and the warmth of it between his legs. Death should mean the end of pain, but it didn't stop. It never stopped.

"Barry!"

Shouting burst through the high ringing in his ears, which then resolved into his own voice, keening a high, desperate note.

"Shhh." Tag pulled him forward into a safe embrace. "Shh. Stop. It was a dream. Barry."

Tag knelt on the floor, rocking him where he sat on the couch and splaying a hand across the back of his head. He clung, tight fists wound into the T-shirt Tag had put on before he went back to bed. He couldn't breathe. His head spun, and dark spots swam behind his tightly closed eyelids.

"Hang on, baby. It's going to be okay."

Barry choked on his own tears. It took a long time for the soothing words and the calming touch to get through. The residual horror hung on at the back of his mind, a tenacious monster he couldn't escape.

Finally, it was the ammonia smell of urine that got through.

"Jesus." He backed away from Tag, yanking the covers over himself. "Sorry."

"Don't be." Tag didn't quite let him go, but kept one hand at his temple, tucking a bit of the tangled hair there back behind his ear. "It's gotten worse." His grey eyes were full of concern.

Barry nodded. "This is a bad one."

"You wanna shower?" Tag pushed himself to his feet and held out a hand. "I'll clean this up."

"I'm sorry, Tag—"

"Jesus, Barry." He yanked, and Barry stumbled forward against him. "Don't worry about it. Just..." This time there was no mistaking the press of lips against the short hair at Barry's temple. "*I'm* sorry. I should have realised." He cupped a hand on either side of Barry's head, held him there and gazed into his eyes. "We are going to get to the bottom of this. I promise."

Barry nodded then pulled free. He couldn't do this. He should never have come here. It was too close to what he wanted, what he didn't have anymore. "I'll go...clean up."

He shuffled off to the bathroom, stood under the steaming spray for a few minutes where he could shake and let his body shiver out the last bits of terror.

When he returned to the main room, a towel wrapped around his waist, Tag had stripped the couch and opened the window to the balcony where the cushions leaned against the fire escape railing. Hints of pink morning light sifted through the smog and the cracked kitchen window to glint faintly on the stainless steel sink.

He reached for his clothes, folded neatly on the coffee table, but a pair of Tag's old sweat pants hit him square in the face.

"You need to sleep, Barry."

"Can't." *Don't want to.*

"I know, but you have to. You know it gets worse if you don't stay rested."

"I don't know if it can get worse." He shivered. The remnants of this dream just wouldn't leave him.

"Come here." Tag was sitting on the edge of the bed, and he patted the mattress beside him. "Talk to me."

"What's to say?" Barry stayed safely in the living half of the apartment, his back to Tag as he dropped the towel and pulled up the sweats. He yanked the string taut as he turned. "I have bad dreams. No one — almost no one — can make them stop."

"Come here," Tag insisted, once more patting the mattress.

"Tag...I can't." *Can't love you again. It hurts too much.* Of course, he couldn't say that any more than he could actually *stop* loving and needing the other man. But he couldn't rely on him, and it wasn't fair to have put this pressure on him again.

"Let me help you."

"For how long?" The bitterness was impossible to hide completely.

Tag closed his eyes, his jaw set. "Deserved." Each heartbeat that passed in silence ratcheted up the tension a little more. "For today. Let me help today," he said at last.

No promises beyond that.

Barry sighed. What, exactly, had he expected? A confession that letting him go in the first place had been a mistake? But then, he dreamed in nightmares, not fantasy. He dragged himself over to the bed and sat a good distance from Tag.

"What was this dream? Did it give you anything at all?"

Barry shivered. "It's one thing," he said quietly, "to dream about...the murders. To be in their skin and know this is the last thing they'll feel, the last punch, last rape, last breath..." He only realised he'd shuffled closer to Tag when Tag's big hand settled on his thigh and squeezed a bit. "You feel the hands close around your throat, or the knife go in, the thud of a bullet. It's terrifying. But it ends. The hurt, the fear, everything. It ends. I'm lucky to get the last bits of their memories, to be able to find who did it and stop it happening to someone else."

"But?"

"This was different."

"How?"

Barry looked up from the floor at last and met Tag's steady gaze. "No one died."

"Well." Tag's brows drew down, and he rubbed his hand across the back of his neck. "That's good, isn't it? Means we're not looking for another body."

"Not yet, anyway."

"What?" Tag turned slightly to face him. "What else? What are we looking for?"

"That's just it. I don't know. I just know all that fear, all that...horror. Someone else is walking around with that shit in their head." For a minute, Barry felt lightheaded and dizzy. "What does that do to a person?"

Tag let out a long breath and, surprisingly, pulled Barry into another hug. "I've been wondering that since I met you."

"Huh." Barry tried to resist the urge to lean into the embrace, to take the comfort for however long it was going to last. He couldn't manage keeping away. This was the only place—inside this warmth, this cocoon—that the dreams couldn't reach. Finally, he had to give in. He did, without asking what Tag meant. He didn't want to hear that the one person he needed to believe in him thought he was crazy.

"Lie down." Tag moved, pushing himself backwards across the bed with his heels. "It's a good day to sleep in." He lay down and patted the sheets in front of him.

For the first time, Barry noticed the sheets were white and not the pale blue stained ones that had been on the bed when he'd arrived. A tiny smile turned his lips, and he flopped into the fragrant, clean smell of them and the warm, earthy scent of Tag, still slightly tinged with Old Spice.

Tag wiggled an arm under him and wrapped it around his chest, pulling him back until the rough feel of his curly chest hair rubbed against Barry's back. He caressed Barry's chest, and his breath fluttered through his hair.

"Go to sleep, babe. I'll be here. Just sleep, and don't dream."

If only. It had been a year and a half since the last full night of dreamless sleep. A year and a half since the last time Tag had held him like this. Part of him wanted the magic bullet. Part of him didn't want the magic to be Tag.

Chapter Six

Birds twittered, alerting Leyton that morning had arrived. He cracked open an eye and peered at his watch. Nine-thirty. Fully rested, he carefully eased away from Lorelei and inched back the covers. He rubbed sleep dust from his eyes and yawned.

He had time to kill — and Charles.

Smiling at the prospect, he stood and pulled open the sink cupboard to check his water level. He'd need to refill it soon, but there was enough there for a wash and some coffee. He'd made the water contraption himself, rigging up a large container with pipes to the tap so it worked just as well as any in a modern caravan. His mother's VW — *his* VW — had served him well since her death, the good old thing still going strong. If it broke down, he knew enough to fix most problems, and if he couldn't, he had the cash to find someone who did.

Leyton lifted out his stove and quietly placed it on the worktop, lighting the gas and putting a half-filled kettle of water on top. The days of living out of this van were coming to an end. His mother had left him money, quite a sum stashed in a large locked tin in the bottom of the wardrobe.

"*I didn't leave you nothin', Leyton.*"

"Be quiet, Mother," he whispered.

He filled the sink and washed all over with cold water, stooping to douse, shampoo, then rinse his hair. No, Mother hadn't left him anything. He'd taken it—and rightly so—as payment for the things she'd done to him. Every time he'd been bad she'd given one of his teeth a twist with her pliers, leaving him in pain for days at a time, toothache raging, him chewing cloves to make the throb go away. After he'd apologised and meant it—and God, had he meant it...anything to make that pain disappear—she'd wrenched the tooth from his mouth.

"And you make me do that to *them* too, don't you, Mother?"

"*I don't make you do anythin', Leyton. That's all yourself. All your own doin'. And as for that money... Hmm, when you found it I was scared you'd turn me in, but instead—*"

"Instead I killed you. Yes, that's right. And why would I return the money? It wouldn't have brought the jewels back you stole from that family, would it? Naughty Mother, stealing from other folks." He grimaced.

Dried and dressed, he ousted Mother from his mind, her bitterness always souring his mood. He didn't need annoyance in his life right now. No, he needed concentration, patience, and hope.

"*Did you enjoy killin' me, Leyton?*"

"Go away, Mother."

"*Did you like pullin' out my teeth and givin' me what I gave you? Those cuts to my face...did they make me pretty too?*"

Clenching his teeth, Leyton squeezed his eyes closed for a few seconds then opened them again, spying his binoculars hanging on a hook by the door. He took them in hand and turned to look at the still-sleeping Lorelei. She would be all right here while he was gone. When he returned he'd explain why he had to leave her, make her understand. And she would, he knew it.

He slipped the strap around his neck and hunkered down beside the bed, quietly pulling out his tool pouch. Selecting a mid-length blade and his pliers, he left the van, locking her in. He headed for the tree. Pleased the sun shone, Leyton climbed, the warmth chasing the chill from the air and his body. He settled on his branch and raised the binoculars, peering at the camp.

Charles sat whittling on a rickety stool, his hand movements sharp, jerky. He must be angry Lorelei was gone. Angry he'd let his control slip. Giving her freedom to walk the camp had been a bad move. The burn ignited inside Leyton, and he pondered on how he would approach and off that nasty bastard.

"How will you keep a hold of her, Leyton? You're no better than Charles. She'd be insane to trust you, and you're insane to think you can make her care for you."

"Shut. Up."

Leyton turned his head and studied Charles, who continued jabbing at the strip of wood. His knees peeked from holes in his denims, and wide biceps stretched the arms of his tight black T-shirt. He worked out, that much was certain.

I can handle him.

Fiddling with the binocular dial, he brought his image closer. Deep wrinkles lined Charles' face, and his skin looked weathered—like worn, cracked cowhide, in need of moisture or...slicing. Leyton gritted his teeth and concentrated.

"Make it quick, boy. It won't be long before she wakes up."

"Don't talk about her like that, Mother."

"Like what?"

"Stressing 'she' like Lorelei... Oh, go away."

Leyton scrabbled down the tree and strode through the woods, eyes keen to the gaps between trunks that indicated the clearing ahead. He slowed as he neared, staring directly at Charles, who carved with angry vigour. The man's hair hung loose and lank, in need of a wash, and the overnight birth of stubble darkened his jaw.

"Annoyed she's gone, Charles?" Leyton whispered and crept closer.

He hid behind a tree trunk, peering out to the side, waiting for the burn inside him to reach the right temperature. He thought of Charles touching Lorelei, and the heat intensified, firing his synapses and urging him to walk out into the clearing.

Charles looked up and scowled, his hands stilling. His lips formed a thin straight line, and he narrowed his almond-shaped eyes.

"Hey, man!" Leyton said, smiling wide and ambling towards him. "I got lost out here. Camped somewhere, but hell if I know how to get back. You got a compass by any chance?"

"Maybe."

Either you have or you haven't.

"It would be great if you do. I can check where I am and be on my way. Leave you to...your craft."

Lies, lies, lies...make Leyton a very crafty boy.

Leyton stifled a giggle, clamping his teeth again.

Charles, gaze staying on Leyton, dropped the wood on the ground beside him but kept hold of the knife. He stood and poked the blade in the air towards Leyton, eyes half-lidded, suspicion pooling there. "Wait here, right?"

Leyton nodded, smile remaining in place.

Walking away with a sour glance over his shoulder, Charles entered his van, disappearing into the darkness within. Leyton eased his hand inside his inner jacket pocket and grasped the knife. The familiar surge of excitement sped through him, notching up his heartbeat. His pulse thudded in his neck, and he experienced a moment of light-headedness as he became accustomed to the changes coming to him all at once. With a deep breath, he brought the knife out and held it to his side, steel pointing behind him.

Charles is taking his time. Inconsiderate prick.

Leyton stared at the whittled wood on the ground, squinting to make out what the bastard had been creating. Two breasts jutted from the thick, barkless branch, the smooth white tapering down to a slim waist and the beginnings of the juncture between plump thighs.

He's making Lorelei. Or is there already another woman on his mind?

Leyton's cheeks itched from their growing heat, and he scratched one with his free hand, fingernails gliding up and over the severest ridge on his skin. Charles stepped out of his van, knife still in one hand, a compass held out with the other. He moved towards Leyton, his strides assured, arm muscles bunching with every step.

Leyton took the compass and nodded his thanks. He smiled again, wider—it hurt his damn cheeks—and began turning in a circle, careful to keep the knife hidden, making pretence of searching for the correct direction. As he swung to face Charles again, he lifted the knife and jabbed it into the man's eye, twisting it ninety degrees and raising the tip a little. Charles screamed, hands automatically rising, and Leyton jerked the blade towards himself. It came free of the socket, eye halfway down the steel, joined to Charles by a straggle of wet, ropey matter. Leyton yanked, and Charles stumbled backwards, blood pouring between his fingers. He fell, a whoosh of air and another scream leaving him, and writhed on the ground.

Snake in the grass…

With no time to waste, Leyton flicked the eye off his knife and lurched forwards, straddling Charles. The burn increased, made him literally see red as he stabbed the man's chest. He wrenched out the knife. Blood spurted, splashing across Leyton's face and wetting the side of his hand. Hacking on, he revelled in the gurgled cries emanating from Charles' open maw, red life spewing from between the rapist's lips.

The body stilled. The screams stopped. Leyton paused.

He cocked his head, studying the dead man.

"How pretty you would look with a slice…there. And another just…there. More…here."

Ah, my canvas. My beautiful canvas.

* * * *

Jessica roused to the sound of birdsong, the melodies not quite loud enough to prod her sleepy mind fully awake or make her open her eyes. She lay for a moment in oblivion, stretching her legs, toes pointed and butting…something hard yet soft?

Quickly, she snapped her eyes open and propped herself up on one elbow.

Oh, shit.

She was in a camper van—*still in the fucking van!*—and there she was thinking she'd dreamed the whole damn thing. Tears burned her eyes as she stared at her feet resting against the back of the front seat. Glancing around, she found herself alone with the stench of cloves filling her nose, the air fusty. She bit back a gag and swivelled to sit up, glancing down at the T-shirt she wore. Last night, the man—Leyton, he'd told her—had said he'd call the police, but she'd fallen asleep before he had. Where was he? Had he gone to the police station?

She shifted the blanket off her and stood. A blush crept into her cheeks. She needed something to cover her legs. Although last night she'd been fine talking to him dressed like this, in the light of day it was altogether different. She rifled through his wardrobe for some jogging bottoms and slipped them on. Too big, but no matter. They were better than nothing.

Maybe he's outside.

Jessica stepped to the window above the sink area and pulled the curtain across. The van's surroundings looked very different to the previous night. Trees crowded around as though floating closer, their branches stretching above to form a leafy canopy that obscured a good portion of the sunlight. Leyton had camped on a speck of grass. Did he want to keep his van out of sight? If so, why?

Chills overtook Jessica, and she gripped the door handle and pulled.

The door was locked.

Panic growing, she moved to the rear door window and pushed the drape aside. More trees greeted her, trunks gnarled and knobby, branches like arms with clawed hands. Yanking on the handle, she tried to open the door. It didn't budge. She turned and staggered the short space to the bed, plunking down on it, suddenly out of breath and frightened. Nausea wiggled inside her, and she swallowed, a flicker of terror beating beneath her left eye. She stared towards the front of the van. Paper blinds hung across the windshield, the door windows covered with drapes that matched the others. Jessica jumped up and clambered over the front seats, eager to try the driver's and passenger doors. Her efforts proved fruitless, and she knew — *knew* deep down — he had ensured she wouldn't be able to get out.

Why, though? Last night he was so…nice. It's not like I need to be here. Unless… Shit, unless he's working with that other bastard!

Jessica slumped in the driver's seat and clamped a hand over her mouth, breathing heavily through her nose to prevent herself being sick. She closed her eyes and rested her head back. Disorientation swept over her, and she snapped her eyes wide to regain her equilibrium. Leaning forward, she lifted the paper blind and peered out.

Ah, Leyton had backed into the trees, then. A small clearing lay ahead, and a huge oak stood a few feet away, leaves jostling languidly. Movement caught her attention — a fleeting glimpse of a shadow in the trees to her right — and she turned her head, steeling herself for what she would see.

Nothing.

Is someone out there, hiding in the trees? Is it Leyton? Or that man?

She scrambled out of the seat and back into the main body of the van.

A kettle sat atop a small portable stove beside the sink, matches on the tiny worktop. A mug with coffee dregs stood in the sink. Why hadn't she smelt it when he'd made it? The scent of coffee always woke her. She thought of home, of her mother trying to get hold of her, of work grumbling that she hadn't turned up. Had the police found Cal's body yet? She'd told her friend she was going there, so surely, if he'd been discovered, the police were looking for her too? She imagined her photograph splashed across newspapers and on the TV, her mother crying at a press conference for her safe return.

Feeling slightly better at the prospect, she tried the door handle again. Something scraped the door from the outside, and she leapt back, palm pressed to her mouth once more. Breaths left her nostrils in quick bursts, her heart beating so fast she waited to faint. Another scrape shrieked, and the image of Leyton's tool pouch he'd slid beneath the bed last night flashed through her mind.

Jessica crouched and patted under the bunk, fingertips touching a bump. She tugged it out and flipped open the pouch with a shaking hand, selecting a long-bladed knife. She stood and faced the side door, weapon poised. A shadow flitted past the window above the sink, eerie through the curtain, then appeared behind the one on the rear door. A scream threatened to bark out of her, and she shook all over, fear pervading every part of her body. Her knees weakened as the shadow whipped past the sink window again, and the sound of a key entering the lock churned her guts.

Placing one foot behind her, the other out front, she adopted a pose ready to lunge. She held the knife aloft in her fist, blade pointed downward, and stared at the door. It yawned open—*so damn slow!*—and Jessica shut her eyes and brought down the knife. A hand clamped around her wrist, and she let the knife go, eyes snapping wide. The pain of the grip sent her fingers into a starfish shape, and she looked ahead at who held her tight. Leyton stood outside the van, his T-shirt blood-soaked, his face splattered with near-black streaks. The scream Jessica had held in burst out, loud and never ending, the sound alien, unlike anything she'd heard before.

Is that me? Am I making that noise? What the hell is he doing covered in blood? Oh my God. Oh my God. Please, get me the fuck out of here. Oh, shit. Shit!

She sank to her knees, pain paralysing her for a few seconds.

Still holding her wrist, Leyton climbed into the van and closed the door, locking it and pocketing the keys. He kneeled beside her, pulling her close to his side. Letting go of her wrist, he draped his arm across her back, hugging her as she sobbed against his chest. The copper stench from his shirt was cloying, too much, and she retched, trying to move away.

"No, no, no. Let me make it all better, Lorelei," he crooned. "Let me hug everything away. You're safe now. I'll take care of you forever."

His breath moved her hair, and she processed his words, one standing out above all the others.

Forever.

What does he mean? Fuck forever! He was going to call the police. He is going to call the police, and I'm going home.

She retched again, nothing coming up but stinging bile, and she swallowed it. Taking a deep breath, she said, "Please, I want to go home."

He chuckled and stroked her hair, his arm about her back clamping her tighter. "Ah, but you *are* home. Well, home for now, anyway." That chuckle again. "But we'll find a house, one we both like, and then make a *real* home."

What the fuck?

"But I *have* a home." She pressed her hands to the dampness on his shirt, and despite shuddering at what she touched, she pushed away from him.

He released her, and she stood quickly, sickened by the transference of blood from his top to hers. To her palms.

"That home belongs in the past, Lorelei." He rose to his feet.

"My name's Jessica," she whispered, fear coiling in her belly.

"And that name belongs in the past too." He took a step closer and cupped her cheek. "You're mine now." Dropping his hand to his side, he gestured to his clothing. "I did this all for you."

She reached out behind her for the bed, needing to sit before her legs gave way. The thin mattress dipped beneath her weight, and she sat, hugging herself, teeth chattering. "Did what?" *Do I want to know? Shit, what the fuck has he done?*

"I killed that nasty man for you, Lorelei. He won't hurt another woman again." He smiled as though proud of himself.

Oh, God. Jesus fucking Christ…

He stared at her, scars appearing livid and new beneath the covering of blood. The skin beside his eyes crinkled, and a dimple of sorts contorted his right cheek.

He's crazy. As crazy as that other bastard.

"Oh, God help me," she whispered and stared at his feet.

"Lorelei?"

His tone made her look up.

"Why would you need God when you have me?"

Chapter Seven

Afternoon sunlight rolled over Barry's legs, its warm caress gently pulling him up from the blank, sound doze. It took a moment to figure that out. There were no windows near his bed. Darkness glowering over him as he rested didn't make it any easier to give in to sleep he knew would bring terror, so he'd moved his bed into a windowless alcove. He turned his head, rolled onto his back, and the faint smell of Old Spice reached him.

"Tag..."

In answer, Tag's big, firm hand slid up his belly to rest on his chest.

Barry held his breath.

Tag moved his hand again. Thick fingers found and teased a nipple to a tight, aching nub, and Barry let the breath out in a tiny, mewling moan.

"Tag? You awake?"

"Yeah." Gently, as though worried he might spook him, Tag inserted his fingers under the waistband of Barry's too-big pants and slowly hauled them down.

"Stop it…" But Barry lifted his hips, allowing the sweats to slide over his ass. Tag got them to his knees, and Barry freed his feet from the tangle.

One of Tag's hairy legs insinuated itself between Barry's and pressured his rapidly growing erection.

"What are you doing, Tag?"

"Want you."

Barry clamped a hand over Tag's wrist before he could molest the other nipple. Before it was too late to stop him. "You had me. Now you don't."

"You're in my bed," Tag pointed out, his voice perfectly reasonable, his lips fastening on the side of Barry's neck.

"Get off me, and I'll get out," Barry growled.

Tag's lips moved away. His tongue played about Barry's ear and his hips ground into Barry. He could feel Tag's wood against his thigh, grinding into him, drawing Tag's breath up, short and sharp with each hard thrust. He remembered the feel of that thickness spreading him, filling him, and the desire to feel it again rippled through him.

"Roll over," Tag countered.

"Horny fucking bastard," Barry snarled as Tag pulled free of his grip and rolled on top of him. He tried to push the heavy man off, but Tag refused to be moved.

"What'd you come here for if not for this?"

Barry compressed his lips, keeping his answer to himself.

"Tell me you don't want it." Tag stared at him, still on top of him, his weight bearing him into the mattress. "Tell me no."

"No," Barry whispered, barely a breath past his lips as he tilted his head back, exposing his throat, and pushed his hips up into Tag.

Tag's mouth clamped down over his Adam's apple, sucking at him, his tongue licking at the sleep-sweat clinging to Barry's skin. Tag's body answered his, gliding with his movements in a smooth, practiced rhythm their bodies easily remembered.

Barry panted — beleaguered by the onslaught — moaned, and let his hands drift up under Tag's shirt. His fingers played lightly in the sparse hair on Tag's back, and he let his legs fall open so Tag nestled between his thighs.

"What do I believe, Wiki?" Tag asked, pulling back to look at him. "Your words or your body?"

My heart.

Trouble was, neither his words nor his body adequately conveyed what his heart wanted.

"Kiss me."

For a moment, Tag merely stared at him, speculation under the lust. How many times had they fucked without that one intimacy? For a while after Tag left and Barry kept showing up on his doorstep, there had always been fucking — hard and fast — blowjobs and heavy petting, and Barry falling dead asleep, safe from dreams for a few hours. But never kissing.

Barry shifted, averting his gaze and turning his head slightly, struggling to accept there was never going to be kissing now.

"Barry." Tag's voice dropped, rough, quiet, onto his cheek like the kisses he refused to give. "It isn't going to be like before."

Barry's chest contracted around his heart, squeezing the life out of it. He shoved at Tag, trying to dislodge him. "Like before when you loved me, you mean?" he spat, heaving against Tag's chest.

The man refused to be removed. Instead, he sat up, straddling Barry and snagging his wrists, pinning him to the bed. "Like when I was trying to pretend I didn't," he said quietly.

Barry's breath caught on the rough edges in Tag's voice. "Why would you?"

Tag closed his eyes, dropping his chin so Barry couldn't see his face properly and he couldn't make him look up with his hands pinned.

"Tag."

Another space of broken heartbeats went by before Tag looked up.

"If this isn't pretending, what is it, Tag?"

Tag leant down, and his lips brushed over Barry's. "I don't know. Can we try it? See where it takes us?"

"Us?"

Tag licked at Barry's lips, covered his mouth gently, and Barry sighed, letting the tentative touch be his answer. He stopped trying to free himself and gave in to the subtle pressure on his lips, opening his mouth as Tag's tongue flicked out to taste him again.

The kiss grew in intensity until Barry was moaning into Tag's mouth and squirming. Without letting go of Barry's hands, Tag slid down on top of him. Barry once again spread his legs, wrapping them around Tag's when his lover settled between his thighs. He didn't dare ask where this was coming from, or speculate where it was leading. He wasn't brave enough right then to hear the answers.

Instead, he concentrated on re-learning Tag, starting with the spicy-sweet taste of him, his strength and weight crushing him into the mattress. The heat of his body and feel of his hair, crisp against Barry's smooth skin, infused Barry with need. He jerked his hips up and tore his lips free.

"Fuck me."

"Wait." Tag moved his hands, wrapping Barry's fingers around the metal bedstead. "Hold on."

"Why?" Barry stared up at him. "I want to touch you."

"You'll get your chance. Let me do this."

"Do what?"

Tag, however, seemed to be done talking for the moment. His mouth roved Barry's body, tickling over his ribs and belly, his tongue leaving a damp trail of tingling skin behind. Barry wriggled himself around to get that mouth where he wanted it, to get his most sensitive spots in contact with that tantalising promise of pleasure. Tag responded by lingering whenever Barry let himself show his appreciation.

It was hard. He'd been so long pretending himself, so many times with strangers who would never be back to retrace their passionate steps. He'd stopped responding to the jolts of pleasure, and learned to appreciate the beauty in a bit of pain that took his mind off the impossibility of ever feeling any of this again. He'd become adept at picking out the men who'd knock him about a bit, jack him hard and leave him sore. Sore meant still alive.

"So gentle," he murmured.

"I want to remember every detail," Tag whispered, lips soft against the skin over Barry's hip. "I want to go back over you, inch by inch, and remember what it feels like to love you."

Barry's fingers tightened on the bed rails. "You forget?" He canted his hips, trying to get his cock closer to Tag's lips and the heat his mouth was spreading over the rest of him.

Tag slid his own fingers into his mouth instead then wiggled back up to lie across Barry. "I want to hear you again. Moaning." He reached down and plied his wet fingers between Barry's legs, dragging them over his hole. "Telling me all your little secrets, giving it all up just by the way your breath catches."

Barry gasped as Tag pried him open with his fingers and pushed inside.

"Just like that, Barry. All the little sounds, the way you twitch and shiver."

He paused to lick at Barry's nipple while he wrested ownership of his backside away from the string of one-night stands and punishing strangers.

He dug in deep, niggling at Barry's prostate. "I want you to remember, too."

Barry's hips jerked. His head dropped back onto the pillow with a muffled thump, and he moaned then bucked again, looking for another tweak inside. "Remember what?"

"Good things, Barry. I want you to remember what this is about. Between us, it isn't fucking. Not today."

"Sometimes," Barry muttered, bearing down on Tag's fingers.

"Sometimes." Tag twitched his fingers, and Barry's grunt ended in a desperate gasp. "But not today."

"Please, Tag. Want more."

"I know." Tag wiggled up a little more and took Barry's mouth in a searing kiss, delving his tongue as deep as his fingers, sliding his other hand up Barry's arm until he could pry his tight grip loose and twine his fingers through Barry's.

Under the barrage, Barry finally began to loosen his death grip on his emotions. Maybe it was real. Maybe it was another dream. Maybe this would be the worst nightmare of all, but he couldn't hold onto himself so tight that he lost the chance to find out. His fingers curled around Tag's hand, his hips rose to meet the next thrust, and he sighed into Tag's mouth.

"Remember what we used to say?" Tag asked. He punctuated his speech with little nips along Barry's torso. "Remember when you'd look me in the eye — beg me to take it all away?"

Barry moaned. His hand tightened on the metal of the bed, his arm shaking with the effort of keeping that grip, of letting Tag lead, trusting where they were going.

"I'm going to do that again, Barry. Relax." He took one nipple between his teeth and pinched.

"Ah!" Barry heaved up under him as that peculiar mixture of pain and pleasure skidded along his skin and sank into his gut.

Another couple of thrusts with those fingers, teeth on his skin, weight grounding him and restricting his movement, drove Barry to panting, reaching madness. "Tag!"

"You always were impatient."

"You always take your bloody time," Barry growled.

"Because you know you want this to last."

Barry blinked, pulled himself up, and Tag's fingers slipped free. "I want us to last."

"I know." He nipped kisses over Barry's tender lips. "One day at a time. Now spread your legs."

Tag reached under the pillow Barry's head was on and pulled out a condom, which he dropped onto Barry's chest. He sat up, pulled his shorts off and tossed them to the floor. "Suit me up."

"I can let go of the bed now?"

"Just for this."

"And if I ignore your little power play?"

"I have cuffs."

Barry's eyes went wider. "You wouldn't."

"Not if you're good." Tag ran his fingers over his own erection, waiting and watching as Barry tore open the packet. "Does it bother you?"

"I want to touch you."

"And I want you to let me look after you."

"I don't need—"

"Right. That's why you're here. Because you don't need me, my help, or—"

"Shut up." Barry pinched the condom tip and rolled it down over Tag's cock, noting it was the pre-lubed variety. His heart pounded a heavier beat at the thought maybe Tag wouldn't slick himself up any more than this before taking him. He certainly hadn't bothered much with his fingers and the burn still lingered.

"You're shaking." Tag ghosted his fingers over Barry's jaw. "What is it?"

A flash of memory, or maybe a glimpse of the future, raced through Barry. He imagined himself easing into his desk chair, his body achy, and wishing he had something other than the hard, ancient wooden office chair to sit on. He lifted his hips off the bed. "What are you waiting for?"

Tag pulled lube out from under the pillow and met Barry's gaze, the question in his eyes.

Barry shook his head slightly, holding his breath, waiting to see Tag's reaction. He hadn't always been into this, hadn't always felt the desire for the sharpness of pain to go along with his pleasure. When the form hovering over him was that of a stranger who cared only about getting off, pain was real in place of nothing else to feel.

Tag swallowed hard enough that Barry could see his throat working, but he dropped the tube and nodded. "Whatever you want."

Barry contemplated letting go of the bed and turning onto his stomach, but Tag wasn't a stranger. Instead, Barry lifted his knees, planted his feet. "I want you. All I ever wanted."

Tag pulled one of Barry's feet up, draping his leg over his shoulder, and positioned them both. His gaze never wavered as he moved, forcing his thick cock past the tight ring of Barry's opening.

"Jesus." Barry hauled in a breath.

"Stop?"

"No!" His body sizzled with the burn of stretching—his legs shook with the effort of keeping them apart when his instinct was to push Tag out.

Tag wound his fingers around Barry's cock, and Barry let the breath out again in a hissing sigh.

"Fuck, yeah. All the way."

The burn eased towards pleasure as Tag seated himself, and Barry had a moment of heart-stopping realisation, lying under Tag, seeing the way his face went slack and his eyes glazed over. He might be the one symbolically shackled to the bed, but Tag was entirely in his grasp. This was what he'd missed. This completely safe, secure feeling—knowing he called all the shots and nothing would happen he didn't want. Anonymous sex couldn't give him that. It was never a sure thing. He might exhaust himself physically, but he couldn't let down his guard. When everything else spun out of control, Tag gave him the reins, gave him back his life, reminded him he was strong enough to deal with the rest.

"Tag..."

His lover blinked rapidly, shook his head slightly, as though clearing fog. His brows drew down. "What?" He hovered over Barry, muscles in his arms bunching with the effort.

"I remember."

The fog cleared. Tag's grey eyes locked with his. A smile twitched his lips. "Now I can fuck you," Tag whispered, leaning down to claim his mouth and to piston his hips, moving his length in and out of Barry's body—hard, short and forceful.

The kiss quickly degenerated into sloppy, tangled tongues and teeth, and Barry now hung onto the bed out of self-preservation. He used his grip as leverage, meeting Tag's thrusts and holding himself from smacking his head against the headboard under the force of Tag's movement.

"Harder!" he panted.

"You're gonna eat me alive."

A grin lifted Barry's lips, lifted his being, until the dreams and the last year dropped away. "Maybe."

He tilted his hips up slightly so Tag's cock drove in at just the right angle. Lightning pleasure zinged through him. His balls tightened—fast, almost painful—and everything went white and crackling as his orgasm crashed through him.

Tag pumped him hard a few more times before pounding his hips tight against him and burying his face in the crook of Barry's neck. His beefy arms curled around Barry's torso, wrapped him up, carried him along with Tag's shaking. He moaned through his own orgasm, leaving traces of whispered promises on Barry's skin with his breath.

Glued together with sweat and cum and bonds that hadn't broken under the past year's strain, they lay still a long while. Barry released the metal, flexing his fingers and lowering his arms to stroke his hands down Tag's damp back. He lingered on the tickling hair of his ass, sighing and letting his eyes float closed.

"'S good," he mumbled. "Home."

Tag shifted, pulled off the condom, and tossed it into the trash without getting up. He settled his head on Barry's chest, kissed him. "Stay."

He sounded drowsy, half asleep. Barry didn't say anything, not entirely sure if he'd heard right, or if Tag had really meant to ask. He held him a little tighter, though, and drifted into the hazy, satisfied sleep that came after complete release.

Tag let himself hover near the edge of sleep. If he hadn't said he'd stay, at least Barry wasn't bolting for the door like so often in the past. Not that Tag could blame him for being angry. How often had Barry accused him of indifference? Had their situations been reversed, Tag was fairly certain he would have had a lot worse to say.

"That's the difference between you and me." He'd moved from Barry's chest to lie beside him where he could see his face, watch him sleep. "You forgive." He fingered a few corkscrewed curls and moved a little closer, where he could smell Barry's musky, sweet smell. "Maybe you have to. Maybe..." Tag nudged closer still, until his nose bumped against Barry's skull, buried in the thick, black waves. "How do you live with what you see?"

It was one thing to see the aftermath, the absolute brutality of what men were capable of. He couldn't imagine living it even once, a victim of that kind of treatment. He had no idea how Barry made it from one end of the day to the other, why he wasn't high all the time, or passed out drunk. Or dead.

"I'm not strong like you, Barry. Wish I could fix it for you."

"You do."

Tag scrambled back. "Sorry. Didn't mean to wake you."

Barry sat up, looked around a little blearily, and shook his head. "My stomach woke me. I'm starved." He fixed his gaze on Tag and smiled—crooked, shy, like he wasn't sure he was using the expression right. "And you do fix me. For a while." He patted the bed. "This is the only place I know for sure I have a say in what happens to me. You don't know what that's worth, Tag."

Except when I'm not there for you.

Tag bit into his cheek and frowned, suddenly concerned he'd let his own heart overrule what was best for his lover. "I can't *actually* chain you to my bed. You know that?"

Barry laughed. "Not asking you to." He shimmied down and around where Tag was still lying then stood up. "You don't have to do anything except believe in me. You've never let me down there."

"Everywhere else, maybe."

"Let's not, okay?" The smile slipped away from Barry's face. "Let's not analyse everything we've done wrong. Like when a perp gets off and we sit for hours, days, trying to figure out how we screwed up. Whatever it was we had before..." Barry waved a hand in the air. "It's gone. Got away. You said it yourself. It can't be like it was."

"It can be—"

"No." Barry sat back down on the bed, dipping the mattress so Tag rolled into him. "No. I'm not going to try and figure it out. I'm not—"

"Getting your hopes up," Tag inserted.

"Fine. If you want to look at it like that."

Barry leaned over, placing a hand on the pillow beside Tag's head, looming—his dark eyes full of shadows, secrets, dark places. Tag didn't even want to imagine what lurked there. "You want to roll me over and fuck me stupid, I'll let you. It's the only time I feel I belong in my own skin, that I belong to me. You think I don't know how much pressure that puts on you?" He leant down, demanded a kiss that Tag freely gave, and pulled away just when Tag was ready to do exactly what Barry had suggested and plough him into the mattress.

"I'm not going to hold you to anything."

Tag licked the faint taste of his lover from his lips. "I don't want you to think you can't count on me."

"I don't think that." Barry tilted his head, ran tender fingers through Tag's hair and kissed him again, soft and brief. "I know I can't." He shrugged, straightened. "Life is what it is, and right now, it's about the funky stink, my sore ass, and my empty stomach."

Without a backward glance, Barry rose and disappeared into the bathroom. A second later, the sound of the shower came.

Tag lay still, trying to catch his breath, trying to pull the shards of himself back together, trying to find a way to imagine he hadn't deserved that.

The smart thing to do would be to walk away. Where Barry Whittaker was concerned, though, Tag seemed to be about as smart as a post.

So instead he got up, made coffee and read the paper while he waited for Barry to return from the bathroom. Once the shower shut off, he busied himself making eggs and toast, setting the table, tidying. For the first time since he'd leased the place almost a year ago, he took a good look around. It was a dump. Cracked windows, peeling paint, and the air of a derelict bachelor pad.

"You always did do domestic well."

Tag turned around to find Barry leaning on the bathroom doorframe, towel around his waist, arms crossed over his chest, something approaching peace on his face.

"Except when I only had me to worry about." He hefted the empty pizza box and beer cans in his hands. "Thought maybe it was time I cleaned up."

"For me?"

Tag grinned a crooked little expression. "Maybe, yeah."

Barry levered himself off the doorframe and held open the garbage can while Tag stuffed the refuse in. "You even made breakfast."

"Don't I always?" Tag brushed light fingers over the slight swell in Barry's towel. "You'd best get dressed or breakfast will be a cold, congealed mess before you ever get a bit into you."

He was straightening the tableware, conscious of the long silence when Barry finally spoke.

"Is that all it takes, Tag? A bad dream, a good fuck?"

"What else do you want?"

Again, Barry let the silence stretch. How much had he been hurting that he couldn't answer that simple question? If Tag had missed him until nothing could fill the void in his life, how much worse had it been for Barry?

"I know you don't want to believe in me, Barry." Tag turned and leaned on the arm of a dining chair. "Probably, you can't. I get that. And you're going to question everything I say, everything I do. Maybe I'll never earn back the trust. But I am going to try."

Barry nodded. The room remained quiet while he slipped into his jeans and T-shirt then settled a button-down loosely over his shoulders. Even when he sat at the table, he didn't say anything. Once, he'd been a talker, needing to fill the void and keep a running commentary on everything, just to keep the vague images from his dreams out of his mind. That's what he'd told Tag, anyway. Now, he attacked his eggs and toast with vigour, but whatever was going on in his head, he kept to himself. It was eerie. The shadows never left his dark eyes now and Tag worried he'd left this reconciliation too long. What if Barry was, as he'd always feared, losing himself in that shadowy, terrifying dream world, even when he wasn't asleep?

The idea his lover might be walking half in the dark all the time was too much to contemplate right then. Tag picked up his own fork and poked his eggs around his plate while he tried to think of something to talk about, something to break the gloomy silence.

Maybe the only way to loosen the dreams' hold on Barry was to face them head-on, drag them into the light and hopefully, take away their power over him. It was worth a try. What was the worst that could happen?

"Famous last fucking words," he muttered to himself, at last stuffing a forkful of food into his mouth.

"What?" Barry glanced up, just as Tag jammed the fork in.

He shook his head, swallowed a scalding gulp of coffee to wash the eggs down, and stabbed at his toast. "Nothing. Talking to myself. So..." He heaved in a deep breath. "This morning. The dream you said didn't end. Tell me about it."

"Guess I was done eating anyway." Barry's fork clattered onto his plate, and he sat back. "I'd rather pretend we're just an ordinary couple of homos fuelling up for the next go-round, if it's all the same to you."

"It isn't, actually." Using the food as a focus, Tag readied another bite before asking the question again. "What was it about?"

"I don't remember."

Tag kept Barry's gaze as he chewed, hoping he looked patient and calm, because he sure as hell didn't feel it.

"Okay." Barry relented and leant forward, though he did shove his food away and wrap his hands around his coffee cup—an old, old habit that seemed to give him some sort of comfort. "It felt like someone was constantly changing the channel. Like I was in this—I don't even know—could have been a kid, even. I was in his head, and then...like he didn't want me there, he pushed me out, made me go somewhere else, but he was the one in trouble. He was the one..."

For a long, still moment, Barry stared into his coffee. When he looked up, the expression he'd had on waking from the dream was there, deep in his eyes, like he'd tried to bury it but it wouldn't stay down.

"All that pain. It's like he's guarding it, keeping it all for himself, to dole out whenever he wants, visit it on whoever he thinks worthy, and he didn't want me anywhere near it." He shuddered. "I hate to think what kind of mind imagines itself capable and justified to visit that amount of horror on anyone."

Tag set his fork down gently, wiped his mouth, picked up his coffee, and set it down again. "Barry."

How did he say his lover sounded insane? How did he even think it? But to imagine someone else was dictating what Barry did or did not dream about...

That had never been an issue before.

Barry stood, his movements stiff, contained, like he might fly out of his own skin if he moved too fast. "If you're going to say that sounds crazy, don't. Just don't open your mouth, don't get up, don't fucking do anything." He backed away from the table, turned and hurried towards the door.

Tag jumped up, caught his thigh in a searingly painful blow against the underside of the table edge that tipped the coffee mugs and set the plates rattling. He almost toppled from the jarring pain, and Barry had his shoes on and the door opened before Tag managed to blink away the smarting tears.

"Barry!" He ran after him, hobbling and slow, bare feet slapping unevenly along the threadbare, sticky-in-places carpet of the hallway. "Barry!"

"I don't need you, Tag. Don't need another lecture on getting a shrink."

"You didn't even let me speak, you stupid fuckhead!" Fury took over as Tag limped hurriedly through the pain after him.

Barry was down the stairs, at the door to the street and pushing on it when Tag's words registered and he stopped.

"You didn't give me a fucking chance to say word one. You have no clue what I was thinking, what I was going to say. Don't you assume you know anything about what I'm fucking thinking or feeling, Whittaker! I've watched you tearing yourself apart for a year and half, knowing it was my fault you had no one, and you don't think that killed me? I get that you're mad. I get that you might never forgive me for it or trust me again, but for fuck's sake! When you say there's someone else in your fucking head controlling these goddamn fucking dreams, give me two minutes to process that shit before you decide you know how I'm going to fucking react!"

Running a marathon would not have left him breathing harder or his heart pounding in a heavier rhythm—thudding a deep, throbbing pulse through his whole body, including his aching leg. He didn't take his eyes off Barry's back or release his death grip on the stair railing. As long as he stood there, even with the door partially open, there was hope Barry would turn around and come back.

"It *sounds* crazy," Barry said, turning. Even from above like this, Tag could see the sunlight glint too brightly off his dark eyes, reflecting off unshed tears. "I know it sounds crazy."

"So can we just move past the crazy, then, and try to figure it out? Please, Barry. Don't fuck off without at least trying."

Barry nodded, visibly pulling himself together, shifting his shoulders back and swallowing, and frowning. "What the hell did you do? You're bleeding?"

"What?"

Barry was already jogging back to him, springing up the stairs two at a time. "What did you do?"

He crouched, and Tag looked down at his leg, the focus of Barry's concerned gaze, and the gash in his jeans and across his thigh.

"Oh. Huh." There wasn't a fantastic amount of blood, but enough to soak through the denim in a dark, slowly spreading stain. "Hit it on the table."

"Rather hard." Barry stood and slipped an arm around Tag's waist. "Come on."

They manoeuvred back around, and Tag tried not to focus on the ache of putting weight on the leg. It hadn't hurt as much when he didn't know he'd broken the skin, when he was focused on not letting Barry run out on him.

"You're an idiot," Barry complained. "What were you going to do? Run out in the street after me in your bare feet?"

"If I had to."

"Oh, please tell me you didn't lock us out of the apartment."

"Uh."

"Oh, for the love of —!" Barry threw a hand up in the air and let it drop again. "Car keys? Wallet?"

Tag shook his head.

"Neighbours?" Barry suggested.

Tag started laughing. The absurdity of it, standing there, shirtless, shoeless and bleeding in his own hallway struck him as inappropriately hilarious, and he laughed until tears ran down his cheeks.

"You done?"

"Ahh. Fuck me." He wiped the moisture away and nodded. "Shit."

"So now what?"

Pulling himself together, Tag hopped around so he was facing Barry. He took his head in his hands and glared, eyebrows raised. "You take off in a huff, this is what happens. I lose my mind. Barry, believe me, don't believe me, but I will give up a lot of shit before I lose you again, and I will not let you just walk out."

"Okay." Finally relenting, Barry closed his eyes, leant forward and slid his arms around Tag's waist. His head rested on Tag's shoulder, and for a few minutes they stood there, breathing.

"Okay." Tag finally shuffled back, keeping a hand on Barry's shoulder for support. "This fucking hurts like a beast. I have spare keys in my desk at the station. Can you get a cab?"

Chapter Eight

Jessica sat on the van floor, hugging her knees to her chest with arms bound together at the wrists. The silver tape, dull and wrapped several times over, pinched her skin. Even the slightest movement ripped out the fine hairs growing there, and she winced. She'd draped the T-shirt front over her knees, the hem reaching her ankles. Oh, he hadn't done anything untoward, not like *that* anyway, but she still remained on edge in case he did. Who knew what people like him thought about? Who knew what they were capable of? Shit, he'd admitted killing the other bastard, and if he could do that, then he could do *that* too.

She stared ahead at the blind-covered windshield and tried to zone out the man's presence. He was too *there*, though, and she failed.

What time was it? With no clock that she could see, and thinking of what had happened so far today, she'd guess it was afternoon. Late afternoon, judging by the light behind the blind. It had dulled since he came back and subdued her, and she'd closed her eyes when he'd taken off his bloodied shirt and washed at the sink. Thankfully, the stench of copper had lessened once he'd plunged the shirt into a bowl of water, but it was still there in her nostrils and at the back of her throat.

It reminded her of Cal, and the terror he must have felt while being killed made her eyes tear up. Her throat clogged—thick and tight and so damn painful—and she willed herself to try and forget the horrors. She doubted she'd be able to—they were ingrained in her mind, after all—but she'd have to try.

She refocused on Leyton. So he had killed that man for her. That concept scared her in one way and awed her in another. Who was bold enough to rescue a woman from a monster then go back and kill him? What kind of person was he to have done that? Bad? A monster himself? She didn't know, because people did kill others, didn't they, but it didn't mean they were evil. Circumstances presented themselves and a person acted accordingly. But to kill just for her? That was damn creepy. From what he'd said, she'd gleaned he was fixated on her, thought they belonged together, but they didn't. She couldn't love a man like him.

His steady breathing indicated he'd fallen asleep on the bunk to her left. If she could quietly reach beneath the bed for his tools, she could smack him over the head and...

And what? Break free? Get away?

I'm not sure I'm strong enough, but I'll give it a bloody good go. I can't stay here with a crazy guy.

But how would she get out?

I'll smash a window.

Her back ached something fierce, her shoulders too—the kind of constant burn that warmed the skin and caused pain at the same time. Her knees had locked—how long had she been sitting here anyway?—and if she stretched them out and attempted to run, she doubted she'd get very far. Jessica stifled a sigh and blinked back the sting of tears. She had no time for them now. Crying hadn't done her any favours when she was with the first bastard and they wouldn't do her any now. No, she was trapped until she could figure out a sure-fire way to get the hell out of here and to safety.

She huffed out a quiet laugh. Safety. What the fuck was that? She didn't know anymore. She'd thought herself safe before, and look what had happened. She'd become one of *those* women seen on the news. The poor bitch who had been in the wrong place at the wrong time and whose picture filled every TV and front page of the newspapers in the country, the good folks racking their minds as to whether they recognised her, whether they'd seen her in the past twenty-four hours.

But what if my picture isn't on the news? What if no one has noticed I'm gone yet? What if Cal hasn't been found?

Jessica clamped her teeth to fight off the panic boiling in her guts. Inhaled through her nose and out through her mouth. The panic turned to anger. Anger that she was here. Anger that the first man had taken her and now *him*. What were the odds of this happening? She was pretty damn unlucky to be taken twice.

I'm going to do it. Hit him. Get the fuck out of here.

Shifting her eyes to the left, she studied the man—*Leyton, but I'll never call him that*—in her peripheral vision. He rested ramrod straight, arms crossed over his stomach as though he lay in a coffin. The image freaked her a little. His eyes were closed, so she dug her feet against the floor and scooted herself around to face him, waiting for the shuffling sound she'd made to spring those eyes open. They remained closed, and as she stared, she appraised his facial scars. They were awful. Like something glued to his face, they appeared unreal, a child's gory Halloween kit to scare the damn neighbours into giving up their candy.

Are they real?

She lifted her hands, the insane urge to touch them pushing her to reach out. Her fingertips came into contact with his uneven cheek, and she almost shied back in repulsion. He didn't move. Jessica trailed her fingers down a particularly prominent and ragged ridge, her breath held as she waited for him to sit upright and chastise her for what she was doing.

He didn't. His eyes didn't even flicker. And the scars were real.

She drew her hands away, intent on hugging her knees again until she summoned the courage to reach beneath the bunk. He'd said this was her home now, that she was his. Should she abandon her plan to escape and play along? Pretend she was happy to live with him? Then, when his guard was down, when he trusted her, she could run away?

"It wouldn't work," he said, his voice startling her so she jumped, her ass lifting off the floor and slamming back down. "I know exactly what you're thinking, Lorelei."

Heart thrumming, she bit back a retort, one where she asked him how the fuck he could know. *Is he a mind reader?*

"Something like that. Let's just say I'm in a place where I know things."

What the fuck? A gasp left her along with a groan, and she cursed herself for showing him he'd frightened her. But then, hadn't he just read her mind?

Or was that just a lucky guess on his part, his response a stab in the dark?

Stab in the dark...

"They can be quite pleasant," he said, remaining still with his eyes closed. "If the victim deserves it."

Jessica shuddered and moved in reverse on her butt until her back met with the small door beside the sink unit. She could keep an eye on him from here, see him move and prepare herself for his approach. And was he inside her head now? Listening in on what she had planned?

"You need to sleep, Lorelei. There are things you must understand, things that will only come if you sleep, if you let me show you."

"I'm not tired." She hugged her knees tighter.

"Oh, you soon will be."

She stared at him, eyes narrowed, immense hatred gnawing her guts—and she didn't care if he knew about it either. Who the hell did he think he was?

"I'm 'The One'. I'm special," he said.

The One? What, for me? Or does he think he's been chosen for something?

"Both. Now shush. Tonight is very important. It will soon be time for me to go out and a deliver a...package, but before that, you must understand a few things. Close your eyes."

Despite wanting to disobey him, Jessica did as he'd asked, leaning her head back against the door. Her body sagged, as though her muscles were liquefying, and as she fought the sensation of falling asleep, she realised she was wasting her time. He had some form of control, somehow directing her body to his will. How was that possible? This kind of shit just didn't happen.

"Oh, it does, Lorelei. It does."

She dreamed of a small boy standing in front of her, their surroundings a dark wheat field, a bright moon shining on them. He smiled, the lone tooth in his mouth like a solitary soldier's headstone in the sea of a black graveyard. He tilted his head, regarding her with eyes that were pure black — no whites — his hair unwashed and greasy, sticking to his forehead in lank strips. His raggedy clothes hung off his spindly frame, and Jessica wondered if he was half-starved. He reminded her of a street urchin in a film she'd once seen — his T-shirt grey, perhaps formerly white, stained with what looked like a month's worth of spilled food. Did he eat so quickly that he made a mess, fearful if he didn't the food would be taken away? She knew this as if he'd told her, and pity for him squeezed her heart.

He reached out a hand, fingernails chewed and dirty, scratches on his arms red and angry.

"I scratch to feel pain," he said. "Makes me know I'm alive and not in some kind of nightmare. She...she hurts me bad."

"How old are you?" she asked, stepping forward to take his hand. His skin was unexpectedly rough, nothing like the softness she had anticipated. "What are you doing out here so late?"

"I'm nine, and I'm out here because I need to tell you things. Make you understand."

Although Jessica knew she dreamed, a part of her went ice cold, his words telling her that she was looking at him as a boy, that he had somehow orchestrated this dream. About to ask how it was possible, she stopped herself. She could ask herself questions later. Now, she sensed she needed to let the dream run its course.

"Who is she?" Jessica looked about, searching the darkness for signs someone else was here. A vast expanse of wheat spread out around them, seemingly infinite, stretching for miles. She turned away from him to look behind her, seeing the same sight.

"Mother."

Jessica spun to face him. His face bore marks now, bloody and freshly inflicted, a couple of slashes gaping wide to show the inside of his mouth. She resisted gagging, pasting on a smile to show him he didn't repulse her. His wounds did, the woman who had trashed his face did, but not him.

"Did she do this to you?" How the hell can a mother treat their child this way and not get caught?

"Yes. She says she wants to make me pretty." He shrugged and let go of her hand.

Dear God…

"And I'm going to get some new teeth, she said." He grinned again, jumping from foot to foot. "I'll be able to eat without making a mess then. She doesn't like me making a mess. I got one tooth left to go. Got to wait until I'm bad before she pulls it out, then after that I got to wait for my big teeth to come. Isn't that great? I'm right excited."

Jessica frowned. Didn't he realise what his mother had done was wrong?

He jiggled on the spot some more. "Oh, and when she makes me pretty, she sews my face up again. The needle stings some, but afterwards, when it's all better and the stitches have come out, she shows me my face in the speckled mirror she keeps in her locked cupboard, and I have to smile and tell her I love my face."

The urge to hug the boy gripped Jessica, and she encircled his bony shoulders with her arms and brought him close. "God… Where do you live? I need to get you away from her. She isn't…right."

He rested his head against her stomach and clutched the back of her T-shirt. "She said no one can do a thing about it. We travel. She said we don't exist, that no one knows anything about me." He lifted his head and looked up at her. "I wet myself when I go to sleep, you know. Wet myself when she leaves me in the van at night to go to work."

A lump expanded in Jessica's throat. Fucking hell... She swallowed and stared down at him. "Won't you let me help you?"

"Oh no," he said, pulling away to dance in the wheat. "It's all right. I dream stuff. And there's this man who comes. In my dreams, I mean. And he isn't really a man. He's got the body of one, all right, but his head is this skull, shaped like a sheep's head, and he has these horns. Curly ones. And he told me that when I'm a man I'll kill Mother and take her teeth out just like she did to me, because I'll need them. She's going to take out my new teeth too, see, so I'll need hers, won't I?" He twirled in a circle. "The man, the dream man, he said Mother's got lots of money, that she works for rich people and steals their things. But if she's rich, how come we live in a van?"

He stopped moving, looked up at the moon as though in thought. Jessica stared at him, not knowing how a boy as mistreated as him could appear so happy. Did the man in his dreams give him hope? Something to cling on to until he had grown?

"Guess what?" the boy said. "I have new teeth now. Look!"

He smiled, drawing his lips back, presenting her with teeth she'd seen before. His teeth. Her stomach rolled over, and her head lightened.

"These are Mother's teeth. I got them made for me, and I put them in with tooth glue. The man in my dream was right. And guess what else?"

"What?" she said, playing along.

"The man said I had an important job to do when I'm grown. I have to stop nasty people hurting others. And when I kill them, I got to take a tooth. And get this..." He leaned closer, whispering conspiratorially, "When I have enough teeth, I got to use them to make me some more new ones."

Sickened, yet at the same time pitying the boy, Jessica swallowed down bile. This child, this innocent had been so corrupted that he believed what he would do as a man was right. A burning hatred for his mother took hold, forcing her to lower herself to the ground in an attempt to process the information before she fainted.

"You all right?" the boy asked, hunkering down in front of her, a frown creasing his brow.

"No, but I'll be okay in a minute." She smiled and stroked his cheek, the wounds now healed scars.

He stood and looked down at her, the moon a halo around his head. "You're going to love me when I'm grown. The man said so."

Her stomach churned, and she battled nausea.

"He said I'm going to save you. That your name is Lorelei."

"Oh right..." She didn't know what else to say. Didn't want to dash any hope this poor child had.

"And we're going to live together in the van for a bit, then buy a house when my work is done."

"That's lovely!" Jessica glanced from left to right, waiting for the dream to end, wishing she'd never been shown this side of him. She felt sorry for him now, understood why he had taken her and wouldn't let her go. This boy had listened to a night spectre — surely only his subconscious — and grasped the instructions, holding them close as something to get him through his childhood. How could she take that hope away? How could she tell him, when she woke, that he was some fucked-up, crazy bastard who needed committing?

"So now do you understand?" he asked, grasping her hand and making a valiant attempt at pulling her upright.

She stood and cupped his face, nodding, staring into those black, whiteless eyes. Why were they like that now, when in reality he had eyes like any other? Perhaps it was just the way of dreams. Things were never wholly right when night terrors visited.

"What will you do next?" she asked. *Tell me so I know what to do next.*

"Oh, I got to take that bad man somewhere, the one I killed, and after that I need to tell Barry where to find him."

"Barry?"

"Yes, Barry. He's a policeman, see. I dream about him too, and he dreams about me. And you."

What?

"Does he know you?" she asked.

"No, but he will soon. He's struggling at the moment. Don't understand he's special like I am. But he will. The man in my dreams said Barry will understand presently." He glanced behind him and stiffened.

Jessica followed his gaze. The van had appeared in the distance, and the side door opened, revealing the shape of a woman, the light inside rendering her a silhouette.

"I got to go. Even though Mother is gone, she's still here. She watches me. I try not to be scared of her, but I still am. The man in my dream said that if I do my work and make Barry understand he's special, Mother will leave me alone. So I got to do what I do. You understand some more now?"

"Yes," she said, still staring at the van. "Yes, I do."

Jessica came to, her dream still lingering in her mind. She didn't want to open her eyes. Not yet. Not if he would be sitting there waiting for her to do so. How could she look at him in the same way now, knowing what he'd suffered as a child?

She laughed inside. *So you believe he really showed you his past and that it wasn't just a dream? Shit, you're as crazy as he is.*

But something inside her told her that whatever the hell was going on was real. He was able to get inside her head—how she didn't know…didn't want to explore the possibilities of such a thing either—and she needed to bide her time, get away the first chance she got.

Jessica cursed herself. *He can read my damn mind. I have to stop thinking like this.*

"Now that you understand—and it's better you don't try and find a reason as to how everything works—you know I must leave you here now to do my work."

She kept her eyes closed. "Barry. How do you know where he lives? Did the dreams show you?"

"Yes. I have much to do before Barry understands. I have to deliver Charles and then meet with Barry in his dreams. It will be tough to make him accept who and what he is. That he is special. That his dreams are not just dreams but information given by... Would you like some food before I go?"

Jessica opened her eyes. He sat on the bunk, legs apart, hands hanging between his knees as though he had no worries, that what he was about to do was normal.

"Please," she said, knowing what she would do once he was gone but refusing to think it.

"A cheese sandwich, I think. Yes, that will do you nicely."

She nodded and hugged her knees closer, hiding her toes beneath the hem of the T-shirt. He stood and took the two steps needed to reach the sink unit. Busying himself making her sandwich, he hummed—an indecipherable tune she struggled to recognise. She had thought she would hate him when she'd opened her eyes. That despite the sadness of the boy's life, the fact that he was a man now who should know better would colour her judgement of him. It didn't. She still felt sorry for him.

Shit.

"Funny how things turn out, isn't it, Lorelei?"

She nodded slightly, fighting against the bubble of laughter that pushed to come out. He placed her sandwich on a plate and put it on the bed, indicating with a flick of his wrist that she should stand then sit on the bunk. She struggled, gripping the side of the unit and pulling herself up. Her knees and legs were indeed weak, and she staggered towards the bunk, her muscles numb and her bones seemingly non-existent. Plunking her ass down, she sat and eyed the sandwich. She'd eat when he had gone, needed the strength the food would give.

Making her mind blank, Lorelei smiled up at him. And waited for him to leave.

Chapter Nine

Leyton locked up and leant back on the side door of his van. He concentrated so he could peer into Lorelei's thoughts, to get a handle on what she planned to do while he was gone. Surprisingly, he picked up on the fact that she intended to stay, to let him love her as the man of his dreams had predicted. Relieved, he stared up at the now-dark sky and silently thanked the sheep-head man for steering him on the right path. Everything was going according to plan.

Pushing off the van, he walked towards the forest, mind going over what he had to do next. It had taken him some time to get to this point, to understand how to reach into Barry's dreams and show him what he had done. Barry wasn't as receptive as Leyton had hoped. The policeman hadn't believed at first that what he dreamed were real images, Leyton trying to show him where to go and who had committed the awful crimes. And, of course, it was all new to Leyton too, but once he'd shown Barry certain things and they had helped him solve crimes, the policeman had begun to accept he had a gift—albeit a gift of what he termed nightmares, but a gift all the same. Now it just needed to be honed. The cop needed to relax more when he slept and let Leyton have control.

But he's too stubborn for that. Questions everything he sees, preventing the whole picture from emerging. But tonight I'll press him harder. Show him that he can dream even when he's sleeping, and supposedly safe, with this Tag person. And Tag might prove to be a bind. He needs convincing Barry's gift is real too. Otherwise... Well, Tag might find himself meeting with a little accident if he doesn't believe in Barry. That would be a shame. Seems a nice chap. But being lenient here isn't an option. Barry is needed for bigger things, and if Tag gets in the way then...

I need to tell Barry where to find Charles, force him to wake and investigate. I may bring the sheep-head man of my dreams along too. Maybe he will have more success in showing Barry that he must stop fighting, stop trying to find a logical explanation and just...be who he is.

Striding towards the tree line, Leyton donned his night-vision goggles and stared at Charles' van. As far as he could tell in the darkness, everything remained the same as he had left it. To anyone who might happen by, it appeared as though someone had camped here and had just gone off out for the evening. Sorry, no one is at home. Yet Charles was indeed at home, sliced and diced in his van, awaiting the next leg of his journey.

Leyton chuckled and relived the murder in his mind. He had perhaps been a little easy on Charles. He could have inflicted more pain, drawn out the torture, but he'd just wanted him dead and unable to hurt Lorelei again. Leyton would have to be careful. He couldn't allow his emotions to get the better of him. If he had more work to do after Charles, he'd have to put Lorelei out of his mind and concentrate solely on the job at hand. The man in his dreams wouldn't like him messing up.

He stepped out into the clearing, walked to the van, inserted the key he had taken earlier, and opened the door. The stench of a fresh kill assaulted him, and he stood still for a moment, breathing in the scent of a good day's work. Ah, that ripe aroma always got to him, made him feel whole and alive. The smell of his own blood when Mother had sliced open his face had been the beginning of a love affair with the coppery scent, and he relished the whiff of it with every flick of his blade.

Climbing the steps, he went inside. He picked up a flashlight from beside the sink and switched it on, positioning the beam so it shone on the bed.

Charles lay on his back, the canvas of his face so pretty and dark red that Leyton silently congratulated himself on such fine work. A folded-over flap of forehead skin exposed a sliver of skull beneath, dried-out flesh surrounding it, and Leyton wondered if it would be hard to the touch yet. He stepped closer to the bed and reached out, fingertips brushing the wound. It *had* hardened, yet still retained a sense of springiness. With the beam shining directly on Charles' face, Leyton studied the open gashes and how the blood had congealed around them. Such a shame they would never be sewn up and resemble the fine scars Leyton possessed.

He had work to do before he could take the body to where it needed to be. Leyton slid his backpack off his shoulder and dumped it on the floor. Hunkering down, he unzipped it and pulled out his tool pouch, unrolling it and selecting his set of shiny pliers. He stood then leaned over the body, cocking his head as he studied his artwork once more. He could stare at

Charles for hours, congratulating himself, but the next phase must be done tonight. The dream man had said so.

With the fingers of one hand, Leyton pushed up Charles' top lip to reveal the teeth beneath. He shone the flashlight on the site and inspected them, dithering on which one to choose. He had killed so many men — women too — taking one or two of their teeth as the dream man had instructed. They were currently clean and in a jar beneath the sink in his van, and one of Charles' would soon join them. He nearly had enough to make a full set. The dentist he had visited to make dentures from Mother's teeth would be seeing him very soon, and he knew to keep quiet. Knew what was good for him. The money and the threat in Leyton's voice saw to that.

"I think I'll have...that one, Charles."

Leyton lowered the pliers and inserted a front tooth between the grippers. From past experience he knew the tooth would either come away easily or remain stubbornly stuck in the gum. He wasn't in the mood for struggling tonight.

He wrenched hard, and the tooth moved some, but not enough. He tugged again, a swift, sharp movement that had the tooth popping free of its captivity with a creak and sending Leyton's torso backward. Righting himself, he held the pliers up and illuminated them in the light. The tooth's bloodied root looked so wonderful Leyton had the urge to return to his own van and clean it right away. But no, that wasn't possible. He turned and placed the flashlight next to the sink, then opened the pliers to drop the tooth onto the small worktop. Inspecting it for cracks or imperfections, Leyton deemed it worthy to have a home in his mouth and slipped it into his jeans pocket.

Pliers back in the tool pouch and his backpack secured, he left the van. Using the keys for Charles' vehicle, he unlocked it and dumped his backpack on the passenger seat, then opened the rear door, ready for Charles. Back in the van, he easily scooped up the stiff body, carrying it to the car and wedging the corpse inside. He had to force the legs to bend at the knees—rigor mortis was a bitch—but he managed it well enough.

"I've had enough experience," he said jovially and leaned inside the car. "I wonder, Charles. Do you see anything with that lonesome eye of yours, or are you gone, dead of soul as well as in body? That would be nice, wouldn't it? To know nothing of you exists now. Even Hell is too good for you."

Leyton got into his van and drove out of the clearing, through the trees, and onto the main road. It was only a short journey to Barry's, and although he knew what the policeman's home looked like, and knew the general area, he had a fair bit of driving through the streets to do to find it. His dreams didn't give him an address or conveniently show him the street sign and house number. No, part of his job was to seek it out, and he liked that. It gave him a sense of being a detective, someone who was righting the terrible wrongs in this world.

He cruised the streets, driving up and down them and turning into the next when the previous didn't house the place he sought. Thankfully, hardly anyone was out tonight, and him driving up and down wouldn't register as odd. After all, people did this all the time. Now, if he'd driven erratically or even too slowly, *then* he could imagine his presence being noted, but he'd perfected this part of the process, had become a master at it.

Minutes of travel passed, and then a sense of familiarity cloaked him. He spied the house of his dreams and parked beside the kerb. Scoping the street for activity, he peered at every window of the nearby residences to check whether anyone stood watching. He saw nothing to alarm him, so got out of the car and swung open the rear door, gripping Charles beneath his armpits and pulling him out. He glanced around again then dragged the corpse to Barry's place, positioning Charles close to the door but to the side of it so only Barry would find it. Of course, he ran the risk of some nosey neighbour discovering a grim gift, but he believed in his dreams and trusted what they had shown.

Pleased with his work so far, Leyton got in the car and drove back to the clearing. He parked up and dug inside his backpack for the cleaning agents he'd brought with him. Humming a melody, he set about cleaning the inside of the car, even going so far as to use his hand-held vacuum cleaner to collect the microscopic fibres his eyes couldn't see. He realised he wouldn't pick them all up, that some part of him would remain, but with no fingerprints—hell, no record of his existence at all—Leyton surmised he was as safe as he could be.

He gave Charles' van the same treatment, although he left the beautiful bloodied sheets intact. It would give whoever found the van a nice bout of sickness, maybe even make them faint. That thought had him smiling, and he whistled as he locked up and wiped the keys with a cloth. He placed them on the top step and walked away, into the trees where the darkness encompassed him and gave him the invisibility he loved.

He reached his van in good time, even though he hadn't rushed back. Lorelei would be inside, of that he had no doubt, so rushing hadn't been a priority. Besides, he liked to take the time to savour his actions after he'd killed then delivered packages. Think about everything he had done to make sure he hadn't fucked up. Plus, he needed a bit of time to go over the next phase. Tonight he would need sleep to come quickly so he could instruct Barry. Lorelei would have to understand that she must remain quiet and not ask him questions he wasn't ready to answer. The dream he had given her would have to be enough for now. She'd probably been chewing on it while he was out and had all her queries ready for when he returned, but he'd stall her. Tell her everything tomorrow.

At his van's side door, he stopped to check out his surroundings, get a feel for whether everything was as it should be. He stared at the van. Nothing appeared untoward, but a nagging sensation tugged at his mind. Something wasn't right. Upon closer inspection, he saw the door was open a tiny bit. The keeper hadn't latched properly. His guts rolled over. Had he done that in his haste to deal with Charles?

No, I leaned on the damn door. It would have clicked into place had I left it like this.

Had she dared to leave? Had she? She couldn't have. He'd have sensed her departure.

Controlling a sudden burst of anger, Leyton flung open the van door and peered inside. She was gone.

"Oh dear, oh dear, Lorelei."

He stood and homed in on her, detected her past movements as though he'd watched them as they'd occurred. She'd found his spare key – so stupid of him to have left it in the bottom of his wardrobe, but he had trusted her, trusted his dreams, damn it! — and fled into the forest behind the van. Wrists still bound, she'd run fast, too fast, and stumbled, banging her forehead on a rock. She lay somewhere out there, unconscious and cold, his T-shirt bunched at her waist. And that wouldn't do. No, he would go and find her, bring her back to prevent anyone else seeing her like that.

Putting his backpack inside then closing the van door, Leyton followed her trail, her lemony scent still lingering in the air. She'd only recently fled, it seemed, and he pulled all his senses together, using them to follow in her wake.

The forest went on for some time here, ending beside a motorway. But she hadn't reached there. No, she nearly had, but fate had stepped in, tripping her over and leaving her on the ground for him to find. He walked on quickly, not in any rush to find her before she woke but because he must stop someone else seeing her half-naked state. Not that they would. The sheep-man had said they belonged together, and Leyton didn't doubt him.

Lifting his night-vision goggles from their place hanging about his neck, he secured them over his eyes and scoured the forest. Ah, there she was up ahead — her white skin pronounced in the darkness, the slash of blood across her cheek even more so. The fact that she was hurt upset him, and he rushed forward, arms outstretched. He should be angry at her, should want to wake her and tell her how bad she had been, but it wasn't in him. He loved her, had waited so long for her, and he wasn't about to ruin that now with a fit of temper that would do nothing but create a barrier between them. And it seemed there was one there already, didn't it? One he would have to work on erasing.

She would trust him in the end.

Kneeling, he lifted her into his arms and held her close. "Oh, Lorelei. You silly thing. What were you thinking?" He stood and settled her comfortably against him, began the walk back to his van. "This part will be over soon, then I'll have more time to devote to you. We'll get to know one another, and you'll see I'm the one for you. I'm prepared to wait, to let you come to me on your own terms, but you must never, *ever* attempt to run from me again. The man in my dreams wouldn't like that."

She didn't stir, just hung limp, and he sighed as his van came into view. Taking her inside, he laid her on his bunk and covered her with a blanket. At least she wouldn't be asking him questions now. Perhaps that's why she had been allowed to run. Maybe the dream man had made it this way so it solved Leyton's problem of having to explain his need for quiet this evening.

He locked the door and made sure the windows were covered. At his wardrobe, he pulled out a rolled-up sleeping bag and put it on the floor beside the bunk. He took off his goggles and hung them on the hook next to the door, turning back to look at Lorelei. She slept on, and he smiled, not allowing any anger to seep into him. It had all been for a reason—he accepted that.

Taking Charles' tooth from his pocket, he dropped it into a glass and squirted enough bleach inside to cover it. After a few days, the squidgy matter surrounding the root would float to the top of the bleach, making it easier for Leyton to remove the remaining fibres. He smiled as he stared at the tooth and imagined laying them all out on the side to resemble what they would look like as a set of dentures. He'd have fun moving them around, working out the best position for each one.

He turned from the glass and settled on top of the sleeping bag with the next phase taking over his mind. It was time to contact Barry. To get the cop to see his dreams properly, to have him understand the images instead of fighting to have them make sense.

"If you would just...*be*, Barry, everything will become clear."

Leyton closed his eyes, hands clasped over his stomach, and went to the place that went beyond dreams. The place he could contact others like him. Where he would see the sheep-head man.

A cave mouth came into view, the inside walls lit by the reflection of prancing flames. A pitch-black night sky surrounded the cave, as it always did, and no stars or moon penetrated the gloom. The sheep-head man appeared in the opening, his hairy chest bare, his legs encased in tight black breeches, feet bare on the gravelly ground. The light glanced off his horns, and the holes where his eyes should have been glowed orange. He nodded at Leyton, lifting one arm to beckon him with curled fingers.

Leyton smiled, at peace, and walked towards the cave. The sheep-head man turned and disappeared around an internal corner, his shadow large and looming on the rear wall. Inside the cave, Leyton trailed him, going through a low tunnel and coming out into a room carved out of the rock. The sheep-head man sat on a large stone seat, his taloned fingers curled around the end of the armrests. Leyton went down on his knees before him and awaited the familiar touch of the man's hand upon his head. It came, the heat of his palm searing, and Leyton closed his eyes, letting a trance consume him.

A trance that would take him to Barry.

Chapter Ten

Barry sighed, waited for Tag to transfer his weight to the doorframe of the locked apartment, and shucked his overshirt. "You are so lucky I'm fag enough to layer." He peeled off the stretchier T-shirt and handed it to his partner. "Put this on."

"Thanks." Tag balanced precariously on his bad foot to pull the shirt over his head and smooth it down his chest and abs.

"Damn."

"What?"

Barry made a noise, deep in his chest. "Keep it. Never looked that damn good on me." He watched Tag's hands slide over the fabric again, a self-conscious gesture that only made him sexier. Unable to resist, Barry yanked him forward, caught him against his chest when he grunted in surprise and swallowed a tight groan in a hard kiss. He didn't let go until he felt Tag relax into him, kiss him back, and allow Barry to take his weight again.

"How do we do this? You have no shoes."

"I'll wait just inside. Hail a cab and I'll come out when it gets here."

"You know we'll get looks when we get to the station if you walk in barefoot and bleeding."

Tag nodded. "I'll wait in the cab. The key is taped inside the top drawer of my desk, on the underside of the desktop."

"Convenient."

"I don't need it to be convenient. I just need it to be there."

"And how do I get into your office and into your desk?"

"Ross."

His partner. Barry knew the intake of breath at that was audible. Not that he didn't like his partner. The man was a good cop and had proved remarkably accepting of all Barry's flaws and idiosyncrasies. But that Tag had trusted him with access to his private sanctum when he didn't trust Barry stung more than it logically should have.

"Something wrong?" Tag asked.

"No." They had made their slow way back down to the door to the street, and Barry waited for Tag to shift his weight again before going outside and hailing a cab.

The ride to the station was a silent one, with the cabby eyeing them through the rear view mirror at five-second intervals, like a nervous twitch. When Barry shifted for the fifth time, Tag slipped a hand across the seat and took his, squeezing his fingers.

"What is it?" Tag asked.

"Nothing." He cast an irritated look at the back of the driver's head.

Tag nodded.

Glad he had managed to pass off his antsy behaviour as irritation with the nosey driver, Barry gazed out the window, away from Tag's scrutinising gaze. Fact was, his head buzzed, his ears rang, and it felt as though he had sand under his eyelids. He couldn't tell Tag this constant edginess was his life now. There was a cocoon of safety in Tag's bed where the buzzing feeling of being watched didn't irritate him—as though the place was shielded from whatever made him dream. Whatever gave him the feeling he was never quite alone inside his own head could not penetrate there. Even the touch of Tag's fingers over his eased the constant whine of white noise.

It certainly didn't help that, however well he'd slept over the past day and night, it wasn't enough to make up for the weeks and months of deprivation. It was just a tease. He stifled a yawn, but not before Tag noticed.

"Just this quick run," Tag said quietly. "We'll get back and you can take a nap. I'll make some supper. We have all weekend."

Barry nodded and glanced at his lover. "Thanks." Part of him wanted to sink down and put his head in Tag's lap, let the rumbling movement of the cab lull him to sleep. There was no guarantee he'd be dream-free out here, even with Tag at his side, and he had no wish to let his boss see he was that far gone, lover and best friend or not.

At the station, Ross was, indeed, at his desk, sifting through paperwork.

"What the hell you doin' here, Davey Jones?" he asked, without lifting his gaze from the form he was filling out.

"Old school, much?" Barry tapped the paper. "We have those online, you know. Fillable forms and all."

Ross just grunted.

"Hey." Barry perched on the edge of his desk and lowered himself, trying to get in Ross' line of sight. "Jerry."

"Oh." Ross lifted his head. "You did not just call me Jerry."

"I need to get into Tag's office."

"Why?"

Barry tightened his lips, not wanting to hear the slight suspicion in his partner's voice.

"Ah. We raised the Titanic last night. Locked ourselves out. Can you please?"

"Raised—? Oh!" Ross grinned. "Really?"

Barry gave a quick glance around. Though the room was otherwise deserted, he still felt eyes and ears everywhere. "Can we?" He nodded at the captain's office. "Not really wanting to talk about this out here."

"Sure, sure." Ross got up and led the way to Tag's door, fishing keys from his pocket as he went. He found the right one and opened up, letting them both inside and closing the door behind them.

"So. Just for clarity's sake, is this one of those on again, off again things? Because if we're partners, I gotta know when you're fucking my boss."

"I fucking hope it's not. It's a long story." Barry pointed to the desk. "Top drawer, please."

Ross nodded, complied. "We're partners, Barry. I got all the time in the world."

"Most of it you wouldn't believe and I can't exactly prove."

"You make it sound sinister and sordid."

"It is. Both."

The drawer was unlocked, and Barry drew it out, setting it carefully on top of Tag's desk. Unlike his apartment, the office was pristine. Not a paper sat out where anyone could look at what they had no business looking at. Everything was under lock and key, including the captain's laptop—not just password protected, but stashed away inside a metal file cabinet, safe from prying eyes.

Barry crouched in front of the desk and felt around until his fingers encountered the key, taped just where Tag had said it would be. He pried it free with his fingernails and replaced the desk drawer. "Thanks."

Ross nodded. "Listen, Wiki, I'm not an idiot. I've read the case files. I know how many cases you and Tag solved together. You've got one of the best closing records on the force...and one of the worst personnel files. I won't lie and say that closing rate isn't attractive. If I wanted to get anywhere, a record like that would go a long way. I'm not against slamming the cage on a few shitheads myself, but I gotta tell you. Some of your methods..." He held up a hand and rocked it back and forth. "Sketchy." He moved to stand in front of the door, blocking Barry's exit and crossing his arms. "I'd say you've got one hell of an informant, but no one could possibly have tipped you off on all those murders, and if you have that many snitches, I'll lick that coffee pot clean."

Barry made a face.

Ross just raised an eyebrow.

He had a point. And with the current case and his dreams spiralling so fast out of control, he really should bring Ross into the loop. He and Tag had managed alone before, but Tag had been his partner then, not his boss, and Barry knew he would have to keep a professional distance this time.

"I can't explain it all right now, but I will." He glanced through the office windows. "And not here. Tomorrow. We'll go for lunch. I'll call you."

For a minute, Ross remained where he was. Barry hoped he would accept the concession. The cab ride wasn't getting any cheaper, and Tag needed his leg looked at.

"One more thing," Ross said.

Barry sighed.

"You and Tag—"

"Partners on the force about seven years."

"No shit. I can read."

"About five. Then he made captain. It's been mostly off since then."

Ross dropped his arms at last and eased his stance. "And now?"

"I'm not sure. One day at a time. But not common knowledge. It won't help his position if rumours started up. He should have kept his distance from my not-so-great personnel record, but…" Barry drew in a breath and met Ross' gaze.

"But he loves you."

"Maybe."

Ross blinked, made a face and stood aside. "The two of you are not hiding anything around here. I hope you know that. For what it's worth, you both should know you do have friends in this precinct."

"That is…good to know." Barry shuffled past and made his way to the station door before he turned back. "I'll give you a shout tomorrow."

"Sure."

Back in the cab, Barry handed Tag the key without a word.

"I'm going to have to talk to him about filing paperwork on his days off," Tag said.

"When else is he supposed to do it?"

"Maybe you could push a pencil or two yourself there, big guy."

Barry snorted. "He knows about us."

"Sure he does." Tag kept his gaze fixed out of the windshield. "He's a perceptive guy."

"Too perceptive. He wants to know why our record is so high."

"And what did you tell him?"

Outside, the rain began to fall again and the streets turned a dull, splashing grey that got on everything and washed out the colour. "That I'd call him tomorrow. Go for lunch."

"You want me to come?"

"Probably."

"He does need to know, Barry. You can't hide it from him forever, and I think he'll…if not understand, at least keep it under wraps and try to cover for you."

"He shouldn't have that on him. It'll just drag him down. He's a good cop."

"And a good man. That's why I assigned him to you. Because he *is* a good cop. He wants to catch the bad guys and save the good guys, and in case you forget which side of that equation you're on, you're one of us. A good guy."

Barry didn't say anything. He never really put himself on the other team, but crazy was a bit of a limbo place to be sometimes, especially when a conviction slipped through his fingers because he couldn't take the stand and say "I was there. I dreamed it, I saw it, it happened." What good was being the last testament of all those souls if he couldn't use it to put away the pieces of shit who had done it? Some days, he wished he could shuck the badge and the veneer of civilisation and go and take out the creeps himself.

Then he looked at Tag and knew he could never betray the man's trust or undo all he'd done to keep

Barry on the force and somewhere close to sane. And what if, one day, he had *that* dream? The one he feared the most, where he wasn't just the victim? What if, one day, he was in that place, that black abyss, staring down the barrel of his own service revolver? He had a hard time convincing himself, especially lately, that it wasn't an inevitability.

Finally back at Tag's apartment, they let themselves in with a little sigh of relief. Tag let him dress his wound, which, though obviously painful, was not all that deep. Once that was done, Barry also searched out the culprit, a broken piece of metal bracket on the underside of the table, and removed it. A few screws did the job of holding the table together in its place.

"Thanks." Tag was slouching on the couch watching a muted football game while Barry put away the tools. He joined him, and Tag slung an arm over his shoulder, drew him close.

"Not a problem." A jaw-cracking yawn later, Barry smiled and rested his head on the back of the couch.

"Bed's more comfortable. Why don't you get some sleep? I'm not going anywhere. I'll wake you for supper."

Relatively sure he'd be safe from the dreams wrapped in the comfort of Tag's bed and scent, Barry nodded and padded over to their sanctuary, flopped out, and was asleep in minutes.

The darkness that surrounded him when he opened his eyes smelt of wet, cold and dank, like rotten concrete or maybe ancient mineral deposits. The stench burned his nose and made his eyes water.

"What the fuck?"

There was no one around. He wasn't bound or restrained. He was completely alone in the echoing darkness with no indication of which way was out, or even if there was an 'out'.

He cautiously made his way forward, feet slipping and rolling on loose gravel. Arched windows appeared, blacker night showing through against the grey. Sometimes he glimpsed rock walls reflecting wavering light and dancing, demon-shaped shadows. There was no way to tell where the light came from. It wasn't enough to illuminate more than the narrow path at his feet a few metres at a time, like peering through the fading glow of an LED flashlight whose charge was dying.

The place had all the earmarks of so many dumpsites — abandoned buildings, echoing warehouses, empty subway tunnels — but it never really lost the feel of a dark, oppressive cave in the middle of nowhere, either.

He felt at his side. No holster. Nothing at the small of his back, and when he reached down to check his boot, he found he was in bare feet. Every step after that, the stones cut into his flesh until he was biting his tongue in agony. The thought of stopping never occurred to him.

There was something down there and it was waiting for him. It didn't care that he wanted to turn and flee in the other direction.

The trek went on and on. At one point, he felt a presence, like an arm draped over his shoulder, and the step-stump of Tag's familiar, uneven gait travelling beside him. When he looked, there were only shadows.

"Tag?"

A far distant cry that could have been his name sounded, but it moved away. He shivered. Warmth wove around him, cocooning him, but it couldn't reach inside to where the cold really dwelt.

Don't leave me, Tag.

The shadowy presence grew fainter, came back and faded again. The warmth of Tag's hands on his skin was only surface warmth. Not even his lover could help him. He'd have to open up, and if he did that, darker things than Tag's love would get in. He couldn't allow it. Those dark things could never be allowed to touch what Tag was, what Tag offered him, even if it meant rejecting that offer. He pushed the hands away, steeling himself for the cold of being alone.

The sound of footsteps softened to disappear behind the erratic thud of his heart. Tag couldn't reach him here. He was on his own.

At the foot of the torturous path, the way forked around a still, black pool. It occurred to him that his mind could be reflecting something out of every other horror movie he'd seen as kid – movies he'd stopped watching once his mind made its own terrifying images for him. Horrible because they were real and he couldn't turn them off or refuse to see. He pried his gaze away from the still water and looked around.

To his right, he could barely discern two figures. Shadows danced and spun around them, impossible to identify them. One might have been kneeling. One might have had horns.

"And a forked tongue and tail, Barry. Get it together."

To his left, the glow intensified, orange and sulphurous. It took a moment for him to recognise the glow of streetlights. He frowned. The path bled into the street, and the street rose up in familiarity that made his gut twist. He hurried forward, past the Chinese market on the corner, dashed through the tiny court in front of the subway entrance where the newsstand stood abandoned – magazines flapping, papers blowing off down the street – and skidded to a halt in front of his building.

The shadows of his doorstep contorted around something lumpy and out of place. He turned away. He didn't want to know. He pelted back towards the dark path. The cave curved and threw him back into the street in front of the café on the far corner. He whirled.

In the dark distance, a figure walked towards him.

"Stay away!"

"You have to look, Barry." The voice was soft, male, calm.

Barry reeled away from him, back towards the path that turned into foggy street, escaped news rags flapping against his shins, rattling away past him. The lumpy pile in his doorway was still there. He backed, swivelled his face away again.

"This doesn't make any sense!"

"It does. It will. If you let it." That voice again. Calm. So fucking calm.

Barry's heart pounded. Sweat dribbled down between his shoulder blades. "Stop it," he whispered. "Just stop! Stop." Every time he turned, the street was there, the steps up to his door, the contorted shadows.

"This is what you need to see, Barry."

"Leave me alone!"

"Look."

"No." Barry stopped spinning, dropped his gaze to his feet and the rock-strewn pavement under his bleeding soles. Mist swirled around his ankles, hiding and revealing the ground in twists of cracked pavement, stones and rock.

"Look." The voice was right in front of him now. The man, not two feet away. "Look." He spoke softly, cajoling. Almost kind.

"Please don't." Barry kept his head lowered, squeezed his eyes shut.

The world tilted. He fell, landing hard on his knees, and the jolt threw him forward. Someone grabbed his hair, yanked his head up. Cold metal and hard fingers pried their way into his mouth. He screamed. And screamed and screamed and screamed.

"This is a gift, Barry," the gentle voice whispered. "If you don't learn to use it, it will destroy you."

Chapter Eleven

"Barry!" Tag shook him again to no avail. "Shit! Barry, wake up!"

He tried not to panic, got up, paced to the kitchen, back to the bed, back to the kitchen where he ran a towel under cold water. Bringing it back to the bed, he draped it over Barry's sweat-damp forehead. "Come on, babe," he murmured. "Come back. Please."

He'd *never* not been able to wake him. Barry had never had a dream like this sleeping in their bed. Never.

The cloth had no effect. Tag paced again, hand scrubbing through his hair. "Fuck!"

Barry had slept a good long while before Tag had noticed his breath had changed from the easy, rhythmical swell of sleep to a choppy, dream-tossed pant. Sweat broke out, and he had begun to twitch. Tag had been torn between waking him immediately and letting the dream run its course in hopes it might give them the much needed break they were looking for. He felt like he was betraying his lover, letting the torture continue, but he knew Barry would have woken frustrated and angry either way.

Instead, he'd climbed into the bed to hold him, hoping his presence might mitigate the anxiety already etched across Barry's face. He'd wrapped his arms firmly around him, held him close so their heartbeats melded, and whispered about never leaving him again.

Barry had continued to tremble, to moan, and eventually, to pluck at Tag's hands on his chest, prying at them, using nails and then feet, kicking to get free. Tag had had no choice but to release him. Even a soft hand on Barry's shoulder met with fearful retreat.

"Let me help."

But no. Not even his pleas did any good. The man slept on, dreamt, and Tag's heart made awful tearing sounds in his chest. At least, he imagined it did, from the pain.

When twitching turned to tossing, the broken panting to murmurs and fretting, Tag tried to wake him again but couldn't. Now Barry cried out, curled in on himself, mumbling incoherent words that sounded too much like begging, and Tag threw himself towards the bed, unable to bear the fear he heard in those incomprehensible words.

"Barry. Please." He touched his lover's shoulder, prised it until Barry finally straightened. He caressed the black mess of curls, touched his face, bent and carefully pressed a kiss on frantically moving lips.

Barry screamed.

The sound threw Tag back onto his ass on the floor.

The screaming went on and on, no matter how Tag shook him or shouted.

Barry's distress stopped as abruptly as it had begun. He sat up, shock and fright shooting across his face, and the silence in the room crashed down on them.

For once, Tag was glad he lived in a neighbourhood where no one ever heard anything. Of course, they could have been murdering each other, and that would still be true, but right now, Barry needed all his focus.

"Barry?" Tag didn't dare touch him. He didn't need physical contact to feel the shaking. It was bone deep and rattled the bed against the wall. He didn't need to touch to know Barry was covered in clammy sweat, didn't want to frighten him more.

Barry's dark eyes were unfocused. A bit of spittle flecked his cheek, too pale and lax.

"Couldn't get out," Barry mumbled after a minute.

Tag nodded. "I know. But it's okay. You're safe now. Tell me what happened?"

"Can't—"

"We can fix this, Barry. I just need you to tell me what you saw. We'll figure it out together, I promise."

"Cold."

Tag couldn't tell if he meant now, or in the dream. He was about to ask when Barry turned his head and his eyes at last took on a deeper, more alive light.

"I couldn't get out," he repeated. "He wouldn't let me go."

"Who?" Tag risked laying a hand on his lover's thigh. Barry immediately grasped it up and squeezed his fingers painfully. Tag kept his expression calm under the bruising grip. "Who wouldn't let you go?" He was proud his voice didn't give away the pain, either. "Could you see him? Do you know who you were in the dream? Where he was holding you?"

Barry's eyes met his again, this time, full of a deeper, angrier fear. "I was me. I don't know who he was. He..."

Silence pulled tight, dangerous and fragile.

"He what? Barry, I need to know."

The idea Barry had dreamt a dream that was not about some anonymous victim ran Tag's blood cold. He could handle it, could find a way to stifle his own fears if he knew Barry always dreamt about some other poor soul. Not when Barry was the victim. Not when he was the one in danger.

The fear hardened to anger, anger to cold determination to put a stop to whatever was doing this to the man he loved.

"Tell me what happened!"

Barry yanked his hands away from Tag, backed across the bed. "I can't."

"You have to. I can't help—"

"No." The word dragged, soft but sharp as glass over Tag's nerves. "You can't. I have to go."

He scrambled off the bed and hurried towards the bathroom to do what he always did and wash off the stink of the dream. Tag followed, unwilling to let it go. Barry could cut and slash at him all he wanted. He wasn't letting go again.

The door slammed in his face. He had to take a moment to smooth down the bristling fury, knowing it was backed by deep fear for his lover and not directed at him...exactly. The shower came on. Tag stood and listened to the door slide open and close again with a bit too much force. After another minute, he knocked.

"Open." Barry's voice drifted, subdued under the sound of the spray.

Inside, the room was thick with steam. Barry had his back to the door, his round, smooth ass glistening and pink from the heat.

"You know what pisses me off the most?" Tag asked.

"Besides me?"

"About you." He yanked at his shirt, hauling it off, and popped open the button of his jeans. "You never hesitate to come clawing at my door when you're broken. I put you back together, and it's like nothing else I do matters. You turn your cold shoulder, and I get to watch you take on the world until the world and these stupid dreams crush you again." He flung back the shower door, not caring about the water spraying out into the rest of the room.

Barry stood with his back to Tag, still, the water flowing over his shoulder and down his back. Tag lifted Barry's arms and placed his palms on the wall above his head.

"I'm not your fucking clean-up crew, Barry. I'm your partner."

"Were."

"Semantics. I love you. Let me help." He stepped close, smoothed a hand up from the middle of Barry's back, between his shoulder blades to rest on the nape of his neck where he squeezed lightly. "Let me help! Please!"

Barry's head dropped. He sighed softly as Tag's other hand drifted up his front. He was still shaking. The tremors flitted delicately through him under Tag's palms.

Tag reached for the soap, lathered his hands and ran them over every inch of Barry's body, starting at his feet, up his legs and back, over his shoulders, lingering with slippery fingers over his nipples until

Barry was moaning and Tag had gained control of the tremors. He initiated each one now, taking command back from the dreams, grounding Barry in the safety of his touch.

The fucking, when it came, was as slow and deliberate as everything else. When Barry seemed content to drift on the rhythm of Tag's motion, Tag reminded him where he was, what was happening, with a tweak to a nipple that made him gasp, or a hard dig of teeth into the muscle of Barry's shoulder.

"Whatever it takes, Barry," he panted, driving up into his moaning lover. "Until this dream freak gets it into his thick skull he can't ever have you."

He couldn't be sure if the sound Barry made was a sob, but when Barry arched back into him, he took hold of him, gripped his hips and drove harder until the slap of skin and Barry's cries drowned out the pattering sigh of the water.

Tag came hard, black spots stealing his glimpse of Barry's thrown back head, blood rushing in his ears, obscuring Barry's strangled shout. His head cleared to the sound of Barry gasping, calling to him, and he lifted his head.

"You okay?" Barry's hands were on his face, calloused fingers roaming lightly over his cheeks, eyes worried.

Tag nodded.

"Good." Barry spun him, pinned him heavily against the end wall of the shower out of the warm spray. "Bareback, Tag? Have you lost your fucking mind?"

"I..." In fact, he supposed he had, just for a moment, in his desperation to reclaim Barry from the dreams. He'd thought of nothing but making sure the man knew where he was, where he belonged.

"Stupid shit." Barry planted an angry kiss on Tag's lips, giving and taking it away again before Tag had a chance to respond, then he was climbing out of the shower, grabbing a towel and leaving the bathroom.

"Shit." Tag spun the taps closed and hurried after his lover. "Hey! Barry, you've got nothing to worry about. I know I'm clean!" he called, hopping and stumbling as he tried to dry himself.

Barry whirled on him. "Maybe I'm not!"

The world dropped away, and Tag sat heavily on a kitchen chair. "What?" He found himself frantically searching Barry's face, his body, for any sign of sickness.

"Shit, Tag, I don't know." Barry tugged frantically at his hair. "I don't. Fuck! I don't have time for this. I have to go."

"Wait! *Go*? Go where?"

"Home."

"You should stay here. Rest—"

"It isn't even safe here anymore."

"Barry." Tag tossed his towel onto the table and rose. "Calm down. I'm sorry about…that." He waved a hand vaguely towards the bathroom. "We'll deal with it. You'll get tested. If we have to worry about it, we will, but let's not borrow trouble, okay?"

Barry nodded. "Yeah. Yeah, you're right. I mean, it isn't likely. Still. Don't take risks."

He met Tag's eye and the sheen of worry and exhaustion still shone out. His hand came up to cup Tag's face. "Don't take risks. I fucking need you, and I know it isn't fair, but I do."

Tag managed a small smile and hauled Barry close. "I'll be more careful. I'm sorry. Now." He pulled in a deep breath but didn't let go of Barry, who didn't seem in any hurry to get away. "Get dressed and we'll go for supper somewhere. I'll buy a fucking club pack. I expect to get you so exhausted you won't be able to dream, okay?"

"I can't. I do have to go home."

"Barry, please."

"I have to." He did move away then, and looked up a Tag. "The dream told me to."

"Shit."

They dressed in silence. Tag couldn't voice the worries that tripped through his head—that Barry was talking about the dreams more and more like they were guiding him, like they had a consciousness, or his pronouncement that he'd been himself in the dream. He resolved to get the man to talk to him while they drove. Maybe it would be easier if they had that illusion of distraction.

When they were safely on the road and Barry had no way to turn his back or run, Tag finally asked about the dream. It was a low trick, but he needed answers.

"I need you to promise me something, Tag," Barry said, instead of answering the question.

"Anything." He knew they still had issues. Barry had no reason to trust him, but he would figure out a way to change that.

"No shrinks. Don't even talk about it. I'm not crazy, and I'm not making this up. I know it's real. You have to believe me."

"Okay."

"Just like that?"

He felt Barry watching him but kept his eyes on the road and the flashes of cityscape illuminated in his headlights. "No talk of shrinks. Tell me why you think this dream was about you." He'd seen the bodies Barry's dreams led them to. He couldn't imagine finding Barry like that. Or, rather, he could, and that scared him.

"You're going to think I'm finally losing it."

"Barry..." Tag took a breath, rolled up to a stop light, and finally looked over to his partner. "I've seen these dreams lead you down all sorts of unpleasant paths. We've solved a lot of otherwise unsolvable cases. At this point, I'll believe just about anything if it means it'll help us understand what the fuck is going on. What happened today... I tried to wake you up, Barry. I tried to get you out, and I couldn't. That is just not okay with me."

"Me either."

"So talk."

A horn blasted, and Tag turned back to see the light had changed. He rolled through the intersection as Barry described the dream as best he could remember.

"The worst thing is, Tag, I *do* remember it. I shouldn't. It was a dream. Who remembers every single detail of a fucked-up dream?"

"Some people—"

"No. Even with the worst nightmares, up to now, I never remembered them well. Just bits and pieces, vague shadows that only made sense after the fact, after we found what we were looking for. This is different. He said—"

"He?" Tag rounded the last corner and approached the kerb outside Barry's building.

His lover turned in his seat, putting his back to the passenger window and staring at Tag. "I don't know who, so don't ask. But I know he was controlling the dream. He wouldn't let me out. Every time I tried to turn around, to find the way out, he manipulated the dreamscape so I couldn't." There was a moment's pause before Barry spoke again. "He called it a gift.

Said if I didn't learn to understand it, it would kill me."

Tag waited, but there didn't seem to be any more. "A gift," he said at last.

Barry nodded.

"Did he happen to mention a return policy?"

Barry actually laughed, and Tag realised he'd been holding his breath. He let it out in a sigh. "So why are we here?"

"Do me a favour."

"Anything."

"Have a look." He gestured over his shoulder. "At the doorway. What do you see?"

Tag peered through the low-lying fog rolling along the street from the subway grate. "Some bum's sleeping in your doorway, but otherwise, nothing unusual."

"Shit." Barry slumped back into his seat. "Shit, shit, fuck!"

"Wiki?"

"You're gonna want to suit up and call this in, Cap."

"Call what in?" Tag looked again at the irregular, slumped shadows in the doorway. "You mean…?"

Barry nodded. "He brought that dream to me, led me through it to where he wanted me to go. He wanted to show me, and there was no ambiguity, Tag. He knew exactly what I would find. He showed me."

Tag slammed a fist down on the steering wheel. "So who the fuck is he?"

Chapter Twelve

Leyton stayed in his trance and waited on Barry's street, keeping to the shadows inside the bush beside Barry's door. He stared at the subway grate, at the fog creeping out of it like a slow-reaching hand, complete with fingers and long nails. The sheep-head man, in his airy form, coming to make sure everything went as he intended. His orchestration of Leyton's life had given him comfort as a young boy and gave him purpose now.

Everyone needed a purpose.

The fog hand stilled, hovered low to the ground. Waited.

Waited along with Leyton.

A car drew up to the kerb, and Leyton parted the foliage to better see the vehicle's occupants. There they were, Barry and Tag—a little late for Leyton's liking, but there all the same. They talked for a while, and Leyton strained to connect to Barry and listen in. He failed, hearing nothing but his beating heart and steady breath.

Barry should be able to hear me now. Feel me. What the damn are they doing just sitting there like that? Barry knows what he's going to find. Knows what he has to do next. So why the reluctance to investigate? And what were they doing to make them so late getting here?

Barry stared ahead, and then Tag glanced towards the bush.

Ah. At last.

The fog billowed out of the grate some more, thicker, and floated along the path, a rolling mass of ocean-like waves. Tendrils of it snaked towards the car, curling at the passenger door, kissing the window, while the body of it hovered across the ground between the car and Leyton. It thickened further, a blanket of mist, the hand no longer visible. Smoke. It looked like cigar smoke.

Leyton closed his eyes and inhaled deeply, taking in the scene by scent, acknowledging the ages-old aroma of the man in his dreams. Ancient books and dust. Mould and damp moss. The fog, it came towards him then, and he didn't need to open his eyes to see where it was. It crept up his legs, surrounded his body, its coldness so icy he shivered. It caressed him like he imagined the hands of lover might, and the shiver sank beneath his skin into his bones, heating him from the inside.

A car door slammed shut. Someone was angry, then.

Leyton opened his eyes, and the fog eddied beside him, a figure now, shimmering and dense. Tag strode towards the bush, his gait lopsided, his face set in an angry grimace, fists bunched at his sides. He appeared so annoyed, yet at the same time fearful of what he walked towards.

"I wouldn't have thought you'd be fearful, Tag," Leyton whispered. "You've seen more dead bodies than the average cop. Ought to be used to them by now. The sight of them. The stench."

Tag walked on.

Barry remained in the car.

"Why don't you join Tag, Barry? Come on now. This is where you're meant to be."

He pushed the thoughts at Barry, hoping their bond was strong enough now that Leyton's words would transfer. If not the exact words, at least his meaning. Something Barry would sense and just know. Leyton held his breath, sights on Barry's profile, dark and indecipherable in the gloom. Just a brow, nose, and chin that could have belonged to any number of people. Barry ran a hand through his hair, gripped it and leant forward, and Leyton could practically hear him whispering, "Get out, get out, get out!" He appeared to be trying to resist exiting the car.

"I wonder, did you hear me, Barry?"

Leyton tried again.

"Come. Get out. See this through to the end. There is no escape. And he is here, the one directing me, you. It's time to face the truth. There's more to this than dreams, Barry. More to everything."

Barry glanced at the bush, his eyes just about discernible through the passenger window. Heavy, dark clouds shifted, and moonlight glanced off Barry's eyes. They reminded Leyton of his own after waking from a dream. He'd looked in the mirror once, saw the whole of his eyes were black, and watched them change to their normal appearance as the mantle of sleep had worn off. Barry's were similar. Although the whites showed, his usual iris colour was darker than Leyton remembered from his dreams. Perhaps they would lighten soon. Or maybe, if Barry continued to carry the memory of his dreams around with him the way he did, they would stay black.

"Now wouldn't *that* give people pause for thought?" Leyton murmured.

Barry squinted in Leyton's direction.

"Yes, I'm here. You can't see me, but you feel me, don't you? Say you do. Let me know you do. And guess what? He is here. The fog. Don't tell me you can't see the fog."

Barry pressed a palm to the glass, leaned closer, his breath misting the window. His head wagged side to side in slow, belligerent denial.

"Oh, stop being so childish, so reticent. Grow up and get out of the motherfucking car!"

Eyes wide, Barry jerked his head back. His lips moved. Leyton heard the words—"Fuck off. Just fuck off and leave me the hell alone."

"Fuck off? No, I don't believe I will. You have work to do. So do it."

The car door swung open and Barry lifted his legs out. He stood and stared ahead at Tag, who had reached Charles and now stooped over to view the body.

"Jesus," Tag whispered, going down on his haunches for a closer look. "Barry?" A pause. "Come and take a look at this guy. At least I think…" He narrowed his eyes. "Some nutso jerk sliced this one up damn good." Then he murmured "Fuck *me!*" and closed his eyes.

Leyton smiled. "Yes, I sliced him up damn good, but I'm no nutso jerk."

Tag wouldn't have heard him—Leyton knew that—but saying what he had made him feel better. Made him feel part of the scenario, as though he was really there, *really* standing in the bush, the branches jabbing into his arm, the fog chilling him until he thought he might come in his pants.

Barry came up behind Tag and stared down at the corpse. He closed his eyes as Tag opened his, a hand drifting up to rub absently at the back of his neck as he looked up.

Barry winced. "This is...fuck. This is..." He ran a hand into his hair and curled his fingers around until Leyton sensed Barry's pain when the corkscrew locks felt on the verge of parting from his scalp.

"The man who killed Cal Landry."

"The man who killed Cal Landry," Barry said, opening his now normal eyes and swiping his face with his palm.

Tag stood and faced Barry. "And you know this how?"

Barry laughed quietly and gazed up at the sky. He shook his head, teeth bared in a wry smile. "Shit. You wouldn't believe me if—"

"Wouldn't believe you? *Wouldn't believe you?*" Tag gripped Barry's forearm until Barry lowered his head to look at him. "How the fuck you can say that is beyond me. Didn't we just fucking have this conversation? It *all* sounds fucking crazy, but it's *happening*, isn't it? Nothing we can do to stop it. We've solved too much, followed the clues left in dreams too many times, for me *not* to believe you. Listen..." He grasped Barry's upper arms and shook him a little. "Forget how crazy it sounds, all right? How it might sound to someone who doesn't give a shit about you. And just tell me." He touched his forehead to Barry's. "Just open your goddamn mouth and talk to me. Please."

"Tell him, Barry, before the poor man implodes." Leyton chuckled.

"Fuck off!" Barry gently pushed Tag away and hunkered down beside Charles.

"Fuck off? Barry... What the hell's wrong with you?" Tag scrubbed hard at the back of his neck.

"Not you," Barry said. "I didn't mean you." He shook his head as if to erase Leyton's words.

Tag flexed his jaw muscles. "Who *did* you mean? Him? The one you told me about? The dream guy?"

"If you can call Freddy Krueger a dream guy," Barry muttered.

Bending over, his hand on Barry's back, Tag rubbed slow circles there, and his face... Leyton would give anything for someone to look at him with love like that.

"Fuck." Barry sighed, an angry, frustrated exhalation, and dropped his head. "I can hear him, Tag. In my head. I can't—" A shudder went through him, and Tag's hand stilled between his shoulder blades. "I can't have him there all the time. He *is* nuts. I don't want to be nuts."

He said it all quickly, probably thinking if he spoke that way it wouldn't sound so insane. Leyton understood how he must be feeling. At least he'd had this kind of thing happening for years now, had become acclimatised to it. Barry was relatively new to all this, and he didn't have a damn clue how to handle it, from what Leyton had seen and felt.

"In your head?" Tag asked, widening the circles on Barry's back once again.

"Yeah. In my damn head. Like he's inside it. Like he's *here*." Barry glanced around nervously then stood, his movements abrupt.

Leyton picked up on the panic. "*Yes, I'm here, but you don't need to fear me. Just because you can't see me, doesn't*

142

mean I'd do you harm. We're in this together. We're partners. Whether you like it or not."

"Here?" Tag straightened and looked around too. "Right. Uh…right. Where is he?"

"I don't fucking know!" Barry whirled away, stalking towards the car, head bent, hands shoved in his pockets.

Tag stayed put, staring after him, his knees creaking as he moved from foot to foot. "Who the *hell* is he hearing?" he muttered.

"Me," Leyton said, reaching through the bush to brush his hand across Tag's arm. The man shivered, looked down at his arm. Shivered again. *"Yes, you feel me, you know I'm here. But it's a little bit too weird for you, isn't it? But I'm telling you now, you'd better start really believing this business, because if you don't, I'll have to do what the man in my dreams said and…get rid of you. I don't want to do that, Tag."*

Tag lifted his arm and cradled it in his other hand, rubbing up and down its length. A shout from Barry's direction drew Leyton's attention. He glanced away from Tag to see Barry bounding back across the grass, a scowl on his forehead and his fists clenched.

Barry turned in a circle, head darting to and fro. "Whoever you are, you leave him the fuck alone! I don't know who you are or what the hell you want until you explain yourself fully, in ways I can damn well understand instead of the pathetic, half-assed dreams you give me, but you'd better fucking believe me when I say I will hurt you! If I'm like you, and I can do whatever it is you do without being seen, I'll work it. I'll figure it out and come for you if you hurt one hair on his head!" He paused, breathing heavily, sweat breaking out on his face. "Do you hear me?"

"Then make sure he understands. Believes. Because if he doesn't, if he starts putting roadblocks in our way, I'll have to do what has to be done."

"Barry?" Tag took a step towards him, one hand reaching out.

"Fuck off." Barry reached a clutching hand towards Tag. "Not you, him." Barry swivelled his head around, trying to see in every direction at once. His fingers closed on Tag's forearm, and he tightened his grip. "Jesus Christ, please, just leave him the fuck alone. Tell me what you want. I'll do whatever I can. Act on whatever you show me. But just leave. Him. Alone."

"As you wish. Providing you do what you say and he doesn't pose a threat. A problem."

"He won't." Barry looked at Tag. "I know. This looks...crazy. Hell, if I were you *I'd* think I was crazy too. Fuck!" His hand flew up and tangled in his hair. "I already think I'm nuts. But Tag, you need to believe me. I don't know what he wants, but I have to do it. Whatever it is. And you have to let me." He peered through the dark, thick air to see into Tag's eyes. "No matter what. Don't get in the way. All right?"

Tag nodded, his face showing emotions ranging from love to concern. "I believe you. I do." He took another step, hand coming into contact with Barry's arm. "Just tell me what needs to be done, and I'm there. All over it."

Barry nodded.

Tag cleared his throat. "So, can you...you know, ask him now who that guy is?" He jerked his head in Charles' direction.

Looking sheepish, Barry asked the air, "Who is he? What's his name? Why did he kill Cal? And where the fuck is the woman who was in the victim's apartment?"

"Tsk-tsk-tsk, Barry. You're the cop, aren't you? Those are things you need to work out for yourself. I just off them. Get rid of them." Leyton pushed through the bush, giving Charles' leg a kick as he walked past and headed to Barry's side. The fog followed him as though attached. *"But I will answer one of your questions. The girl. She's with me."*

"With you?" Barry's eyes widened, and he turned, looking directly at Leyton but not seeing a goddamn thing.

At least Leyton didn't think he could see him.

"You'd better not hurt her." Barry lunged at the fog.

"The fog isn't me, Barry. And no, I'm not going to hurt her. I'm going to make her love me."

"Love you? Jesus. You're—"

"Don't say it, Barry. Don't say I'm insane. After all, we're not that different, you and I. Aren't you trying to make Tag love you? Haven't you been trying to do that ever since you met him?"

Barry breathed through his nose, nostrils flaring. "That's different." He glanced at Tag, who stood staring their way, eyes narrowed, mouth downturned. A picture of someone trying to work out what the hell was going on. "I think he—"

"All right. You got me. He loves you. But Lorelei? She'll love me too before long, you'll see." Leyton rolled his shoulders and glanced at the fog, now slinking away from him, back to the subway grate. *"The fog's going. You see that?"*

Barry turned and watched it disappear. "What does that mean?"

"What does what mean, Barry?" Tag asked, moving closer to his side.

"Hang on. I'm talking to *him* still. Just give me a minute, yeah?" Barry turned back to where the fog had been and, by instinct or just coincidence, stared right into Leyton's eyes. "Why has the fog gone? What *is* the fog?"

"It's him, Barry. The man in my dreams. The one who directs me. Like I direct you. We're a chain, all linked, all giving instructions. He gives me mine, I give you yours, and you give out directions and…solve the puzzles."

"Forgive me for getting pissed and impatient here, but you didn't answer my first question. Why has the fog — the man — gone? Where? And you'd better be quick, because we called this corpse in and the guys will be here any minute." Barry bit his bottom lip and gave Tag a quick, sidelong glance.

"He's gone to get his instructions from… Yes, he's gone to find out who will be next."

"Next?"

"Oh, yes, Barry. Next. This process will happen all over again. As it has ever since you began dreaming. Only this time…" Leyton walked back a few paces. *"It won't be so difficult to make you understand where you have to go and who you have to find. We've come a long way, baby."* He laughed heartily.

"Don't you baby me. I —"

"Oh, shush. Just do your job. Find out the name of this jerk — I called him Charles, by the way — and await the next time I contact you. Forget about Lorelei. She's safe."

"I need to know where she is. For her family. I have to make sure she's okay."

"No you don't. Goodbye, Barry. For now."

Leyton slid inside the bush, pleased with how the night had gone. Barry had finally breached the barrier, stepped over to where he needed to be in order for their partnership to work properly. He lowered himself to the ground, gave one last look towards

Charles, sniggered, and closed his eyes. He concentrated on reversing his journey, leaving this place and finding his way back home. Still, he couldn't help feeling a little sorry for Barry and his confusion. He let go of a fleeting memory showing Charles' car, his licence plate, flashed through some of the more pleasant reminders of his work over the past day and night, of Charles' van, bed, the key on the doorstep, and the turnoff where that van was parked. Not a lot and nothing that would implicate himself. Just enough for Barry to know where to look and how to recognise what he found. Sure, it was cheating a bit, but just this once—just to show him how well they could work together—Leyton felt sure it would not be frowned upon. The clues laid, he smiled to himself and concentrated on his own future. Home and Lorelei, who he hoped still slept soundly, unaware he'd ever gone anywhere. Still, if she'd woken up, tried to rouse him, it would appear he was just in a deep sleep. She'd have to wait until he awoke by himself. Until the man in his dreams allowed Leyton's soul to return to his body.

The shift was quick. He felt himself filling his body, the thin sleeping bag beneath him, over him. Opening his eyes, he leaned up on one elbow to stare at Lorelei in his bunk. She slept on—perhaps she had concussion from that bump to the head—and he resisted waking her so he could wash the dried blood from her face. It didn't look right on her. She was pure, his angel, and the red splashes reminded him of the people he'd killed. Of their faces, wreathed in the claret that had once given them life. A life he took with pleasure.

Her chest rose and fell steadily, and the sight calmed him.

But what if she doesn't wake in the morning? What if she has more than concussion?

He snaked a hand out and gave her a little shove. She stirred, brushed at his hand, and Leyton lowered himself back to the floor, relief bleeding into every part of his body so he grew tired. So very tired.

He settled down and closed his eyes, ready for a dreamless sleep or one where the sheep-head man would show him Leyton had another task to do. It was an oblivion of sorts either way, and he welcomed it. His life was almost perfect. Everything had happened as the dream man had predicted.

Now all he had to do was wait for Lorelei to love him.

Chapter Thirteen

Jessica had stirred just before *he* came back, her face tight, like the skin had been daubed with glue that had now dried. With her eyes still closed, she reached up to touch her cheek. A crust met her fingertips, and she frowned. It smelt like dried blood and reminded her of Cal again. Tears stung her eyes.

Fuck. Don't think of him now.

Opening her eyes, she sat up. Her head spun, and she blinked to try to orient herself. She was on his bunk. In the damn van. Looking around, she searched for him, finding him down on the floor beside her. He was in that weird position, ramrod straight, arms folded over the top layer of a sleeping bag. His eyes twitched — *REM* — and his lips moved as though he spoke to someone.

He's so damn weird.

She shuddered and shifted her gaze away from him and to the door. Remembered getting out of here when he left the van, whenever the hell that was. And running into the forest, adrenaline spurring her on. But her eyesight had blurred, as though mist or fog swirled in front of her, and she'd pitched forward, landing on her knees. A shove to her back sent her sprawling, and she'd lurched into thicker fog, a pain streaking through her head as it struck something hard.

Was it the night of the afternoon she'd fled? Or was it days later, with her having slept the hours away? Not knowing freaked her out, and she started breathing erratically. Her chest tightened, and she clutched at her neck as her lungs failed to allow more air in. Getting up, skirting around his prone form, Jessica stumbled into the sink unit. She clutched the edge, told herself to calm the fuck down, and blew out the previously trapped air to hike in a fresh breath. Her head swam again, and her knees jolted as they lost their rigidity. Trying not to panic, she clutched the edge tighter, repeating the mantra, *It'll be all right. Just calm down. It'll be all right…*

She had been free, damn it! Had got away, tasted liberty, and now this. Back here in this damn-fucking-shithole of a van.

Shit.

Jessica ground her teeth and breathed through her nose. Her equilibrium returned, as did her sense of what she must do. She looked over her shoulder at him, saw his eyes still moving rapidly, and moved quietly to the wardrobe. Riffling through it, ensuring the hangers didn't scrape the pole, she selected a jogging sweater and a matching pair of bottoms. They would drown her, but she didn't have time for vanity now. If she could just find a way out while he dreamt, she might be well away by the time he woke up.

The key. She'd hidden it before she'd left last time, wedging it under the sink unit between two crude slats of wood that acted as a shelf and its bracket. She marvelled at her foresight—she must have known she'd need it again. Or maybe her survival instinct had kicked in, working out a way to help herself if he caught up with her and brought her back. If she could get to that key now, without making a noise…

With as near-silent movements as she could manage, she slipped into the jogging bottoms then drew the sweater over her head and down her torso. With no shoes, running through that forest again would be hard on her feet, but what was a bit of pain in return for freedom?

She pulled the string tie tight about her waist and rolled the fabric over so the crotch lifted away from near her knees. While folding the sleeve cuffs to her elbows, she moved towards the sink unit. Slowly. Her breathing sounded so loud, like it had been amplified, and she prayed he would sleep on. Prayed to God or whatever the hell was up there that she would get away.

If God is good, I'll make it. If God helps those who help themselves, I'll get away.

She inhaled deeply and opened the unit door. It squeaked. Jessica winced. Looked down at him. Waited with her breath held for him to move. He remained in place, eyes still flickering beneath the lids, so she hunkered down with him inches behind her. If he awoke now, he could grip the sweater hem and yank her back onto the bunk. Tie her wrists and tape her mouth.

No, I'm not going through that again. Not for any fucker.

Reaching inside the unit, she felt in the darkness for the shelf, keeping her fingertips to its edge so she didn't upset anything on top. She smoothed along the bracket where she'd jammed the key. Its coldness and the jagged cut of its stem made her spirits soar and her heart race.

Don't lose it now. Don't celebrate until you're out of here.

She immediately put a barrier up in her mind, remembering he could read it, might know what she was doing. Maybe he wasn't dreaming. And maybe, if he was, he could still see her from that place he spoke of. Perhaps his arm would fling out when she stood and his hand would clamp around her ankle and —

Stop it. Just stop it.

Latching onto the key's end with her fingernail, Jessica prised it loose, reaching her other hand inside the unit and cupping it beneath the bracket. She needed to catch the key if it fell. The tinkle of it hitting the contents below was something she could do without, and even if that sound didn't wake him, her scrabbling about to find the key would. The stem came free with an agonisingly loud squeak, the wood protesting. Jessica paused and glanced behind her. She could only see the bottom half of the sleeping bag, but from what she could tell, he hadn't moved.

Turning back to face the unit, she gripped the key between finger and thumb and eased it out. Just holding it infused her with hope, and she stood, pulse throbbing in her throat, light pains streaking across her chest. Anxiety pains. Lord, but if she had a panic attack now…

Not daring to look at him, she stepped to the side door, almost groaning when the floor moaned beneath her tread. Lifted the key and moved it towards the keyhole. Silently cursed her heavy breaths. Wished this part was over and she was outside in the fresh air.

But you're not. So get on with it.

She slid the key into the lock, holding her breath, sure the dull, heavy beating of her heart could be heard outside her body. The key went in with only the barest scraping sound, and she turned it, hoping the damn keeper didn't click too loudly.

It didn't.

Blowing out through pursed lips, she took the key out and tiptoed back to the unit. Kept her gaze off *him*. Closed off her thoughts. Placed the key at the back of the shelf behind a large bottle of bleach. No time to wedge it beneath the shelf. No time to hang around.

Back at the door, she pulled down the handle and pushed the door open only enough that she could slide through the small gap. She didn't want a sudden burst of cold air to sweep inside and startle him awake. Squeezing through, she jumped down onto the ground. Held her breath again—her heart thumping and her legs weak. And she couldn't resist checking on *him*.

Jessica pushed the curtain across, closed the door, and stood on tiptoe to look through the window. He slept on—she thought, hoped—eyelids flickering more rapidly, fingers twitching now, their tips drumming against the backs of his hands. Wherever he was, he wasn't here, wasn't anywhere that alerted him to her presence.

Or lack of it.

She ran then, into the deeper darkness of the forest, tears streaming down her face, barking sobs hurting her throat. The damp ground chilled her feet, debris biting into her soles, but she ploughed on, her pace relentless, unwavering. Trees, so many trees, and well-trodden paths that spiked off in several directions. Which way? Which path led to civilisation? Jessica veered left, away from the path she'd taken before, away from that dreadful mist she was sure had come out of nowhere, intent on thwarting her. But that was silly, wasn't it? To think like that?

Captivation sends people crazy. I feel fucking crazy.

She upped her pace, jumping over exposed tree roots and mounds of fallen leaves. The wind whipped into her mouth, drying her throat, and she swallowed in an attempt to wet it. Pushing on, fists bunched and legs pistoning, she strained her ears for the sound of cars, peered ahead for a break in the trees that indicated a highway or even a country lane was nearby.

And then the mist came again, thick and fast, filling the forest in front of her like a menacing, all-knowing *thing* that wanted her. She knew it wanted her, felt it in her marrow, her gut, and her goddamn heart. How she knew she wasn't sure, but that knowledge was as real as any truth she'd ever learned.

"Shit!" she screamed, anger leeching into her, obliterating any fear. She slowed to a walk, determined not to make the same mistake as before. The mist would *not* stop her. "Fuck you! I'm going home. Home, you hear me?" The mist grew denser, enveloped her. She stilled, cocooned in its cold embrace. "Yeah, you can try and scare me, but I'm not the one for him. He thinks I'm called Lorelei, but I'm Jessica. Fucking *Jessica!* You hear that? He's got the wrong girl. *You've* got the wrong girl."

The mist stopped swirling and hung around her like a thick shower curtain, solid and grey. She stared at it, watched it thin ever so slightly, and waited. Time seemed to stop, and it was as if she could hear the trees pause in their growth, waiting with her for the consequences of her outburst.

"Yeah, you know it. I'm not the right one, am I?" She glared at the mist. It thinned some more. "You fucked up, whatever the hell you are. *He* fucked up. So go and make it right. Go and find whoever this Lorelei is and let her fall in damn love with him, because I'm fucked if I will!"

The forest seemed to sigh, the trees releasing their collective held breaths. The mist moved as though sucked towards a vacuum cleaner in front of her, coagulated and formed a gooey, liquid man. He was just a shape, but the curly horns on his strange skull looked like they belonged to some animal. Jessica swallowed down the fear threatening to overcome her and stared at him...*it.*

"You need to go," she said, voice steady, belying the terror churning inside her. "*I* need to go. Home. Where I belong."

The figure lifted its hands, beseeching, cocking its head. Clearly confused.

"I'm not her. Not the one you want." *Please, let me go. Please, please, please...*

The figure collapsed, seeped into the leaves and mulch, just a wet remnant of what it once was. Jessica closed her eyes for a second and released a long breath. When she opened her eyes again, the ground was dry.

"Thank you, God. Fucking thank *you!*"

Jessica ran on, fresh tears falling, relief spreading into every part of her. Suddenly weary, she had to force herself forward, the trek seeming too much, too hard. Until a break in the trees and the swoosh and swish of traffic made her more alert.

Running faster, she broke through the tree line and down into a ditch beside a busy highway, one knee jolting as she stumbled on the uneven ground. She scrambled up the other side of the ditch, digging her fingers into the earth and pulling herself up on long clumps of grass. On her belly at the top, she shimmied towards the road, using all the strength she had left to haul herself upright.

She took a moment to acquaint herself with her surroundings. Cars streamed past, their drivers either unaware or uncaring that she stood in too-big clothes, no shoes on her feet, in what she assumed was the middle of the damn night. Several sets of headlights approached, and hundreds of tail lights twinkled in the distance on the other side of the central barrier. So many people, yet still she was alone.

But she was free.

Jessica glanced back into the forest, suddenly expecting to see the mist or *him*.

Nothing but trees met her gaze.

But what if he'd awakened? What if, right now, he was running through the forest to find her?

She turned back to the road and waved her arms, frantic for someone to stop, to help. No one did. Each car sped past, some drivers giving her a glance as though she was crazy to be out at this time.

"Yeah!" she yelled, fists punching the air, anger gripping her. "It *is* fucking crazy to be out here in the dark, right? It *is* crazy to be abducted — twice, can you believe that? — and have no bastard stopping to help me. To take me home."

She almost caved in to grief. Almost. But the need to see this through grabbed her harder, overtaking her need to crumple to the ground and beat it with her fists. To rail at the injustices she'd been served, the ordeal she'd been through.

Gritting her teeth, she waved at the cars again, and when no one stopped, when they all cruised along as if she didn't exist, she stepped out onto the road.

Right into the path of an oncoming truck.

Chapter Fourteen

Barry immersed himself in the normalcy of the flashing lights and frenetic activity that was a crime scene and tried not to reflect on how screwed up his life was, that this was normal. About every five minutes, Tag glanced at him, finding an excuse to approach or lay a hand on his shoulder.

"I'm fine," he muttered. "If you want to be a little bit more obvious, why don't you just slap my ass?"

Tag chuckled. "Was that a joke?"

"Only halfway."

"Look, we're surrounded by police detectives, Barry. Put yourself outside the scene for just a second and tell me what you see."

"Couple returns home to find a body on their doorstep. First place I go is — someone's trying to send them a message." He met Tag's eye. "How ironic."

Tag's eyes flashed, and Barry could see him mentally resist the urge to grab his wrist and yank him closer. The knowledge that Tag wanted him that close, wanted to protect him, was gratifying in itself.

"The word couple seems significant, doesn't it?" Tag murmured as a pair of detectives rose from examining the body and exchanged a few words with the coroner. "You think these guys haven't all already joined those dots?"

"Once again, I put your career in a hand basket."

"You let me worry about that."

The flash of resentment that coursed through Barry, white-hot, left him in a shaky, cold sweat.

"Don't worry." Now Tag did pull him a step closer with a hand on his shoulder. "Not like last time. That will never happen again. You need me, and I intend on being here. I promise."

"And if they find a way to squeeze you out?"

"They won't. I have no intention of walking their straight and narrow. Not anymore. They want to call foul, listen to me scream discrimination even louder. I can play hardball." He tightened his arm around Barry's shoulder and acknowledged the detectives who approached. "Danielle, Jacob." Tag nodded his greetings to the partners and they returned grim smiles.

"Hey. Sorry I'm late." Before any questions started, Ross sidled up to stand on Barry's other side. "I had a quick look. Gruesome."

Danielle made a face. "That's one word for it." She made eye contact with all three of them, one at a time. "You know I have to ask. Any of you know him?"

"How could a person recognise that?" Ross asked.

Tag shook his head.

Barry dropped his gaze. "No idea, Danny, sorry."

"Well," her partner Jacob chimed in, "there's nothing on him. It'll take time to get an ID. Any idea why he was dumped here?"

"Barry is not the only one who lives in this building," Ross pointed out.

"I'm the only cop, though," Barry said, letting his gaze travel over the scene and the uniforms standing around trying to look busy while they hoped for a glimpse of the horror propped against his door.

"Still," Ross persisted, "there is also the coincidence factor to consider."

They all exchanged glances.

"Let's just cut to the chase, shall we?" Tag said, drawing Barry a little closer, himself up taller, and giving his belted jeans a tug. "We came back here to pick up a few things. Barry hasn't been home all weekend." He waved towards the apartment entrance. "We found a dead guy in the doorway. I suggest you canvas the neighbourhood, do a door-to-door, and get started on IDing the guy. Let me know when you find something."

"Sure thing, Cap." Jacob gave a curt nod and handed over his notebook. "What we do know—he was stabbed, cut up good after he died, but not here. This was just the dump site." He glanced up one side of the street and down the other. "Plenty of less visible places to dump a body." He motioned to the street light just a few yards away. "This is a visible enough spot to not risk hauling a body from a car on the kerb"—he motioned with his arms along the path a person would have to travel, right under the street lamp—"to the doorway. Unless you're being specific. I can't imagine anyone would pick that doorway unless they meant to."

"Agreed." Tag nodded, returned the notes Jacob had shared, and left it at that. "Ross, I need you back at the station. You two"—he wagged a finger between Danielle and Jacob—"start pounding the pavement."

He turned abruptly and headed back to the car.

Barry snatched Jacob's notepad, tore out a page and borrowed his pen. He scribbled a string of numbers and letters down and stuffed the page into his pocket before handing back the pad and pen.

"What's that?" Jacob asked.

Ross eyed him thoughtfully.

"Just a number I need to remember." He glanced uneasily at the body and turned away from them. "Nothing to do with..." He waved his hand vaguely and followed Tag.

Slipping into the car's passenger side, Barry leant far back into his seat.

"Okay?" Tag asked as he started the car.

"No." Barry pulled in a deep breath and looked back to find Jacob watching them ease away from the kerb. The man gave him a small nod before focusing his attention back on his duty. "Yeah. Maybe." He reached and Tag met him halfway, lacing fingers through his and squeezing. "I don't know."

"Listen." Tag palmed the steering wheel, guiding the car smoothly around the corner. "Don't worry about this." He squeezed Barry's hand again. "Anyone says anything about us, you let me deal with it. You just concentrate on figuring out who it is that's getting into your head and what he wants."

"God, you say that like it's a normal, everyday occurrence."

"For you?"

Barry glared at him, feeling the tension knotting at the base of his skull.

"Here's the thing," Tag continued mildly. "You have always had these dreams. They have to be coming from somewhere. It isn't like you were actually there, so how could you possibly know what those victims felt unless something else is going on? I feel slightly more comfortable with the idea that someone might be orchestrating all this than with the idea your brain randomly taps into some freak radio wave that we can't control. A person, an entity, whatever...*something* behind it means there's a chance we can stop it." He spared a quick glance for Barry. "It means I can protect you from it."

The elusive ache at the back of Barry's head suddenly swelled, sending him into a dizzying spiral of ferocious pain. He screamed, grabbed at his head, and doubled over. Somewhere outside himself, tyres squealed, horns blared. The car lurched and spun, and Barry felt everything tumble out and away before the vehicle came to a devastating stop.

For a long minute, he remained still, trying to work out what had happened. The world was dark around him. Night air whisked across the back of his neck, cooling the sweat, and slowly, the awareness of a horrid, shrilling blast broke through. The car horn bled sound on and on, out into the night.

"Tag?" He blinked and shook his head, which sent the world spinning around off its axis. "Tag..."

The steady drone of the horn was his only answer.

Finally managing to right himself, Barry blinked at the deflated air bag in his lap.

"Oh shit."

His brain clicked into gear, and he looked to the driver's seat.

"No. This is *not* happening. Tag!"

Gently, he touched his lover's shoulder. No twitch of movement, no moan, no response at all. Blood dripped in a steady *plop, plop* off the base of the steering wheel.

"I tried to warn you, Barry."

"Not now! Tag!" He scooted closer, reached for both Tag and the radio. "Code thirty! Code thirty! We've gone..." He glanced around, unsure where, exactly, they were. "Off the road under the west turnpike bridge. Send a fucking bus! Tag!"

Dumping the radio in favour of carefully prying Tag back from where he slumped over the steering wheel, Barry tried to peer around into his captain's bloodied face. "Tag, come on. This is not a good time for you to check out on me. Please."

"You should have listened."

"I said... Not. Now!"

"Now is all there is."

Barry tried to shut out the voice in his head as Tag finally made a low, guttural sound in his throat. Blood bubbled out of his mouth, and he coughed, a weak, pathetic little bleat.

"Oh, God. Okay. Tag, it's going to be okay. Just..." He glanced around. They weren't that far from the crime scene. Where the hell was everyone? "Just try and relax."

Outside the window, he could see only low rolling fog and tendrils of mist snaking along through the grass. Anything beyond that was gone—the road, the traffic, the light of the sirens that should have been there... It was like they'd dropped out of the world.

The mist shrouded everything, clawed up the side of the car and curled around Tag's open window. Barry's two worlds meshed into one, horrifying reality. He dived across Tag's lap as he began to choke, the mist roiling up along his neck and into his mouth, his nostrils, seeping into his hair and ears.

"No! No, no, no!"

Frantic, Barry twisted the window lever round and round, but the fog was already inside with them, already forcing Tag's mouth wider, climbing down his throat like a thing alive.

"Stop!"

He shook Tag, tried to wipe the stuff away. It clung in clammy, sticky globs to his flesh.

"Stop it! Fuck! Leave him alone! You promised!"

There was nothing to grab onto as Tag choked and convulsed, trying to get air into his lungs. His eyes opened finally and fixed on Barry, pleading for help he couldn't give.

"What do you want?" Barry shouted. "What? I already said I would help. I said. Don't do this." His voice drained to a hoarse whisper, and he dragged Tag into his arms. "Don't. You said you wouldn't hurt him. Jesus fuck, please. I'll do anything, just don't take him."

"He will interfere, Barry. Distract you. You need to focus."

"He *is* my focus." Barry petted Tag's hair, rocked him, tying to ease the pain and fear knotting his lover's muscles, trying not to listen to the dying sounds he was making. "I'll do whatever you want. Leave him out of it."

"Can you leave him out of it?"

"What? No! I need him!" Barry tightened his arms. "You want me? You only get me if I have him. I can't do this alone."

"He can't threaten us, our mission, Barry. Not even in words. You make him understand. It doesn't stop. You have a gift. You must use it."

"Okay! Okay, just… Let him go!"

In his arms, Tag heaved, convulsed, then the fog was withdrawing, snaking back out the window, and Tag was hauling in breath after breath, shuddering and panting in Barry's arms.

"It's going to be okay," Barry whispered, over and over with each stroke of his hand through Tag's hair.

Even after Tag was breathing somewhat normally again, Barry held onto him, stroking him, rocking, whispering his mantra.

Chapter Fifteen

"Barry?"

Tag shoved himself upright, out of Barry's too-tight embrace. Barry blinked at him, eyes too wide and bright, and Tag dragged a hand over his own sticky, wet lips. His hand came away covered in saliva and blood. Barry trembled.

"Barry." He snapped his fingers, and Barry blinked again. "Come on, babe. It's over."

Tag tried to keep his voice calm, even, but Barry cringed at every word, like a kid trying to climb into a corner then into the wall and make himself disappear...make himself vanish into nothing.

"Focus, Barry." Like Tag had waved a wand, Barry drew in a ragged breath and an angry, frightened growl snarled his lips.

Tag swiped at the blood dripping down from his broken nose, glanced out the car window. They were five minutes away from the crime scene, but the fog had rolled in so fast, so thick, he'd slowed to a crawl. Then Barry had howled, doubled over with his head in his hands, and Tag's reaction had been instantaneous and disastrous, jerking around, dragging the wheel — and the car — towards the sound of his lover's distress. He'd driven them right off the road, into the ditch off the exit ramp, and gravity had taken over, slamming them into a light standard at the bottom.

Between the ripping shock of realising what he'd done and the shattering impact, Tag had had one heartbeat to see Barry's head come up, his face a mask of horror, then nothing.

He couldn't be sure how long he was out, but it was evidently long enough for Barry's fear to latch onto him. Tag reached again and found the back of Barry's neck wet and cold with sweat. He let his fingers curl into Barry's hair and rested his own head back on his seat rest.

Off upward, he heard voices, sirens. His face ached. His head throbbed. He tightened his fingers, pressing them against Barry's damp skin. "Okay, babe. They're coming. It's going to be okay."

The EMTs were quick and efficient at assessing the damage, figuring out how to get them out of the wreckage. Tag wanted nothing more than to go home, take Barry with him and keep him safe there, but he knew they had too much work to do and the rescue team wouldn't let him leave.

Stretched out on the gurney, he was helpless to do anything as Barry stumbled out of the car, wobbled a few steps to stop and stare at the ruins. Fog tumbled and rolled around his ankles — a spectral puppy, hiding his feet, blurring his connection to the real world. Tag lifted his head and let out a groan at the heavy, dull ache the tiny movement rippled through his body.

As if he'd heard the noise, though, Barry's head snapped up. Their eyes met, and he finally moved, leaving the fog behind and hurrying to Tag's side.

"I'm sorry, Barry. Stupid of me—"

"No. Shh. We'll talk later." Barry elbowed his way past the EMT at Tag's side, earning them both a disapproving look from the matronly woman.

"Let Ross take you home," Tag insisted.

Behind Barry, his partner found Tag's gaze and nodded. "Sure thing, Cap. He can stay with me tonight."

"I'm going to the hospital," Barry assured Tag. "I'll be there."

Tag met his gaze. "I need you to get a good night's sleep."

Barry snorted. "Like that will happen."

He glanced up and around, giving the emergency worker a fierce look. She only shrugged and diverted her gaze as she continued her work securing tubing to Tag's gurney.

Barry lowered his voice. "Like I could without you there." He found Tag's hand and brought his knuckles up to his lips. "Sitting up awake with you in hospital is better than the nightmares," he whispered.

"You have to talk to Ross, Barry. Tell him everything."

Barry cocked his head. "No." His whisper was fierce. He lifted his gaze again to the woman just trying to do her job. "Could you?"

She gave them an exasperated grunt in response, but she did move off towards the ambulance and her partner to help him put his equipment away.

"He needs to know," Tag said, "and you need someone besides me watching your back."

Barry tossed a look over his shoulder at his partner. "What makes you think he'll understand?"

"A hunch. We can't do this on our own, Barry. We can't stop it—"

Barry slapped his hand down over Tag's mouth. "Don't. Don't even think that."

"Think what? About figuring out how to give you your life back?"

"No. That's why this happened. This *is* my life. We can't stop it. We have to deal with it, and if you even think about trying to free me of this…" He shook his head. "I can't keep him—them, whoever—from hurting you, Tag. I can't. The only way you stay safe is to accept this is who I am. If you can't do that…"

Something deep in Barry's eyes gave way, and Tag had a clear view of the terror the other man lived with on a daily basis. He knew he was the only thing standing between that dark mass of destruction and Barry's mind.

"If you can't do that, Tag, walk away now. I won't survive you getting hurt because of this."

"You won't survive without me."

Barry pursed his lips into a tight, hard line. His eyes darkened, going almost black, and Tag shuddered. That wasn't his Barry. It was the shell, the veneer of protection that Barry hid behind when he had no other choice, but it wasn't him. Tag knew that's what his lover would become if he walked away. He didn't need any confirmation to know he was right. Barry needed him.

"I'm not going anywhere." He squeezed Barry's hand and swallowed his own fear. "We'll do whatever we have to, to get through this. You need to rest."

"I'll rest when we get to the bottom of this. I'll go to the station. See what I can dig up on the dead guy, on

Cal, his girlfriend, and whoever this Lorelei woman is." Barry let out a breath. "Somewhere, there is a connection between whoever left that body and the rest of this mess. I'll find it."

Tag nodded. "Come get me, then. Soon as they're done taking pictures of my head. I'll call."

The EMT came back, eyebrows elevated, and he gave her a faint smile. "Sorry. We can go."

"Oh, you are sure right about that, sugar." She tossed a look of sympathy in Barry's direction. "You should be going to the hospital and all, boy."

Tag managed a weak smile at the woman calling his lover a boy, but Barry merely shook his head.

"I'm fine."

"You a doctor?" She shook her head. "Mm-mm, honey. I can't force you, but in *my* experience—"

"I'm fine." To Tag, he nodded. "Call soon as you're ready. I'll come get you." He gave Tag's hand one last squeeze. "Take good care of him."

"You know it, loverboy." She flashed him a curt, confident nod to her partner and together they wheeled Tag off over the uneven ground.

* * * *

Tag knew he and Barry had to talk. The black circles under Barry's eyes when he picked Tag up at the hospital spoke volumes about the sleep Barry was avoiding.

"Barry, you can't just not sleep—"

"Don't lecture me, Tag."

Barry guided his rust bucket through the grey city streets in silence. His dark eyes glittered, darting about incessantly, as though he expected something to step out from behind the next lamppost.

"Doesn't the sun ever come out?" Tag wondered aloud.

Barry only grunted.

"Can I voice my concern without it being a lecture?" Tag asked, trying not to let the annoyance he felt colour his voice.

"I need to sleep." Barry glanced over. "I know. So do you. We can do it together."

"I might not be there every night, Barry."

"I know."

Someone in a dark coat and fedora emerged from an apartment building up the street, and Barry flinched.

"There's something else," Tag said.

"It's nothing."

"Don't bullshit me."

"You almost died, Tag."

"It was a bump on the head." He reached up and touched the bit of tape over his nose. "Don't start jumping at shadows now."

"It was more than that. You don't remember?"

"Remember what?"

"The fog."

"Yeah, I remember. It got thick, and I slowed down. That's probably the only reason we're both still alive. At least I wasn't going that fast."

Barry pulled into the parking lot in front of Tag's building and turned the car off. "After the crash. The fog. You don't remember?"

"I was out."

"No." Barry slumped back, defeated. "He tried to kill you."

"Who?"

Barry turned a look on him, and Tag realised it was a foolish question. "But you stopped him."

"No. I begged. I told him I'd do whatever he asked. I might as well have sold my soul, and we have no idea who to. He made me promise to tell you not to try and stop whatever is happening. If you threatened to stop it..." Barry shook his head. "He can take you whenever he wants, Tag. I have no control."

"Well, then let's not give him reason." Tag got slowly out of the car, testing his balance and the efficacy of his pain meds. "He wants this puzzle solved, we solve it. After a good night's sleep." He raised his gaze up into the dusky grey sky. "You hear that? For God's sake, let the man have a good night's sleep! I'm no threat to you. You want this shit solved, we need to be able to function."

He glanced at Barry, who only shrugged. Time would tell if his tirade had had any effect.

"Come on." He held out an arm, and Barry slipped under it. "I want to get this hospital stench washed off, maybe eat some real food and then sleep."

"Sure. You shower. I'll order."

If life could only be this normal. For one night, at least. Please.

Whether his little speech had been heard or their tormentor was just busy driving someone else mad for the rest of the night, Barry slept soundly, curled tightly, his back jammed up hard against Tag's chest. For hours, Tag lay and listened to Barry's even, peaceful breathing and stroked an occasional hand through his hair.

"Is this so bad?" he asked the night. "So hard to just let him be? Let him have a night? A life?"

Something fluttered outside the window above the bed, and Tag looked over to see a pair of doves, heads tucked neatly under their wings, tiny bodies pressed close. He smiled.

"Thank you."

As if the sight was a sign, he felt his own eyelids grow droopy and heavy, and when he next knew anything, he was lying on his back, Barry's warm body half draped over him, the man's big hand tracing a slow, gentle path down the centre of his chest.

"Morning." Tag didn't open his eyes, but a smile curled his lips. His headache was gone. Even his broken nose didn't ache so much.

Barry's hand stopped its downward trajectory.

"Oh, no." Tag fastened his fingers around Barry's wrist and urged it on again. "Don't stop. You aren't there yet."

"Make love to me, Tag."

Barry's whispered request sent goose bumps then heat slithering in a delicious trail from his neck, where Barry's lips tickled his skin, straight to his groin.

Tag moved his hands down his lover to his hips and nudged him. "Make it easy on me. I'm injured." He opened his eyes at last and looked straight into Barry's clear, brown gaze. "Get on."

"You didn't used to be this bossy," Barry muttered, though he did swing a leg over and straddle Tag's hips. His ass nudged at Tag's erection, teasing, as he slipped his entrance back and forth through the wet leakage.

"I didn't used to be your boss."

"In bed too?" Barry's gaze didn't waver.

Neither did Tag's. "You haven't resisted doing what I tell you...yet."

Barry spat into his palm, reached around, and slicked the wetness over Tag's cock. Heat steamed up, visible in Tag's gaze, sparking between them. Barry lifted himself and came down again, engulfing Tag completely. His lips parted in a huff as he sank all the way onto Tag.

"No," he conceded, "I guess I haven't."

Tag groaned, grabbed Barry's hips and pushed, tipping his hips up to take every last inch of his lover he could reach. He already knew this wasn't going to be enough for either of them.

"Fuck it." He sat up, wrapped an arm around Barry, and in an awkward tangle of limbs, flipped them so Barry landed on his back.

He didn't waste any time retaking him, or building up to a hard, fast rhythm that had Barry clutching the sheets and panting. Little groans interspersed with cussing filled the apartment for the next few minutes, until Barry's eyes widened and his back arched.

Cum shot over his chest, and whatever he shouted was too garbled to comprehend.

There was nothing like the sight of his lover letting go of everything in the face of pure pleasure to get Tag off. His own orgasm slammed the breath from him and knocked him blind—a kaleidoscope of spots dancing before his eyes, fading slowly as he came back to the present.

Barry lay limp and panting beneath him while Tag licked and kissed the sweat and spunk off his chest. Finally satisfied Barry was comfortable, he flopped over, half covering him still.

"We should talk about condoms," Barry said, his voice low, sated, lacking any sort of edge at all.

Tag let out a sigh and played through the hair on Barry's chest. "Go to the clinic today."

"I will." Barry turned his head to look at Tag. "You?"

"Had them do it at the hospital. Should have results on my desk today."

"It takes—"

"I know how long it takes to be sure. Don't lecture me. I also know the next call you go out on could get you shot."

"I don't think he"—Barry tapped the side of his head—"is willing to let that happen. If just anyone could do what I do, it wouldn't be such a big deal. He needs me."

"Hmm." Tag rested his chin on Barry's chest. "Maybe so, but you still belong to me. He's just going to have to deal with that."

Barry smiled, and it was like the room lit up. "I'll be sure and let him know next time we're in the middle of a torture scene."

"Do that." Tag sat up and swung off the bed. "In the meantime, we have a puzzle to solve." He held out a hand and pulled Barry to his feet. "Breakfast on the way?"

* * * *

Ross was already at his desk when Tag and Barry entered the station. He was flipping through papers and frowning, a mug of tar at his elbow, too tepid to steam. He absently picked it up, sipped, made a face, and placed it back.

Across the room, the usual police station chaos reigned, and for a few minutes, Tag stood there and enjoyed the fleeting moment of his world spinning in the direction it should.

"I can't watch this atrocity any longer," Barry muttered and strode across the room to Ross' desk. "Delivery."

He set a paper bag and fresh coffee on the desk, taking the cold coffee Ross had been torturing himself with and handing it to a passing uniform. "Do something with that, will you?"

The man gave him a look, but took the mug and wandered off.

"You are a saint," Ross said, picking up the paper mug and popping the lid off.

Barry grinned, but the expression faded quickly. "Here." He dropped a slip of paper onto the desk. "We need to run this tag."

"What is it?"

Barry shrugged. "A hunch." It was all he could tell his partner at this point and he hated the idea of not being truthful. They depended on one another. Half-truths could get either or both of them killed.

Next to Barry, Tag grunted. "My office, both of you. We have to talk."

"Now, Tag?" Barry turned a pleading gaze on him.

"We agreed. No point putting it off. Come on."

Barry slumped slightly but didn't argue further as Ross got to his feet. They both trailed Tag across the room to his office. Tag closed the door, and Barry nicked the blinds shut.

"This serious?" Ross looked between them but still plopped his ass on the couch and dug into the bag Barry had brought him. "Breakfast waits for no man."

"Go ahead," Tag told him. "This could take a while."

Ross had got through about half his bagel as Tag and Barry explained the dreams and everything surrounding them before the food ceased to hold his interest. In the end, he sat with his hands clasped between his knees and an indecipherable expression on his face.

"So, you...believe all this?" he asked Tag.

"You asked how our record is so good." Tag lifted a shoulder and let it drop.

"I know it sounds crazy," Barry put in, "but—"

"A lot of things sound crazy." Ross leant back into the couch, spreading both arms along the back. "The world is full of crazy shit. Coincidence, déjà vu, people who swear they can hear voices, see the future, see dead people." He shrugged and looked up into Barry's worried face. "Maybe the incredible part isn't that you have these dreams, but that you managed to figure them out and still stay sane."

"So you believe us?" The hope threaded through Barry's voice just about broke Tag's heart.

"Six impossible things before breakfast, right?" Ross asked, picking up his bagel again and taking a healthy bite.

A knock sounded at the door.

Tag sighed. "Come."

"Cap?" Jacob stuck his head in the doorway. "You need to see this. You're never going to believe who just showed up after walking from about twenty miles outside town. You remember the missing girl? Landry's girlfriend?"

Ross chewed, swallowed, and grinned as he stuffed the remainder of his bagel into the bag. "That's two. Four to go. Looks like I might even make my quota today." He waved a hand towards the door. "After you, Cap."

In the hallway, he pulled the slip of paper Barry had handed him earlier out of his pocket and looked at it. "A hunch?" he asked, holding it up.

Barry shot him a glance. "Just look into it and tell me what you find."

"Aye-aye, *partner.*"

Barry grimaced. "Sorry."

Ross just grinned and stuffed his hands back into his pockets. "You're too easy, Wiki. Too easy."

Chapter Sixteen

Jessica stood at the main desk in the police station, lost, left alone while the kind policeman went to find whoever it was she needed to speak to. Everything around her was chaotic—a miasma of blurred faces, people scuttling back and forth—too much action to handle. A couple sat in chairs against the back wall to her right, their faces pinched, hands linked in a scribble of fingers. They looked as though they awaited bad news.

Vulnerable, in *his* clothing, her bare feet cold on the linoleum, sore, the skin broken from walking all damn night with no bastard stopping to pick her up... She gripped the hems of the sweater sleeves and glanced back out through the glass doors to the street. It was too dark out there for this early in the day, and passing car headlights gave the somewhat misty air an eerie, undulating appearance. She shuddered, wondering if the man with the horns had come, making himself look like common fog.

And would *he* know she'd come here? Would her captor follow, even at the risk of being caught? He'd be angry she was gone, seeing as he'd convinced himself she was the one for him. If he still thought so, if the man with the horns didn't make him believe otherwise, the craziness in *him* left her in no doubt he'd try and find her.

You'd think I'd feel safe standing in a fucking police station. Instead, I feel exposed, like they're out there, watching me through the glass.

Another shudder rippled through her, and she turned away from the front doors to stare at the door the policeman had pushed through. What was taking him so long? And why had he left her here, as though what she'd told him was of no importance? Fucking hell, she'd been abducted twice, her boyfriend had been — Yet she'd been left in the company of milling officers and one behind the desk who looked bored shitless?

Angry at their apparently uncaring attitude, she moved closer to the desk, sucking in a breath at the pain in her feet, and rested her forearms on top of it. "Umm, excuse me?"

The desk cop looked up from a form he was filling out, pen poised midair, his weathered face and age — around fifty-five, she guessed — telling her he was just waiting out the years until retirement. "Yes, ma'am?"

"Uh, I've been abducted, twice, and umm, I've been left here like this?"

Maybe they thought she was some crazy, some mad bitch who regularly cried kidnap for want of attention. Dressed as she was, she couldn't blame them, and God only knew what state her hair was in.

"Ah. Let me just check where Detective Riggs is."

He picked up one of the two phone handsets and poked at a few numbers. Handset pressed to his ear, cradled on his shoulder, he glanced up at her with an apologetic smile. His greying hair, swept back at the temples with an oily quiff between reminding her of Elvis, looked in need of a damn good wash. As must hers.

Jessica's anger only simmered now. At least something was being done. At least she was getting closer to spilling her story and having that…that monster caught.

"Has Detective Riggs forgotten he has a victim at the main desk?" he asked, rolling his eyes as if to let her know he was on her side. That a cop leaving her here alone wasn't the done thing.

And it damn well isn't. I'm tired. I just want…just want to get this over with and go home.

A fierce yearning for her mother gripped her, and tears stung her eyes. She eased her arms off the desk and hugged herself, pretending her mother's embrace held her tight, taking every bad thing that had happened away.

But it won't go away, will it? It'll always be in my fucking head. Replaying, reminding me I was almost killed, almost taken God knows where to live with him. Reminding me how lucky I am to be alive, although right now I just feel…confused. Empty yet full of crap at the same time.

Tears stung harder.

Fuck, don't lose it now. You've come this far.

"Ah, right," the desk cop said. He placed the phone down, shouting to a guy at a desk behind him, "Bill? Look after the desk a sec, will you?" Then he turned to Jessica. "Come along with me. The detectives are on their way to see you now."

He scooted around the desk and took her through the side doorway, stopping abruptly in a pea-soup-coloured corridor so she slammed into his back. She peered around him, seeing three men in dishevelled suits, one of them adjusting a too-loose tie, their faces stoic, features set firm, as though they were on a mission.

"Jessica Claire?" one asked, the bandage across his nose indicating it had been broken recently.

She nodded.

"Thank God you're all right," he said, grasping her elbow and guiding her from behind the desk cop. "We need to get you looked at by the doctor." He glanced at her feet and winced. "Then I'm afraid we have many questions to ask you. We'll telephone your mother and ask her to bring you some fresh clothing. It may be easier for you if she's not in the room with us when—"

"I understand," she said. No, she didn't want her mother knowing what *they'd* done to her. Maybe she'd tell her in her own time. Later, when she'd come to terms with it better herself, but for now...

Relief surged through her at the thought of seeing her mother, leaving her legs weak. Despite not wanting to go over what had happened, to relive what she'd been through, Jessica told herself to close her mind off and recall all the small details she thought she'd missed while with him. *Them.* People said it was the minor things that meant the most sometimes, insignificant to the victim but very telling to the police. It seemed like so much time had passed since she'd been initially taken by the first man. What day was it now anyway?

And what if he can still read my thoughts? He'll know where I am. What I'm doing.

Jessica went over her nightmare from beginning to end in her mind, perhaps to steel herself for the grilling the police would undoubtedly give her. If she told the tale to herself, it might be easier recounting it again.

* * * *

The interview room was stark, an uninviting place to spew everything inside her. Jessica supposed it had to be like this—bare, unwelcoming for the criminals whose lies seeped into the very walls every time they were arrested. Wasn't me, sir. I was home alone, watching some shit on TV. You ought to go looking elsewhere, cop.

But what about people like her? What about the victims? A bit of comfort would have gone a long way to putting her more at ease. Instead, the room made her feel like *she* was the one who had done wrong, despite the expressions of two detectives sitting in front of her and one leaning against the back wall telling her they had every sympathy for her plight.

She traced circles with her finger on the Formica-topped table, skirting around a cigarette burn and then a scorch mark from the bottom of a hot drink placed there God knew when. The only thing in the room that didn't look like it had come off the set of *Barney Miller* was the sleek recording device sitting on the table in front of her. She'd never seen anything like it, but the captain didn't bat an eye as he touched the screen, then tapped it a few times once it lit up. He gave her a curt nod.

"We're ready."

Jessica pulled in a deep breath and let it out, then told her tale from the start, when she'd been at Cal's and everything had been so right and happy. Occasionally the policemen opposite, named Captain Taggart and Detective Whittaker, interrupted her for clarification. The other, Detective Ross, took notes and chewed the end of his pencil from time to time.

"And then the second man took you, you say?" Captain Taggart asked.

She nodded. "Yes. He said he'd come to save me. That he'd ring the police. But he didn't. He took me to his van."

Detective Whittaker frowned. "So the *second* man had a van too?"

"Yes, except his was a VW. He took me there, said I needed sleep before he'd ring the police. And I *believed* him. Shit!" She swallowed, forcing herself to tell the rest—where his van was situated, or as close as she could remember anyway. She finished with, "And he told me some things. Weird stuff. Like he really believed it."

Like I believe it. The mist...shit, should I tell them about that? They'll think I'm fucking nuts. Maybe I am. Maybe being cooped up with them sent me nuts.

She stared down at the table, again circling the cigarette burn.

"Tell us *everything*, Jessica. Don't leave anything out, no matter how crazy it seems," Detective Whittaker said.

She snapped her head up at that. Something about his voice, the tone or the cadence, told her he'd believe whatever she had to say. Did they know something she didn't? Were they aware that mist had the ability to form into a damn man and shit the bloody life out of her?

Jessica laughed, startling them.

I can't tell them that. They'll say I was hallucinating. That my ordeal had made me see things that weren't there.

"Okay," Captain Taggart said, reaching to the touch screen on the recorder again. She listened to the flat thumps of his finger pad on the device then met his pale gaze as he looked up. "If it makes you feel better, we know about the mist. The fog. We know the second man has the ability to...do certain things."

What?

"You do?" She stared at the three in turn, part of her disbelieving the captain, the other part grabbing hold of what he'd said and hugging it to her like a buoy. *Or are they trying to trip me up for some reason?* She sighed, unsure what to do. *Fuck, I just don't know.*

"Tell us what's troubling you," Detective Ross said, pushing off the wall and approaching the table. He leaned his hands on it, and it creaked under his weight. "It may sound a little...odd, but if you know something about the mist... Jessica, we need to know everything. No one in this room is going to think you're insane, I promise you that."

She glanced across and up at him, took in his features and decided he was sincere. After taking a deep breath she said, "He—"

"Sorry to interrupt," the captain said. "But does *he* have a name? Do you know it?"

Shivers rattled up her spine. She didn't want to say it, didn't want that name tripping from her lips, but she had to tell them, didn't she? To have him caught? "Leyton," she whispered. "That's all he told me."

At a nod from the captain, Detective Ross walked out of the room.

"Carry on," Detective Whittaker said, reaching out a hand as though to cover hers, but instead lowering it to his lap.

She blew air out through pursed lips, her cheeks inflating.

This is all so stupid, isn't it? So weird and unreal. Tell them. Just get it out. Let them think whatever the hell they like.

"He said he goes somewhere when he sleeps." She paused, then added, "Somewhere...not here. Like, another world or something." She gazed down at the table.

Please don't be staring at me like I'm crazy when I look up.

She lifted her head. It seemed the colour had drained from their faces, although they made a good show of trying to keep their expressions neutral, she'd give them that.

Rushing on, she babbled, "I'm just going to say it, all right? Whether you believe me or not. He said some guy directed him to kill people. That he was sent to rescue me and that I was the one for him. That the guy, someone with horns, for God's sake, told him what to do all the time—like he was in a cult or whatever that enabled him to talk to weird fucking men who looked half animal, half human." *Tell them about the mist.* "And d'you know, I believe him. How mad is that? Something fucking weird is going on with him. Like, when I ran the first time..." She held her breath then pressed on. "When I ran the first time, this mist came. I couldn't see where I was going, and I fell. And he—Leyton—came and found me. Took me back. Then when I ran again—God, this is going to sound whacko—the mist tried to stop me again. It formed into a damn *person!* With *horns!*"

She released a sob she hadn't been aware was brewing, finally getting the insane things out of her head and into the stunned silence of the room. And the policemen were stunned, she knew that. Stunned by her stupidity in believing what she'd told them.

Calming herself, she sniffed, accepting the tissue the captain produced out of nowhere.

"So now tell me I'm a candidate for the funny farm, because I sure as shit would if I were you." She laughed, the sound a croak.

"We believe you," Detective Whittaker said.

Jessica stared at him, trying to see the lie in his face.

She didn't find one.

Confused, she asked, "So what the hell does it mean? The man with horns, the place *he* goes to when he sleeps? This shit just doesn't happen, right? And the second time I ran, I *knew* that mist was real, a thing, a person or whatever. And I *told* it to let me go, that I wasn't the one for *him*, and I felt like he knew that too."

Detective Whittaker eyed her with sympathy, his face showing signs he didn't sleep too well, that he was troubled.

By this case?

"The captain turned the recorder off because..." The detective glanced at the captain, who gave him a nod. "Because this isn't something other officers apart from us and Detective Ross are aware of. When I turn the tape back on, after I've skipped it back a bit, tell us the tale again, leaving out the mist and the man with the horns, all right? We're still trying to come to terms with this...this case ourselves, so the fewer people who know about that part, the better. You okay with that?"

Jessica nodded, understanding what he meant but unable to accept that the police, of all people, believed she wasn't crazy.

Just do as they ask. Trust them.

She laughed inwardly.

Will I ever trust anyone again?

Detective Whittaker stood. "Listen, we'll break here. You must be hungry. We'll take you to the cafeteria. You can sit with your mom for a while and work out, in your mind, the part of your story you'll tell for the record. And then we'll discuss where you go from here."

The captain stood too, adjusting his belt around his waist with an absent little tug. "I think it would be prudent that you stay elsewhere for the time being. Somewhere other than your home."

He smiled, a gentle curve of his lips that expressed so much about him—more than he'd care for someone to know, Jessica would guess.

"If he knows things from the dream place he visits," the captain said, scrubbing a hand over the back of his neck, "and I don't want to alarm you here, he might know where you live. If he's fixated on you, thinks you're the one for him... And you said he called you Lorelei? We need to figure out who she is." He turned to the detective. "We'll set that in motion while Jessica takes a breather."

Detective Whittaker nodded. "I can do that. I've got a few ideas to look into as well."

A strange glance passed between the men and Jessica shivered, certain there was sudden tension where there had been none just a moment ago.

"Don't worry about it," Detective Whittaker said, voice a little tense. "I'll let you know."

The captain frowned but returned his gaze to her. "Detective Ross will be doing a search on that name you gave us and also sending a team out to try and find where his van is, although I suspect he'll be long gone by now."

Jessica followed them out of the room and down a corridor. She crossed her arms beneath her breasts, trying to warm herself from the chill that had suddenly settled deep in her bones.

Is that him? Is he letting me know he's watching? That he's still with me in my mind?

A brief vision of the man with horns entered her mind, but not the form she'd seen him in. He wore black, skin-tight leggings, and his chest was bare. He stood at a cave mouth, flames behind him, his horns seeming to glow in the firelight. Leyton — she cringed at thinking his name — stood beside him, tears coursing down his face.

His voice filled her mind. "I won't let you go, Lorelei. Please come back. Don't listen to him." He jerked his head towards the horned man. "He's wrong. You *are* the one for me. Please, meet me at the Jubilee Mall tomorrow. I can't...I can't live without you. Not now we're so attached. I know you can hear me. That has to count for something, right? Two o'clock. Outside the chocolate shop. You know the one? It's beside Just Sports. Please. I miss you."

Jessica blinked. The vision faded, and she blurted, "I just saw him. He just spoke to me."

The two men stopped and spun around.

"Who?" the detective asked, holding her forearm lightly. "How?"

"Leyton. In my head. I saw him and the man with the horns. Outside a cave. *He* asked me to meet him tomorrow."

"Shit," the captain said, looking at the detective. "What the hell do we do now?"

"What do you mean?" Jessica asked, incredulous. "You go there and arrest him!"

"I don't think we can," Detective Whittaker said. He lowered his voice, glancing behind her before he continued. "There are things going on you're not aware of, though I suspect now he's been able to contact you like this, you'll soon understand what we're dealing with."

Chapter Seventeen

Leyton leaned against the outside of the cave wall, tears streaming down his face. The man with horns—Rivald—had told him he'd let Lorelei go when she'd escaped Leyton's van.

Why did he do that after telling me she was the one? After I got attached and started loving her? When I'd dared to hope that for once in my sorry fucking life I'd get something worth having?

He turned to Rivald now and voiced his thoughts, staring at the man who had orchestrated his life for such a long time now. What answer did he expect? That Rivald had got it wrong? How could that be, when he knew everything? When whoever told Rivald what to do knew everything? If they had got this wrong, what else had they fucked up? Had Leyton killed people he shouldn't have?

Rivald ignored Leyton's questions and instead said, "I hear your thoughts, Leyton, remember that. You should not have asked her to meet you. Not when she is not the one we thought she was. That she is…one of us." Rivald turned and walked inside the cave, calling,

"Come. Let us discover what happened. Let us find out where the real Lorelei is."

With no choice but to follow, a force pushing him inside the cave no matter how hard Leyton resisted, he followed Rivald into the depths, into the room where Leyton always received his instructions.

Rivald sat in his chair, fingers cupping the edges of the arm rests, and closed his eyes. Getting information, no doubt. Leyton, out of habit, kneeled before him, head bowed. Thoughts of Lorelei entered his mind again, and he tried to reach out to her once more, to stress that she must meet him. They could run away together, start afresh elsewhere. He could be loved.

A blinding pain ripped through his head, stabbing at the inside of his skull.

"Sorry. I'm sorry. I won't try and contact her again unless you say."

Leyton waited for what seemed a long time, his head throbbing with remnants of the pain, and picked through his confused thoughts. Perhaps the being who instructed Rivald had got his wires crossed. Perhaps Lorelei — *Jessica, think of her as Jessica now* — the woman for him, was out there waiting. Maybe Jessica's appearance had confused the being, making him think she was the one when she was — what had Rivald said? — one of them.

Jessica hadn't struck him as such. She hadn't displayed any signs that she dreamed like he did, like Barry did. But then, maybe she'd needed contact with Leyton in order for her gift to manifest? That had happened with Barry. The cop's ability to hear Leyton had come on quickly.

I don't know. I just know I fell for her. How can I love another now? How can I work with Jessica, remain aloof?

And he knew he'd have to. Jessica would be used to help them in their quest now. He'd have to visit her dreams and relay messages. Tell her what to do. Could he do that? Could he keep his emotions out of the equation?

"You will have to," Rivald said, his loud, sharp tones bringing Leyton out of his reverie. "She will soon discover she is a part of something she never dreamed possible."

Leyton lifted his head and looked at Rivald.

The horned man opened his eyes and stared at him. "The information got...muddied. I did not fully understand what I had been told. It is my fault you are feeling this way. But I know who Lorelei is now, and she is not what I first thought. Not your love."

"What do you mean?" Leyton's heart thumped hard. Something was coming, something he didn't want to hear. He felt it, knew it with such certainty he couldn't breathe for a moment.

"There is no one for you, Leyton. You have always just been destined to kill. You are not the kind who can live without doing so. It is in your blood."

"But Lorelei—"

"Lorelei is your next victim." Rivald heaved in a deep breath and let it out, a burst of orange flames coming with it. "I am sorry. You are destined to be alone throughout your life, here to serve Him, as am I."

An ache grew in the pit of Leyton's stomach. *No one for me? Alone?* "But I...I wanted... This isn't right!" He scrambled to his feet, anger replacing the ache. "All this time I've been promised a normal life, and now you say I can't fucking have one?"

"I am sorry." Rivald stood and reached out to touch him.

Leyton sprang back. "No. Don't touch me. This is your fault! Giving me false hope. Making me think...*fucking hell!*" He buried his hands in his hair and pulled, the pain something to focus on other than his collapsing heart. "Mother said...she said if I listened to you, if I just did as you asked..." Incensed, he paced the room, clenching his jaw until his teeth hurt. Rage bubbled so hot inside him he couldn't see straight. He should have known better than to trust Mother. When had she ever done or said anything to him that didn't hurt? Didn't scrape his insides bare and leave him hollowed out? He stopped his pacing and glared at Rivald. "So I don't get anyone to love me?"

I sound pitiful. So childish.

"No."

"All I get is instructions to kill people?"

"Yes."

Leyton stopped pacing and stared at the cave ceiling. Murderous fury erupted inside him, overtaking his emotions until only the desire to kill presided. It was strangely calming, filling him, leaving no room for love or even hate. "Where do I go next?"

"You need to move your van first. The police are coming. Barry must be warned that in future he must keep the information he receives about you quiet. Jessica told him where you are." Rivald pursed his lips, then said, "You must go to a basement in Moore Street. I will show you which house when you arrive. Lorelei has a victim there. If you hurry, you may get there before she kills. She was...one of us, but she defected. She must be caught. She has information about us that cannot be repeated."

Leyton let out a giddy laugh, half from hysteria, half from astonishment. They just expected him to continue as though the prospect of living a semi-normal life with Jessica hadn't been an option? "So, what's Jessica's part in all...this? What role is she going to play?"

"She will be used most times as bait. To lure those with intent to kill. You will have to make sure she *is not* killed. If you love her..."

You bastards! You know I'll make sure she isn't harmed. Was this their plan all along? Did they use me, make me think...

"I'll do this, but only because I have to." Leyton flexed his jaw muscles. "Now I know how Barry feels. Manipulated by me into doing things he doesn't understand. Fuck!" He balled his fists and slammed them down onto his thighs.

"You have no choice, Leyton. Besides, as I have already said, murder is in your soul. However much you try and tell yourself you can be normal, you cannot. You would be wise to stop listening to your mother's voice and only listen to mine."

"What? When you give me false information! Jesus fucking—"

"Enough!" Rivald roared, spewing flames. "It is not for us to question our instructions. We are placed on a path from birth, and we must be ready to do His bidding. Now go. And tell Jessica your little meeting is off and that you will be contacting her soon with some instructions. If you tell her anything else, I will know. *He* will know."

It would destroy Leyton to do that, to send her out there knowing she might be killed. The pressure was on him to save her every time. His old, assured self seemed to crumble. The strength he'd had to threaten Barry and make the detective do whatever he was told appeared to be teetering on the brink of extinction.

Suddenly, with no prize or repayment for what he was doing in sight, Leyton had no desire to continue. All this didn't seem worth the effort now.

"Oh, but it is," Rivald said, lowering back into his chair. "After all, if you give up, who will protect Jessica?"

Anger boiled inside Leyton again, the urge to find this Lorelei and take out his frustration on her propelling him out of the cave and back into his body. If he couldn't have Jessica, he was fucked if he'd let her come to any harm. He was stuck in this mad life and vowed to continue the way he had before he'd met her, taking enjoyment from every murder he committed.

"That is right," Rivald said, his voice echoing in Leyton's mind. "You cannot deny what or who you are. Think of that moment of wanting what you cannot have as a blip. Before the promise of Jessica, you enjoyed your life. Enjoyed what we sent you to do. And you will enjoy it again..."

Opening his eyes, Leyton turned to see his bunk empty, the covers mussed from where Jessica had slept. He swallowed down the hurt, the lies and the deceit, and zipped open his sleeping bag.

I'll do as he says. Go back to who I was before I met her. Before I hoped.

He thought of the many kills he'd committed, how the burn had infused him to take the lives of those who had harmed others. Wasn't he just as bad as them? Wasn't he being used to do good by ridding the world of terrible people, when he was a terrible person himself?

"*Do not think too deeply,*" Rivald said. "*Just...be who you are.*"

Leyton nodded as though the horned man could see him. "All right. *All right!*"

Quickly shoving Jessica from his thoughts, he stood and took the two steps towards the driver's seat. He checked his pocket and pulled out a bunch of keys, then climbed into the front of the van. Gunning the engine, he careened out of his hiding place, mind intent on where he'd camp next. He couldn't afford to think about Jessica and what might have been now. No, he had to remain detached, hard and unforgiving, focusing on the jobs at hand.

If he didn't, he knew they would kill him. Or Jessica.

* * * *

Leyton decided to forego finding a place to camp first and headed straight for Moore Street. There would be plenty of time after he'd killed the woman — the real Lorelei. Questions formed, ones he wanted to know the answers to, but at the same time didn't. Who was he to question who *they* were, the ones who instructed him? If their requests assuaged the burn inside him to take a life, then he'd obey them every time.

And because it means saving Jessica now.

"*Stop it,*" Mother snapped. "*Stop thinking of her like that.*"

"Fuck off, Mother. I don't need you here right now."

Leyton swerved into Moore Street, slowing as he concentrated to connect to Rivald. "Which house? Where is she?"

"*At the bottom,*" Rivald said. "*The house that stands alone on a plot of scrubland. When you get there, park behind the trees to the right of the property. I see you have taken your van. Foolish. Someone may see you.*"

Leyton cursed himself. He hadn't been thinking straight.

Doing as Rivald had instructed, he parked up, slipping on his leather gloves. Through the windshield, he scoped the area to check out the other houses. The one he sought stood away from the others—far enough away that if anyone was looking, they'd have to focus hard to make anything out—like him, prowling the surrounding land, creeping towards the white clapboard structure with ancient shutters that swung in the breeze.

A 'For Sale' sign stood drunkenly in the front yard, on its last legs. The house was a wreck, and Leyton couldn't imagine anyone wanting to buy it, even with the prospect of doing it up until it resembled what it once was. No lights blazed behind the curtained windows. He briefly wondered who lived there, if anyone still did, and why Lorelei had chosen them to kill, but pushed the thoughts away. He had to concentrate. Had to get rid of her. It wasn't for him to question.

He climbed over the seat and into the body of his van, pulling his tool pouch from beneath the bed. Selecting a flick knife, he left the vehicle, slipping his keys and knife into his jeans pocket. Upon reaching the back door of the house, Leyton peered through the glass into a darkened kitchen. Shadows lent the room an ominous air, as though they were real and knew something terrible was happening in the bowels of the property.

Or has already happened. What if I'm too late? What if she's gone?

"*She has not,*" Rivald said.

Seeping from beneath a door to the left, a parallelogram of light bled onto the floor. *The basement?* Leyton cocked his head, pressing his ear to the doorjamb in order to detect any sounds from within. He heard nothing and, turning the handle with the thought that the door wouldn't open, he was surprised when it did. Perhaps Lorelei had left it unlocked so she could escape quickly, something he would have done.

Clever woman.

"Be careful, Leyton. She may detect you are coming. Do not forget she was one of us. Although she is not directed by us now, she may still have retained her abilities to sense things. To know we are closing in on her."

"Shh!" Leyton said, irritable now.

Rivald hadn't been with him the previous times he'd killed. He'd been allowed to go his own way, to execute as he saw fit. Having company distracted him.

"I have been asked to watch over you. I have no choice."

Leyton bit back a retort for Rivald to leave him the fuck alone and entered the kitchen, his nerves bunched tight. He didn't feel right. *This* didn't feel right. It was as though Leyton's control had slipped. He was no longer the puppetmaster, the boss of his own actions.

It rankled.

Leyton padded over to the door on the left and eased down the handle.

"Wait!" Rivald said. *"She knows you are here."*

"Shit! Will you just go? You're making me nervous. If this goes wrong..."

Leyton eased open the door, trying to ignore the fact Rivald watched him. He looked down a set of rickety wooden stairs into a basement lit by a bright halogen lamp positioned in one corner. A man was pinned against a wall rack, duct tape holding his wrists and ankles so he resembled a human star, and the light played off his naked, sweating body. Blood trickled down his torso from wounds left by the slice of a knife, and the burn inside Leyton surfaced. Yes, this was what he was born to do, just as Lorelei had been.

The man must have sensed his gaze and looked up, his tawny hair drenched in sweat, his eyes pleading. Leyton stared at him, wondering if Lorelei had chosen this man for the reasons Leyton chose his victims — because he was bad and needed eradicating. Somehow, he got the sense this wasn't so — that the man was innocent, chosen for reasons so far unknown.

"Welcome," came a voice in Leyton's ear.

A real voice. One so close he felt warm breath kissing his cheek.

He spun to face where the words had originated, finding a woman standing behind him, her smile wicked in the light spilling through the doorway. Blonde hair cascaded down to cover her breasts — breasts as naked as the rest of her — and drying blood streaked her stomach and arms. His heart rate kicked up speed, and for a moment he was stunned into a paralysis that even prevented thought.

"I knew you would come," she said, her voice calm and level, melodic. "It will be so nice to perform for an audience. Maybe even have you help me."

"*Do not let her tempt you!*" Rivald said, panic leaching into his tone.

"Oh, do be quiet, Rivald," Lorelei said, flapping her hand midair as though swatting an irritating fly. "Wasn't it you who said I was the one for Leyton, hmm? Wasn't it you who told him if he found me, he'd find the chance of happiness?"

Confusion overtook the paralysis, and Leyton stared at her, wanting to believe she *was* destined for him, for them to live a life with one another, killing together.

"Now wouldn't that be fun?" she asked, taking Leyton's hand in her delicate grip. "You've been so lonely, haven't you, Leyton. I understand all about that."

Her voice mesmerised him, pulled him in.

"And they used you the same way they used me. They pick your deepest desire and manipulate you with it. For you, it was love. Mother didn't love you, did she, Leyton?"

He shook his head, conflicting thoughts warring with one another. *Who do I listen to? Rivald? Her? Myself?*

"For me it was the promise of living a life without detection. Being able to kill without being caught. Then they revealed it had all been a lie, that they had reeled me in just so I did their bidding. Is that what happened to you, Leyton?"

He stared into her eyes—black as the night, no whites—and nodded numbly. He struggled to make sense of what she'd said, what Rivald had said.

"Do not listen to her," Rivald said. *"She knows how to make you think—"*

"Oh!" Lorelei sighed. "Listen to him trying to make you ignore me. But you're thinking, aren't you, Leyton? Your mind is ticking. Asking questions. Putting two and two together." She smiled again, head tilted, and squeezed his hand in hers. "Come down into the basement with me. There is someone I would like you to meet."

Chapter Eighteen

Barry flopped restlessly onto his back. He should be exhausted. *Was* exhausted. Still, sleep remained elusive. Beside him, Tag had drifted off. Their lovemaking had been slow, almost lethargic, with Tag taking methodical care, almost like he was painting his claim over Barry's body with every kiss and caress. His firm, just-short-of-forceful possession had been a comfort, and Barry played through the memory in detail, feeling the tingle over his skin and down through his being, just as he had when Tag touched him. He rolled onto his side to face Tag and watch him sleep.

Their interview with Jessica had been long and gruelling for the girl, but she'd been a trooper throughout. It hadn't been difficult to convince the powers that be that she should not go home. Her captor, after all, was still out there, somewhere. Of course, they kept back the niggling detail that her captor was never going to be caught. Not in the traditional, stopping-him-from-murdering-people sense of the word, anyway. But until they could find and talk to this Leyton character, convince him to leave her alone, it was better to keep her as far out of his reach as they could.

Barry's attention drifted to the lights wheeling across the wall, and he fell onto his back again to watch their progress along the ceiling. How out of reach could she ever really be, though? Leyton might still have an inside track to her every thought, and even if he didn't, he had one to Barry. Because of that, he'd told Ross and Tag not to tell him where they'd stashed her. It was safer for her if Barry didn't know.

A wide yawn caught him, cracking his jaw and making his eyes water. It wasn't the first time he'd been this tired and unable to sleep. He didn't want to admit he was afraid of the darkness behind his own eyelids, but there was really no other reason he should still be awake.

Beside him, Tag shifted, threw an arm over his chest, and his body lazily gravitated across the mattress before he curled around him, moulding to his side. He lifted a hand and dragged his fingers through Tag's greying hair.

"Go t'sleep," Tag muttered.

"Easy for you to say." Barry yawned another huge yawn.

Tag's lips pressed to his shoulder. "Let you off too easy. Shoulda made you fuck harder. Wear you out."

Barry chuckled.

Tag lifted a leg, slinked it between Barry's, and his soft cock fell into the crease of Barry's hip. They were like a jigsaw puzzle, pieces worn at the edges, some of the bright colours scuffed off, but they still fit perfectly together.

"Love you," Barry whispered through another yawn.

"Mmmm," Tag murmured agreeably and slipped an arm around Barry's waist. The weight of his limbs was an anchor, holding Barry in place, protective. "Now sleep."

"Yes, sir."

Tag's lips twitched against the skin of his shoulder. "Better."

That 'held down' feeling followed Barry into sleep when it finally came. The warmth of Tag's nearness did not. He still felt tired. He knew immediately it was a dream. For a fraction of an instant, he let the knowledge chase away the fear.

Then something struck his skin, cold, like ice trailing across his abdomen, leaving a sharp chill of pain in its wake. Every few minutes it came again on a different part of his body – arm, calf, the top of one foot, the inside of his thigh – and he tried to move away from the frigid touch.

Warmth trickled down his skin. He didn't have to look to know the cold touch was a knife and the warmth his blood. Mixed with the sweat of fear, it stung like hell as it ran into new cuts. The bright slice of pain traced the upper edge of his thigh, along towards his privates.

"God, no, please." He couldn't help the words bleating out.

They were met with a low, throaty chuckle.

"What do you want?" He blinked, but sweat ran into his eyes and he couldn't focus.

"I have what I want." Lips pressed to his cheek. "I have everything I could possibly want right here." The voice was a whisper in his ear, too quiet and close to identify. He'd expected it to be Leyton's, but it wasn't. It was too soft, rounded and husky. He couldn't imagine the man who fit that voice. A hand lifted his flaccid cock, played with it, let it fall again. The knife traced the same path along his other thigh, and he cried out helplessly.

Barry sat up in bed, jostling Tag awake. Weak morning sun filtered around the edges of the blind, and Barry found himself running questing fingers over his body, tracing the delicate curve above his thigh.

"Fuck."

Tag scowled at him. "Another body?" he asked, peering past Barry at the clock.

Barry sighed, looked down at him briefly before rolling on top of him and kissing him senseless. "Fuck me first."

Tag didn't argue. He did push Barry off and roll him over, issuing commands Barry didn't hesitate to follow. Tag's possession was hard, forceful enough to leave behind a few bruises, fast enough to have them panting with the exertion, and complete, both of them sated and limp after a few, frantic minutes. What it had lacked in build-up, he made up for with his careful lather, rinse and repeat of Barry's entire body in the shower.

"Okay?" Tag asked from where he stood in the tub towelling off.

Looking in the bathroom mirror, Barry examined the aftermath of the session, pushing the edge of his towel down to look at the finger marks. He trailed a light touch over them, relishing the dull ache and the marks as real and tangible indications that there was a fundamental but important difference between the dream world and the real one.

"I'm sorry." Tag appeared in the mirror behind him, laid his fingers over the marks, showing off the perfect fit. "Didn't mean that."

Barry shook his head, laced his fingers between Tag's. "Don't be. The more of you I have on me, the less of me the rest of it can touch." Maybe it sounded foolish, but with the memory of that sharp blade slicing skin just deep enough to bleed and hurt, not enough to kill, he felt the truth of it.

Tag leaned on him, watched him in the mirror, his chin resting lightly on Barry's shoulder. "Tell me."

Barry did, detailing the dream to his partner in a monotone that shook ever so slightly around the edges.

"Your memory's getting better," Tag observed.

Barry nodded. They were still standing in the bathroom, watching one another in the mirror. Tag had wrapped his arms around Barry's chest and pulled him back so they stood fused as one, Barry's ass pressed against his lover's crotch. Only a slip of terry cloth separated them, and Barry felt the security of Tag's protection as he talked. It made it easier, both to remember the atrocities of the dream and to share them.

"So." Tag kissed the side of his neck, sucking up a bit of skin between his teeth, leaving a mark there before he backed off and let Barry go. "Where's the body? Any idea?"

Barry shook his head, shed his towel, and headed back out to the main room. "No body."

"Wait." Tag hurried after him. "No body? Then what the hell are we doing? If she's not dead why are we fucking around? We need to get moving—"

Barry shook his head. "Leyton would tell me."

"Tell you?" Tag stopped where he was, standing beside the bed, shirt in hand. "Tell you what?"

"If we needed to act." Barry kept his gaze on the floor at Tag's feet. "If it was urgent, he would tell me."

"So we just let him kill her?"

Again, Barry shook his head. "I don't think it's a her."

"Barry?"

Sinking onto the edge of the table, Barry ran a hand through his hair. "It felt different. This victim was...different, and the dream..." He shook his head, scrubbing at his scalp with the palm of his hand, like a genie's lamp that wasn't giving him any answers. He let out a long sigh. "The guy is terrified and he's hurting and still in danger, but I don't know where he is. I have to wait for *him* to tell me."

"Barry!" Tag advanced, fist clenched tight around his shirt. "We can't just sit on this! We have to do something. If he's being held, tortured, we have to do something. We're cops!"

"No shit."

Tag leaned in, getting low and in Barry's face, forcing him to look at him. "Think, Barry. Any detail you can remember that will help us find him."

"There are no details."

"Try."

"You think I haven't?"

"There must be—"

"There's nothing!" Barry pushed past his lover, snatching up his rucksack and dropping it on the bed. He dug through for underwear and socks, pulled out a T-shirt. "I have to get more clothes from my apartment. People are going to start noticing I'm wearing the same two suits."

"Suits?" Tag grabbed for and caught Barry's wrist. "Fucking suits you're worried about? Barry, a man's being held against his will. Maybe tortured, maybe killed—"

"I know!" Barry yanked, pulling Tag off balance and spinning, slamming him against the wall. "I know! What the fuck do you want me to do?"

"Remember."

"There is nothing *to* remember. When it's time to act, I'll know. That's all I can do, Tag."

"It isn't good enough."

"What do you think? I'm doing it on purpose? I'm happy leaving him there?" It hit him then why the voice from the dream was off-kilter. "A woman." He frowned, shook the realisation away. It was the victim that mattered. That was his purview. The degenerate belonged to Leyton. "I was in his skin, Tag! In his skin while this…bitch sliced it off in little chunks, and you think I *like* not being able to do anything about it?"

"Of course not." Tag was so infuriatingly calm. "I don't for a minute think you like it. I don't think you want this." Tag raised his free arm and cupped Barry's face gently. "But you can't just accept it. *I* won't just accept it. I'll solve their fucking puzzles for them, but goddamnit, they are going to help us in this. Bad enough you have to go through this shit every time you close your eyes. I will not let them torture you with making you know it's happening and not letting you do anything about it."

Barry relaxed his hold, leaned until his forehead rested on Tag's shoulder. "What do you propose we do? They didn't give me any answers. Some guy held somewhere by some woman who is so not right in the head it makes me want to vomit just thinking about it. She didn't care about him—who he is, where he's from, what he does. He's some random guy. She just wants to peel him, hurt him, watch him bleed. For fun. And I can't do a damn thing. And neither can we. If you butt in… Remember what can happen?"

Tag's arm slid around Barry's back.

"I hate this, Tag."

"I know."

They stood like that for a few moments, Tag's arms around him and Barry wondering how much compassion and patience his partner had to bleed out before he snapped under the pressure. He had to find his own strength, or eventually Tag would leave again. Get fed up or driven off. Barry didn't want to be alone with this, so he had to pull himself together, be strong enough to partner Tag, give back enough so his lover didn't run out of strength to deal.

"Okay." Barry disentangled himself from Tag's hold. "Okay. Enough. Nothing gets done standing here."

Tag just nodded.

Barry squared his shoulders. "I need to eat. Talk to Ross." He looked up at Tag, still leaning on the wall in his boxers, shirt dangling from one hand. "Next time Leyton drops in," he tapped the side of his skull, "I'll be sure and give him your list of demands, all right? But don't bank on him listening. Until then, there's nothing I can do. Dwelling on it will drive us both nuts. Let's pick up some breakfast and start going over missing person's reports. It's all we've got to go on right now."

"You're right."

"Sometimes I am." Barry found a smile and plastered it on.

After a second, Tag returned it, or made a half-hearted attempt, anyway, and pushed himself upright. "This is a fucking nightmare," he muttered.

For a split second, the room crackled with silence.

"Oh, shit. Barry…"

For the first time in what felt like a million years, Barry's smile turned genuine. He grinned. "You think?"

Chapter Nineteen

Tag resisted kicking himself mentally over the thoughtless comment. Barry grinned at him, and the expression brought back their first year together, before the dreams had got really bad. Was it possible, he wondered, that the relentless fucking, the hours spent loving every inch of Barry, inside and out, was going to get through to him? Maybe his fears that his lover would never trust him again were overblown.

He watched Barry as unobtrusively as he could while they finished dressing. "You want to swing by your place on the way to the station? Pick anything up?"

Barry shook his head. "On the way home, maybe."

Tag couldn't help a small smile. "Home."

Their gazes met. "That a problem?" Barry asked.

"Kinda small place for two grown men."

Barry glanced at the bed. "Plenty of room for me. I like cosy." He shifted his shoulders in an exaggerated shrug. "No room for the feeling like someone's sneaking up behind me."

Tag nodded. "Neighbourhood sucks."

"It does."

"You've had that apartment of yours a long time."

"Dead guy on my doorstep."

Tag fell silent as they holstered their weapons and made a last pass for wallets and watches. "Doesn't really matter where you go, Barry," Tag pointed out quietly as he fished in his sock drawer. "*He* can always find you."

"I know."

"Here." Tag held something out to him. "Thought you might want this back."

Barry lifted his hand, and something cool and heavy dropped into his palm. A thick gold band nestled among his calluses. "You kept it?"

Tag gave his belt a little tug, then slid a matching ring on his left ring finger. "Course."

"Of course?" Barry turned the ring over in his hand. "Saving it for the next guy? Or were you just that sure I'd take you back?"

"I made some bad choices, Barry." Tag took the ring, took Barry's hand in his. "I'm sorry."

Barry nodded.

Tag slipped the ring into place. "It's all different now. No matter what happens, you have me."

Barry nodded again. "We should find some place nicer. Little more uptown." He closed his hand into a tight fist, the ring glinting in a shaft of sunlight that finally broke through the morning haze. Barry met Tag's eye. "Once this is done and I have Leyton where he can't hurt you, we find a place he doesn't know about."

"How?"

"Not sure yet. But if I'm stuck with this gig, time I got to make some of the rules. Not going to live my life always scared, always on the edge of crazy.

Whoever this Leyton guy is, maybe that's okay for him. I can't live like that, and neither can you. So..." He smiled, one of the darker expressions he'd adopted during their separation. "We have coffee to pick up and a date with the missing persons database. And" — he opened the door to usher Tag out — "with any luck, a lead on Leyton. A real lead."

"Okay," Tag said, trepidation clear in his voice.

"I caught something the other night. As we were leaving the crime scene. Didn't want to say anything, in case. But there's been nothing else even remotely close, so I'm hoping it was a bit of Leyton slipping up and letting me see something he didn't want me to see. Like his car, complete with licence plate, and maybe his camper. Ross ran the plates while he was doing his looking, so we'll see what he's got."

Tag nodded. "We'll see."

* * * *

It was Ross and Barry who trolled through the endless reports of missing loved ones while Tag fielded a dozen phone calls from superiors about the fiasco that was him driving into a telephone pole and then not taking any time off for recovery, and not putting the mystery of a dead man on one of his most controversial officer's doorsteps on the highest priority.

"I know how to run my department, sir." His head ached slightly, the dull pain radiating from his broken nose and settling just behind his eyes. "I give the cases we have a hope in hell of solving the highest priority. There's nothing I can do about that case until I at least have an ID on the corpse."

"Or, you're putting it on the back burner in hopes of keeping your pet out of trouble."

"Whittaker had nothing to do with the man's death."

"And you know that how?"

Tag sighed, pinched the bridge of his nose between thumb and forefinger, stifled a yelp and dropped his hand with an exaggerated thump onto his desk. He leaned both elbows on the hard surface and closed his eyes. He'd hoped this bit would have taken at least a few more days to come up.

"Because I know Barry."

"Quite well, or so rumour has it."

"We were partners for seven years, sir."

"Taggart, let me give you a piece of advice."

"Not necessary, sir. I know my job. Now, if we're through here, perhaps I'd be free to go do it."

"Whittaker is going to drag you down, Taggart." The voice on the other end of the phone didn't change timbre. "When Internal Affairs gets going on this —"

"Wait. Internal Affairs?" Tag stood, leaning over the phone. "Why?"

"Because this is one too many odd coincidences surrounding your lover, Taggart. I suggest if you don't want them on your back, too, you cut him loose."

"Not going to happen, Gallagher. He has skills this department needs, and I mean to protect him. You go after him, rest assured every discriminatory action you've ever taken against us, or anyone else, will hit the table."

Silence.

"I didn't get this job because I was afraid to play hard ball, Arty," Tag said. "You let me play with the big boys, be prepared go hard, because I am not an easy mark, and neither are my friends."

Tag hung up, his chest still heaving, his head throbbing with adrenaline and the leftover ring of crashing metal and the whoosh of airbags. Outside his office, he could see Barry looking over a file Ross handed him, and shake his head. He went out to see if they'd had a more productive morning than he had.

"Well?" he asked, approaching them.

"Dead end after dead end," Barry muttered, glancing over a file in his hand. "Fuck!"

"What's that?"

"The plate Wiki had me run," Ross replied when Barry didn't look up from the page. "Belongs to a Michael Dagson."

"The serial killer we've been after…" Tag sighed. "Cal's murderer."

Barry nodded and tossed the file on his desk. "Dead end."

"It closes how many cases?" Ross pointed out. "All we have to do is find that car."

Tag was watching Barry and somehow, he knew what was coming before his lover opened his eyes. "When they find it, it'll be clean as a whistle," he said quietly. "Because Dagson's dead." He met Tag's gaze and there was such darkness there it took Tag's breath away. "Somewhere, there's a caravan out there with bloody sheets. A crime scene to correspond to the dump site that was my front doorstep. It was no slip up on Leyton's part, Tag. It was a puzzle. A nice, easy puzzle to show me who's got who by the balls. Find the car. Find the caravan. Find the link to the body. Close a dozen cases without the court costs or burden on the prison system of one more fucked-up serial killer, and Leyton walks off into the sunset with his horned freak." He sighed.

Tag wanted to reach out and touch him, drive that dark out of his eyes, but he refrained. Barry wouldn't thank him for the impulse here. "What about the missing persons?" he asked instead, hoping they'd had more luck finding the mysterious victim from Barry's latest dream.

Barry just shook his head.

It didn't pass Tag's notice that a grimace of frustration passed over Ross' face. He felt for the guy. It was one thing to accept the dreams. Quite another to be able to accept their limitations.

"How do you know?" Ross took a swig of his coffee and made a face. "Cold." He set the cup down in disgust.

"I know," Barry told him.

"What?" Ross asked. "Was there a mirror in that dream? Did you see his face? How?"

"I. Just. Know."

Tag recognised the signs Barry was getting a headache. The way his mouth pinched at the corners and his eyes dulled, his gaze drifting to the corners of the room.

"What say we go grab some lunch," Tag suggested.

Barry nodded.

Ross picked up his cold coffee and stood. "Sounds good to me."

"Leave that," Tag told him, waving at the offending cup.

Ross shook his head. "Necter of the gods, is caffeine." He gulped down another swallow and grinned. "Lifeblood."

Tag made a face. "Suit yourself."

They settled in a small diner on a quiet corner where other cops didn't eat. Ross sat in the corner of the booth, arms draped across the back of the seat, one ankle propped on the other knee, looking exactly like a Don surveying his domain—all casual, easy threat. Tag watched Barry gingerly place his back to the now-streaming sunshine. He reached for his lover's hand, and it was a measure of Barry's discomfort that he tiredly laced their fingers without protest. He wasn't generally in favour of public displays.

"Okay, babe?"

Barry shook his head. "Took a few aspirins. Doesn't seem to help."

"Is it *him?*"

A shrug shifted Barry's shoulders. "Don't know. It's like he's... I don't know. Out of tune. Like a radio with too much static covering the broadcast."

Tag leaned a little closer, put a hand on Barry's leg. "Maybe you should lie down. Get a bit of sleep."

Their eyes met, and Barry cocked his head. "I know what you're doing."

"What?"

"Trying to tune me." He smiled a tired smile. "And if I thought that was the problem, I'd do it. I'd go in and let him find me, but this time, I don't think it would help."

"What do you mean?" Ross moved, setting both his feet on the floor and placing his elbows on the table, clasping his hands before him. Tag had seen him use the squared-off pose to put victims at ease during statements, to make perps feel like they could trust him. The ease with which he changed gears was amazing. And potentially useful.

Barry shot his partner an irritated look but settled back in his own chair and picked up the beer the waiter had set down before him. "The dreams. They're relayed through Leyton, the guy you couldn't find in any database."

"A first name isn't much to go on."

"True." Barry sighed. "Don't worry about it. I didn't expect you to find him. He's in my head and I can't find him."

"Back to the point," Tag said. "If you don't think it will help, what will?"

Barry shook his head. "It isn't me, Tag. I want to find the victim as much as you do. I'm open. If Leyton's trying to reach me, he's failing. I don't know why. He's the one out of focus, not me." For a few minutes, Barry's attention turned to his beer and the bottle's label as he shredded it. "I think..."

When he didn't continue, Tag prompted him again.

"Jessica," Barry said, reluctance stilling his fingers on the shredded label. "She said Leyton acted like he was in love with her before he ever met her. That he kept saying she was meant for him."

"So?"

"So...what if her escaping has messed him up? What if he's gone rogue?"

"*Gone* rogue?" Tag almost laughed.

"No, I'm serious. If it was Leyton in the street that night, when we found the body, if it was him, he acted like he was just a messenger. Like there was someone else directing him. So what if he's gone off programme?"

"We don't even know what he's programmed to do."

Ross' phone rang as Tag and Barry stared at one another. Tag didn't pay much attention to the content of Ross' conversation. He was too concerned with trying to figure out the ramifications for Barry if what he was surmising were true.

"I think…" Ross hung up his phone, a thoughtful look on his face. "That was Danielle Cornwall. She ran with the plate ID." He fixed his gaze on Barry. "You were right. We got an ID on the dead guy." He looked from one to the other of them. "We can show Jessica a picture, but ten to one says he's the guy who took her out of Cal's apartment. It was his escapades Cal was writing about. He killed seven women, and Cal wrote columns on every one, pleading for information, anything, to help find the guy doing it. Seven vics, every one in the paper and him doing our job before this degenerate caught up with Cal and killed him. He died because we had our heads up our asses. Jessica was just in the wrong place at the wrong time. Bad luck that she was exactly this creep's type. Or maybe good. Maybe if she wasn't tiny and blonde, he would have just killed her instead of taking her. Anyway, Leyton did us a favour killing him. He was scum."

"Too late for Cal, though," Barry muttered, remembering every dream that started out with the vague idea of Tag and ended…the way they all ended. He shuddered and Tag's hand skimmed down his clammy back.

"So? What does that have to do with anything?" Tag asked.

"We solve the puzzles," Barry mused. "What if the dreams are not *from* Leyton, so much as *about* him? Or about his next target?"

"The girls?" Ross asked. "But you said last night's captive was a man. Doesn't make sense."

"No." Barry let go of Tag's hand and sat forward, beer forgotten in his excitement. "Not the girls. The killers. He's after the killers."

"Why put you in the skin of their victims?" Tag asked, disgust coiling in his gut. "That's beyond cruel."

Barry snorted. "How better to get into the head of the creeps doing it, than to know exactly what they're doing and who they're doing it to? How many of these assholes have we caught? How many has Leyton got to first? Think about it. We're about fifty-fifty. It's a wonder Internal Affairs isn't on our asses for murder."

Tag's gut clenched again.

"No matter how fucked up they are," Barry said, poking a finger into the table and glancing between them, "murder is murder, and we're the ones not bringing anyone in for it."

Tag congratulated himself on keeping his calm. No need for Barry to have that stress on top of everything else.

"We don't get to play judge, jury, and executioner," Barry said.

"Leyton does." Tag made a face. Leyton's pastime, albeit supposedly forced on him, was going to get them all hung.

"So we're supposed to stop him?" Ross asked.

"I think we get the ones we can prove," Barry said. "He gets the rest."

"As long as we get there first," Tag muttered.

"As long as we get there first."

"So what about this guy you dreamed last night? Is he real?" Ross asked.

Barry frowned. "They're all real. He's real. I just have no idea how to find him."

"Because Leyton can't tell you?" Tag asked.

"Or won't." Barry met his gaze. "I'm not sure which. Now that I know more, it seems like I should be able to contact him if I want, but I can't. Okay" —he held up a hand when Tag would have protested —"I know I have no idea how, but still. There should be some sort of…channel or something. But there's just static. Like he's keeping me out on purpose. Or like he's not completely in control of this one for some reason. Like maybe he's in trouble."

"Enough to get him killed and the fuck out of our lives, I hope," Tag snarled, feeling the hope and wish grip him and pushing it back ruthlessly. Hope was a cancer that only made his will weak.

"Tag." Barry leaned in, making Tag look at him. "If I don't have these dreams, if I don't try to help these people, they all die. Whether Leyton gets the perps or not, the innocent still die. If I can save any of them… Tag, I know how it feels to see the end and not be able to stop it. If one person goes home safe because I lived their death and found them in time, then it's worth it. Tell me you understand that."

Tag nodded, though his heart hammered and his gut twisted. He hated the reality, but loved his partner for his conviction, for being able to keep doing it when it so obviously gave him so much grief. He resolved again to give Barry enough brightness to combat the darkness.

"So." Barry sat back once more as the waiter brought their usual lunches. There was something to be said for being regulars. Once the food was delivered and the waiter gone, Barry picked up his fork. "Here's what I think. Whatever's going on to foul the lines of communication, it's either beyond Leyton's control, or it's his fault. I won't stand for the little shit jerking me around. I need to go to the source."

Ross looked up from cutting into his slab of liver.

Tag's fork slipped from his fingers and hit his plate with a clatter. Mashed potatoes flew in all directions. "What?"

Barry glanced at him. "Jessica's horned man. I need to talk to him." He popped a forkful of sauerkraut and sausage in his mouth.

Tag's first reaction was to forbid it, as stupid as that would be. He could ask if Barry was sure, but the determined look in his lover's eyes was answer enough.

"How do you propose to do that?" Tag asked at last, knowing he wasn't going to talk Barry out of it.

"Not entirely sure." Barry caught Tag's eye across the table. "But we'll figure it out?"

Tag nodded. "Eat." Picking up his fork, he wiped off the handle and cleaned up the mash off the table. "Then I want you to go home and sleep off the headache." He didn't look at Barry. Was it perverse of him to hope Barry would dream again, get enough information for them to act without having to chance contact with some mystical horned creature who sounded way too much like a devil to be good?

Chapter Twenty

Leyton sat with his back to the wall opposite the hanging man. He sighed, having been awake all night, tired right down to his bones. Well, he'd closed his eyes some, but never slept. Now, well into the later part of the next day, eyes gritty and sore, he rubbed them with the heels of his hands. His muscles went through phases of aching then going completely numb, until he felt as though just his soul existed and his body had disappeared God knew where.

An odd sensation.

Twenty-four hours he'd been here, awake for a whole lot more.

His mind ticked over, sluggish with the new knowledge he had gained during the night. The things Lorelei had done... Shit, when he did them, it felt right, *was* right, but to see someone else doing them...

"*Are you doubting who you really are now, Leyton?*" Mother asked.

"Fuck off," he whispered. "Please, just fuck off. I'm too tired to deal with you. And her. And thank God Rivald has shut up. He was —"

"*Driving you insane?*" Mother's voice held a hint of amusement.

"Yes. Like you are. Like you do. Like you always have."

"*Aww, my poor child. My poor creature, who kills and maims and hurts and —*"

"Fuck. Off!"

"What was that, Leyton?" Lorelei's voice streaked through the echoic basement.

"Nothing."

Her footsteps tapped down the stairs, dull patters on the wood. What had she been doing since she —

"Tired?" Lorelei asked, her bare legs visible through the balustrades.

He jumped, her tone making him uneasy. He was on edge now, as wired as a damn drug addict needing a fix, and wanted to yell that yes, he was tired — tired of her being in control. Of Mother and Rivald and whoever the hell else dictated what he did. It wasn't fun anymore. Wasn't such a game. Not since they'd directed his actions, where he went, what he saw.

"Perhaps you should eat something," Lorelei suggested, rounding the newel post and waltzing towards him as though she'd slept like a baby.

Perhaps she had. Maybe she'd gone upstairs after...after...

Yeah, she'd slept all right. She looked fresh as a fucking daisy, the skin on her cheeks rosy beneath the streaks of that man's blood.

She has no conscience. Like me, yet...

For the first time in his life, guilt plagued Leyton. Had dogged him while he rested against the wall for who knew how many hours, his ass numb from the cold concrete. Poked into his mind, waving its bastard hands at him as he'd taken a look into Barry's head and seen him dreaming of what Lorelei was doing. Barry's horror matched Leyton's. And why *was* that? How come all of a sudden Leyton saw killing as the horrific thing it was?

Only when she did it. When it's me it isn't wrong. I kill killers. She killed some man for fun.

"I wonder..." Lorelei cocked her hip and planted a hand over the jutting bone. Her slender fingers tipped with black-polished nails could have belonged to any woman, except those fingers had held instruments of torture and given an innocent man so much pain it wasn't funny.

Will she ever get some fucking clothes on? Wash that blood off?

"No, I won't. Not yet," she said. "As I was saying, I wonder if Mr Jack Yemen there has been missed yet."

Jack Yemen. Up until his dying moment, a man with a wife, three kids, and a border collie. A man who had what Leyton thought he'd get when Jessica came into his life. He swallowed the lump in his throat. No sense in thinking about her now. The life he could have led. It was gone, all bloody gone.

Out of my grasp. I'll never have what Jack had. An SUV parked outside my large house beside a front lawn bigger than the grounds of the local park. A wife who waits for me at dinnertime as I breeze through the front door yelling, "Honey, I'm home!" A child who runs towards me, arms outstretched, pleased her daddy is back from a hard day, ready to spend time with her.

"You should never have entertained the scenario." Lorelei laughed, the sound jarring and mean. A laugh that told him she found his situation more than amusing. She took pleasure in it, knowing someone else had been duped. That she wasn't the only one caught up in a web of lies. That she wasn't alone in trusting someone else with the direction her life should go. "I can't believe you actually took Rivald at his word. He's a lying bastard. They all are."

"You did," he said, pushing on the floor to stand. "You're just as stupid as me."

She tilted her head, regarding him with eyes that were blue now, the black of last night gone…until she felt the burn inside her again, Leyton suspected. "Yes, you're right." She sighed dramatically, turning away from him.

To hide her face? The emotions on it?

"Yes, yes, Leyton. To hide my embarrassment." She whipped her head around to look at him again. "Still, that's all in the past, isn't it? I have you now, and you have me. Isn't that delightful?" She twirled in place, her corn-coloured hair fanning out. Blood gave that hair pink streaks, held the tresses in hard clumps.

Christ, she needs to wash it. Get rid of it.

Leyton's stomach bunched.

"I'll have a bath when I'm damn good and ready," she snapped, coming to a stop and putting her finger beneath his chin. "I *like* having them on me. It's…divine. The smell. Like copper pennies."

She trilled out a laugh and snatched her finger away, her nail scraping Leyton's skin. He hid a wince, sensing she'd enjoy knowing she'd inflicted pain. He nearly allowed his thoughts to roam but stopped them. She didn't need to know what he really thought of her. She'd listened in on him enough last night to gain a good insight into how he saw her. A monster. A bitch. An insane, insufferable bitch.

Lorelei walked over to Jack and leant forward, nose almost touching his torso. She inhaled deeply and released a sigh, clearly relishing the man's deathly scent, almost certainly seeing what she had done playing through her mind. Leyton had done the same in the past, although he couldn't recall smelling them. No, that was just too weird.

Mother laughed. *"Like taking out your victims' teeth isn't weird? Like fashioning them into dentures to wear yourself isn't weird? You're weird!"* she screeched.

Leyton clutched the hair at his temples. *I know, I know, I know… Leave me alone. Please, for God's sake, just leave me alone. Let me think. Let me regroup. I need to contact Barry but that bitch has done something. Stopped the contact somehow.*

"You also need to stop thinking," Mother said. *"She'll hear you. Good job she's otherwise occupied at the moment."*

Leyton stared at Lorelei, who poked one finger into a congealed wound on Jack's chest. She withdrew her digit and sniffed it, then turned to face Leyton, finger pointing at the ceiling.

"Would you like to eat him?" she asked, her mouth a parody of an innocent smile. "I'll bet he tastes good."

Disgust uncoiled in Leyton's stomach, and he took a few seconds to ponder why. Would he have done the same at one time? Would he have evolved into a man who took the ultimate kill trophy — digesting a part of his victim? He didn't know, would never know, because seeing the globs of red matter on her finger put a stop to him ever wanting to try.

"Leyton, you really must get over this squeamishness. I thought you were stronger than this. I thought I'd found someone who understood me. Someone who would partner me, go through kills together." She popped her finger in her mouth and sucked, slowly drawing it out. Clean.

Mother sighed. *"She's a bad one, boy. You know what you need to do, don't you?"*

Leyton nodded.

"Ah," Lorelei said. "So you agree with me. Good. We're getting somewhere." She faced Jack again, sliding her fingers inside a particularly nasty stomach gash and, gripping the skin either side, yanked.

Her strength surprised Leyton. She was such a dainty thing.

"*Oh*, did you *hear* that?" She glanced over her shoulder, eyes alight with excitement. "Did you hear how his skin *ripped?*"

Leyton had heard it all right, and despite his guilt, despite wishing himself out of this basement, the sound had called to him. Woken up his inner burn. He nodded again. Smiled. Took a few steps forward. He stared at Jack's entrails spilling out of the gaping hole and slapping into the floor. Lorelei held her hands up, marvelling at their new colour.

"You really should have something to eat, you know," she said, bending to scoop up a mass of innards. She held them to her belly, rubbed them over her skin, eyes closed and lips in a disturbing smile.

Mother whispered, "*Look at her. She's in another world.*"

Leyton shot a look towards a chest of drawers, his open tool pouch on top. Lorelei had used them on Jack. Sullied them with the blood of someone who had done nothing more than be in the wrong place at the wrong time. As Jack had babbled, answering Lorelei's rapid-fire questions about himself, it had come to light they'd met in a parking lot when Lorelei had feigned losing her keys and needing a ride home.

Jack's first mistake had been to approach her as she'd stood crying. His second had been giving her a ride 'home'.

Lorelei continued her strange behaviour, moving the innards upward to cover her breasts. She hummed

Twinkle Twinkle Little Star, swaying to the melody. Leyton took careful steps to the drawers and reached out his hand, grasping the handle of a corkscrew. Yes, he'd used it before to kill someone after wondering how much damage the metal spiral would cause. How much pain his victim would suffer as he twisted the implement inside their body. Lorelei stopped humming and panted, short, sharp gasps that heralded the onset of an orgasm. She bunched her eyes tight, rubbing the mass of red up her neck and back down towards her cunt. A whimper left her, and her pelvis juddered.

"Do it now, Leyton. Now!" Mother screamed.

He swiftly moved in front of Lorelei and lunged forward. The corkscrew entered one of her eyes, and he twisted it, wrenching it out to the beautiful sound of her anguished cries. She dropped the innards, lifting her hands, fingers splayed, and covered her face. With her blood-streaked torso open to invitation, he thrust the corkscrew into her belly and yanked, her screams the perfect accompaniment to his action. *Her* innards streaked out, attached to the spiral, and she lowered her hands to stare down at the length of intestine that hung between her body and the tool.

She looked up, her face and eyes full of questions Leyton refused to answer. "You...? Why did you...? I thought—"

"You thought wrong."

Leyton rammed the corkscrew into her time and again, the spray of blood fuelling the burn inside him. She sagged to the floor screaming, and he bent over, hacking and hacking, rage building, justice being served. Her body spasmed, and she clutched at his jeans before her body went slack, her hands falling to rest limply by her sides. Leyton stared at the desiccated mess of her stomach, gaze devouring the carnage he'd created. He stood upright, chest heaving from exertion, adrenaline thrumming through his veins.

Stepping back, he stared at Jack. "There. Doesn't she look pretty now?"

At the small steel sink beside the drawers, Leyton washed the bitch from his corkscrew and cleaned his hands. He placed the tool in its slot and closed the pouch. His mind cleared, free of the clutter Lorelei had put there, and he took a deep, calming breath.

"Everything is all right now. Everything is back on track."

Infused with strength and purpose, he left the basement, pouch under his arm, and found the bathroom on the upper floor. He stripped, piled his clothes and pouch on the floor, and stepped into the tub. A half-full bottle of shower gel stood on the bath ledge, and he jabbed the 'On' button for the shower, washing that filthy whore from his skin.

As the water pattered over him, he thought of Jessica. What was she doing? Where was she? During the night, Rivald had put a block on Leyton contacting her. Not surprising, given Leyton's state of mind back then. He'd still wanted to run away with her, to have the life he'd been promised, but now? No, he understood, if she was one of them, that a romantic involvement would muddy things, make him sloppy in his work. He couldn't have that. Not if it meant putting Jessica in danger.

Bait. Why does she have to be used as bait?

Oh, he knew why, just didn't want it to be her.

He allowed his mind to roam, reaching to contact her, just in case he could. He sensed she slept—and she *would* be tired after what she'd been through, of that Leyton had no doubt. But it must be lunchtime around now. Surely, if he probed hard enough, he could wake her.

Mother huffed out a breath. *"But you don't want to wake her, stupid! You want her to be asleep. You're a Dreamer. You need for her to be asleep so you can make contact. Jesus Christ, boy, haven't you learned anythin'?"*

Leyton gritted his teeth. Mother's teeth. Dentures that would be replaced soon now he could add one of Lorelei's molars to his collection. "Yes, Mother. I hear you. I forgot."

"Well, you'd better start payin' more attention, because things are about to heat up around here. Are you listenin' to me? Do you understand what I'm tellin' you?"

He nodded, letting the water play over his face and fill his mouth.

"So get a hold of her, boy. You need some clean clothes."

Leyton concentrated, infiltrating Jessica's dream state, expecting Rivald to step in any second and stop him. Quickly, he pushed harder, screaming at Jessica.

"Listen to me. It's Leyton. I know you don't want to know me, and I don't blame you, but this is bigger than what you think. This...this thing we're involved in. You're a part of it now whether you like it or not, and I need your help."

He felt her tensing. He couldn't see her, was just in a black void, but she was there, able to hear him.

"I need you to bring me some clothes. Can you do that?"

"Go away. Please, just go away," she whispered. *"Get out of my fucking head!"*

"I can't. You're involved now. You have a job to do, a role to play, and there's nothing you can do about it. The horned man...he'll contact you soon with instructions. You have to do as he asks. You have to do as I ask."

"*Shit. I don't want this crap.*" She released a quiet sob. "*Just go. Leave me the hell alone. And tell that horned bastard he can do the same. The pair of you can kiss my damn ass.*"

"Jessica, please. You mustn't fight it. You have to—"

The air around Leyton heated up, swirled over his skin, then grew cold. As cold as wintry fog.

"Fuck. He's here."

"*Who is?*" Her voice sounded small. She was afraid—fear radiated.

"*I am,*" Rivald said. "*The 'horned bastard'. Not a term I would have used, but still... You must do as Leyton asks. He needs clothes. Now. Wake up, find some clothing, and take them to Moore Street. I will direct you as to which property you need when you get there.*"

"*Oh, Jesus. Oh, no. Please...I don't want this,*" she said, voice bordering on panic.

"*It doesn't matter what you* want," Rivald said. "*What matters is what He wants.*"

"*I'll tell the police. I'll tell that Whittaker guy. He'll know what to do,*" she said.

Leyton butted in. "You can tell Whittaker—*after* you've brought me the clothing."

Rivald eddied around them in the darkness. Leyton knew what the being was doing. Gaining command of Jessica, making sure she understood exactly what was at stake if she refused his request. In his mind's eye, Leyton saw Jessica's mother then, her body broken and lifeless.

"*No!*" Jessica said. "*Don't hurt her. Please don't hurt her. I'll do what you ask. Whatever you say.*"

"*Good girl,*" Rivald said. "*Now, wake up and get Leyton some clothing. He has some place he has to be, and arriving there naked is not a good idea. Remember, Moore Street, then await my instructions."*

Leyton felt Rivald slip away, the coldness replaced with a fierce heat that must have been emanating from Jessica. Although helpless, she was angry—angry that she had no control over the rest of her life.

"It doesn't feel good, does it?"

"No."

"Now you'll begin to understand why I do the things I do."

"Yes," she said. *"Yes…"*

He opened his eyes and blinked, taking a moment to orientate himself. Switching the shower off, he stepped from the tub, scooped his clothes into a ball, and tucked the pouch beneath his armpit. He carried them downstairs—damn he was cold—and shoved the clothes into the fireplace in the living room. Finding a box of matches on the mantel, he lit the fabric and watched it burn for a few minutes. The flames mesmerised him, and he found himself reaching out to Barry.

The policeman's sigh sounded as though the man was relieved. *"Where the hell have you been? What the fuck were you playing at last night, giving me mixed messages? Showing me shit I didn't understand? I thought you'd stopped playing games now. Thought we'd come to some sort of arrangement where we help one another out?"*

"We did—we have," Leyton said. "I tried to show you what was happening without her knowing what I was doing."

"Her? Who the fuck is her?"

"Lorelei."

"What?"

"Lorelei."

"Oh, God. Did you kill a woman? Is that how it is now? You're killing women?"

"I kill whoever needs killing, Barry."

"But you showed me a man. You killed a man, right?"

"No, I killed a woman. A bitch. Lorelei killed the man. An innocent man."

"Oh, Jesus. What the hell is going on?"

"It's too much to explain in detail now. Lorelei tried to make me...she...she was bad, all right? So I killed her. Jessica...she'll be bringing me some clean clothes."

"Jessica? Fuck. Leave her out of it. Haven't you done enough to the poor girl?"

"She's one of us, Barry."

Silence hummed along with the crackle of the fire.

"So where are you?" Barry asked.

"I can't tell you that."

"Does Jessica know?"

"The street, yes, but Rivald will be with her. You'd do well not to interfere. Tag—"

"Yeah, yeah. I get it. Tag will get hurt." Barry sighed. *"You pair of motherfuckers. I hate you, d'you know that? Fucking hate you."*

"Yes, well, I'm not too fond of you either, but we're stuck with one another. You, me, and Jessica. Oh, and Tag, *if* he behaves himself."

"He will. Leave him out of it." Barry paused, then said, *"So what's going on? What's happening next?"*

"You'll be discovering the innocent man's body once I've left here, that's what's happening next. After that? Who the hell knows? Rivald said he has something for me to do, so I'm guessing Jessica will have her first try-out as bait. She'll lure a killer, I'll kill him or her, and you'll clean up the mess."

"*Fuck. I don't know how much longer me and Tag can keep doing this without arousing more suspicion.*"

"Find a way. There's always a way."

"*Right. Find a way. You say it as though it's easy.*"

"Isn't it?"

"*No, dealing with Internal Affairs isn't damn well easy.*"

"Nothing I can do about that, Barry. I'm just a link in the chain the same as you."

"*A damn link I don't want to be. Unlike you.*"

"Deal with it. Suck it up, you big baby."

Chapter Twenty-One

Jessica woke, immediately aware of the foreign surroundings. The apartment block she'd been taken to wasn't half bad, but what was the point of being here now? That dream — *no, it wasn't a fucking dream, it was real* — had made it quite clear that wherever she was, they'd find her.

She stared at the ceiling, at the streaks of sunlight illuminating the semi-darkness. Dust motes danced in the shafts. She glanced at the clock on the bed side cabinet, saw she'd slept through last night and most of today. Damn.

A safe house. Some fucking safe house, when they can contact me in my damn dreams.

She laughed, the sound brittle, bordering on hysteria. Tamping down the urge to laugh until she cried, she swung her legs out of bed and waited for the feeling of disorientation to pass. Their voices had come to her, out of a vast blackness that seeped into the movie that had been a normal dream. One where she and her mother were out shopping, cramming all manner of things into a cart overflowing with items she knew they couldn't afford.

She shook her head and padded over to the window. Flinging the drapes back, she expected…what *did* she expect? The horned bastard to be standing out there on the small patch of lawn that separated the apartment block from the road? A road where two policemen sat in an unmarked car to ensure she never went out alone?

"How the fuck am I going to get past them?" she muttered, turning from the window to grab her clothing from a chair in the corner. Sitting, she put on her socks, panties, and jeans, refusing to entertain the many questions that roiled inside her mind. She didn't have the energy to analyse this crap and knew from her time in the forest when she'd seen the fog that something weird was going on. And shit, she believed in all things unexplainable now. Ghosts, beings, whatever the hell they were, *did* exist. Just that your average person didn't see them.

"And, God, I wish I was average."

She stood, slipping her bra on and pulling her sweater over her head and down her body. Dressing just like any other day. As though she was *normal*, as though her whole life was now normal, whatever that was. She laughed again, then thought of what they'd told her to do. Where the hell was she going to get clothes from, let alone the right size for Leyton? She jammed her feet into her boots and shrugged on her coat, a plan forming in her mind. Pinching her cheeks to make them red, she left the bedroom and made for the front door. She took a deep breath and ran down several flights of stairs, bursting out into the daylight and heading for the police car.

An officer got out before she reached their vehicle, his hand held aloft as though that action would stop her from running.

"There's..." Jessica panted, bending over, hands on her knees. She glanced up. "There's someone in the apartment. He told me to get my coat on. That I had to go with him. I pushed him. He fell. He's—"

"Get in the car, lock it, and stay there," the officer said, rapping his knuckles on the driver's-side window. "I mean it—do *not* get out of that car until we return." He ran towards the apartment block, drawing his gun.

The other policeman got out and followed, the pair disappearing through the double glass doors. Jessica waited for a beat, long enough for them to have taken the first flight of stairs, then ran down the street. She glanced back every so often, convinced the policemen would catch on to what she had done and chase her down.

No, not yet. They wouldn't have reached the empty apartment yet.

At the corner, Jessica stopped, glancing left and right, trying to recall which way led to town. She took the right and kept running, her focus on finding a shop where she could get Leyton some clothes.

I don't have any money, so I'm going to have to steal them. Shit. How the hell did I get into this mess? When did I become a criminal? Why me?

"Go left at the end," a male voice said.

Jessica gasped and whipped her head around to look behind her. No one was there. Nothing but a street devoid of people, houses lining the road.

What the hell?

"It is I, Rivald."

Holy fuck...you!

Jessica turned left and continued running, her chest heaving, her lungs fit to burst.

"Slow down. And calm down. Everything will work as it should if you just do as I ask. There is a house here, on the right, with a package on the front step. There, you see it?"

Jessica's head was moved for her, and she shuddered at the intrusion of Rivald directing her body like that. What the shit kind of being was he? She saw the package and approached the house.

"No one is inside. They have gone out. Walk up the path – casually – *and pick up the package. Then walk back the way you have come."*

"But the police," she said, feeling insane speaking to someone she couldn't see.

"They will not pose a problem."

"Oh, no. What have you done?"

"Never you mind."

"Shit!"

Jessica strolled up the path, looking left and right in case someone watched her from inside one of the houses. And if they did? She was certain Rivald could deal with them. She wondered briefly whether he had infinite power, whether he ever got tired from exerting it, taking hold of people like this.

"That is not your concern," he snapped.

She picked up the soft package and went back down the path, retracing her steps.

"Now," Rivald said. *"When you reach the street of the safe house, keep walking."*

She did as instructed but peeked down at the safe house apartment block. Jessica squinted, making out two people sitting in the police car.

"They are quite safe," Rivald said. *"They have no recollection of you coming out and speaking to them."*

"What about when I go back?"

"Who said you're going back?"

Oh, God.

Tears stung her eyes, and she fought the urge to cry. If she thought about what she was actually doing, what she was involved in, she'd crumple right here on the ground and cry until her tears ran dry. But the threat to her mother… No, whether this was insane or not, whether the rational side of her argued that this kind of thing just didn't happen, she'd do as she was told.

"You are a Dreamer now," Rivald said. *"One of us. We have big plans for you."*

"Wonderful. Just fucking wonderful."

Anger replaced the tears, and Jessica strode on, legs rigid, one arm swinging beside her. Later, when she'd delivered the clothes and had gone wherever the horned fucker sent her, when she had some time to herself, she'd think about everything. Come to some form of acceptance. It was plain she had no choice, that she'd have to suck it up and follow instructions for the foreseeable future.

"For the rest of your life," Rivald confirmed. *"Now take a right."*

His shocking words registered, but she filed them away for later. She spied a sign ahead—Moore Street—and headed towards it, her stomach in knots. Her heart rate sped up, and she bit her lower lip as she turned into the road. She stopped and stared at the houses.

"Which one?"

"See the property at the end? Go there."

She dragged in a deep breath and walked towards the house. It was clear, even from this distance, that it needed renovating. As she neared it, she caught a glimpse of Leyton's van hiding behind some trees. She shuddered at the memory of being inside it. Of escaping from it. The smell of it.

"Walk across the grass and find the side door," Rivald said.

Jessica obeyed and knocked on the door, the thought of seeing Leyton again freaking her the fuck out. What was she doing here?

Keeping my mother safe. Helping a killer. That's what I'm doing.

She swallowed bile and waited, her stomach clenching tighter as a figure came towards the door, visible through the two patterned glass panes. She let out a ragged sigh and clutched the parcel to her chest. The door swung open, and Leyton ushered her inside, stepping back to allow her entrance. He closed the door, the click of it sending a chill up Jessica's spine. She stared ahead at a kitchen and made her way there. An open door allowed light to spill into the room. Where did it lead to?

The rustle of plastic told her Leyton was opening the package behind her, and she waited while he dressed. She didn't want to look at him again anyway— wouldn't ever if she had her way.

After a short time, he moved to stand beside her. "There's something you should see. Something that will prepare you for the future. You have a job to do, whenever Rivald calls you to do it, and the result of what you do will look like what is down here."

Leyton walked to the open door and beckoned for her to follow. She took in the fact that he wore a grey tracksuit now but studied him no further. She couldn't without shuddering, recalling...

Trailing him down some wooden steps, she dreaded to think what he was about to show her. An indescribable stench wafted up to greet her, and she knew then, without a doubt, what she would see in the basement.

It smelt of the last time she had seen Cal.

Oh, God. I miss him.

Even knowing what it was, it didn't prepare her for the shock. The place was so *red*, so *disturbing*. A man—*Oh, God, he's dead…oh, God, he's dead*—was attached to a wall rack, his body shaped like a star. His chin rested on his chest, longish hair hanging down like a sheet, and his belly had been cut open. It seemed everything inside him had fallen out, piled on the floor at his feet. Blood—there was so much of it. Too much for one body to hold. And then she saw the woman, her naked body a short distance from the man's insides, her stomach resembling his. She lay on her back, arms flung out beside her as though she merely slept, yet her eyes were wide and staring, completely black. Jessica frowned.

"Those black eyes…we all have them." Leyton shrugged. "But she was a bad Dreamer."

"And you're *not?*" Jessica blurted, backing away from the carnage, unable to move her gaze from it, and reaching blindly behind her for the newel post. She suppressed a gag. If she vomited now, she'd never stop.

"No, you mustn't vomit. It will contaminate the crime scene. Involve you in ways that you shouldn't be involved. Get Barry into trouble."

Although she hadn't wanted to, Jessica stared at Leyton. "What do you mean, get Barry into trouble?"

"He's a Dreamer, and if you are known to have been here too… Who knows, with you having been in the police station so recently, interviewed by him, his superiors might suspect something more is going on. We must not be linked together. Do you understand?"

Her hand came into contact with the newel post, and she quickly snatched it away. *Fingerprints...* She nodded, turning from him to busy herself with wiping the post with her sleeve where she'd touched it. To stop herself thinking about the bodies behind her. Had he killed them both? He must have done.

"No, I only killed her."

"*Only?*" she huffed out.

"Not all Dreamers are bad, Jessica. Only those like her."

She glanced back and found him staring at the dead woman. "But *you're* bad. You *kill* people, for fuck's sake!"

"I do, but only bad people. I have never killed anyone who didn't deserve it. And I had no choice. *Have* no choice. Just like you. It just so happens that I enjoy what I do."

Fear invaded Jessica, and she shook her head, thoughts racing. "Oh, no. No way. I'm not killing anyone. No damn way. You can forget it." *But my mom...*

"We do not want you to kill anyone, Jessica."

Relief winged through her. "Then what *do* you want me to do?"

"It's quite simple. You will bring the killers to me."

"What? How?" *This is damn well crazy.*

"Rivald will let you know what you must do. When he has been informed of a killer, he will no doubt send you to find him or her. We know how men are. How predatory men are. They love a pretty face. Suckers for them. And you're so pretty... They won't be able to resist you."

"What? You want me to speak to these crazy bastards?"

Leyton smiled. "Oh, it's a little more than speaking to them. You must go with them."

"Go *with* them? Are you insane?" She paused then added, "No, don't answer that. You are. You're fucking nuts. Oh, God, what the hell am I going to do? I don't want to be here, don't want this crap. I just want to go home."

He chuckled. "We will be with you all the way. Know where you are at all times. And once you're where we need you to be, I will come and…take care of things."

The image of what was behind her loomed up in her mind, bright and vivid. The man. The woman. Their insides. The blood.

"I'll be classed as an accomplice. And if I'm still there once you arrive, when you do what you do…"

"Oh, no. You'll be gone by then. Off home. Back to your *mother*."

"Right." She knew why he'd stressed the word—his way of making sure she knew what the stakes were. Spinning around, a rush of nausea taking hold, she ran up the stairs, away from that *mess* and *him*. At the top, she took a few seconds to catch her breath and still her rambling thoughts.

I'm going to be in danger every time I do as this Rivald asks. Relying on Leyton to get there in time. What if he doesn't? What if he —

"He will," said a man.

She snapped her head around. The horned bastard stood in the doorway between the kitchen and a living room beyond. Her pulse quickened, and God…it felt like her heart was going to burst, it thumped so hard and fast. She bit back a scream and clamped her hand over her mouth. This was all too much. The bodies, seeing Leyton again, and now *him*.

"I have seen the future, know what it holds." Rivald stepped towards her. "You will always be safe."

"Get away from me."

He continued advancing.

"I *said*, get away from me!"

"Or what, Jessica? What will you do if I do not obey?"

"I'll...I'll—"

"You will do nothing. Now stop being so childish. There is something I want you to do."

She lost the ability to breathe. Her head spun, and she looked about wildly for something to hold onto before she fainted. The room tilted, and she fought to inhale.

"Fingerprints," he said. "You may hold on to me."

Despite being revolted at the thought, she reached out and gripped his forearm. Closing her eyes, she at last managed to take in a deep breath and concentrated on being calm.

Later. Think about everything later. For now, do as he asks. Just get through the day minute by minute.

"Good girl," Rivald said. "Now, keep your eyes closed and listen to me. There is a man I wish for you to meet tonight—your first job, how about that, hmm?—but first I want you to go and have lunch with a mutual friend. He is currently eating with two colleagues. I will direct you there once you leave this house. You will have enough time to fill your belly and tell our friend everything you have learned, and then I'm afraid he will have to leave you and come here."

Jessica opened her eyes and looked at Rivald, taking him in properly for the first time. He was surprisingly good-looking, in a demon kind of way, a typical tall, dark and handsome man...albeit with horns jutting out of his head and feet like a goat. Was he some ancient being, or had he only recently become...what? What was he?

"It is best you do not know," he said, his dark eyes growing darker until they turned black and the whites disappeared. "Ah..." Something dark and contorting passed over his features, flitting away almost before Jessica could register it. "Time is pressing upon us, urging us onward. You really do need to be going. You have an hour to spare before our friend needs to be here. Go."

Unsteady on her feet, Jessica stumbled from the house and rushed across the ratty lawn. The pavement jarred beneath her feet compared to the soft grass, and she barrelled out of the street, seemingly directed by an unseen force. Her mind was blank, no thoughts swirling there until she reached the place where the detectives were eating lunch. She saw them through the window, deep in conversation, forks pausing mid-air as they hashed out whatever the hell they were hashing out.

"Go inside and tell Barry that he must change his plans." Was Rivald's voice in her head thinner than before, or was that just the contrast with how it had sounded rich and too enticing in person? *"He has no need to make contact with me. He must be made aware that he deals only with Leyton. If he does not... Remind him of how much he loves Tag."* He was gone in a whiff of dark, shadowy thought.

Frowning, Jessica repeated Rivald's information in her head and pushed open the door. She stepped inside, the scent of different meals assailing her and making her stomach growl. Hunger propelled her towards Barry's table, and she weaved between the tables, catching his attention with a wave of her hand.

His eyes widened a second before he stood and dropped his fork to his plate. "What the hell...?"

She reached his table and stood beside it, looking down at their half-empty plates.

"What the fuck are *you* doing here?" Barry asked, placing a hand on her shoulder and pushing her down into the seat beside his. "How did you get out of the apartment? How did you know we were here?"

"Leyton, he..." Her stomach growled again. If she didn't eat soon, she'd pass out. "Could I please have something to eat?"

Chapter Twenty-Two

Barry waved their waiter over and he took Jessica's order of a BLT and fries and a glass of water, which she guzzled as soon as it arrived.

"All right," Tag muttered, lips pursing, turning down at the corners as he watched her set her glass down.

She turned to look at him, face pale, latent fear in her eyes. It ripped at Barry's gut to see that expression and know, intimately, how it felt. How it never went away completely. He reached and found Tag's hand under the table, squeezed his fingers tight.

"Tell us what happened, Jessica," he said, gently as he could, also knowing he couldn't spare her. If anything any of them was going to go through was to make a damn bit of difference, none of them could be spared the difficult feelings. They'd just have to get used to it.

She told her story, a little haltingly at first, but gradually her voice dulled, the emotion leaching out until she sounded grey, flat. She paused only to accept the food that was set before her and occasionally to take a bite.

"So we're too late," Tag said as she wound down. Anger slammed the words onto the table between them.

Jessica's chin trembled.

"We were never going to find him, Tag," Barry said quietly, not looking at his lover.

"You knew that when you woke up, didn't you?"

Barry didn't say anything, not wanting to confirm in his own mind that he had known the guy was going to die no matter what they did. If he stopped hoping now, when he knew he was never going to escape the dreams, he might as well be killing them himself.

"This is too much," Jessica whispered. "Too..."

Ross was the one who finally answered her. "As horrible as it is, what it would be without us is worse. They'd die and no one would know. No one would be able to save that bit of them that Barry holds inside because he was there. He's special, and those little bits of innocent people he keeps with him are what makes it worth it."

Barry stared at his partner, shocked to silence at his insight.

"But you didn't *see*," Jessica protested, her small fist thumping on the table. "The blood and the...the..." She splayed her other hand wide, waved it in the air, as ineffectual at conveying her horror as her words.

Ross touched her shoulder, then her wrist, his fingers light and reassuring. "But you did," he told her, as if his confirmation was some sort of validation for her.

Maybe it was, because she looked up, met his eye, and it appeared some of the confusion diminished.

"You know what you saw was just a body." He smiled slightly. "Just a shell. That man —"

"Jack," she said

"His name was Jack," Barry spoke almost at the same time.

Her brow tightened. A shadow flitted through her eyes and was gone again. She gasped like she'd been holding her breath, and her gaze met Barry's. "Do you ever get used to it? To someone in your head, directing you?"

He just shook his head. No point lying to her about it. "But you won't have to. This horned man, Rivald. I'm going to have a chat with him. Make him leave you alone. Somehow."

"Don't!" She almost sprang from her chair, and Ross' hand on her wrist flattened out, keeping her seated. "Don't try to contact him."

"You don't need to be mixed up in this," Barry insisted.

Jessica's gaze flitted, for the barest instant, to Tag. "I can take care of myself. Just don't try and talk to Rivald, please."

Barry glanced at Tag, too, half expecting to see fog curling around his throat. He swallowed convulsively. "Why? What did he tell you?"

"Just...he said to remind you how you love Tag. And to keep your communication to Leyton."

"Leyton doesn't *know* anything!" Barry brought his fist down on the table, making the plates and silverware dance.

"Barry." Tag touched his hand. "Calm down."

Barry snarled, fury pulling him tight as a bowstring. "They're *playing* with us, Tag!" he spoke through clenched teeth. "Dictating. Not giving us any choices. It isn't *fair!*"

"How does that saying go?" Ross asked mildly. "Life is shit and then you die?"

"You don't know fuck all," Barry shot back, glaring at his partner. "You're just along for the fucking ride and the cold coffee, so keep your smartass fucking comments to yourself." Furious, Barry got up, his chair slamming back against the wall, and left the restaurant.

"You're not mad at Ross," Tag said a few minutes later, having followed him out. "Don't take it out on him. That's what isn't fair."

"Don't, Tag. Don't fucking tell me how to handle this."

"We can't afford to alienate him."

Barry bit back another curse. He knew Tag was right on both counts. He wasn't mad at Ross, and they did need him. He shook his head. "If he could just…"

Tag turned Barry around to face him. "Just what?"

"Freak out. Act normal, like this whole mess is as fucked up as it is. Just once, he should be…freaked out. Not act like it's another day at the office. This isn't the fucking *X-Files*."

"Isn't it?"

Barry snorted. "You know how that ended. Internal Affairs buried their asses in the alien desert, or some stupid thing."

"You let me worry about IA."

"So it is an issue."

"Not for you. Come back inside and finish your coffee. That girl needs you to show her she can get through this. Be as mad as you want at Ross or Leyton or Rivald or whoever the fuck, but in front of her, be calm. She needs that."

"It isn't right, Tag. She doesn't deserve—"

"And neither do you. But there it is and we have to deal. Come on." Tag took hold of his arm and led him back inside.

Barry took comfort in his lead, in the firm hold and the direction. If the dreams were precarious, frightening puzzles, Tag's love and support was not. He clung to that.

Back inside, he managed to meet Ross' eye and mumble an apology.

Ross waved it off. "Nah. I get it. I am on the outside looking in, but you need that, too. Perspective."

"Well, I don't need to be reminded my life is shit, thank you very much."

Silence fell around the table.

Barry bit his lip. "Tag, I didn't mean—"

"I know." This time, Tag found his hand under the table and squeezed.

"So what now?" Ross asked. "Is there a point to the safe house anymore?"

"I want to go home," Jessica said. "I want to go home. I want to see my mom." Her fist rested on the edge of the table beside her plate. The fries still sat, untouched.

Ross reached over, took one and popped it into his mouth. "Best you return to the safe house for now. Too many questions from higher-ups if we allow you to go home before we catch your second abductor. Yeah, we know he won't be caught, and eventually you'll be allowed home anyway, but keeping up the pretence is best at the moment."

A tiny sob escaped Jessica, and she slumped.

"What?" Ross touched her hand as he had before, and she shook even more.

"I hate fries now. I used to order them for Cal."

Barry could hear the tears under her voice and from the concerned look on Ross' face, so could he.

"I'm sorry," he said, as though it made a difference.

"Not your fault. He knew his job was dangerous. He knew..." She shuddered. "Anything could happen, and there, it did, didn't it? Now maybe... They want to use me as bait, you know. To draw out these men so Leyton can get at them. He's supposed to keep me safe. They're using me to keep him in line just like they're using Tag and my mom."

Jessica drew in a deep breath and managed a wan smile. "Every girl, you know? She wants a knight in shining armour. I get gay cops and a freak of nature with unnatural dentures."

"Hey, now." Ross rubbed her arm and smiled at her. "Don't count me out. Even with my unhealthy obsession with the paranormal, next to all that"—he waved a hand in Barry's direction—"I'm practically normal." He patted his huge barrel chest and grinned. "Though I doubt they make armour in my size."

Jessica actually giggled, and Barry found himself smiling. When he looked over, Tag was at least not frowning, and finally, it was easy to see how Ross fit into the sorry mess. Perspective was a good thing. Barry couldn't help feel a pang of sympathy for Leyton, so far outside the normal workings of everything, and further, now that he knew he could never have what he most wanted. So much about it all was not fair, and Barry had a sudden recollection of the most terrifying dreams, the ones that centred around a small boy. He always knew when they couldn't be saved and it killed him just a little to know that that was one victim he'd never be able to save. It was far too late for that boy. The Dreaming was all that kid had left, and how much did that suck?

Swallowing down the last of his coffee, he brought their attention back to the immediate issue. "We're gonna get a call soon, I expect." He eyed his partner, watched the way Ross was gazing at Jessica and sighed. "Cap." He leaned over and smacked a kiss over Tag's lips. "Better get back to the office. Ross and I will take her to the safe house."

Tag stared at him, dumbfounded. Barry didn't blame the man. So much of their past relationship had been spent in hiding. Barry didn't care anymore. If Tag was here for him, then he could be out about it. Or all the lip service in the world wouldn't make a difference.

After a protracted moment, Tag reciprocated, grabbing the back of Barry's head, twining his fingers in his hair and pulling him into a searing kiss that coiled a warm, anticipatory glow in his gut, and left him breathless.

"Don't do anything stupid," Tag warned.

"Course not." Barry remained slightly off-kilter as Tag got up and tossed a few bills onto the table. The captain left the restaurant smiling, got into the replacement car that the department had finally given him, and drove off as Ross settled the bill, a huge smirk on his face.

"You can wipe that look off your face any time," Barry growled.

Ross just laughed. "If you could see your face. That man fucking owns you."

Barry opened his mouth to make a scathing retort but closed it again. He met Ross' eyes over the top of their cruiser and shrugged. "Better him than a freaky horned dude, right?"

It was good to hear Ross laugh. The big man might not be as embroiled in the nightmare as the rest of them, but that was probably a good thing. They needed to hear laughter once in a while, needed to know the world still turned outside their little circle of horror.

* * * *

The call came over the radio just after Ross returned from securing Jessica inside the apartment and giving the officers outside some cock and bull story about him taking her out earlier for police business. He felt bad for letting them think they'd missed seeing him leave with her, but needs must. "She's strong, that one," he said as he folded himself back behind the wheel.

The radio crackled to life as he started the car, the dispatcher's bored voice spouting the call sign and address. Barry responded, unsurprised that they were the closest vehicle to the crime scene. Nothing much about the so-called coincidences shocked him anymore. He might have taken time to wonder how things always seemed to work out that way, but he suspected the answer was too far-reaching to be a comfortable one.

"Fun times," Ross said, throwing the car into gear and wheeling them out into traffic.

"Aren't you worried?" Barry asked as he watched Jessica's building disappear in the rear-view.

"About what?"

"This…thing. Horned man, mist, whatever you want to call it. Rivald. It almost killed Tag. It's threatening everyone. And you just jump in with both feet like it isn't the most fucked-up thing ever."

Ross glanced at him. "Sure. It's weird and scary shit. But it isn't the most fucked-up thing ever. Have you listened to the news lately? Or looked at the cold case files? Something has to change, Barry. Maybe this is it. Maybe the only way for now is to frighten people into taking notice. Maybe once they're convinced we'll do this thing because it needs doing, they'll stop threatening everything we love. In the meantime, we do it, and I, for one, am not going to stop looking for the good and the strength and the joy that might be there. That's no way to live."

"You're just a fucking Guru, aren't you?"

Ross grinned. "You ever think that there's a light and a dark side to everything?"

"And you're the light?"

"I know." Ross' grin didn't diminish. "A thankless job, but someone's gotta do it."

"If I wasn't sure you were crazy before, I am now."

Ross just continued to grin.

The house at the end of Moore Street was a dilapidated little wreck of a place. Still thinking about Ross' comment—*light and dark side to everything*—he suddenly had a vision of the tiny house, whitewashed and tidied, with a picket fence and a flower garden. He stopped, standing just inside the open door of the cruiser and gazed about. His attention caught on the 'For Sale' sign leaning haphazardly in the yard. How crazy and sick did it make him to even contemplate living in this house, knowing what had happened here?

But what if Ross was right? The dark had touched it. What would happen if no one brought back the light?

He felt eyes on him and looked up to see Ross watching him.

"Now you're getting it." Ross nodded at him. "Ready? This is going to be one crapfest of ugly."

Barry nodded, pulled out his notepad and wrote down the real estate agent's name and number.

Amusement tinged Ross' eyes as he led the way inside.

"We'll have to contact her," Barry reminded him. "Find out whatever there is to know about the place. Who owns it, why they're selling."

"Of course."

"Shut it," Barry grumped. But he felt lighter than he had in quite a while.

They weren't the first to arrive on the scene. A patrol officer claimed he'd seen a curtain moving inside and a van parked around the corner—on the edge of the street, but tucked behind bushes in a way that made it look like someone had purposely tried to make it inconspicuous. He'd gone ahead to investigate the action around the house he knew was supposed to be empty, found the bodies, and by the time he'd done retching and reached his radio to call it in, the van had gone.

"Well done," Barry muttered, not entirely sure if he was addressing the pale-faced officer or the invisible crew in his head.

"Now, now," Ross said under his breath, trying but failing to keep the smirk from his face.

They entered the building through the side door, which opened directly into the kitchen. A flash of gore, blood, bodies, complete human destruction, flashed through Barry's head, and he groaned.

"Fuck." He had to stop, hold his head as a dizzy spell swayed him on his feet. He grabbed for the back of a chair and encountered Ross' arm instead.

"Steady. You all right?"

"The stench..." Barry started to say, realised they were alone and he didn't need to make excuses, and shook his head. "They're showing me shit." He shook his head, as though that might dislodge the gruesome images. "Leave me the fuck alone," he addressed the air. "I'll see with my own eyes in a minute."

The visions faded slowly, leaving a dull, red ache in his head, lodged just behind his eyes. He glanced up.

Ross gave him a curt shake of his head. "Your eyes," he whispered, sharp, shocked. He pushed Barry's head back down, as though administering a remedy for fainting. "Head down. Let it pass."

Barry blinked, lowered his head as the beat cop entered behind them.

"Go wait out front for the coroner," Ross snapped at him. "Before you puke on the crime scene."

The cop didn't hesitate to get the hell out, obviously not wanting to have to view the bodies a second time. As soon as he was gone, Ross lifted Barry's chin and peered into his eyes.

"Okay." He gave himself a little shake. "Now that was...disconcerting."

"What?"

"Your eyes." He shivered again, and Barry took a perverse thrill in finally seeing him rattled. "They had hardly any white. Your irises were black, black...weird."

"Like this whole fucking set-up isn't weird as fuck." Barry straightened up, ignoring the residual spin of the room and addressed the invisible. "Leave me alone to do my goddamn job. You keep interfering and you're going to get me sent to the loonie bin. No help to you in there, am I?" He shook Ross' support off. "Wish they'd just back the fuck off."

"Just trying to help, Barry," came a murmur in his head.

"Well fucking don't."

"*This is not your everyday crime scene*," the voice persisted.

"And I'm not your everyday cop. Let me do this my way." He clamped his mind closed to outside interference, or imagined he did and hoped to hell it would work, and he examined each detail as they made their way to the top of the basement stairs.

If Leyton had been in the room, there was no sign of him. The floor was covered in dust, disturbed by footprints, but there was no way to know whose. At least three people had wandered through here. Two of them were dead, and the other was the cop now standing guard safely out in the front yard. Only Barry and Ross knew Leyton and Jessica had ever set foot in the house. The most important thing to ensure was that there was no sign or hint that either of them, especially Jessica, had ever been there.

Barry glanced over at his partner and received a curt nod, as though Ross knew precisely what he was thinking.

"She can't be connected," Barry said.

Ross nodded again. "I know."

Together, the partners followed the disturbed dust trail to the door at the top of the stairs and down, slipping on latex gloves along the way.

The disembodied voice was right about the scene. Not your everyday murder.

"Jesus fuck," Barry muttered. Even knowing what he was going to see, first from Jessica's description, then through the vision, he faltered. "Jesus *fuck!*" He felt the blood drain into his soles and was glad he'd remembered to don gloves before entering the house as he needed the support of the handrail to keep his balance.

"This is some fucked-up shit," Ross whispered.

Barry studied the body on the wall. He didn't much care about the dead bitch. She'd got what she deserved, and although it disturbed Barry that thought came so easily—so certain and irrevocable—he didn't wish he hadn't thought it. He could see the lines of sliced skin where she'd played. Each memory from his dream had a corresponding mark on the man. His feet, his arms, lines down his thighs, where she'd sliced just the skin then peeled it away to hang in ribbons at his knees.

Barry made his way down the stairs to stand as close as he could get without stepping in the mess. He needed to see the guy's face. He needed to see the humanity—even the death mask of fear and pain was something human and real he could remember. She hadn't touched his face. Somehow, he knew it was because she'd wanted to see every tear, every expression of loathing, pain, and terror as it distorted his perfect features.

"Where's the light now?" he asked.

Ross' hand fell onto his shoulder. His partner's voice was strained but determined. "You tell me. If you were here when she did this to him, why? Why let you see it but not stop it?"

"If I knew that..." Barry shook his head.

"If it was you, Wiki, wouldn't you want to know you weren't alone? Look at him."

Barry did, taking in the wide brown eyes, tangled hair, clenched teeth still set into the contortions of pain.

"Look in his eyes."

"You're a sick fuck."

"Just look. Really look." Ross stepped back. "I've seen dead people look a whole lot more frightened than that, Barry. Maybe, somehow, he did know.

Maybe we don't fear death so much as we fear facing it alone." He moved to the other body and gazed down. "Now that." He pointed. "That's fear."

Finally, Barry forced himself to look away from the poor man on the wall and down at his killer. Her face was twisted in hate and utter terror. He had to wonder what she saw at the last, what it was that gnawed into her soul and ripped it out through her eyes and left her with nothing but that devastating fear in her expression.

"Maybe she saw herself..."

This time, Barry didn't shush the voice that whispered through him. He couldn't think of a single argument for the sentiment.

Chapter Twenty-Three

Tag sorted through the mail and phone messages on his desk, then flipped through his emails. He skimmed the reports. It hadn't taken Riggs and Cornwall long to follow the licence plate to the car and the car to the abandoned caravan. He wasn't very optimistic the investigation of either would lead to Leyton, though he wished it would. Give him an excuse to haul the creep in and deal with him on his own terms. The report was only going to be filled, eventually, with confirmation of what he and Barry and Ross already knew.

Nothing held his attention like the empty desks on the other side of his window anyway. He knew there was nothing for him to do for the partners but get his own job done the best he could. Keeping the brass off all their backs was the very best thing for them all. It didn't stop him wanting to be out there at Barry's side making sure his lover was safe. He trusted Ross — had handpicked him to keep Barry out of trouble — but he was still a substitute.

"Get a grip, Taggart," he griped.

Barry was a seasoned police officer, a grown man. He could look after himself.

Irritated with himself for worrying, for not being able to stop the worry, he slumped into his desk and pushed aside the paperwork in favour of the phone messages. He balled up the three from John Williams, his immediate superior, and tossed them in the trashcan. The man could damn well come down here and talk to him face to face.

Unable to concentrate on anything but the fact his lover was out investigating yet another case they weren't going to be able to solve without having to give explanations, Tag pulled out all the files related to it and began spreading them out, combing through them for anything and everything that linked them. Those were the leads they should be tracking down most rigorously, and he had to make sure none of them led anywhere close to Barry, Jessica, or fucking Leyton. He didn't like the idea of protecting the freak, but he had no choice.

If he didn't give a rat's ass what happened to himself, Barry did. Barry needed him. That much was made obvious today when he flew off the handle at Ross, when he reached for Tag's hand under the table. Tag had to stay on the sheep-man's good side whether he liked it or not.

Two hours spent bent over the files and scarfing down bad coffee left him with nothing but a headache and heartburn. A glance showed him Barry and Ross weren't back yet, but that wasn't really a surprise. One of his officers came in to tell him about the call to the house on Moore Street and to inform him Wiki and Ross had taken it. He nodded and waved the man out, barely lifting his head.

"Sir?"

Tag grunted, shuffling papers and trying not to lose his train of thought.

"You want something to eat, sir? Couple of us are putting in orders..."

"No."

Tag let out an exasperated sigh, clenched a fist around a month-old report, and the man left without another word. He had to go back three steps and start over, trying to trace the near invisible line of reasoning that he thought he saw threading through the cases.

He dropped his reading glasses onto the pile of gruesome pictures in front of him and pinched the bridge of his nose between thumb and forefinger, feeling the sharp tang of pain through the dull ache and knowing if he didn't stop playing with it, it would never heal. This was like playing a game of Six Degrees, only the links he was trying to find were as elusive as smoke.

Closing his eyes, he leant back in his chair and groaned. He was tired. The last few nights fucking Barry, watching him sleep, waking with every sound the man made, had left him exhausted. He drifted off in his chair. Something tugged at his memory, prodding at him to wake up. The nightmare feeling of not being able to breathe jolted him fully awake. His chair rocked, nearly toppling him over backwards, and for a revolting second it was exactly like he was back in that car careening over the embankment, helpless. A dark fog receded from the edges of his vision, and he rubbed at his eyes.

"Fuck me," he muttered, pushing the memory away and picking up his glasses again.

That same memory assaulted him every now and again since the accident, and he never knew when it was going to strike. If it was even a small taste of what

Barry was going through, it was enough to prompt Tag to work out how to anticipate their horned man's moves and try to get a step ahead. He just had to figure out how they chose their targets, and that meant studying the files until he found the connections.

Maybe, if they got to the perps before the bastards found their next victims, he could spare Barry some of the worst of the nightmares. Maybe they could both get a decent night's sleep once in a while, or make love when it wasn't a desperate attempt to push away the fog and the darkness. It might even get the fucking brass off their backs if they managed to bring in a few convictions instead of just more dead bodies.

Even as he had the thought, his cell phone rang. He fished it out of his pocket and flipped it open. "What?"

"Williams is on his way down." The voice sounded whispery, secretive, and Tag glanced out the window of his office. A half dozen of his men were on the phone out there. None of them were looking in his direction.

He got up from his desk, stalked across to poke his fingers through the blinds and get a better view. "Who is this?"

The phone went dead. Confused, he glanced at it, but the caller ID was 'unknown'.

"What the fuck?"

Outside his office, the elevator lights flashed, indicating the lift was coming down and stopping on his floor.

"Shit."

He knocked on the glass, and Jacob looked up from his computer screen. Tag tugged at his earlobe, and Jacob nodded, turning back to his monitor and keyboard. Tag left him to it, knowing the man knew what that signal meant.

Hurriedly, he gathered up the files he had been going over and stashed them in his desk drawer. No need to advertise he was looking into cases more than a year old, cases he and Barry hadn't been able to solve. He knew now they had been Leyton's kills, but he couldn't say so, couldn't bring the guy in. Couldn't do a damn thing about it except find a way to keep IA noses out of those cases and prevent the whole mess ever happening again.

He was sitting placidly behind his desk, going over the most recent cases, when John Williams knocked on his door and strolled into his space.

"David." He nodded a greeting and took a seat across form Tag at his desk. "We have to talk."

"We have talked, John." Tag didn't look up from the notes he was reading, although the words meant nothing to him as his mind raced to figure out what the man wanted this time.

"About Barry Whittaker."

Tag still didn't bother to look up. Blood pounded hard in his head, and he had to fight from curling his fingers into fists but he managed an outward veneer of calm. "Unless you have something new to say" — he silently congratulated himself on the calm tone of his voice — "I don't see that we have anything to talk about." He picked up a pen and made a note in the margin of the page he was reading.

"You want me to keep IA off his back, don't you?"

"No one has any reason to investigate any of my men," Tag said, still calm, although inside he was seething.

"The growing list of dead suspects on his case file is reason enough, Tag, and you know it."

Tag looked up finally, the use of the nickname, more than anything else, catching his attention. The man across from him was ageing, with grey hair ringing the bald dome of his head and a paunch expanding the space between him and the desk. Tag wondered if he looked as old, after their nearly twenty-year acquaintance, as Williams. He hoped not. The man had bags under his faded brown eyes and jowls hanging over his collar, making it look like his tie was tied too tight. Tag recalled years ago when John had been fit—handsome, even. They'd had a decent working relationship until rumours had outed Tag in whispers around the coffee pot and John had got scared their closer-than-working relationship might come to light. That had been years and years ago. Sometimes, it seemed like a different lifetime and that the John Williams he knew now was a different person.

Until very recently, the rumours had stayed just that. Until very recently, no one in the upper echelon of the department had bothered with Tag's or Barry's arrest or conviction rates. But then, John hadn't been in IA's pocket until recently either.

"That list," Tag said, folding his hands in front of himself and lacing his fingers together, "has been on his file a long time. No one seemed to care until you figured out we're fucking."

John's face flushed a deep, angry red. "It has nothing to do with—"

"Doesn't it?" Tag went back to his reading, bowing his head to hide his own burning desire to deck the guy. He hadn't made captain by losing his temper or showing his true feelings for most of the people above him on the food chain. He wouldn't keep his position if he started flying off now, however much he might want to.

"I'm worried about him, Tag."

Not half as much as I am. Tag kept the thought to himself. He knew perfectly well where John Williams's worry stemmed from.

"Tag, you and I, we go back some." John sat back in his chair, flipping the front of his suit jacket as if it might hide the bulge of his stomach. "I'd hate to see you get tangled up in something."

"Like what?"

"Bad cops don't always start out that way, Tag." He said it gently, like he was breaking the news of a death to a loved one.

It was all Tag could do not to snap the pen between his fingers in half. Still, he kept his voice calm. Mostly. "Barry is *not* a bad cop."

"You ever think maybe he's letting stress over his...personal life get to him on the job? Maybe his...issues...are affecting his judgement."

"Issues?"

"I think maybe there is a conflict of interest, here, David. I'm not sure you can be objective where Barry Whittaker is concerned. The fact of the matter is, his sexual orientation is cause enough for concern if it's affecting his ability to get along with the other men or driving him to make poor personal choices that could affect his performance on duty."

That was all Tag needed to hear. He reached over and turned his laptop around. "You see this?" he asked, pointing to a tiny icon along the top edge. "Know what that is?"

John frowned.

"Danielle, Jacob, do you mind coming in here for one minute, please?" he asked. He glanced meaningfully at the window looking out into the rest of the room. Every head on the other side of the glass had turned to stare at them through the open blinds.

Two detectives stood from their desks and headed over to Tag's office door.

"What is going on?" John asked.

"This," Tag pointed to the little icon again, "is a microphone. Easy to link it to all the machines out there." He pointed out into the main room at all the computers on the desks and smiled grimly. "Computer networks. Beautiful things, if you know how to use them."

John frowned at the array of faces turned towards him. No one was smiling.

"David…"

"The thing about building a good case for harassment, John, is proof. Witnesses. Fifty officers just heard you say the only reason IA is the least bit interested in Barry Whittaker's record is because he's gay." Tag set down his pen, took off his reading glasses, and once again leaned over his desk to glare at the man. "How many of them do you think are going to give a statement that he failed to get their backs because he's a homo?"

John clamped his lips shut, refusing to say another word.

Tag grinned at him, punched a few keys on his computer, and leaned a little further across the desk. "Don't fuck with me, John. I was always better at this than you were."

"I am your superior officer," he sputtered.

"But not, I think, the superior man. Don't think for a moment that because you don't *see* my ambition or determination that they aren't there."

"How long did it take you to make captain?" John snarled. "I've been there and done that, Tag."

"Yes. So go out there and ask those men and women your questions. See how many of them remember when you were their captain." He smiled again, going for a not-so-nice expression.

"How many of them are so squeaky clean they can afford to block me?"

"John, I don't care who's in whose pocket or how deep. There is no chance the higher-ups are going to let you tear apart the best precinct in the district for some fucking vendetta."

"You think that's what this is?"

"I think there might be a certain amount of resentment, yes." He stood, crossed his arms over his chest. "Barry didn't take anything away from you, John. We were done the moment you decided to lie to your wife. Barry had nothing to do with that."

"Fuck you," John snarled.

Tag shook his head. "Not anymore. Right now, I kind of wish you never had."

Williams didn't have a chance to find an answer to that. The door opened, and Jacob stuck his head in. "You called, Cap?"

"I did. Would the two of you please assist Mr Williams with any questioning he has for the men? He's interested in getting to know a little more about Wiki and the cases he's been working on. I expect, of course, everyone will be on their best behaviour and answer any and all questions Mr Williams might have. Truthfully, of course." He picked up his glasses, unfolded them, and moved back to his own side of his desk. He took his seat and went back to his paperwork.

"Sure, Cap." Jacob opened the door fully and held it open for Williams. "This way, sir."

"I don't need this crap," Williams said.

Tag said nothing.

"There will be questions, Taggart. You can bet your badge, and your boyfriend's, on it."

"I'm sure." Tag peered at Williams over the tops of his glasses. "Ask away. You'll find Barry and I have nothing to hide."

Williams stormed out and Jacob followed, close on his heels.

Danielle poked her head into Tag's office. "You need anything, Cap?"

"No, thanks." He didn't look up from his work for her either. She knew him well enough, he hoped, to know it was nothing but the need to be alone with his fury for the time being. After a slight hesitation, the door closed quietly and he was alone.

About ten minutes was all he got. A hubbub rose outside, and he looked up to find Barry and Ross had returned. Other officers babbled at them like a bunch of magpies.

Tag rose from his desk, hurried to the door, but by the way Barry had gone pale, his eyes wide, he judged it too late to warn him the entire office was officially in the know about them now.

Nothing to hide, he had told Williams. It was the only way. He'd have to make an appointment with the department shrink for them, put the relationship on record and spend the foreseeable future proving he could be Barry's boss and do it effectively.

Rather than hide, or call them in to his office, he wandered out to their desk. "How did it go?"

Barry glared at him. "We found him. *Dead.* It seemed to go better there than here."

Tag ran a hand over the back of his neck and sighed. "Look. I did what I had to. IA is off our backs. Williams won't pursue it now no matter what his mucky-mucks try and talk him into."

"What did you do exactly?"

Tag let out another sigh. "I outted us."

"Tag—"

"I had to." He held up both hands in front of himself. "And this isn't the time or place to fight about it. We'll jump through all their hoops and it will be fine. What did you find out at the crime scene?"

Barry continued to glare silently at him.

Ross pulled out his note pad and flipped through. "The guy's ID said his name was Jack Yemen. We've got people tracking down next of kin now. Death by exsanguination."

Tag frowned.

"Drained of blood via gutting," Barry supplied sourly. He turned and flipped on his computer. "She did it because it was fun," he said. "No other reason."

"That why Leyton killed her?" Tag asked quietly. "Why not just lead us to her?"

Barry shook his head sharply. He wrote something on a pad on his desk. *He likes it.*

"It was gruesome," Ross admitted as he plopped into his chair. "We should do drinks after shift ends, yeah?" He made eye contact with both of them, and Tag kicked himself for his indiscretion.

"Yeah." He patted Barry on the shoulder, decided there was no point in dissembling, and leant down to give him a peck. Other couples did it. Danielle was certainly fucking the desk sergeant downstairs, and she didn't hold back the affection. "Let me know what you find out about the woman."

Barry just grunted at him.

"Fuckers gave us precious little to work with," Ross told him. "Let's just hope her prints pop or the coroner finds something we can use to identify her."

Barry nodded. "Something about her is off," Barry mused. "I don't know what, but something."

"What do you mean?" Tag asked.

Barry glowered. "I don't know. A round of drinks says she's not in the system. She's smoke."

All three of them exchanged looks at his choice of words. It didn't give Tag much hope for closing up the investigation any time soon. He'd got Williams off their backs, but who was to say IA wouldn't find another pawn to push in his way?

He gazed at the back of Barry's bowed head. Maybe it was time to think of alternate career paths for them both. There were ways to investigate crimes that didn't involve being on the force. He'd managed to fast-track his way to captain when it meant protecting Barry. Ross was plenty smart enough to do the same, and they could still fulfil their obligation to Rivald if Ross was on the inside picking up after them. It was worth considering.

For the first time in a long time, Tag saw a way out that let everyone get what they wanted and stay sane. It was a bit of light at the end of a tunnel he had almost begun to believe would never end.

Chapter Twenty-Four

Jessica woke on top of the covers in the safe house. She was amazed she'd been able to sleep all afternoon after tossing and turning, the events of the day swirling through her mind. God, she'd been dragged into something hideous, no doubt about that. What the fuck choice did she have, though, but to comply with their wishes?

She sat up, head fuzzy. Darkness had come while she'd slept, and moonlight shone through the window, bathing the room in an ethereal glow. Everything had a yellow tinge and looked creepy as hell. She shivered and rubbed her arms, the goosebumps there making her skin taut. Her mother came to mind, and the urge to call her grew fierce.

"No, you must not contact her yet," Rivald said, his voice booming from wherever the hell he was—in her head, in the room, she didn't know. *"Once you prove yourself tonight, you can ask Barry and Tag to allow you back home. By then, you will all have shown you can work together. That you understand you are a team. Then you may go home."*

Jessica narrowed her eyes, glancing straight ahead as though he stood before her. She wanted him to see her hatred.

"Oh, but I feel it, Jessica."

"I wish you'd just fuck off." She stood and strode from the room, making her way to the kitchen. Over her shoulder, she shouted, "And I wish you'd never picked me for your goddamn team. I never wanted it. I never asked for this shit. I wanted…" She faced the wall ahead and closed her eyes, heaving in a deep breath. "I wanted a life with Cal. To be some normal person with kids. A house. A car."

"You have something in common with Leyton, then."

Rivald's loud voice startled her, and she suppressed a yell of surprise. "I have *nothing* in common with him. Don't you *dare* say that again!" She flicked the kettle on and busied herself with the process of making instant coffee — anything to take her mind off the fact Rivald was in the room. He may be transparent, but that bastard's breath was hot, tickling the back of her neck. "He's mental. He's —"

"Your teammate."

Jessica drummed her fingertips on the counter and gritted her teeth.

My teammate. Fucking wonderful. I get to work for the rest of my life with a murderer. I get to go out at night and do whatever the hell this horned freak tells me because I've been 'chosen'. Shit.

Her stomach growled.

"You had better eat something before you go out. We do not want you fainting while doing your job, Jessica."

"Oh, no, that just wouldn't do, would it? Fainting on the job, letting some sick jerk abduct me again. No, that would royally fuck up your plans, wouldn't it?" She lifted the boiled kettle and sloshed water into her cup. The scent of coffee comforted her—something she needed right now—normality, a link to saner times.

"You have much anger in you," Rivald said.

Did she detect a note of sadness there? No, she couldn't have. He was incapable of feeling anything other than spite, that one. She turned from the counter and moved to the fridge, grabbing a carton of milk, the anger growing inside her. She didn't want to answer him, so finished making her coffee and quickly made a sandwich. Whether she'd manage to eat it was anyone's guess. The thought of food churned her stomach, and she swallowed, a sour taste layering her tongue. She stalked out of the room, food and drink in hand, and settled in the living room, the darkness matching her mood.

Sensing he'd gone, she relaxed a little, chewing her food without tasting a thing. The coffee was good, though, and she savoured it as the last one she'd drink before she changed from a law-abiding citizen into a criminal yet again.

And that's what I'll be, isn't it? A criminal?

She slumped back on the sofa, leaned her head against it, and closed her eyes.

I'll just have to get used to it, but what if Leyton doesn't get there in time? What if I end up abducted again? Will I eventually be able to link with Barry so he'll know where I am?

"Get up!" Rivald shouted.

Jessica lurched forward, coffee jumping out of her cup and landing on her leg. Cursing, she stood, pulling her hot jeans fabric away from her thigh. She glanced around, hoping, yet at the same time dreading he'd make an appearance in the flesh. "What's wrong?"

The air chilled, and she shivered.

"You need to get changed. Things have taken a different turn. Our target has decided to go out earlier than he'd planned. Hurry!"

Dumping her cup on a side table, Jessica ran towards her bedroom, intent on doing as she was told. One day she might be able to get out of doing this kind of shit—when her mother was no longer on this earth—but for now...

She opened the wardrobe to find it empty. "Fuck! What am I meant to wear? The stuff I have in my bag isn't exactly the kind that will gain a man's attention."

"Look on the bed."

She turned. An outfit laid on top of the covers, positioned as though a person wore them—a flat person with no substance. *That's me now.*

Quickly, she stripped and redressed, hating the short black skirt, the red halter neck top. What did they want her to look like, a damn hooker? She picked up a black bolero-style jacket, an ugly thing embroidered with red swirls, then lifted the pair of high-heeled red shoes.

Ugly. As. Sin.

After dressing, she tottered over to the light switch, wondering how the hell she'd manage to walk any distance in these damn shoes, and flicked it on. Rummaging through her bag, she pulled out a brush and did the best she could with her hair in the limited time she had. She sat on the bed, applying makeup with the aid of a small compact mirror, and decided she never wanted to see herself in such an alarming state again.

Nothing but a damn prostitute.

"*That is the idea,*" Rivald said.

"Oh, God. Were you here when I was *naked?* While I *dressed?*"

"*No, I was not. I am not the animal you think I am. Now get outside and follow my instructions.*"

"But the police—they'll still be out there in their car." She jammed a hand through her hair, anxiety growing, her stomach in knots.

"*They will, but they will not see you leave.*"

"What if they knock to check on me while I'm out?"

"*They will not.*"

"Why? How can you—"

"*You ask far too many questions. Just do as I say!*" Even in her head his voice sounded thin, sharper than normal.

Forcing herself not to yell at him, lest she just piss him off more, she walked to the front door, the shoes pinching her toes. "If you're so good at magic, then you'll make sure these shoes don't hurt me!" She yanked open the door, bracing herself for a difficult walk.

Outside, she spotted the policemen in their car, gazes ahead, mouths moving. She walked past, but with no idea as to where she had to go, she faltered.

"*I will guide you along. I need to fill you in on our subject and you need to concentrate on what I say,* not *on how you are walking or where you are going. Pay attention. It is imperative you get this right.*"

Trepidation made a quick dash through her veins, and Jessica allowed the horned bastard to have his way. She swore she floated down the street, the shoes comfortable, as though she wore a well-loved pair of sneakers.

"*Stop thinking inane things and* concentrate!" Rivald shouted.

Startled into clearing her mind, Jessica waited for him to tell her what she had to do, trying her best not to focus too much on where he directed her.

"Our subject is entering a club. Dancing Nights. Are you familiar with it?"

"No," she muttered, glancing about to ensure no one was around to see her talking to herself.

"He is looking for a woman to... He is looking for a woman. You will be that woman. You must entice him, make him want to leave with you, and take him down the alley beside the restaurant next door. The name of that establishment is Dennard's Cuisine. Do not take him anywhere else. Do you understand?"

"Yes."

"Leyton will arrive shortly after you go down the alley."

"Shortly?" she shrieked. Any damn thing could happen in the space of whatever time shortly was.

"We will not allow you to be in any danger. We are watching at all times. You may, however, feel in danger. Your reactions will only help matters. He will think you are frightened. He likes his women to be frightened."

"I *am* fucking frightened!" she said, breezing along the road that led towards the club scene. "And these people here. Can they see me floating like this?"

"No. You are invisible at present."

"Invisible?"

"Please stop repeating what I have said. You are annoying me." His 'voice' strained around his irritation.

"Well, pardon me for breathing. Pardon me for being shocked that I'm going down an alley with a damn killer and that I'm currently invisible. I mean, this is all *normal*, isn't it, this jolly old float down the road!"

"Indeed it is."

"Normal to *you*. What you need to wrap your ugly head around is the fact that it isn't normal to *me* — or any other sane person on this fucking planet. Don't expect me to just accept this shit without question. It's weird, fucked up, and totally off the bloody scale."

"Your language is foul."

"Well! Tough. Fucking. Shit! You might be able to direct my body, but you can't stop me from saying what I—"

"Silence!" he roared.

Jessica came to an abrupt halt, raised in mid-air by an unseen hand clamped around her neck. Her eyes bulged, and her lungs fought for air. She flailed her arms and legs, panic setting in.

"I can do whatever I so choose, and at this moment I am throttling the life out of you. If you wish to live, then be quiet and obey orders. If you prefer to die, I will oblige and find another Dreamer for bait."

Oh, God. This is crazy. So bloody crazy... "Let me go. Please, just let me go."

Rivald deposited her to the ground. She wavered on unsteady legs and sucked in a huge breath, her throat sore and her chest aching.

"Now, I shall take you to Dancing Nights and direct you to our target. One wrong move from you, and I will treat you once again to what you just experienced."

Tears burned, and Jessica raised shaking hands to her eyes. She covered them, taking a moment to process what he had done, the ability he had.

"Are you quite composed?" he asked.

No, I'm fucking well not.

"That is a shame. We really must press on. Now, in we go!"

Rivald floated her through the front doors of the club, and Jessica darted her head, eager to take in her surroundings. The place was dark except for strobe lights piercing the blackness, and she envied the frenetically dancing men and women, off their heads in an alcoholic stupor. If it was alcohol powering her movements, at least she'd still feel some semblance of control. She had no hope of catching someone's attention, asking for help. It appeared every single partygoer was inebriated beyond reason.

"They still cannot see you. And if you are thinking of escaping, think again. Your mother—"

"Yes, yes, all right!" She waved one hand. If he would only shut up for a few seconds she'd be okay. With no time to think about where she was or what was ahead... Shit, she felt her panic growing.

"Take a deep breath and calm yourself. I will make you visible once you have done so."

I can't do this. I can't make some man want me.

"Yes, you can. And you will."

Her stomach bunched, and she willed her nerves to settle. "All right. Let's do this."

"Good girl."

Rivald breezed her towards the bar and left her standing beside a man nursing a bottle of beer. She stared at him, taking note of the way he was dressed head to toe in black—jeans, casual jacket, boots. Even his damn hair was black. She felt a subtle shift and knew she could be seen now.

The man glanced up sharply, apparently startled she had appeared by his side. He smiled without showing any teeth, his expression one of kindness, his eyes soft and giving her the feeling they'd got the wrong man.

"Appearances are deceptive, Jessica," Rivald whispered tiredly in her head, as though weary of explaining every little thing. *"This man is capable of terrible things."*

She swallowed then smiled at the man. "Hi." She sounded breathy, as though she'd raced across the club to be with him. Her voice didn't sound like hers. She frowned, quickly erasing it so the man wouldn't think her weird. "You out for a good time, sugar?"

Oh, God. Did I really just say that?

Rivald chuckled.

The man smiled, this time showing his teeth, even and very white in the glare of the strobes. "Yes, you?" He raised his bottle to his lips and took a healthy swig.

"I could be tempted..." She cocked one hip and pouted her lips—damn Rivald for doing this—and looked at him through lowered lashes.

"You want to dance?" the man asked.

Jessica lifted one hand to her mouth and ran a fingertip across her bottom lip. "Not really. How about we go someplace more...private?"

"So help me God, Rivald. Please stop making me say this shit!"

The man tilted his head, probably unable to believe a victim had fallen into his lap like this. "Well, sure, babe. Where did you have in mind?" He eyed her while finishing his beer, then placed the bottle on the bar.

"I like it outside," she whispered, leaning closer, her body inches from his. "I like it in alleyways."

His eyes glimmered, and she knew she'd ignited the devil inside him.

"Just my kinda gal." He crooked his arm. "Shall we?"

Jessica nodded and threaded her arm around his, staring up at him adoringly as he eased them through the crowd. Her pulse thudded in her ears, and her heart hammered way too wildly for her liking.

Rivald made a throat-clearing sound. "Remember — you are not to act frightened yet."

She swallowed and focused her attention ahead. The man propelled them through the front doors and out into the night, unlinking their arms to rest his across her lower back. He hugged her close to his side, and she felt sick to her stomach that she was actually going through with this.

"Down here," she said, a smile spreading on her face, one she knew Rivald had put there. A seductive upturn of her lips. A sex-siren's call. "Let's fuck in the alley."

She gripped the front of his jacket with one hand and tugged him down the side of Dennard's Cuisine, her heart rate soaring. Her heels tapped on the concrete as she walked backwards, her smile still in place. She stared at him longingly. The light from the street made him a silhouette, and she grinned through the shiver tromping up her spine. Turning, she pulled him farther down the alley, hoping to God Leyton would be here soon. She didn't want this man to touch her, kiss her...

She took control, coming to a stop in front of a large dumpster. A faint light shone from above, giving him a menacing look. With a little giggle she hadn't intended, she pushed him up against the side of Dennard's, her hands smoothing up and down his chest.

"Rivald, is this necessary?"

"Yes. We need him to... Just keep doing what you are doing."

"What you're making me do!"

The man lifted one arm and tunnelled his fingers into her hair, gripping it in his fist and flicking his wrist. Pain spread across her scalp, hair roots pulled so tight she thought he'd surely rip her hair out. Fucking bastard.

"Oh, you like it rough, do you?" she asked, her voice gravelly and so damn seductive it freaked her out.

"Yeah," he said, yanking at her hair and closing the fingers of his free hand around her upper arm. He squeezed, stealing her breath, and jerked her closer. "Yeah, I like it rough."

He dipped his head, covered her lips with his, and revulsion spread through her. She kept her eyes open—he did too, and stared at her with glazed eyes that were nothing like the kind ones in the club. His tongue forced her lips apart, and she opened her mouth, allowing him to probe inside. She tried to stop his invasion, but it seemed her mouth had a mind of its own. The creep drew her closer, pushing his erection into her pelvis. God, no, this was as far as she was prepared to go. She began to struggle, writhing in his grasp, but he held her too tight. Biting down on his tongue, she lifted one knee and jammed it into his groin. She opened her mouth as if to scream, and he muttered curses, let go of her arm, and smacked his hand over her lips.

"You fucking teasing whore. You wanted this. You brought me out here."

He took his hand away, lifting it quickly, then gave her a backhander across her face. Her head snapped to the side, and pain radiated over her skin and into her jaw. She whimpered, her hair still held fast in his grip, and brought her hands up to his chest. Pressing her palms against it, she pushed, trying to gain some distance between them. He slapped her face again then cupped her chin, holding her head still.

"Now, you're going to suck my cock, bitch, and you're going to do it good. If you even think about biting…"

He let go of her hair—blessed relief!—and pushed her down by her shoulders. She wrenched away, flinging herself backward, intent on getting the fuck out of the alley, but she propelled herself too hard and landed on her ass. She tried to scream, but no sound came out. Had Rivald made sure she couldn't make a noise? Frightened now, because shit, it didn't feel like Rivald was here and Leyton hadn't shown yet, she scuttled backwards, her spine jarring when it met with the wall.

The man walked towards her, the light above the dumpster only illuminating one side of his face. "Now, you little bitch…now you're going to wish you'd never met me."

Chapter Twenty-Five

Leyton stood at the far end of the alley, surrounded by shadows that seemed to hold him in place. He wanted to help Jessica, goddamn it, but his legs wouldn't move and Rivald hadn't given him permission.

You're going to wish you'd never met us in a minute, you bastard.

The man hauled Jessica upright, slamming her back and head against the restaurant wall. Air whooshed out of her mouth, and she winced.

He's hurt her. He's fucking hurt her...

She looked frightened for her life, just as she had when Leyton had first set eyes on her, and he made a concentrated effort not to allow his mind to wander down memory lane. He had another lane to focus on now, this alley with its stinking refuse strewn on the floor and the scuffle of what he guessed was rats foraging. The damn health officials needed alerting if vermin roamed freely. There was a restaurant here, for Christ's sake.

"*It is not vermin but me*," Rivald said.

"That's a matter of opinion…"

"Since when did you grow so bold, Leyton?"

"Since Jessica was pinned up against the wall by that asshole there."

He nodded towards her and grimaced. The man had pushed his groin into hers, and Leyton had no trouble figuring out how she'd be feeling with an erection digging into her. She glanced about frantically—searching for him to appear, of that he had no doubt—and he made as though to step forward and intervene.

Rivald held him in place with the silk-cold slide of mist over his limbs, and he shuddered, hating and relishing the familiar feel over his skin.

"Not yet, Leyton. He has not done anything wrong at this moment."

What? Not done anything wrong? What part of a woman struggling for a man to get off her don't you get? We know what he's done in the past, know what he's capable of, so why wait? Does Jessica have to be subjected to the whole horrific ordeal before we act? "Get off me," was all he mumbled out loud.

"Of course she does not have to suffer that. We will not let it go that far."

"So then why are we waiting?"

"I want to see how well she acts under duress."

"You're sicker than I thought. Sicker than me." He shivered again as the mist curled around him, holding him still.

"No, I am merely making sure she proves her worth. We thought we had picked an excellent candidate in Lorelei, and look what she did. It is imperative we are sure of Jessica's loyalty, sure of how far she is prepared to go in order to keep her mother safe, to work for our cause."

"She'll do it, you know that. Let me step in. Let me get a hold of the bastard."

The man lifted Jessica's halter-top, her belly a pale swathe in the eerie light mounted on the wall above her. He smoothed his big meaty hand over her skin, and Leyton ground his teeth, excited at the prospect of ripping one of this son of a bitch's out and adding it to his collection. The man kept Jessica in place—no chance she'd be able to get away—and fumbled with the hem of her skirt. Leyton's stomach knotted as she cried out, begging for the man to stop his exploration.

He didn't. Instead, he jammed one knee between her legs and forced them open, then yanked her skirt up around her waist.

"No, no, please no…"

Her pleas tore at Leyton's heart.

"Rivald, come on. Let me have him. For God's sake, let me stop this shit!"

Rivald sighed. *"Very well."*

Leyton lunged forward, rushing out of the shadows and smacking into the man's side. The pervert reeled and lost his footing, crashing onto the ground. Leyton glanced at Jessica, who stood as though stuck to the wall, her arms out, hands splayed against the rough brick.

Leyton caught a movement in his peripheral and, attention on the man now rising from the ground, said to Jessica, "Go back to the safe house. Now!"

She peeled herself from the wall and ran towards the man, clearly hell bent on making it to the mouth of the alley. The man dashed out his arm and caught her around the waist, spinning her around so her back rested against his chest. With both hands holding her to him, he eyed Leyton, menace in his eyes and a hard smile stretching his lips.

"Help me, Rivald!"

Leyton's hand lifted and his wrist flicked. The man's arms flew up, releasing Jessica, and he staggered backwards so fast his feet couldn't keep up. He went down on his ass, the splash of him meeting a puddle loud in the confined space, and gave a strangled grunt.

"You actually listened to me for once. Jeez…"

"Run, Jessica!" Leyton shouted.

She turned, looked at Leyton with terrified eyes then fled, disappearing around the side of the building. More at ease with her gone, he ran at the man and flung himself through the air, landing on top of him before he had a chance to get up.

"You fucking filthy bastard!" He gripped the man's jacket and pulled them both to standing, holding tight as the asshole swung his fists, their hardness connecting with Leyton's head.

Anger boiled inside him, and in one fast move he threw the pervert at the dumpster. The man staggered, falling onto his side, his face showing his shock that someone had overpowered him.

"Not so good when the shoe is on the other foot, is it, asshole?" Sliding his hand inside his own jacket, Leyton withdrew his corkscrew, intent on gouging out the man's eyes so he'd never look at another woman again.

"You will do more than that," Rivald said, his voice hard. *"Kill him and prop him up beside the dumpster. It will make a nice tableau for when Barry and Tag find him."*

Angry that Rivald was still here instead of ensuring Jessica got back to the safe house without incident, Leyton kicked out, the sole of his boot striking the man on the temple. Head snapping back and connecting with the wall, the bastard released a gravelly yell and scrabbled to his knees. The position was perfect. Leyton kicked him again, the crack of bone as his toecap met with nose a beautiful sound in the gloomy alleyway.

"Silence him, Rivald, then go and make sure Jessica gets home safe."

Leyton lifted his arm and brought the corkscrew down in a delightfully perfect arc, jamming the twirl into the man's eye. Mouth open but no sound coming out, the man writhed and jerked, his hands coming up instinctively to cover his face. Leyton yanked the corkscrew out and stabbed again, this time through the webbing between two of the asshole's fingers. He revelled in the task, jabbing over and over, first pulling out an eyeball and then other viscous matter. The man lurched to the side during the assault, resting on the ground as though he needed a nap, and Leyton decided now was the time to give him the longest sleep he'd ever had.

He took a step back, lifted his foot, and stamped down on the man's head.

Repeat, repeat, repeat.

Only when the man lay still did Leyton stop. Then he casually walked over to the puddle, swished his boots through the water, and strolled back to his victim. Hunkering down, he checked for a pulse. Finding none, he melted into the shadows, back the way he had come, pleased with himself for ignoring Rivald's suggestion of propping the corpse up. He had to have *some* form of control.

He emerged onto a residential street behind the restaurant and casually threaded his fingers through his hair, cursing himself when he remembered his blood-covered hands and the fact he hadn't worn gloves. He'd have to alert Barry about that. Corkscrew back in hiding, he slid his hands in his pockets and weaved through the streets until he reached his van. Inside, he poured water into his small bowl and thoroughly washed his hands using anti-bacterial soap. He scrubbed beneath his nails and, once satisfied his hands were clean, he quickly undressed and washed his whole body. Redressed, he opened his van door and threw out the dirty water. He climbed into the driver's seat and drove away, his intention to find a secure place to park for the night.

He mulled over how quick the kill had been — he'd had no choice, what with the location and the chance of being spotted — and told himself next time maybe he could take a more leisurely pace. There were so many deaths ahead of him, so many times he would watch Jessica perform from the darkness of hiding places.

Having her in his life this way was better than not at all.

"*Stop thinking of her like that,*" Rivald said. "*And contact Barry.*"

"Is she home safe?" Leyton turned onto a disused track.

"*Of course. You may contact her later to see for yourself. But only in mind, Leyton. No face-to-face visits.*"

"I'm not stupid." Leyton gripped the steering wheel — hard.

"*Hmm. Sometimes I do wonder... Contact Barry. Tell him where the body is. I have other things to do, other things to plan. Our next victim seems about ready to venture out into the world of murder sooner than we thought. He was at the planning stage, with weeks ahead of him before he took the next step, but the urge to kill has taken rather a firm hold.*"

"I don't think Jessica can deal with another one so soon. She'll have marks on her neck, a split lip. She needs time to heal before you send her out again." The track curved to the right, and Leyton followed it, parking inside a circular stand of trees. "Why are the kills so close together all of a sudden? What aren't you telling me?"

"Jessica will just have to deal with it, wear makeup. We all have jobs to do and we cannot have her protesting each time she has to do hers."

"You didn't answer my question."

Silence.

Sighing, Leyton snapped, "Fuck off now. Please, just go away. I'll contact Barry. I'd rather not hear from you again until I have to."

"Very well."

Rivald's presence disappeared, and Leyton relaxed only for a second before another voice intruded.

"Oh, Mummy's little boy has been naughty again, hasn't he? He's slipping. He killed without gloves. And he forgot to collect another tooth."

"Piss off, Mother."

Damn. The tooth. I need to go back...

"No, you mustn't go back. Do as you're told and tell Barry it's time for him to accidentally stumble upon another body. Ask him to get your tooth, you strange little bastard."

Leyton clamped his jaw, lurched out of his seat and into the rear of his van. He climbed onto his bed, zipping his sleeping bag around him, and settled his head on his pillow. It took a long time for him to calm from Mother's name-calling enough to go into his Dreamer trance—or at least it seemed a damnably long time. At some point, he had to stop listening to her. Stop letting her affect him. It wasn't like he was alone any more. Not like before.

He reached out, broadening his mind in search of Barry. He found him, the cop alert and ready to receive news that the job had been completed. Leyton considered toying with him but decided he couldn't be bothered.

"It's done," he said, his voice as weary as he felt.

"*Is Jessica all right?*" Barry asked.

"Rivald assures me she is. She was fine when she left the alley, if a little shaken."

"*A little shaken? Fucking hell, man, I'd bet she was more than that.*"

"You are quite right, but she'll get used to it."

"*I doubt that very much.*"

Leyton sighed. "Look, I don't like her being involved any more than you do, but we're all bound by Rivald and Him to do their bidding. There isn't anything we can do about it, pointless fighting, and I'm too damn tired from the kill to give much of a shit about anything right now."

Barry's tension seeped into Leyton. His hatred. His spite.

"*Where's the body?*" Barry asked, sounding as though he spoke through gritted teeth.

"In the alley beside Dennard's Cuisine. He's next to a dumpster in rather a sorry state. His head's a little the worse for wear."

"*Jesus Christ…*"

"Indeed. I couldn't help myself. And I forgot to wear gloves, so check if he has anything on him I may have touched. Jacket buttons and the like."

"What do you expect me to do, rip the fucking things off?"

"*I don't care* what *you do, just ensure nothing can be traced back to me. Oh, and I also forgot to take my trophy, so you'll have to collect it for me.*"

"Trophy? Look, I'm not about to take evidence from the fucking scene. How the hell do you think I'll get away with that?"

"I don't give a shit how you do it, just do it."

Barry's sigh gusted over Leyton, and he smelt coffee, a hint of food spice.

"What do you need, Leyton?"

"A tooth. Back molar, to be precise. And make sure it's a nice shape without any cavities or fillings. I don't like fillings."

"How the fuck am I meant to get hold of one of those?"

"Oh, it won't be too much trouble. I'm sure a few teeth will have come out during my assault. Take a torch, there's a good man, and I expect you'll find a tooth on the ground."

"You're a sick bastard. What the hell do you want a tooth for?"

"That's on a 'need to know' basis only, and you don't need to know. Besides, if I told you, you wouldn't believe me."

"I don't think I want to know anyway."

"No, best you don't." He waited a beat, then said, "Off you go then. Perhaps you and Tag could decide to go out for the night and happen to see a man's feet poking out from beside a dumpster. That shouldn't bring up any questions from Internal Affairs. An innocent discovery. Shocking that you can't go on a normal night out without finding a dead man, isn't it, but there you go. Perils of living in such a terrible world."

Leyton closed his mind off before Barry could protest. While still in the trance, he may as well contact Jessica, so he reached out once again, imagining her pretty face and the terror in her eyes as she'd stared at him for the second before she'd left the alley. The poor woman was undoubtedly traumatised, but it wasn't as though it was his fault. She was trapped in this insane situation just like he was.

"Jessica? Can you hear me?"

He felt her trembling, whether from fear at what she'd seen or anger at him intruding, he couldn't tell.

"What do you want?"

"I'm just checking on you."

"What, to see if I've told anyone? See if I've finally gone insane and intend to do myself harm?"

It was anger he'd felt, then.

"No, no, nothing like that. I care about you, remember? I'm here on a genuine enquiry. Are you all right?"

"All right? All fucking right? *How the hell can I be after what that man did to me?"*

He sympathised with her, but hell, she hadn't stuck around to see the worst of it. "Just be grateful you didn't witness his demise, then you'd *really* have something to complain about." He regretted his words instantly but he wouldn't take them back. No, she had to grow a tougher skin if she was to succeed in this business.

"Oh, yes. I'll be grateful. Thank you, Leyton," she said, her voice childish, *"for sparing me the terrible ordeal of watching you kill someone. I'll be grateful forever."* She went silent for a moment then muttered, *"You fucking jerk."*

"I can hear that you're quite all right now, so I'll leave you be."

Leyton cut her off and pulled himself out of the trance, refusing to hang around in the Dreamer state in case Rivald got hold of him. He had to get some sleep, to make sure he was refreshed for tomorrow. From what Rivald had said about their next victim,

Leyton had a suspicion he needed to be ready faster than usual, rested and alert for the coming task. He pondered for a time on how he would kill the next one, which brought his corkscrew to mind. His corkscrew that was still in his jacket pocket. Still dirty.

Although tired right down to his bones, Leyton unzipped his sleeping bag and hauled himself out of bed. He couldn't stand to know his tools were dirty, so he scrubbed the corkscrew at the sink and put it back in its place inside his tool pouch. Happy that he had at least remembered to do *something* right tonight, he returned to bed and relived the murder, his lips stretching in a contented smile and his fingers itching to grip his tools and kill someone else.

Not only was their next victim's penchant for killing growing by the minute, so was Leyton's. Despite not liking Jessica being involved, despite being ordered around by Rivald, Leyton had to admit that he had the best career in the world when it came to job satisfaction.

Chapter Twenty-Six

Barry sank back onto the couch beside Tag with a sigh. They'd both been dog-tired when they'd left the station and decided to order in and spend a quiet night not thinking about work. Instead, they'd fallen asleep in the midst of a bout of light petting and languid kissing. Tag still slept beside him.

"Fuck me if that bastard's going to make me collect his damn trophies. If he's stupid enough to leave evidence, then he can damn well get caught."

Snarling, he got up and shuffled his way to the bathroom to take a piss. He turned to go back to the living room when the odd thought that there was enough filth in his life struck him, and he stooped to wipe the edge of the bowl with a tissue. Tag liked his place clean, and Barry's sleepy aim left a little to be desired. He took a few minutes to wash his hands and splash some water over his face, so he didn't quite catch Tag's first words when his lover's voice drifted from the other room.

He shut off the water and grabbed for a towel. "Be right there."

"Barry…" The uncertain shake in Tag's voice caught his attention this time. "Fuck. Barry!"

Dropping the towel, Barry rushed back to the living room.

Tag was sitting up on the couch, both hands gripping the thigh he'd banged on the table a few days before. A dark, spreading stain seeped through his sleep pants. Thick, red liquid dripped from under the hem to run between his toes.

"Jesus!"

"It won't stop bleeding!" Tag tried to get up but a renewed gush of blood from the old wound dropped him back onto his butt. "What…"

"Leave him be!" Barry shouted at the room in general as he rushed to Tag's side. He knew how much blood a person could lose before it turned dangerous, and how fast it could pump out of the human body. "Stop it!"

"*Leyton gave you instructions, Barry,*" the voice in his head said calmly.

"He asked me to fix his screw-up."

"*And you'll do it.*"

"Fuck!" Barry fumed helplessly as he pressed his weight down on Tag's leg. "Yes! Yes, all right. I'll do it!"

In his head, Rivald clucked his tongue. "*How much are you going to make this poor man suffer while you try to exert power over this situation that you do not have, Barry?*"

"Just make it stop," Barry snarled.

A sigh. "*Very well.*"

Tag groaned sharply, and his leg jerked. "Oh. Shit." He grimaced "Hurts."

"Rivald!"

"Remember who is in charge, Barry, and do as you are told. I do not have the time to supervise you as well as Leyton."

"And if you were fucking supervising that freak, I wouldn't have to be covering his sorry, twisted ass."

"Touché." There was a distinct pause. *"The bleeding has stopped now."*

Barry gritted his teeth. "Thank you."

"You are welcome. We are a team, Barry. We help one another."

Barry dropped his head, anger strengthening his resolve. "You think threatening my lover is helping, think again. You want my cooperation, try showing a little faith and pull your weight. You know how the system works. I can't cover for Leyton. He has to be more careful. I'll do what needs done this time, but make sure he gets his shit together." He backed away from Tag and looked up at his lover. "Get these off. Let's see the cut."

Tag nodded, though his face was pale and there was fear in his eyes keeping him quiet. Barry knew he wasn't meant to see it, but there it was. One more reason Barry needed to get a handle on this situation.

"Transition can be…difficult," Rivald allowed. *"Leyton has never been one to play well with others."*

"Well. He's in my sandbox now," Barry muttered. "He can damn well learn the rules."

Above him, Tag gasped.

"I have the power here, Barry. Never forget who owns the playground."

"You have the power to hurt people," Barry agreed. "You can coerce me into doing what you want. Do you think that's really the best way? If you're so bloody wonderful, magic away Leyton's fingerprints. Make…the rest of what he wants doable." Barry wasn't about to even hint to Tag what he had to do. Tampering with evidence would get them both fired. If he was caught, Tag needed plausible deniability. He didn't bother to think how the omission would feel like a betrayal to his lover. If he was to keep him and his job safe, he'd need that honest reaction too. The idea of keeping anything back from Tag hurt, though.

"Help me out here, Rivald."

A small sigh, like a stale, tired breeze blew through Barry's mind. *"Very well."*

Amazed that Rivald had agreed, Barry gave a curt nod. "Come on," he said to Tag. "Let's get you into the shower and cleaned up. I suddenly feel the need to go out for dinner."

"Now?" Tag frowned at him as he slipped the sleep pants off.

"No time like the present."

He peered at Tag's leg. The bandages Tag had applied that morning were soaked in crimson. The entire leg was streaked in sticky red. When Barry carefully peeled the bandages away, the small cut sustained on the table seemed to have gaped open again, deeper, wider than it had been, like someone had reached in and torn the flesh open with a sharp claw.

Tag drew in a deep, shaking breath. "That was almost healed."

"Yeah."

"What does that shit want you to do?" Tag leaned over to get a better look at the wound.

"Go out to dinner," Barry said.

"What aren't you telling me?"

He should have known it would be no easy task to lie to the man who knew every sordid thing about him. Barry looked up and met Tag's eye, willing the man to believe him. "I'm hungry. I feel like Dennard's." He glanced at his watch. "If we hurry we can make the last seating."

Tag gripped his chin in tight fingers and gave him a little shake. "You're lying to me."

"Tag—"

"Don't fucking lie."

"Then don't ask," Barry said quietly.

Tag's lips tightened. His eyes bored into Barry, like he could root the truth out of him that way. "I won't stand for them coming between us," he snarled, teeth clenched tight to hold back the rush of anger that snapped through his eyes.

"What am I supposed to do? They'll kill you. If that isn't coming between us, I don't know what is."

Tag leaned close, took Barry's mouth in a hard, angry kiss that only just got him reaching for more before Tag pushed him away. Barry flailed back onto his ass, the coffee table went flying, and Tag surged to his feet.

"Ten minutes. We'll take my car."

Tag stormed into the bathroom and slammed the door. The click of the lock was like a hammer to Barry's heart.

"Satisfied?" Barry asked.

"*So much anger.*"

If Barry didn't know better, he'd have thought Rivald almost sounded sad.

"Bastard. You don't know the meaning of the fucking word," he muttered. He couldn't help but think, though. If they didn't want him to be so fucking angry, why did they keep threatening everything that mattered to him? Why not try a little bit of goodwill for a change?

It took longer to clean up the blood than the ten minutes Tag demanded, but he didn't appear from the bathroom in ten, either. Barry had mopped up the mess and righted the furniture, cleaned himself up at the kitchen sink, and changed into slacks, T-shirt and a sweater by the time Tag emerged. His lover dressed in efficient silence and led the way out the door. The drive across town was more of the same, stony stillness.

Barry knew the minute he broke the stalemate, Tag would demand to know what he was keeping back, and he didn't dare tell him. Up to now, they'd done everything by the book. IA could not fault them for breaking rules or even bending the law. Tonight, that changed. Barry couldn't keep Tag safe from Rivald, but he sure as shit could keep him out of any potential Internal Affairs investigation should Barry's tampering become known. Even if it meant enduring his partner's wrath.

There has to be a better way.

He'd give up the force if he had to, before he'd drag Tag's name into the mud with him. Somehow, there had to be a way to do what they had to do without the constant threat of ending up behind bars themselves.

Tag approached the restaurant and slowed, searching for a parking spot in the street out front. A light drizzle had started up, and he aimed for a spot as close to the entrance as possible.

"Here." Barry pointed to the front of the restaurant. "Stop here and duck inside. Get us a table while I park the car out back."

"You'll get soaked."

Barry shrugged. "Just a little rain." He knew the damp was hard on Tag's lame leg and foot. "Better me than you." *Blessed rain, an evidence eraser.*

"Don't fucking coddle me," Tag growled. But he did pull up and get out of the vehicle.

Barry jogged round to the driver's door and reached for the handle.

Standing in his way, Tag took him by the back of the head and pulled him into another of those angry, fierce kisses. "Don't do anything stupid."

Barry gulped for breath, shook his head. What the man did to his equilibrium. "I won't." That was hardly reassuring, said in such a breathy, indistinct way.

Tag searched his eyes, and Barry forced himself to keep his gaze steady. "You'd better not." Fingers tightened in his hair. "Or forget Internal Affairs, and that fucking horn-head." He gave Barry a little shake. "You'll have me to answer to."

Okay. That should not have sent a surge of blood straight to his cock like that. Barry almost bleated out a 'Yes, sir', but Tag kissed him again, stopping him speaking, breathing or even thinking.

Tag had let him go and was walking away towards the front of the restaurant when Barry regained his senses. Shaking himself back to reality, he ducked into the car and pulled it around the block.

Finding parking in the back lot wasn't difficult. It was nearing the last seating, too late for most customers. He breathed a sigh of relief to find a clear path down the alley between the restaurant and the bar next door. Easy enough to slip through, do what he had to do, and get inside to meet Tag. His partner would be none the wiser. They would eat and leave and find the body on the way back to the car.

He ignored the sinking sensation of what he was doing, resisted listing all the ways he was breaking the law and obstructing the justice he'd sworn to uphold.

He had to wonder if this really was the best way to get the job done.

"Like conventional methods have worked so well lately," he reminded himself. He didn't have to go over the list of dead and missing to know the law fell far short of justice for any of them.

Ducking quickly into the alley, he picked his way through the puddles towards the dark bulk of the dumpster nearer the other end. From this distance, he couldn't tell what was discarded trash bags and what was the more unsavoury refuse he was after.

A part of him wished he'd followed Leyton's advice and brought a torch. The more practical side of him knew it wasn't worth the risk. If anyone reported seeing a light in the alley now, things would get complicated. Being seen here before anyone officially found the body would not only raise suspicion on his investigation, it would dump him in the deep end of the suspect pool. No one needed that.

He was close enough now he could see the street lamps' glow reflecting off the beaded water on the trash bags. He could see where the still lump of something else reflected nothing. Masses of wrinkled, slumping darkness appeared, soaked up water, light, even the crisp night air, and gave back a shadowed stench and emptiness. That dark cloud stretched outward, beyond the body, sank into the cracked pavement and slicked like oil over the puddles. It rose, black fog, crawling up the side of the dumpster and seeping into the brick and mortar of the building. It stained the air and tainted every breath.

Barry blinked, coughed to clear his throat, and raised his face to let the rain wash away the veil. This was ended, this creature, this man. Whatever he'd done, he was over and done in the most final of ways.

He'd still been a person—however twisted and wrong, he'd been born to someone. He had been someone's son. Barry frowned into the night and stepped a little closer.

"Why like this?" Peering into the dark, he could make out the vague shape of a large male. "It isn't—" He swallowed bile. Dead bodies were one thing. There was no escaping the fact he'd been a part of this, however obliquely. A life had been taken. He knew it was going to happen, if not when or where or who, he knew.

"Stay on point, Barry."

"Rivald, I'm a cop. This is..." He didn't know, he didn't have words. There was right and there was wrong. And this was neither. There wasn't a word for what this was.

"That is why I exist, Barry. I am the grey. The in-between. Leyton uses a corkscrew. I use him. You use the justice system. We are all on the same side. Whatever light this creature might have snuffed out will now shine."

"Might have," Barry pointed out. "That isn't how the law works."

"The law is broken. Do not tell me you cannot see that."

"This is broken," Barry muttered. He crouched, though, squinting into the shadows at the fallen man's head. Or what was left of it.

"Do not look now." Rivald almost sounded gentle. *"Not what you want to see moments before a dinner date with the man you love. Look to your left. What you are after is there."*

Barry shook his head. "You think I've not seen enough gore and filth that one more mangled corpse is going to make a difference?"

"I hope, Barry, that the day a corpse does not affect you never comes. Now get up. Take the tooth. I will guide you. And then go and enjoy your dinner."

"Fuck you, you twisted, horned freak."

A soft chuckle resounded through Barry's head. Not malicious or sharp. Just amused. *"Close your eyes, Barry."*

Wading through the reluctance, Barry did as he was told. The darkness behind his lids was less fraught. There was nothing in it but his own thoughts, at least for a moment, before Rival stepped into his head, horns, hooves, in all his darkly, fascinating glory.

"See, now *that's* something I didn't need to see before dinner."

Again, the soft laughter echoed through him in an oddly comforting way. *"You are more fun than Leyton, when you are not angry."*

Barry snorted. "The tooth? Can we just do this?"

"Certainly."

Rivald did guide him. He didn't need to see. His body turned, and he reached, fingers contacting the cold, wet pavement.

"A little to your left. That is it. There. Take it to the parking lot and set it on the hood of your car. Leyton will retrieve it before dinner is over. Go. Enjoy your evening."

"Leave us alone, yeah?" Barry asked as his feet retraced his steps out of the alley. He failed to keep the plea out of his voice entirely. "I did this for you. I broke the law. I lied to Tag. Just give us this. Leyton might get off on this shit. I need Tag. Alone."

There was no answer. He was standing beside the hood of his car in the dimly lit car park, alone. He forced himself not to look down at the grisly trophy he'd recovered. Turning his back, he took the long way around to the front of the restaurant and went inside.

Chapter Twenty-Seven

Tag gave the waiter a small nod, then watched as the young man peeled away the foil wrap around the cork of the wine he'd ordered. He was just setting the corkscrew to the soft stopper when the front door opened. Tag watched Barry's face carefully as his lover spoke to the host. He had plenty of practice in detecting lies in the set of that strong jaw, the narrow slant of brown eyes. It had taken Barry a long time to confess about his dreams at first, and even longer to admit to the drinking and the random sex.

Those were long ago confessions, though. Tag pushed the thoughts away. No use dwelling on the past, on the disintegration of their first relationship. He'd been as much to blame for that as Barry. Now, today, he was determined not to let it happen again.

"Hey." Barry nodded to the waiter and pulled out his chair.

His coat was damp with rain, Tag noticed, before the host took it from him and handed him a coat-check ticket.

"That took a while." Tag kept his gaze directed to the waiter and the sure, smooth movements of his hands as he filled their glasses. "I went ahead and ordered the wine."

"Thanks." Barry settled into his seat and folded himself forward a bit. "Found a spot around back and walked around the long way. Didn't realise the alley went straight through."

"Never mind." Tag took his hand, just resting his palm over Barry's fingers and warming his lover's rain-cooled skin with his own. "What do you feel like eating?"

The waiter took that as his cue and rattled off the specials.

Barry chose the salad and soup option, and Tag ordered something quick and not too filling. The waiter moved to leave but Barry stopped him, nodding at the corkscrew sitting on the table. A slight shiver racked his big frame. "Forgot that," he said, pushing at his fork which nudged the corkscrew.

The waiter nodded his thanks, picked the tool up and left them in peace.

"I thought you were starving," Tag said, willing Barry's attention back.

Barry nodded, clearly distracted. He sipped his wine, but his gaze returned, again and again, to Tag's face. There was something hurried and needy in his eyes, and it set Tag's heart thudding.

"What's wrong?"

"Nothing."

Tag drew his hand back. He could see the lie. It was so plain, and he had to wonder if Barry knew he could see and just didn't care.

"Tag, please. Don't do this interrogation thing. I'm not one of your suspects."

"I can't help if you won't tell me what's going on."

"The best way for you to help is to do just exactly what you're doing. Let me worry about the crazy shit, and just be my lover."

Tag couldn't help the soft snort that came out. "You are the crazy shit, Barry."

A tight smile flitted across Barry's face. "I know." His voice drifted softly across the table. His fingers twitched where they still lay, pale against the deep red of the cloth. "I know."

"All right." Tag downed a good portion of his wine, sat forward and clasped his hands in the middle of the table. "I'll say this, so you know what's in my head, so we can get past it. Once and only once. The last time you started lying to me, everything fell apart. I got pissed. I didn't help. You went elsewhere."

Barry's lips tightened to a white, thin line.

"I'm not saying that's what's happening here—"

"It's not."

"But I'm at a disadvantage here, Barry. I'm up against a guy who can get inside your head and convince you of things before I ever even know there's anything going on. All he has to do is make it look like he might hurt me and you cave. You do whatever he asks. How am I supposed to compete with that?"

"Compete?" A deep grimace curved Barry's lips, lines of confusion marring his brow. "This is not a competition, Tag." He took both Tag's hands in his. "I love you. I'm not going anywhere. And I refuse to get drawn into one of those pointless who-did-what-to-whom shit-fests. We both got hurt. We both screwed up. We're both back. One hundred per cent."

"Then tell me," Tag demanded. "Tell me everything. Don't keep shit from me. I can't protect you if you do."

Barry's fingers tightened painfully. "I don't want your protection."

The pain of grinding knuckles disappeared under the new stab of rejection. Tag swallowed around it and forced himself not to draw away. "I'm your boss. That's my job."

Disgust flitted across Barry's face just before he yanked free, slamming himself against the back of his chair. His lips pinched into that tight line again, Barry remained closed-mouthed as they sipped through half the bottle of wine in shifty-eyed silence before their meal came.

The rest of the wine evaporated. Barry ordered another bottle and poured for them both. That bottle, too, emptied quickly. Their meals disappeared. Every time Tag looked up it was to find Barry glaring at him. His eyes seemed too dark, the pupils swallowing the colour, the whites shrouded in anger. When his spoon clattered into the bottom of his soup bowl, he pushed his chair from the table.

"We done here?"

Tag shrugged.

A sharp nod, and Barry lifted a hand. The waiter appeared almost immediately. "The bill. And call us a cab."

Tag frowned.

"I'm not driving." Barry pointed out. "You?"

"No." He should have been paying more attention, shouldn't even have ordered the wine in the first place. Some things, Barry was not good at saying no to.

He was about to say something when Barry's cell rang. He watched his partner's eyes darken even more as he answered. A deadly smirk crossed Barry's lips as he listened to whoever was on the other end.

"So call the fucking cops," he snarled into the receiver and snapped it closed.

"What was that?"

Barry turned the phone off. "Rivald's learned a new trick." He waggled his cell phone in the air. "I suppose he thought it would be amusing to use technology instead of popping into my head and reminding me —" He cut himself off, shrugged like he was readying for a football skirmish, and held out a hand towards the door. "Never mind. Come on." He dropped a pile of bills on the table and took off for the door.

"Our coats?" Tag followed hurriedly.

"Later." Barry grabbed his hand and hauled him out into the rain.

A cab stopped on the kerb, disgorging a laughing young couple who hurried inside. Barry jumped into the empty back seat, and Tag could do nothing but follow.

The ride back to Tag's apartment was achieved on the same thin ice of silence as their meal. Tag didn't know what to say to fix this. He hadn't said anything that wasn't true. Perhaps the best thing was just to wait until the cab delivered them, and they were alone. When the car pulled up to the kerb outside the building, Barry practically flung a few bills at the driver and jumped out.

"Thanks," Tag muttered as he hastily followed his lover.

If the cabbie responded, it was lost in the slamming cab door. Tag found he had to chase Barry down the hallway to their door, and it was with a mix of annoyance and warmth that without ever talking about it, he'd already begun to think of things as theirs again. That realisation shouldn't come in the middle of a fight he didn't even understand. But it was still a nice thought.

Barry was already fitting his key in the lock and opening the door when Tag caught up. "You know," he snapped, as he followed Barry inside, "it would be nice if—oof!"

Barry had him by both arms and had pushed him back until he impacted the door with a thump and cut short his complaint with an angry kiss that stopped his breath along with the words. He pinned Tag, thrusting deep, fighting well past his guard and slaughtering any attempt at coherent communication. Not that Tag wasn't fluent in the language of lust Barry was using. His lover definitely had a way—a *force*—that Tag could never resist.

But this combination of alcohol and sex that Barry used—it had hammered a wedge between them once. Tag refused to let it happen again. He gripped Barry, clinging to both arms at his elbows, and drew him closer. Trying to take the kiss—and his wits—back, he dug in, sliding tongue against tongue, hauling him in and spreading his legs to give Barry a comfortable cradle of safety against his hips. If he didn't want to talk about what was bothering him yet, then Tag could fuck it out of him. The last time, he'd refused to use sex to communicate, and Barry had found his release elsewhere. This time, he'd speak the man's language and get past it to what was really going on.

At last, Barry sank against him, hands finding the back of his neck and his hips and melding them together. The tongue dance deepened, robbing Tag of more of his faculties.

They should talk.

Barry clearly wanted to fuck.

Tag couldn't tell if it was the dreams spurring him on or something else. He couldn't tell if he cared as Barry drew him into the moment and out of his own head. He decided he didn't give a rat's ass what was causing it when Barry sank to his knees and started undoing Tag's pants.

"Ungh...Bar..."

Once again, Tag lost the thought in the slick heat of Barry's mouth as he wrapped it around his dick. Barry gripped his ass, hard, strong fingers digging in and holding Tag still while he licked and sucked every thought out through his cock. He drove Tag up, up and up until thought blended into thought and into a white sheet of need.

"Bar—" Unable to complete even the word as Barry swallowed around the head of his cock, he resorted to the same, strict non-verbal communication his lover would understand. He dug his fingers into Barry's hair, gripped close to the scalp and yanked.

Barry groaned. His eyes, long since drifted closed, opened, and he gazed up. Deep brown, completely devoid of any outside influence, that gaze drew a sharp gasp from deep in Tag's gut. How long had it been since he'd been allowed to look so deeply into his partner? How long since the dreams had erected that dark barrier he could never get past?

Hauling hard, Tag brought Barry's face away from his groin and stared down at him.

"Jesus," Tag muttered.

With his lips red and still parted and glistening, his chest heaving, and a bit of spittle dripping through his stubble, Barry had never looked quite so fuckable.

"Get up," Tag demanded, voice grating over his lust. He tightened his hold in Barry's hair and watched

Barry's face as he winced and swallowed hard. "God. Fuck. I need to be in you. Now. Up."

At last, Barry stumbled to his feet and they both fumbled and groped to get his jeans off, getting in one another's way, glancing sloppy kisses over each other's faces until Barry finally hissed in annoyance and slapped Tag's hands away.

Tag didn't back off for long. As soon as Barry had his jeans around his ankles, he was back, grabbing him, spinning him, and planting a hand at the base of his neck. They didn't make it to the bed. Not for that first round. Spit for lube and fuck the condoms, Tag took and Barry grunted with the effort of receiving him. He had only the hard kitchen table to hold himself up against Tag's insistent assault. If it hurt, Barry didn't seem to care. He just pushed back, answering Tag's force and need with his own.

It was a brutally hard fuck that left them both sticky and panting and far from sated. Ignoring the mess of spunk dripping from both their bodies—and the table—Barry hauled Tag to the bed, spread him out and renewed his own original agenda. He licked and nipped, kissed, caressed, owned every part of Tag's body until he had him once again bucking and grinding in search of release. He was relentless. And near silent.

Tag gave in to every demand. Every liberty Barry took, Tag allowed. This wasn't about sex. It was about control, and of all the people in this fucked-up scenario, the one who needed it most was Barry. For that, Tag could be his balance. His anchor. Anything he needed. If only he would just say something. Talk to him. Let him help…

Not even Barry could go forever. Eventually, they both came again, Barry long and hard down Tag's throat, and Tag, most unusually, with Barry's fingers up his ass. He wondered if that was a precursor of things to come, and if he should maybe warn his lover to be more careful next time. Not that it hadn't felt good after the initial intrusion, but his sadly neglected hole needed more TLC than Barry had offered this time.

Not a conversation he cared to have right this minute. For now, he was content to lay still, breathe, enjoy Barry's weight spread over him, and stroke his fingers through the tangle of black, sweaty curls hiding Barry's face. They hadn't turned on any lights. Most of the sheets had been kicked and scuffled to the floor. The room, lit by the sulphur-orange glow of streetlights slanting through the slats of the broken blinds, cocooned them in comfortable, sated silence. The faint city noises gave the quiet a heartbeat, breath, a life they both knew, inside and out, good and bad.

"I don't need your protection," Barry said, a quiet, determined ring to his voice.

Tag searched back, back—hours…days, it seemed—to the restaurant and his bone-headed *'I'm your boss'* comment. "Barry—"

"I need you to trust me."

"I do."

"Really trust me." Finally, he lifted his head and looked Tag in the eye.

Once again, Tag was struck by the purity of his gaze, the utter lack of outside influence. The light that was Barry's, unshadowed by the dark the dreams brought. He swallowed hard at the reminder of just how deep his love for this man went.

"Sometimes, I *can't* tell you," Barry went on. "Sometimes, you need me to protect you."

"How can I help" —*how can I keep* this *light*—"if I don't know what's going on?"

"This." Barry laid a hand over Tag's pounding heart. "This is how you help. I want something, sometimes, that isn't touched by them. There has to be a place for me outside the dreams. You're my place. When everything is dark, there should be this. Us. You help by not getting involved. Is that asking too much?"

"No." Tag pulled Barry back down, holding him tighter. He wanted to feel his weight, the sticky cling of skin on skin, the rasp of hair over his body. "But can you blame me for wanting to fix things?"

"No." Barry struggled free of Tag's clutching grip, once again looking him in the eye. "But I'm not broken. This is who I am. You can't make it go away. Tell me you can love me as I am. Or tell me you can't. But know there is nothing to fix."

For a long moment, Tag searched Barry's eyes. The truth of that ate at him. The knowledge that sometimes, he would look into those gorgeous eyes and see the shadows, the darkness, and that those things were as much a part of Barry as this light, struck fear into him. He touched Barry's face, ran fingers along his lips, over his jaw. "I love you, Wiki." There was no doubt in him about that. "I love you."

He reached for a kiss and got it. Barry opened to him now as surely as he'd drawn everything Tag was out of him just hours before. As tender as the rest of the evening had been rough, the kiss was just another piece of the complex puzzle. When Barry pulled back to look at him again, he forced a small smile.

"Those dreams tear you up," Tag said, placing a finger over Barry's lips as he opened his mouth to speak. "I see it in your eyes. The fear. You know they aren't real, but the terror is there just the same. You don't know how much I want to take that away, to see you happy. How am I supposed to ignore that?"

"You're not. But you have to let me deal with them in my own way. Sometimes, you're not going to like what I have to do. Sometimes, it will mean I have to not tell you. Sometimes, I have to protect you." He offered another tender kiss, and Tag drank it up. "And sometimes, you have to hold me down and fuck me, love me. Just give me something solid to hold on to."

"If you go breaking laws and I find out…"

"I won't. Bending is another matter, but I will always figure out a way to stay within the letter, I swear." This time, the kiss he planted on Tag was another of those mind-melting, searing numbers that left him breathless and foggy. "Sometimes, I just need your hands on me, lover. Your cock in me. I am not going to be another Leyton. My life is mine, and I intend to keep it that way.

It shocked Tag to realise either of them had the energy to get it up again. But they did. Release was a long, slow climb to get to and almost painful when it came, but it threw them both into a much-needed and refreshing sleep.

* * * *

He wasn't at all surprised to find Barry gone when he woke to sunlight streaming across his bed. He didn't ask where he'd been, seeing his lover walk into his office an hour after Tag finally made it to work. He gazed silently at the neat, white envelope Barry set on his desk. For a few minutes, they both sat on either side of the desk enjoying the quiet underlined by the soft whir of fans and the constant murmur of voices from beyond the glass walls of Tag's space.

"You're sure?" Tag asked after a few minutes had passed.

Barry nodded.

Tag picked up the envelope and poised it over his outgoing mail. "You know once it's in Williams' hands, he'll never let it go. He's been waiting for this moment. He won't like that you're taking his thunder, but he won't let you take it back, either."

"I know." Barry smiled. "I know. This is for both of us. You and me. If I'm off the force, you don't have to cover for me. And I can do things I could never do as a cop with Williams breathing down my neck. I thought this through, Tag. I'm resigning from the force." He leaned over, pushing to his feet and planting a firm kiss on Tag's lips. "Not from us. Never from us."

Tag dropped the envelope into the mail tray and nodded. "Okay."

Chapter Twenty-Eight

Jessica had fumed well into the night after Leyton's visit inside her mind. Anger at him bugging her after she'd done such a disgusting thing had burned all expectations of sleep away — that and the fact she'd turned to him in that damn alley, knowing thanks had shone from her eyes. Thanks! She was thanking him for coming to her bloody rescue when he'd got her into this mess in the first place. Irony had a lot of answer for, the bitch.

She lay awake now, gaze glued to a ceiling pocked with beige blobs that told her the previous people who had resided here were heavy smokers. Hell, she couldn't blame them. A cigarette would calm the serrated edges of her nerves right now, but she couldn't bring herself to get out of bed and find a shop that sold them. Besides, cops would be out there, asking where she was going and why. She had no energy to deal with them. And she'd stopped smoking for Cal. To make him happy. No way was this shit-fest going to take that away from her, too. She clamped her jaw down on the ache and turned her mind away from going down that miserable road.

Her body felt like it was a part of the mattress, that she'd sunk really low in more ways than one, her skin fusing with the bed. She'd ask if she could call her mother today, just to hear her voice and let her know she was okay, but who the hell did she have to ask? Leyton? Rivald? Barry or Tag?

Rivald had made it clear he was in charge...of their team anyway. But who was 'He'? Who was the guy Rivald answered to? She suspected that was more information than she needed at this time. The less she knew about the weirdoes of the team, the better.

Team.

She snorted. Yes, they were a team, but none of them wanted to play the game. Except maybe Leyton, although she'd bet he'd prefer to go his own way, killing whoever he saw fit and not being told who needed doing in. And Rivald...yeah, he seemed to enjoy this business a bit too much for her liking.

You're stuck in this shit. Nothing you can do about it. So shut the hell up with your moaning and wait for your next job.

Job. Would she be getting paid for this gig? How was she supposed to earn a living if she had to go off at a moment's notice and do her part in snaring killers? It wasn't like she could just ring in sick, or nip out of the office, calling out to her boss, "I'll be back in about half an hour. I just need to quickly change into some gross clothes and make some guy want to fuck my brains out then kill me."

No, her working life would have to revolve around this load of bollocks now, but she wasn't in the right frame of mind to work out what kind of job would suit her best. When she'd gained some semblance of normality — whatever that was now — she'd talk to Barry about where they all went from here.

She tried moving her arm enough to fling the quilt off her body, but failed to lift it. "Fucking Rivald. What now?"

"You are very perceptive, Jessica."

Shit. He was in her room again. His voice had been loud, but not in her head. And then the chill came, heralding his presence, making goose bumps spring up on her arms despite being warm beneath the bedding.

"You hardly slept last night. Even if you are lying still it means you are getting the rest you need for tonight."

"Tonight?" She would have shot up out of the bed if she'd been allowed. "D'you mean to tell me there's another one *already?*"

"Yes. He was not supposed to be dealt with just yet, but he has decided to embrace his inner demon faster than we anticipated."

She stared at a beige ceiling blob in the shape of a question mark. "So he hasn't killed anyone yet?"

"No. You will be his first — his first attempt. Better to get rid of him now before he actually murders someone."

In a perverse way she agreed. "Right. So what's the plan? And when? Will I have time to get used to this, or do you expect me to be ready now?"

"Tonight. He has tonight in mind. He has been loitering outside the cinema lately. He plans to abduct someone there after the late-night movie."

She sighed, accepting her fate. "So, what movie am I going to watch?"

"You will be watching two. Just in case he changes his mind and decides to venture out earlier. He is sleeping currently, so I am unable to give you more information until he wakes and I can access his current plans. He does not appear to be dreaming about what he wishes to do."

"Right." She tried to move again, angry that she couldn't. "Would you please let me get out of this damn bed? I'll take a nap this afternoon if I have to, but I can't lay here a minute more."

"Very well. I will leave you to it and contact you later. And yes, you may telephone your mother today. I think it is wise you set yourself up in a rented apartment once the police let you out of here."

"Oh, yeah. I can rustle up the deposit from thin air and pay the rent with the buttons ripped off my clothing by perverted freaks."

"Do not worry about money. There is a...fund. Donations are given by... Donations are given. You are not required to work unless you wish to. You work for us now. There are funds in your bank account, invisible to anyone but you. No tax issues. No one snooping as to where it came from."

"How is that possible? How can you *do* these things?"

Silence was her answer.

She knew he had gone. Not just because his eerie voice had stopped, but because the room warmed up and she was able to get out of bed. She wandered into the kitchen, her mind full of questions — the burning one, *Why me?*

Staring out the window, she eyed the cops, different to the ones who had been there last night. If only her life was as easy as theirs — stuck on watch duty with nothing but talk, coffee, and doughnuts to pass the time.

Fuck. What a mess.

She made coffee, sipped it absently while looking back out the window at nothing in particular. Her vision blurred, the view disappearing into something of her mind's creation. The alley. That creep. Leyton coming out of the shadows.

How had he killed him? And did she really want to know?

The phone trilled, startling her stupid. She placed her cup on the counter and went into the living room, reluctant to answer in case the call brought more bad news. There was only so much a person could take. Reaching out, she lifted the receiver and held it to her ear, the plastic cold on her skin.

"Hello?"

"Jessica?"

Relief poured into her, and she relaxed her rigid shoulders. "Barry! I'm so glad it's you."

"Are you all right?"

"Um, yeah. For the most part. I don't like this shit, but..."

He grunted out a sound that might have been amusement. "Not like we have a lot of choice. Believe me, I get it, though."

"I need to speak to you. *Someone* —"

"Don't say anything. Just don't say a word."

He laughed, a little too maniacally for Jessica's liking. She couldn't deal with the policeman losing his grip now. Not when she needed him — he and Tag were the only sane ones in the team. She didn't count herself. She'd been feeling slightly crazy ever since Leyton had taken her.

"Listen, I'm coming over to get you. I'll take you to lunch. I have some things I need to discuss with you."

"Okay. I have to talk to you too. What time?"

"Will you be ready in half an hour?"

"Damn right I will. I need to get out of this pissy little shithole."

* * * *

He took her to a small café opposite Dennard's. Not somewhere she'd have chosen to be so soon, but her stomach growling overtook any protests she would have made. She chose a large ham and salad roll, chips on the side, and Barry toyed with a cheese sandwich.

"So what did you need to talk about?" he asked.

Jessica swallowed her mouthful and sipped from her glass of Coke before responding. "First, I want to call my mother today. Rivald said it would be all right."

"Rivald?"

"Yeah, he visited this morning. The creepy fucker kept me pinned in bed. Said there was another job on tonight."

Barry widened his eyes and scratched his chin. "Already? Shit, I thought the next one would have been well after I left…"

Left? "You're *leaving?*" she asked, panic fluttering in her chest. Her stomach stopped grumbling, her roll suddenly unappealing.

"The force. I can't do this…this fucking shit while still a cop. It's too dangerous. I don't want Tag in trouble—and he would be in the end. We can't keep making out we *just happen* to stumble over all these dead bodies."

Somewhat calmer, she took another bite of her roll then said around the food, "So you'll have to deal with this one tonight before you leave your job." She shrugged. "No point in whining about it. We *have* to do this. Life without Cal, well, it'll be hell, especially if I let myself think of him, but if I put my all into this job, this *team*, maybe the pain of losing him won't hurt so bad. I've decided—just this morning, actually—that if this is my lot, I may as well accept it and live as best I can despite it."

He nodded. "Something I've been coming to terms with too." He paused to take a gulp of coffee. "So is that all you have for me? Anything else?"

"Yeah." She lowered her head and leaned to her right so he could hear her. "We get paid for this shit."

"*Paid?*" Barry said, his voice too loud. He glanced around then bowed his head to meet hers. "Paid? How? Who by?"

"I don't know. Rivald said there was a fund," she whispered. "That I can get myself an apartment and it will all be taken care of. He said I didn't need money, that there are funds in my bank account no one else but me can see. Weird, right? So damn weird. That must go for you too, right? That must be how Leyton survives. He doesn't work. I wondered how the hell he afforded to live."

"Jesus..." Barry rammed his fingers through his hair, nudging his plate away from him with his free hand. "This is so...fucked up. If I hadn't seen it for myself, I wouldn't believe *anyone* who told me this kind of crap happened. People talking inside your head. Invisible money."

He laughed like he had on the phone, an eerie little chuckle that darkened his eyes and stretched his lips thin over his teeth. It unnerved Jessica, and she stared at him, recognising the fact that he was releasing pent-up tension and that if he didn't stop laughing he'd end up crying.

She placed a hand on his arm and squeezed. "Barry, stop it. I know exactly how you feel, but for God's sake, *stop laughing.*"

He did, glaring at her with watery eyes, his mouth twitching as though it would stretch into a smile again any second. "Fuck." He breathed out, slow and long. "Just…fuck."

But shadows left his eyes and she breathed a sigh of relief.

"I know."

She picked up her Coke and stared out the window, giving Barry a moment to compose himself. God knew she understood how he felt. The alley made her shiver—just the sight of it brought everything back. That man's hands on her. His tongue in her mouth. His breath…

Another thing you have to get used to. Many hands, many tongues…

She shuddered and focused on the crime scene. Police tape barred entry into the alley, bowed low where she supposed numerous cops had climbed over it during the night. An officer stood beside the dumpster, and she made out a guy in uniform down on his haunches, poking about on the ground with what appeared to be a pencil.

"So you didn't have to deal with that?" she murmured.

"No. I expect I'll be in shit for it at some point, but I went there before… Listen, Tag doesn't know this, all right? But I have to tell someone. I went there before we ate in Dennard's late last night. Rivald helped me find a trophy Leyton wanted."

"Trophy?"

She didn't bother to turn back to look at Barry. A man had caught her attention. Bearded and wearing a beanie hat, he approached the alley mouth at a slow pace, the officer at the dumpster coming to stand guard, eyeing him with suspicion.

"Yeah, you don't want to know. I'm guessing I did what I had to do last night. That I wasn't the one to deal with the aftermath is neither here nor there, but I'm guessing Rivald and his boss won't see it that way."

"Look at him," she said. "Look at that man out there."

"Fucking freak. There's always one. Anyway, now I've handed in my resignation, they'll have to accept it. No point in a cop being involved, anyway. They've already set themselves up as judge, jury and executioner. I can do more off the force than on it, if they aren't going to let me bring any of these fuckers in alive. I can filter information to Tag, make out I'm an informant, my real name protected, but other than that they—"

"Barry."

"What?"

"Look at that man."

"I just did. It happens all the time. People see this shit on the news and can't resist coming to have a nose."

"No, *look* at him."

Jessica's stomach bunched, a hard knot forming. She'd know those eyes anywhere. The beard, the hat, did nothing to disguise him. Not from someone who had studied his facial features in order to brand them into her mind for when she broke free and could help the cops with an identikit picture.

"Fuck me," Barry breathed out. "What the hell is *he* doing out there?"

Leyton approached the policeman, engaging him in what looked like casual conversation. He shook his head as though saddened by the atrocities that went on in the world, hands in pockets, his profile showing how appalled he made himself out to be. Jessica held back a heave—she hated him. Yet at the same time there was a vulnerability to him that made her want to befriend him, to understand him. How had he come to this? Exactly where along the line of his life had he been called into this mess? Wasn't he just doing as he was told like they all were?

"He's putting himself at risk coming back here," Barry said, anger tingeing his words. "What the fuck is he doing?"

Jessica nodded. *"What the hell are you doing here, Leyton?"*

He nonchalantly turned towards the café, bobbing his head once in her direction as though he had heard her thoughts.

"Did you hear that without tuning in to me first?" she asked.

"Yes. Your abilities are manifesting. Rivald will be pleased."

"Jesus fuck, Barry," she said. "I just spoke to him in my head. Spoke to him first, and he heard me. You try. See if you can get hold of him."

She turned to look at Barry, who closed his eyes.

"Ah, hello, Barry! Calling me a motherfucking prick for coming here really isn't what I wanted to hear this morning, but good day to you too."

"I heard that," she said to Barry. "He heard you. Did *you* hear his response?"

"I did. Shit. This is…it's like we've gone to the next level. To his level. How is that possible? How the hell can we speak with our minds?"

"I don't know." She looked out at Leyton again. "Let us both try and speak to him. See if we both hear his answer. See if I hear you talking to him, and you hear me."

"Leyton, go back to your van," Barry thought.

"I heard you, Barry. Now see if you hear me," she said.

"Yes, do what he says," Jessica added. *"It's too dangerous that you're here."*

She looked at Barry. He nodded.

"Ah, at long last. A three-way conversation." Leyton casually lifted one hand in a wave that could be passed off as him swatting a fly. *"Now isn't our future going to be fun?"*

Chapter Twenty-Nine

Leyton had slept heavily until noon, waking refreshed and ready for another kill. He liked the idea of offing a man who, at this present moment, he was sure, was enjoying the prospect of committing his first.

"Too bad you won't get the chance, fucker."

He chuckled and unzipped his sleeping bag, getting off his bunk to wash in chilly water that shocked the fuzz of sleep away. The molar he'd taken from the bonnet of that car last night sat beside the sink, slightly yellowed and in need of a good scrape and scrub to get rid of some hardened plaque near the root. Not something he felt like doing right now, so he popped it in some denture cleaning solution in a glass and let the wonder agent do its thing. Hopefully the plaque would be easier to remove with his little tool later tonight. It would give him something to do as he came down from his killing high. Something soothing and banal.

As he dressed, he heard the distinct clearing of a throat and waited for Rivald to speak. The horned beast had been doing a lot of that lately, just dropping by instead of waiting for Leyton to find him in his dreamstate. He supposed things *would* move on like this, though, and knew he'd just have to accept these unplanned visits as the norm in future. There was nothing he could do about it.

"You seem happy today, Leyton."

"Yes, I am rather. I have the last tooth."

"Jolly good, although why you do not touch the funds in your bank account and buy yourself a brand-new pair is quite beyond my understanding."

"I don't expect you to understand."

"No. Well, I have some news for you. It changes things somewhat."

"Oh, right? What's that?" Leyton perched his ass on his bunk and pulled on his socks and boots.

"Barry has handed in his resignation."

Leyton lifted his head and stared around, trying to get a handle on exactly where Rivald was. He stared at the door, imagining him leaning against it, arms crossed over his belly, horns almost touching the low ceiling. "So where does he fit into this now? The idea was we used him to find the bodies."

"We still have Tag. I put the idea into Barry's head that he could become an informant, filter the information to Tag that way. That will do for now, but he is entertaining ideas of setting up as a Private Investigator. I am not sure that is such a good idea. What if, by a strange quirk of fate, family members of your victims go to him for help? He would be in a compromised position and not be able to tell them why he could not help them."

"Then deal with it! Don't come here chattering on to me as though we're just shooting the shit, like we do this all the time!" Leyton snapped. "What the hell has this got to do with me?"

"What has it got to do with you? I am glad you asked. You are going to tell Barry he must only work for us now. Tell him about the funds. How things work. That he must ensure Tag remains in his job so the police can clean up the mess you leave behind without arousing suspicion."

"What if Barry refuses to get Tag involved like this? Tag would be working alone, without Barry there to guide him in the right direction."

"I have ways and means. Why, just a few short hours ago I opened a wound in Tag's leg and would not stop the bleeding until I had Barry's full cooperation again."

"Oh, so you'll just keep making the guy bleed, is that it?"

Rivald chuckled. A nasty, eerie sound.

Leyton sighed. Lately he hadn't found the sick side of this shit funny. Since Jessica... He'd gone soft in some respects, that's what it was. And he couldn't help himself asking the next soft question either. "And what if Tag leaves the force too? What then?"

"There is that other fellow who knows about us. Detective Ross. He will do nicely should Tag give up his badge."

Leyton shook his head. "And the net widens. Do you think you can just recruit anyone, at any time? Don't we all have to be special? That's the impression I got. That we're all chosen because we have some kind of ability." *Please let it be that we're special. Just let me have the belief that I am special to someone, somewhere.* "That's why Tag can't hear our thoughts, get these dreams, because he's not really one of us. He's just a vessel, someone we use to our advantage. Isn't that right?" He imagined Rivald nodded. "How many people do you have working for you? How many cities, towns, *countries* are involved?"

"*That is none of your business. All you need to do is control your team. I am quite capable of controlling all of mine.*"

"So there *is* more than one team. Jesus..."

Leyton's mind filled with thoughts of hundreds of people doing His bidding. It awed him, made his mouth gape open as he pondered the fact there were more men like him out there—men who could assuage their need to kill by killing for the good.

"*Barry is having lunch in a café opposite Dennard's at present. With Jessica. I suggest you go and join them. Let them know how things stand.*"

"Isn't it a bit risky, me going back there so soon?" Leyton stood and walked towards the driver's seat, climbing into it and jabbing the key in the ignition.

"*Do not worry about that. I will erase the minds of those who see you.*"

Before turning the key, Leyton cocked his head, the sudden thought coming to mind that Rivald had been playing some kind of game with them all along. "If you can erase people's memories, why the fuck do we ever need to worry? Why don't you just do that all the time when I kill? Why didn't you do that with the Internal Affairs guy? Save Barry and Tag all that worry, that hassle?"

I am going soft...

"*Ah, worry and hassle are character building, Leyton. If I eased your passage all the time, you would never have any fear, never make sure to cover your behind when you go out on a job.*"

"But now I know you *can* do that—"

"*You will continue to be careful. Do not rely on me to sort out your mistakes. I may not be able to do these things as soon as they are needed.*"

So there were limitations.

"And where would you be if I am not able to cover for you, hmmm?"

In jail, probably.

"Exactly. Now go. And eat a hearty lunch. You will need the sustenance for tonight. I had my first glimpse of our fellow this morning. He is a brute. It will take all your strength to take him down."

The burn inside Leyton began, and he relished the coming challenge. A fight would go down nicely prior to dimming the light in his victim's eyes. Yes, he would enjoy tonight a lot.

He pulled out of his parking spot and made his way to town.

"Oh, and Leyton?"

"Yes?"

"You are special."

The burn changed to a warming glow of happiness, and tears stung his eyes.

Rivald had been gone five minutes when Mother piped up.

"Mornin', you strange little bastard. How is my boy today?"

She had the ability to sour his mood in an instant.

"Rivald? Are you still here even though I can't feel you? You promised you would make Mother go away. Is it time now?"

"It is, Leyton," Rivald said. *"Although this could have waited. I am busy. Your interruption is not appreciated. Goodbye for now. Again."*

Leyton sighed, feeling the weight his mother had been slide off him. And for the last time said, "Fuck off, Mother."

* * * *

Leyton pushed open the café door and strolled inside, heading right for Jessica and Barry's table. He sat, lifted a menu, and began reading—and waited for Barry to begin a tirade about how they shouldn't be seen together, blah-de-fucking-blah.

He did, and Jessica joined in. Their hushed voices meshed into one, the tones and pitches prickling inside his mind like pins on skin despite their softness. He'd been fine until Mother had spoken. Had woken happier than he had in a long time, and to know he was special...

Fucking old cow always did ruin a good day.

"Oh, be quiet, will you?" he said. "Anyone would think you were a pair of fishwives, the way you're prattling on."

Leyton glared at Barry, who stared back with his mouth working, and thankfully, no sound coming out.

Silence is golden...

Barry lowered his voice. "Prattling on? Fucking prattling on? We're sitting in here, all *three* of us, opposite a shitting crime scene we have more knowledge of than is good for us, and you're not *worried* about that? Jesus!" He slapped a palm on the table, toppling an empty Coke can onto its side. "It's all right for me to be seen with Jessica, but you as well? No damn way. Get out. We'll meet somewhere else." He glanced about the café furtively, then out the window.

Leyton waved a hand dismissively. "Oh, don't worry about *them*." He jerked his head towards the window, indicating the cops. "Rivald is dealing with them."

"*Dealing* with them?" Barry asked. "In what way? Don't you *dare* tell me he's going to have them kill—"

"Oh, behave yourself, Barry. You never struck me as the hysterical type until now."

He smiled at Jessica, who scowled back, her eyebrows like thin, angry caterpillars squirming above her eyes. She glanced to the cops then back to him and Barry in turn.

She was beautiful, and he loved her.

"It's all right. Rivald, just this once, will erase their memories, and those of the people in here. They won't recall us ever being here."

Barry looked up into the corner. "But he can't erase the damn CCTV."

"Oh, you'd be surprised what he can do." Leyton levelled his gaze at Barry and smiled, wondering how it would feel to smile with his new teeth. His tummy flipped at the prospect. "Or maybe you wouldn't now."

Barry shifted as though uncomfortable beneath Leyton's gaze, and it pleased him, though he would prefer it if they could become friends. Maybe in time they would. Maybe Barry would learn to tolerate him, at least.

"It has come to Rivald's attention that you have handed in your resignation. He asked me to tell you a few things."

Leyton related what he'd been told to say, watching with amusement as Barry's facial expression flashed from incredulity to shock to anger, and back to incredulity again. He knew it would be difficult for a cop to take unearned money—money that had no origin to speak of, and didn't even exist as far as anyone else was concerned.

"So, I get paid for filtering info to Tag, and no one is going to ask questions as to how I manage to live? A detective's salary isn't too shabby, but it isn't enough to sustain my living expenses for the rest of my days as though I've been saving all this time. People will start asking questions, wondering if I've been on the take these past few years, whether I'm working and not declaring it. No, it's too risky. If I'm going to take this money — and d'you know what? I fucking well will. I'd have earned it for all the crap and upset this shit has caused — then I need a legitimate cover. The PI angle will do it. Besides, Tag can never know about the money, so I *have* to work in order to explain the cash. Tell Rivald it's a no-go on working solely for him. If he wants me in, he has to allow me to cover my ass in the real world." He laughed bitterly. "Because his world sure as shit isn't the same as ours. Things work differently here."

"I haven't touched my funds," Leyton said. "I live off the money my mother left me when she died." *When I killed her whiny fat ass and stole it from her.*

"I think I'll do the same," Jessica said, her voice firm, as though she'd fed off Barry's assertiveness. "My mother will only start asking questions if I set up in an apartment by myself and have no job. I'll start some kind of fake home business or something. It should keep her from asking questions. What business that will be...well, I'll deal with that later. I need to get tonight off my back before I contemplate thinking about anything else."

"Good girl, Jessica."

"And I heard that. Don't patronise me, Leyton," she said. "I'm not some insipid woman who needs your approval."

Her hard glare and sharp words hurt his heart.

"You can come work for me," Barry said to Jessica. "Secretary or something. I'll pay you a legitimate wage that you can declare. I'll do small jobs to keep a trickle of money coming in, cash *I* can declare. All right?"

She nodded. "Thank you."

"So," Barry said, turning to Leyton. "You can tell Rivald what we're doing."

Leyton sighed. "Very well. I'll relay your messages. I'll contact you via thought later on when I have more details of where we all need to be. Rivald needs to finalise the plans first."

He stood, staring at them, a challenge to see if they'd dare protest again.

They didn't.

He walked out of the café, the smile back on his face, the lightness returning to his step. He was in charge of those two and they knew it. That they were all beholden to Rivald and Him was just a fact of life, something they all needed to accept without quibbling the ins and outs of the cat's asshole. But yes, Barry and Jessica had to do what he asked, otherwise the people they loved the most would find themselves on the other end of Leyton's curly corkscrew.

He went back to his van, realising too late he hadn't eaten anything in the café. He drove away, stopping at a drive-thru McDonald's to buy himself a Big Mac Meal. Slurping the Coke as he drove back to the previous night's campsite, wedging the cup between his legs when he needed both hands on the wheel, he looked forward to telling Rivald those two weren't as easily moulded as the horned bastard had thought.

"Well, if you've chosen them as Dreamers, as part of the team, you'll just have to accept their terms," he muttered. "They just want jobs as a cover, that's not too much to ask, is it?"

"No, I suppose it is not," Rivald said.

Leyton jumped, and his hands jerked the wheel, his van veering towards the centre of the road. He righted the vehicle and coached himself calm. His heart pattered wildly — damned if he'd let Rivald make him feel this way again — and said, "I wish you'd clear your throat *every* time you visited without an invite."

"But that would be no fun, Leyton."

He imagined Rivald sitting in the passenger seat and glanced that way. "You're a devious little bastard."

"As are you. And I agree. They should work as a cover. He will have to accept that it is a necessary evil."

Leyton pulled up to his hiding spot and killed the engine. *That's not the only thing I'll be killing today.* He laughed loudly and slapped the middle of the steering wheel. The horn blared.

"Something funny, Leyton?"

"Uh, no. Nothing that you would find amusing, I don't think. And before I forget, the café had CCTV."

"Duly noted. And now we have things to discuss. So! About tonight…"

Chapter Thirty

Barry stared at the paper in his hand. More specifically, at the number at the bottom.

"Is there a problem, Mr Whittaker?"

Barry glanced from the page to the bank official sitting across the desk from him. "Uh." He frowned. A week ago, he'd been unable to raise the limit on his credit card by five hundred bucks. Today, they'd approved him for a mortgage that was easily four times what he'd need to purchase the sad little house with the crooked picket fence and blood in the basement.

"Mr Whittaker?"

"No!" Barry set the paper down on the desk as though it might go up in a puff of smoke any second. "No problem."

The bank lady—Patrice, he thought her name was—smiled at him. "Good." She stuck out a slender, well-manicured hand. "Very good. All you have to do is sign a few papers, and I wish you happy hunting."

Barry brought his head up with a start. He didn't see a gleam in her eye. Did he? "Hunting?"

"House hunting, Mr Whittaker. Happy house hunting."

"Oh. Of course."

Idiot. All this business with Leyton and Jessica had him on edge to the point carrying on a coherent conversation with a regular person was next to impossible. How the hell did he expect to run a business, let alone one where he would have to instil trust and confidence in his clients?

Papers signed and poor Patrice left in a state of confusion at his ineptness, Barry hurried out of the bank and took out his cell. He'd already talked to the real estate agent. She'd seemed happy to get the derelict house off her hands and hadn't quibbled much about the lowball price he'd offered. He contacted her and she agreed to let him know when the crime scene clean-up was complete.

"Now what?" Barry gazed around at the sun-brightened street. Warmth soaked up from the pavement through his sneakers. He pulled his sunglasses down over his eyes and wondered what he'd missed out on the night before. He hadn't heard anything about the business at the movie theatre. Perhaps Jessica and Leyton had played their parts well enough his own part in the whole thing was no longer necessary.

"Don't get your hopes up, Barry."

Barry snorted. *Rivald.* At least he was with it enough not to talk out loud to the disembodied voice. *"And to what do I owe this pleasure?"*

There was no answer, however, causing Barry to frown deeper.

"Such a dark expression."

Barry glared at the twink-ish young man falling into step beside him. "Fuck off."

Blond eyebrows rose up to disappear behind a fringe of stylish bangs. "And rude," he murmured in a soft, silky voice. "Rivald didn't exaggerate."

"Wait." Barry stopped cold on the pavement. "Rivald? You know —"

"Shush." The young man reached out and took Barry's hand, tugging him into motion again.

"You know Rivald?" Barry whispered, leaning closer as they resumed walking.

Shapely lips curled up in a distressingly plain smile, and the stranger turned his face slightly towards Barry. "Intimately."

Barry shuddered and tried to pull his hand free.

"We should talk."

"Who the hell are you?" The grip holding him was frighteningly strong. Barry took another look at his companion. The young face turned towards him, and for a fleeting instant, Barry thought he saw pure terror in the sky blue eyes. "What is going on?"

"Please make this as easy on everyone as possible, Barry. You've asked, times too numerous to count, why you. Why you and not some other poor sod? How is it possible, and a hundred variations of those questions. Yes?"

Barry frowned again.

"Yes," the man answered. "And so Rivald has asked me to explain to you, once and for all."

Barry said nothing.

Fingers squeezed his until he winced.

"Once and for all time, Barry, yes?"

Barry nodded, a grudging dip of his chin, and the painful grip eased.

"Good." Their walk slowed to a stroll. "As to who I am" — he shook his head — "time and memory are funny, loopy things. What you think is straightforward…well, it isn't. I am generally referred to as He."

Barry narrowed his eyes at the slight young man next to him. "And here I thought you'd be so much more…more."

"Don't be fooled by the vessel, Barry."

A swift brightness passed through Barry's head, temple to temple, and left behind a ringing pain.

"Now stop interrupting. I don't want to have to smite you, charming as the wit and banter are."

Barry growled. "Fuck you."

He sighed. "Again. Yes. Now where was I? Despite how people refer to me now, I can only say I was once you."

"What?"

"*Like* you, I suppose. Very, very much like you. Only I did not have the guidance you do. My *He* wasn't strong enough to stop me growing, harnessing my strength as it grew and taking over. You carry bits of those victims around with you, don't you?"

Barry glanced at the twink, hated the smirk he saw on his face. He nodded.

"This *should* give you strength. You could gather it in, try and usurp me. The game would be fun. I get rather bored at times, only telling Rivald and the other leaders what to do, visiting crime scenes occasionally to leave behind a drop of blood. Purely to confuse the authorities, you understand. An amusing pastime."

Barry clenched his jaw tight. A thought came to him then, sudden and harsh. "Leyton. Could he harness his powers too? Does that freak take a bit of the victims with him?"

"He does, although without realising it, he uses it to fuel the burn he so fondly refers to when anticipating a kill. Without it, I don't think he'd be so effective.

Yes, he was born to kill, but without our guidance, without that burn, I do believe he'd become sloppy. You all have that in you. You could *all* take me down. Interesting, hmm?"

The thought of what Leyton could become if he used the residue of dead people's souls to grow in strength frightened the shit out of Barry.

"Don't worry," the twink said. "I have him under control. I don't fancy my chances fighting with him for the top spot, but you... Hmm, there's something a little weak about you. You're vulnerable to a high degree when it comes to your gammy-legged man."

Barry bit his tongue on another *fuck you*. His companion shot him an amused expression.

"Such a one-track mind. Tag must love that about you."

"Leave Tag out of this."

"I wish I could, Barry. But he is the key to you, isn't he? You couldn't care less what happens to you. No. Tag is very much a part of what we do."

"What we do." Barry curled a lip. "What *you* do. I just want my life back."

"But what life? You've always had the dreams, haven't you? Despite what Tag thinks, they've always plagued you. I didn't do this to you, Barry. It is just who you are. I have no explanation for why you are that way, and believe me, I searched for a very long time to find one."

"Why?" Barry watched the pavement slide past under their feet. "Because you were 'like me'?"

"Because I suspect that as many Dreamers as we find, there are so many more we never get to in time. Do you really think there is any such thing as crazy? Or are there simply things about the human brain we can never understand?"

Barry had no answer to that.

"All I can tell you about what I found on my search is that there is a peculiar relationship between mothers and sons who turn out to be Dreamers. It is a pattern to look for, to save those I can."

"What? Like male pattern baldness and Dreaming share the same DNA marker?"

He actually laughed. It was short-lived, though. "It is a trial, Barry. A mother knows. A mother who Dreams knows more. Too much. And to know you've given that 'gift' to your child..." He shook his head, a sad expression on his face. "It is a difficult burden for a woman, for anyone, to bear. Some..." He shook his head. "How did you get along with your mother?"

Barry grimaced. "She died when I was very young."

"Suicide."

"Shut up about my mother."

"You were one of the lucky ones, Barry."

"What's that supposed to mean?" He didn't think growing up without a mother, knowing she'd taken her own life in a fit of post-partum depression, was exactly lucky.

"Well. Let us just say, I would not wish Leyton's childhood on even the worst offender I have ever brought to justice."

Barry pursed his lips as a half-heard, plaintive wail drifted across his mind, like fog from an old dream. "He's the kid I keep dreaming about."

"The fact he is as sane as he is—"

"Is a miracle."

He turned his face to Barry again, eyes shining with an eerie, otherworldly light. "Funny how that works. Isn't it?"

"A fucking laugh riot."

They walked for some time in silence.

"So. You're saying this shit is genetic," Barry said.

"As genetic as enjoying the taste of dick, yes."

"But you can't figure out how to stop it," Barry enquired, not bothering to figure out if that was a slight or not.

"Why would you want to?" *He* stopped walking and drew Barry's focus to a petite, dark-haired woman on the other side of the street. "Look at her, Barry."

"Who is she?"

"Look at her. Think about it. You know who she is."

"No, I—" A flash of distorted memory seared through Barry's mind. "Shit."

"A memory that never happened, thanks to last night. You don't even remember having the dream, because the event never took place."

"But I did have the dream. Weeks ago. She…oh, shit." Barry's stomach turned over, his knees went weak, and he stumbled back until his heels contacted the base of a cement planter. He lowered himself to the edge and leant forward, trying to combat the vertigo. "It was horrible, what he did. Over and over…"

"Barry." *He* crouched in front of Barry. "Barry, look at me. It never happened. It was a dream you had that never came to pass. One I saw no benefit to you to remember." Hands on Barry's shoulders soothed away the cold chill. "That's where time being less linear than most people think comes in handy."

"Loopy time," Barry muttered.

He smiled. "Loopy time, yes."

"We stopped that. What happened to her."

"We stopped it. It never happened."

A few more moments passed. Hard heels clicking along the pavement brought Barry's head up and a tiny, wiggling mass of fur squirmed between his feet.

In front of him, an equally tiny boy stared at Barry with huge, dark eyes. And behind him, the woman with the dark hair. Who wasn't tortured or dead.

"I'm sorry," she said, her voice soft. "Andy's not used to holding the leash, yet."

"It's okay." Barry reached down and lifted the puppy, held the squirming mass out to the boy. "Here you go. He's okay. You take good care of him, hear?"

The boy nodded vigorously and took the dog.

"He's going to be big," Andy pronounced.

"I bet." Barry gave the dog a quick pet. "And when he is, he'll take care of you."

Again, the boy nodded. A moment later, they were gone again, off down the street and about their lives like nothing had happened.

"Because nothing *has*, Barry. And if that doesn't answer your questions as to why, I can't imagine anything ever will, and very likely, you'll end up like the woman who died in the basement of your brand new home."

"She was one of us."

"Us. Now you're getting it. Yes. She was. But she never understood."

Barry nodded.

"One last thing." The young man stood, held out a hand to Barry and helped him to his feet. "I cannot always predict what will happen when I leave a body I have borrowed, and I cannot use just anyone. Only potentials."

"You mean this kid" — Barry looked the lean form *He* had possessed up and down — "is a Dreamer?"

"He has potential. And now he is going to be confused. Disoriented. Possibly dangerous. His name is Jason. Please look after him. Help him. Goodbye, Barry."

The young man's face went impossibly pale. His knees buckled. Barry only just caught him before he hit the pavement. A collective gasp went up around him from the passers-by.

"Somebody!" Barry called as he lowered the limp form to the concrete gently. "Someone please call an ambulance?"

Chapter Thirty-One

Some instinct told Tag he knew where Barry was taking him, even though he had his eyes covered. He'd known since the day he saw Barry's notes in the murder book involving that dilapidated little house what Barry would do. The way his partner had circled the name of the real estate agent on the page was enough to tell him what Barry intended. Tag just couldn't decide if he approved.

Now the journey was over and Barry was helping Tag out of the car. His boots crunched over gravel and he could smell the wet scent of pine gum after the rain they'd had all afternoon. Tag recalled the crime scene photos. The little house had two tall pines on either side of the front gate. A slow creak and Barry guided him onto a pavement and the creak came again behind him.

"You have a gate?"

Barry laughed. "What good is a white picket fence without a gate?"

Tag grunted.

"Come on. Few more steps." Barry led him up one step and removed the blindfold. "Ta-da!"

It had been months since Barry had left the station after his final shift. He hadn't been idle with his time off. A fresh coat of paint graced every surface, inside and out. New shutters and a bright blue door greeted them as Barry led the way up the walk. The original tiny cement steps and porch had been replaced with a wide wooden deck housing two comfortable-looking chairs with a table between, complete with a full roof to ward off the rainy weather.

Inside, carpets had been ripped up, floors sanded down and refinished, and mouldings repaired. The concrete floor in the basement had been dug out and replaced, and the walls no doubt scrubbed and buffed within an inch of their lives before being white-washed and new storage shelves bolted to their surfaces.

The upstairs bore no resemblance to the dusty, faded memory it had been. It was bright and cheerful, exposed to afternoon sun coming through the clouds and new windows with wide open blinds.

"So?" Barry closed the door at the top of the stairs behind Tag and came round to see his face. "What do you think?"

"I think it looks great." Tag ran a hand over the granite counter between living room and kitchen. "I think cops don't make this much money."

Barry flushed. "Okay, I admit. Don't kill me. I did what you told me not to, and I used every penny of the mortgage they approved."

"Barry, that approval was some sort of mistake."

"Maybe, but they never corrected it, and look at this place. It's a new house, practically."

"Why?" Tag asked, still unsure what had motivated his lover to do this.

"Why let it rot and fall apart? Why let the last thing anyone remembers about this place be something so…" Barry trailed off, as unable as Tag to find a word strong enough to encompass what this house had seen. "If this is the only good thing the Dreaming ever gets me, Tag, I wanted to make sure I did it right. Made it worthwhile."

Tag nodded. He couldn't argue with that. Not really. This place, whatever its history, clearly made his lover happy, and happy was something Barry deserved infinitely more of.

"So." He pulled Barry around and wrapped him in a bear hug. "It's kind of out of the way, Wiki. You expect me to drive back into town tonight and get up early for work in the morning? Because if so, you'd better show me the bedroom now."

"You'd better fucking not drive back to the city," Barry growled, nuzzling his way up until his lips caught at Tag's throat and meandered along his jaw. "No. You're staying here, tonight, Captain Taggart. As you say, I haven't even shown you the bedroom, yet."

"So what are you waiting for?" Tag pulled Barry's head back by his hair and planted a firm, very demanding kiss on his lover's mobile lips, thrusting his tongue deep without even the preamble of a caress.

Barry moaned into his mouth and melted into his body, forming the perfect fit Tag had been dreaming of all day. Not having Barry just on the other side of the glass window of his office was proving more of a distraction than he ever thought possible. He had grown used to being able to look up and know his lover was safe, sound, easy to keep his eye on. The man was on his mind every moment they were apart now, and Tag was beginning to hate the little house not because of its past, but because its future meant Barry would no longer be gracing his own bed as often.

Eager to act on a few of the other things that had been occupying his mind since he'd last been with his lover, Tag pushed his advantage and ground his hips into Barry. "Bed. Now," he growled.

"Mffn." Barry planted both hands on Tag's chest and pushed. "Not so fast, Horndog."

"What?" Tag made another grab for him, but Barry evaded and pointed at the counter between the rooms.

"Sit," he ordered. "Eat first, then fuck to your heart's content."

"Hey. I thought I was your captain," Tag muttered, gripping the back of one stool and pulling it out. He had to admit, he'd totally missed the wine and glasses and the two plates set on the countertop.

"Were," Barry reminded him.

"Right." Tag knew he sounded disgruntled. The issue of Barry leaving the force was still a contentious one, even though the deed was done.

"And will be again," Barry promised, giving him a quick peck over a hot casserole dish he'd pulled from the oven. "Just as soon as you've eaten and I don't have to worry you'll give out on me mid-fuck."

"That only happened that one time."

"Right." Barry set the dish down and fixed a serious expression on Tag. "And what did you eat for lunch today?"

Tag picked up his napkin from his plate, seated himself and spread the cloth over his lap. He didn't meet Barry's eye.

"What I thought. What about breakfast? Or dinner last night?"

Tag remained silent as he poured them both wine.

"You'll keep your ass in that chair and have a plate of food, then a shower and wash off the precinct stink." Barry shook his head as he dished out food. "I'm going to have to have a serious talk with Ross. You'll waste away now I'm not there to look after you."

"Fine." Tag sipped from his glass, gazing at Barry over the rim with all the heat in his trapped, aching erection in his eyes. "Then I cuff you to the bed and–"

"Oh, Captain, my captain," Barry leered.

Dinner passed agonisingly slowly for Tag. Barry seemed to enjoy his discomfort way too much. Tag had been kidding about the handcuffs, but if his lover kept that smug look on his face much longer, there was a good chance Tag would seriously consider getting them out.

"I've eaten, all right? Can we?"

"We can." Barry grinned at him, picked up the new wine bottle he'd just opened and their glasses, and led Tag to the bathroom. "This way to the shower, Horndog."

"You have to stop calling me that."

Barry grinned over his shoulder. "Horndog."

Tag couldn't really be angry. How long had it been since Barry was this relaxed? Loose enough to joke? He hurried after his partner, catching him just outside the bathroom door. "So, that was actually good. When did you learn how to cook?" He pulled Barry back against his chest, rubbing his hand down across Barry's pecs and reaching for his wine. He sipped over Barry's shoulder. "Last time I checked, you were in the habit of burning water."

"Busted." Barry turned in his embrace. "Jase cooked it for me."

"Jase." Tag backed off, fingers tightening around the stem of his wine glass. "He still here?"

"Yes, Tag, the kid is in the next room listening to our verbal foreplay. Don't be a jerk. Of course he's not still here. He went home hours ago."

Tag sipped his wine again, let go of the hand Barry had grabbed. "You know he wants you, right?"

"Do you think I want him?"

"He's always here."

"He helped me fix the place up."

"He sleeps in your spare room."

"Slept. For three days while he was looking for a new place. The spare room is my office, or did you forget that?"

"How could I forget? You keep bringing it up, this whole PI thing."

Barry scrubbed both hands over his face. "Tag. Really? Now?"

Tag tipped his head. "Why not now? If not now, when?"

"How about never? This is ridiculous. I'm not doing the kid, and I am not coming back to the force. This is my life now. This is what I want. This is what's best."

"For you."

"For us, Tag. We don't have to live in each other's back pockets twenty-four-seven. We don't have to hover—"

"I can't protect you here," Tag blurted.

"Tag." Barry cupped his face, rough hands gentle against Tag's five o'clock shadow. "I don't want or need your protection. We've been through this. My life, remember?"

Tag nodded, hating himself for wanting desperately not to be going through this again. It felt too much like breaking up, like letting go. But this was good for Barry. Tag could see that. Barry should be strong. He should be able to stand on his own two feet, have his own life and not need Tag. It sucked that Tag wanted to be needed, but that was Tag's issue and he had no right to put it on Barry.

"That doesn't mean I don't want you to be a part of it. You *are* my life."

Again, Tag nodded.

"Good." Barry took him by the hand, led him to the shower and proceeded to undress him and get him inside. The soaping up and rinsing off went a long way towards distracting Tag from the hollow feeling that eventually, he would have to leave, go back to his empty apartment and his empty bed.

"Stop thinking so hard," Barry admonished as he dragged a towel over Tag's back.

"Can't help it." The gruff sound of his voice made Tag wince inwardly.

"Sure you can." Barry reached round from where he was standing behind Tag and gripped his semi-hard shaft. "I bet I can get you to stop thinking about anything at all." He spread kisses and hard little nips along Tag's shoulders, stroked him and played a palm over his nipples.

"Ah."

"Better," Barry whispered, drawing his tongue over the shell of Tag's ear.

The next few minutes were taken up by the constant rhythm of Barry's hand on his cock and lips on his neck, his warm chest pressed against his back and his strong arms around him. For the first time since Barry had come knocking on his door again, Tag felt the unmistakable need to give in. To just stop trying and fighting and striving.

"Remember this, Tag? Back in the back of beyond, when I wasn't so much work?" Barry pressed his hips forward, his full cock sliding between Tags cheeks. "You've carried everything for so long. Let me."

Tag nodded, pushed back into the promise of Barry's touch.

"Bed," Barry suggested, pushing Tag ahead of him.

They landed on the bed, Tag on his back, Barry fitting his slim hips neatly between his thighs. Tag lifted both knees, cupped Barry's face.

"Really?" Barry wedged an arm between them, rolled Tag's balls out of the way and coasted his fingers lightly over Tag's entrance.

Tag gasped.

"You'd let me?"

"Let you?" Once again, Tag's words came out gruff, jagged around the edges. "Want you to." He feathered a light touch over Barry's cheek. "Been so long."

"It has." Barry squirmed around, fumbling lube from the nightstand and dropping it on the bed beside them. He spent the next little while lavishing every inch of Tag's body with attention, soft touches and sweet kisses, sharp nips of his teeth and his firm, grounding grip when Tag felt himself losing control.

Lube, fingers, teeth, lips, it all blended into one long, blissful ride. The sharp tang of sensation when Barry penetrated was an accent, a high point leading to better things. Tag hadn't allowed anyone to top him since he'd first left Barry. When he had sex, it had never been like this. Anonymous fucking had nothing on what Barry was doing to him now.

His heavy thrusts left Tag panting, bucking against him, drawing closer and closer to oblivion until Barry stiffened, hands gripping Tag's hair, pulling his head back into the pillow so his lips could fasten onto Tag's throat. It felt like a claim was being staked and Tag was the prize.

That thought threw Tag into orgasm. He came, hard—cum spurting warm and slippery between them.

It took more than a few minutes to finally feel Barry's weight crushing him into the bed, all bones and angles, and he shifted, dislodging the other man to sink into the soft mattress at his side.

Barry patted the white linen with one lazy hand. "Been waiting to sleep here."

Tag frowned. "Huh?"

A laugh rolled up from Barry's tousle of curls. "You sound so well fucked."

Tag grunted.

After a few moments, Barry rolled over, rested his hand on Tag's chest and his chin on his hand. He could look right into Tag's eyes from there, and Tag noticed there was no darkness, just deep, brown pools of contentment. "Bought the bed last. Had it delivered last week."

"So where have you been sleeping?"

"Couch."

"Why?"

Barry shuffled his weight, pulling himself to sitting. Tag noticed the slight sheen of sweat and spunk on his belly, the way his dark curls stuck to his forehead and cheeks, and smiled.

"I'm not the only one who looks well fucked."

Barry grinned.

"So why sleep on the couch?" Tag ran a hand over the soft, expensive cotton sheets. "This is a big, comfy bed."

"Made for two," Barry pointed out.

"So what are you going to do when I go home? Sleep on the couch again?" Tag's stomach shifted, grinding the realisation home that he would have to leave. If not now, at least in the morning.

"Don't go home," Barry said.

Tag blinked at him.

"I mean it. Don't go."

"I have to go, eventually. All my stuff —"

"Packs into boxes." Barry got up and went to the closet, pulled it open to reveal a huge space only half full of his own clothes. He pointed to twin tall boys on either side of the bathroom door. "His and his."

Tag pushed himself to sitting. "You're serious."

"It didn't shock you when it was your place we co-habited."

"But you had your own apartment."

"Okay. So this is different. I'm asking. Officially. Live with me. No more rat-infested apartment buildings, no more crack-whore neighbours. Come home every night to me. To us."

Tag glanced at the empty closet, the dressers, one of which had Barry's things on top—a bowl with keys and a cell phone in it, the box that housed Barry's father's army medals...a framed picture of Tag. "You really..."

"Yes. I really." Barry came back to the bed and knelt between Tag's legs. "I really, really want this. You. I want us." He took Tag's face in his hands, kissed him hard. "I love you."

Tag closed his eyes, forehead leaning against Barry's, their breath mingling, hands tangled in one another's hair. "Yeah. Okay." He kissed Barry, demanding and possessive. "My stuff is not going to fit in with yours."

"Your stuff sucks," Barry pointed out.

"True." He pulled back to look into Barry's eyes. "You're rebuilding everything. From scratch."

"Without you?"

Tag opened his mouth, realised he didn't know what to say. Not without him. Just without needing his help. It hurt and it didn't.

"For you," Barry whispered. "For us. My life will not be about the Dreaming. It's about what we have."

Tag nodded.

"You deserve this, Tag. Everything you've done to protect me. You deserve this."

"So do you."

Barry shifted around till he was once again cradled in Tag's arm, head on Tag's chest. "So that's a yes?"

"That's a yes." Tag kissed the top of his head. "Do we have to keep the house boy?"

Barry squirmed, and Tag knew his answer before his lover spoke. He sighed into the inevitable. Barry was his own man. No doubt about that. Tag was just going to have to get used to sharing.

"We're keeping him. He's a good cook, and he needs the job." Barry ran a hand through the hair on Tag's chest. "He has a hard time holding down a regular job."

"Why?"

"Same reason I had to leave the force, Tag. He needs us."

Tag shook his head. "Fuck me."

"Again? Already?" Barry lifted his head, a deep, lustful twinkle in his eyes.

Tag let the issue of Jason go and pulled Barry on top of him. "Somebody's getting a dick up the ass before the night's over."

"Excellent." Barry wiggled until he was nestled once more between Tag's thighs.

Yeah. It felt like home. One venue or another. Tag wrapped both legs around Barry. This was one dream of his lover's he was going to make damn sure came true.

About the Authors

Jaime Samms

Jaime writes, romance, fantasy, urban fantasy, shifter stories about men, about life, about love. Her work is populated with mostly men, most of whom are into each other, and yes, we do mean into each other. You can find plenty of free reading on her website.

She also reviews for Dark Diva Reviews, mostly the same types of stories, and will happily spout her opinion on the books she reads to her kids, who she home schools. Finally, she's occasionally gainfully employed. She writes for the love it, and hopes to pass on that love to her readers, her kids, and anyone else who comes along.

Sarah Masters

Sarah Masters is a multi-published author in three pen names writing several genres. She lives with her husband, children, and three cats in an English village. She writes full time and is also a cover artist and blog designer. In another life she was an editor. Her other pen names are Natalie Dae and Charley Oweson.

Sarah is busy co-authoring with Jaime Samms. They have several books in mind so will be writing for a couple of years to come! She also needs to finish her M/M novel, the tale she's dubbed The Book That Doesn't Want To End. She's at the last chapter but is afraid to open it in case that last chapter isn't really the last chapter...

Jaime Samms and Sarah Masters love to hear from readers. You can find their contact information, website details and author profile pages at http://www.total-e-bound.com.

Total-E-Bound Publishing

www.total-e-bound.com

Take a look at our exciting range of literagasmic™
erotic romance titles and discover pure quality
at Total-E-Bound.